SLIGHTLY WICKED

"Sympathetic characters and scalding sexual tension
make the second installment [in the Slightly series] a
truly engrossing read. . . . Balogh's sure-footed story
possesses an abundance of character and class."
—*Publishers Weekly*

SLIGHTLY MARRIED

"*Slightly Married* is a masterpiece! Mary Balogh has an
unparalleled gift for creating complex, compelling
characters who come alive on the pages. . . . A Perfect
Ten." —Romance Reviews Today

PRAISE FOR THE NOVELS OF MARY BALOGH

THE SECRET MISTRESS

"Regency romance doyenne Balogh . . . pairs a staid young nobleman with a vivacious debutante in this top-notch tale. . . . An unusually accurate portrayal of Regency society, laden with colorful period detail, makes a sparkling backdrop, and the supporting characters are delightful. . . . The charming mixture of sensual passion and hilarious confusion makes Balogh's delightful tale a must-read for Regency fans."
—*Publishers Weekly* (starred review)

"A treasure . . . No one tells 'secrets' better than Balogh." —*Library Journal* (editor's pick)

A SECRET AFFAIR

"This neatly choreographed romance . . . will fascinate readers as Balogh gradually peels away the layers of [the] complex, secrets-laden story with tantalizing skill and sympathetic care. . . . Poignant, thought-provoking, deliciously sensual, and completely enthralling, this polished gem is the last in the Huxtable quintet and one that Balogh's fans have been anxiously awaiting."
—*Library Journal*

"Balogh has saved the best for last; Constantine—dark, wicked, and cryptic—has a perfect foil in Hannah, and their encounters are steamy, their romance believable. Though series fans will be disappointed to see it come to a close, they couldn't ask for a better way to go out."
—*Publishers Weekly*

"Mary Balogh has masterfully woven a romantic tale of the importance of family, of compassion, and of love and forgiveness in this fifth book in her series about the Huxtable family. *A Secret Affair* will not disappoint, and you'll be pleasantly surprised by the 'secrets.'"
—Fresh Fiction

SEDUCING AN ANGEL

"With her inimitable, brilliantly nuanced sense of characterization, elegantly sensual style, and droll wit, best-seller Balogh continues to set the standard to which all other Regency historical writers aspire while delivering another addictively readable addition to her Huxtable family series." —*Booklist*

"One of [Balogh's] best books to date."
—A Romance Review

AT LAST COMES LOVE

"Sparkling with sharp wit, lively repartee, and delicious sensuality, the emotionally rewarding *At Last Comes Love* metes out both justice and compassion; totally satisfying." —*Library Journal*

"*At Last Comes Love* is the epitome of what any great romance should be. . . . This novel will leave you crying, laughing, cheering, and ready to fight for two characters that any reader will most definitely fall in love with!"
—Coffee Time Romance

THEN COMES SEDUCTION

"Exquisite sexual chemistry permeates this charmingly complex story." —*Library Journal*

"Balogh delivers another smartly fashioned love story that will dazzle readers with its captivating combination of nuanced characters, exquisitely sensual romance, and elegant wit." —*Booklist*

"Mary Balogh succeeds shockingly well."
—Rock Hill *Herald*

FIRST COMES MARRIAGE

"Intriguing and romantic . . . Readers are rewarded with passages they'll be tempted to dog-ear so they can read them over and over." —McAllen *Monitor*

"Wonderful characterization [and a] riveting plot . . . I highly recommend you read *First Comes Marriage*."
—Romance Reviews Today

"Peppered with brilliant banter, laced with laughter . . . and tingling with sexual tension, this story of two seemingly mismatched people struggling to make their marriage work tugs at a few heartstrings and skillfully paves the way for the stories to come."
—*Library Journal*

"The incomparable Balogh delivers a masterful first in a new trilogy. . . . Always fresh, intelligent, emotional and sensual, Balogh's stories reach out to readers, touching heart and mind with their warmth and wit. Prepare for a joyous read." —*Romantic Times*

"A memorable cast . . . refresh[es] a classic Regency plot with humor, wit, and the sizzling romantic chemistry that one expects from Balogh. Well-written and emotionally complex." —*Library Journal*

SIMPLY LOVE

"One of the things that make Ms. Balogh's books so memorable is the emotion she pours into her stories. The writing is superb, with realistic dialogue, sexual tension, and a wonderful heart-wrenching story. *Simply Love* is a book to savor, and to read again. It is a Perfect Ten. Romance doesn't get any better than this." —Romance Reviews Today

"With more than her usual panache, Balogh returns to Regency England for a satisfying adult love story." —*Publishers Weekly*

SLIGHTLY DANGEROUS

"*Slightly Dangerous* is the culmination of Balogh's wonderfully entertaining Bedwyn series. . . . Balogh, famous for her believable characters and finely crafted Regency-era settings, forges a relationship that leaps off the page and into the hearts of her readers." —*Booklist*

"With this series, Balogh has created a wonderfully romantic world of Regency culture and society. Readers will miss the honorable Bedwyns and their mates; ending the series with Wulfric's story is icing on the cake. Highly recommended." —*Library Journal*

SLIGHTLY SINFUL

"Smart, playful, and deliciously satisfying . . . Balogh once again delivers a clean, sprightly tale rich in both plot and character. . . . With its irrepressible characters and deft plotting, this polished romance is an ideal summer read." —*Publishers Weekly* (starred review)

SLIGHTLY TEMPTED

"Once again, Balogh has penned an entrancing, unconventional yarn that should expand her following."
—*Publishers Weekly*

"Balogh is a gifted writer. . . . *Slightly Tempted* invites reflection, a fine quality in romance, and Morgan and Gervase are memorable characters."
—*Contra Costa Times*

SLIGHTLY SCANDALOUS

"With its impeccable plotting and memorable characters, Balogh's book raises the bar for Regency romances." —*Publishers Weekly* (starred review)

"The sexual tension fairly crackles between this pair of beautifully matched protagonists. . . . This delightful and exceptionally well-done title nicely demonstrates [Balogh's] matchless style." —*Library Journal*

"This third book in the Bedwyn series is . . . highly enjoyable as part of the series or on its own merits."
—*Old Book Barn Gazette*

The Famous Heroine

The Plumed Bonnet

MARY BALOGH

DELL

NEW YORK

The Famous Heroine and *The Plumed Bonnet* are works of fiction. Names, characters, places, and incidents are the products of the author's imagination or are used fictitiously. Any resemblance to actual events, locales, or persons, living or dead, is entirely coincidental.

2011 Dell Mass Market Edition

The Famous Heroine copyright © 1996 by Mary Balogh
The Plumed Bonnet copyright © 1996 by Mary Balogh
Excerpt from *The Proposal* by Mary Balogh copyright © 2011 by Mary Balogh

Published in the United States by Dell, an imprint of The Random House Publishing Group, a division of Random House, Inc., New York.

DELL is a registered trademark of Random House, Inc., and the colophon is a trademark of Random House, Inc.

The Famous Heroine was originally published in paperback in the United States by Signet, an imprint of Dutton Signet, a division of Penguin Books USA Inc., New York, in 1996.

The Plumed Bonnet was originally published in paperback in the United States by Signet, an imprint of Dutton Signet, a division of Penguin Books USA Inc., New York, in 1996.

This book contains an excerpt of the forthcoming title *The Proposal* by Mary Balogh. The excerpt has been set for this edition only and may not reflect the final content of the published book.

ISBN: 978-0-440-24543-8
eBook ISBN: 978-0-345-53250-3

Cover design: Lynn Andreozzi
Cover photograph: © Herman Estevez

Printed in the United States of America

www.bantamdell.com

9 8 7 6 5 4 3 2 1

Dell mass market edition: October 2011

The Famous Heroine

1

THE DUCHESS OF BRIDGWATER, FORMIDABLY ELE-
gant in her purple satin evening gown with matching turban and tall plumes, bedecked and sparkling with
the family jewels, looked Miss Cora Downes over with
slow and methodical care, beginning at the top of her
elaborate coiffure, and ending at her slippers, which
were already cramping her toes.

The slippers were cramping her toes because she had
unwisely taken the advice of Lady Elizabeth Munro, the
duchess's elder daughter, to buy the smaller of two sizes
in footwear when in doubt, as gentlemen did not admire
large feet. Cora's feet were not extraordinarily large, she
had decided, holding them out in front of her, unshod,
as she sat on the edge of her bed soon after the advice
had been given. And really she did not care much for
gentlemen's strange preferences in such matters. Did
they crawl around on hands and knees examining a
lady's feet before going to any other lengths to discover
if she was someone with whom they would not mind
dreadfully spending the rest of their days on this earth?
But there was no escaping the fact that her feet were
somewhat larger than Elizabeth's and decidedly larger
than those of Jane, Elizabeth's younger sister. But then
Jane was more than usually small and dainty.

And so Cora had bought the slippers in a size smaller

than she ought because she had persuaded herself that she was in doubt. She now meekly bore the consequences of her own folly, though she knew she had not really begun to bear them yet. There was a whole ball to live through, a whole evening of dancing—if any gentleman could be coerced into dancing with her, that was. Cora would have squirmed with discomfort at the very real danger that none would if her grace had not been still examining her appearance.

Do not let her use her lorgnette, she instructed some unseen power without moving her lips. *I shall die of mortification.* At the horridly advanced age of one-and-twenty she was decked out in virginal white and blushes and was about to make her debut into the *beau monde.* Jane, who was a mere eighteen years of age, had already made her curtsy to the Queen the year before, though she was still dressed this year in what Cora thought of as "the uniform." When one added to the age difference the fact that Cora was larger than Jane—in *every* way, not just in the matter of feet—the result was depressing.

Elizabeth, who was nineteen, was dressed in pink and had put on, with her gown, a look of ennui that bespoke the seasoned lady of the *ton.* She, of course, was already nicely settled indeed, being betrothed to a marquess of enormous wealth and consequence and alarmingly advanced years—he was three-and-thirty—who happened to be in Vienna this year with the result that the wedding had been postponed indefinitely.

The duchess handed down her judgment at last. She inclined her head once and set her plumes to nodding a dozen times. "You will do, my dear Cora," she said.

That was all she said, but it set Elizabeth to smiling graciously in almost comic imitation of her mama's regal manner and Jane to squealing and squeezing her arm and exclaiming in glee.

"I *told* you you looked beautiful, Cora," she said.

Which was a very loose paraphrase indeed of what her mother had said.

Cora tried not to look sheepish and giggled instead. It was strange how laughter, which she had always indulged in with unself-conscious spontaneity, had become giggling as soon as the Duchess of Bridgwater had taken her so determinedly under the ducal wing. Giggling, it seemed, was not a ladylike attribute and must be curbed at all costs. The most a lady could allow herself in company by way of displaying amusement was a well-bred titter. On the few occasions when Cora had practiced tittering, she had ended up with her head beneath a cushion, smothering the bellows of unholy mirth it had given rise to.

"We will be on our way, then," the duchess said, smiling at all three young ladies who had joined her in the drawing room.

She really looked remarkably beautiful when she smiled—and even when she did not, Cora conceded in something like envy. It must be wonderful to have that kind of poise and grace and self-assurance. It was hard to believe that her grace could be the mother of Elizabeth and Jane and of Lord George Munro. It was almost impossible to believe that she was also the mother of the present duke, to whom Cora had been presented for the first time but yesterday. His grace was all elegance and formality and ducal hauteur.

Cora had had the uncomfortable feeling that his grace did not approve of her, even though he had bowed over her hand and even raised it to his lips—she had stood rooted to the morning-room floor, stupidly awed by the knowledge that he was a *duke,* a real live duke—and assured her of his pleasure in meeting her. He had even thanked her over the little Henry incident. Little Henry was his nephew, of course, and heir to his grace's heir. But even so it had startled her to find that the Duke of

Bridgwater had heard about the little Henry incident. He had even called her a heroine and she had resisted only just in time the urge to look over her shoulder to see to whom he was speaking.

But then, of course, he must have wondered why his mother had brought to town a mere Miss Cora Downes, daughter of a Bristol merchant—a *prosperous* merchant, it was true, and one who had recently purchased a considerable property and renovated a grand old abbey that had been falling to ruins on it—with the intention of taking her about in society with her own daughters, his own sisters. He would have thought it very strange indeed. And so, of course, the explanation of what had happened with little Henry would have been given.

The truth was—at least, it was not *quite* the truth but what was perceived to be the truth—that Cora had saved little Henry from drowning in the shadow of the Pulteney Bridge in Bath and that out of gratitude the duchess, little Henry's grandmama, had taken Cora into her own home to mingle with her daughters and to be elevated to the ranks of gentlewomanhood long enough to be found an eligible gentleman.

The Duchess of Bridgwater was going to find Cora a husband. Not from the ranks of eligible dukes and marquesses and earls, of course, amongst whom she had already plucked a mate for Elizabeth and planned to pluck one for Jane. But nevertheless, a gentleman. A man of fortune and rank and property. A man who had never soiled his hands or enriched his coffers with trade or business. Despite all the wealth of her father, Cora could never have aspired so high if she had not saved little Henry—well, sort of saved him, anyway—and so been catapulted into the benevolent good graces of the Duchess of Bridgwater.

Her grace and the girls would not even have been in such a questionably fashionable place as Bath at such an unfashionable time as spring if Lady George had not been suffering through a difficult confinement. But her grace was fond of her daughter-in-law and of her grandchildren and had deprived herself and her daughters of all the pleasures of the first half of the Season in London. Perhaps fortunately for them, the incident of little Henry seemed to have precipitated the arrival into this world of his sister, who was delivered a mere two days later. Mother and child were doing remarkably well and were now being coddled with affectionate indulgence by the proud father.

And so at last, when it was already June, her grace had set off for London with two impatient daughters and a rather alarmed protégée, who wondered how a usually strong-willed young lady like her could find herself in such a predicament. Over the past few years, she had turned down no fewer than three proposals of marriage from remarkably eligible men merely on the grounds that she felt no more than a passing affection for any of them. As if *that* had anything to say to anything, her father had commented each time, rolling his eyes at the ceiling and making clucking noises of frustrated disgust.

Her father was rather tickled over the idea of her marrying a gentleman. So was Edgar, her brother, who had pointed out that she must marry someone and it might as well be a gentleman who might awe her into something like meek ladylike submission. She would make a horrid spinster, he had warned her, all stubborn will and bossiness with no domain over which to exercise her tyranny. She was fond of Edgar. It was a pity that some people had concocted the idea that he had behaved with cowardice in the incident of little Henry. How stupid and how totally untrue. But public opinion was remarkably difficult to manipulate, she had found.

Cora frowned and contorted her face until she could

bite the flesh of her left cheek. But she was seating herself in the carriage as she did so and the duchess was seated opposite, watching her.

"You are nervous, dear," she said with gracious condescension. "It is understandable. But you must remember that you are dressed as well as anyone and that you have the manners to equal anyone else's. And the fact that you have my sponsorship will silence any question about your eligibility to be at Lady Markley's ball. Bridgwater has undertaken to present you with some eligible partners. I will do the like, of course. Now do smooth out the frown and the facial contortions, my dear. They are not becoming."

Cora had already smoothed out the frown and had stopped biting her cheek. And a wonderful antidote to her sense of unfairness over what had happened to Edgar with reference to the little Henry incident was remembering why she was in the carriage so grandly dressed—with clothes Papa had been quite adamant about paying for.

She was on her way to a ball. Well, there was nothing so remarkable about that. She had danced at assemblies at Clifton and Bristol and of course in Bath. She loved the vigor of country dances.

But this was a ball in *London*.

This was a ball exclusively—well, not quite exclusively, considering the fact that she was going to be there—for people of the *ton*.

Cora's stomach chose that inauspicious moment to rouse itself out of its quiet and comfortable lethargy in order to tie itself in knots. And then her dinner decided to protest the fact that it was sitting inside a knotted stomach.

She smiled vacuously at her carriage companions.

* * *

"SHE IS A diamond of the first water, Frank," Lord Hawthorne said, sighing and gazing at the lady in question across the expanse of the ballroom. "She refused me a dance last week. Said her card was full. And then granted a set to Denny when he arrived late."

Lady Augusta Haville's bad manners in behaving thus only enhanced her reputation in his eyes, it seemed. Such was the extent of his cousin's humility and confidence in his own charms, Lord Francis Kneller thought as he raised his jeweled quizzing glass to his eye and gazed through it at the lady. But then Bob was young and a trifle gauche and had doubtless blushed and stammered as he stood and bowed before one of the *ton*'s brightest jewels.

There had been only one lady all Season to rival Lady Augusta and she was now gone—to Highmoor Abbey in Yorkshire. As the wife of Carew, damn his eyes. Samantha. Lord Francis's heart took a nosedive to land somewhere in the vicinity of the soles of his dancing shoes, a place where it had resided with disturbing frequency for several weeks past.

He was nursing a broken heart—in the soles of his shoes. He had not even realized quite how deeply in love with Samantha he had been until she had announced quite out of the blue a mere few weeks ago, as she was on her way to the park with him in his phaeton, that she was going to marry the Marquess of Carew. Carew! Lord Francis had not even known she was acquainted with the man. And yet he himself had been faithfully courting her and regularly offering for her for more years than he cared to remember.

"Yes," he said absently. "An Incomparable, Bob."

Lady Augusta was of medium stature, slender, graceful, and elegant. She was gracious and charming—except when she was rejecting gauche boys and then favoring more suave admirers. She had skin like the finest porcelain and hair like a golden sunset.

She was aware of his scrutiny across the ballroom, despite the distraction of a largish court of admirers and was indicating in a thoroughly well-bred manner—nothing that would have been remotely apparent to any casual observer—that she would not take it at all amiss if he strolled about the floor and stopped to pay his respects and add his name to her dancing card.

"She would dance with *you*, Frank," Lord Hawthorne said with faint and humble envy. "Ah, there are the fellows. Excuse me." And he was off to join a group of other very young gentlemen, who would bolster up one another's esteem and courage for the rest of the evening—probably in the card room, a more comfortably masculine domain than the ballroom.

Lord Francis lowered his glass and wondered what he was doing in Lady Markley's ballroom. It was the last place he felt like being. But then these days any place on earth was the last place he felt like being. And yet he had realized with some logic and some regret during the past several weeks that there really was no other place to be than any place on earth.

So this place was as good as any.

"An Incomparable," a haughty and rather languid voice said at his shoulder, unconsciously repeating the word he himself had used only a few moments before. "You are thinking of attaching yourself to her court, Kneller?"

Lord Francis turned to greet the Duke of Bridgwater, who was in the way of being a new friend. Though they had been acquainted for years, it was only in the past couple of weeks or so that they had had any dealings together. Bridgwater was Carew's friend and Lord Francis was Samantha's—yes, he was, he admitted ruefully, even though he had wanted to be very much more than just that—and they had closed ranks, the two of them, he and Bridgwater, when that fiend Rushford had insulted Samantha and Carew had been forced to challenge him despite a partially crippled leg and arm. They had both become his seconds, Bridgwater by Carew's request, Lord Francis by his own. They had gone to Jackson's boxing saloon to witness the slaughter and to pick up the pieces of Samantha's husband—and had remained to bask in the wonder and glory of Carew's victory.

The clubs of London still had not ceased buzzing with the story, which might have seemed to be considerably embellished to anyone who had not been there to see it.

Bridgwater had been the one to advise Lord Francis that it was not the thing to wear his heart on his sleeve in quite the manner he was doing. Lord Francis had been ready to challenge Rushford himself, even though Samantha had a husband to look to her protection.

Discovering, as he had done just after the fight, that Samantha actually loved Carew and had not married him simply for his vast fortune had done nothing in particular to raise Lord Francis's spirits. Neither had his begrudging admission that Carew was worthy of her.

"I am thinking of it," he said now in answer to the duke's question. "One likes to keep up one's reputation as a connoisseur of beauty, you know."

"For my part," his grace said, "I would find it unsatisfactory to be merely a part of someone's court. I would prefer to be the one and only. My pride, I daresay."

"But then there is danger in being a one and only," Lord Francis pointed out. "The danger of finding oneself netted. Or caught in parson's mousetrap, to change the image but not the meaning."

"I have a small favor to ask of you," the duke said, causing Lord Francis to swing around to look full at him, his eyebrows raised. He felt a flicker of interest.

Life had been so desperately devoid of interest for weeks now. He must be impoverished indeed, he thought, if the mere mention of a favor he might do grabbed his whole attention. Perhaps his grace merely wished to know if a lock of his hair was sticking out at the back like a cup handle.

"My mother has arrived in town," his grace said, raising his own glass to his eye and beginning a languid perusal of the occupants of the room through it, "with my two sisters—and a protégée."

The slight pause before the final words and the almost imperceptible pain in the duke's voice as the words were spoken alerted Lord Francis to the fact that the small favor had something to do with the protégée. It would hardly concern Lady Elizabeth Munro. She was betrothed to old What's-His-Name, who was in Vienna, reputedly dazzling the world with his diplomatic genius. And Lady Jane Munro, though young and unattached, was unattached only because Bridgwater had rejected a string of suitors whom he considered unworthy—if gossip had the right of it, as gossip had a habit of not always being. Lord Francis Kneller was the son and brother of a duke, but it was extremely unlikely that he would ever attain the title himself since his brother had already been brilliantly prolific in the production of sons.

No, it could not be Lady Elizabeth and would not be Lady Jane. It would be the protégée.

"I trust they are all in good health?" Lord Francis said politely.

"Ah, yes indeed," his grace said, his glass pausing for a moment and his lips pursing. Yes, she was pretty, Lord Francis thought as he followed the line of the duke's quizzing glass to the young lady on whom it was trained. The quizzing glass resumed its journey. "I would appreciate it, old chap, if you would dance a set with the protégée. Miss Cora Downes." He said the name with something like distaste.

"Glad to," Lord Francis said and wondered what was wrong with Miss Cora Downes. Apart from her name, that was. Her two names did not blend together into anything resembling poetry or even pleasing symphony. "Miss Cora Downes?"

His grace sighed, "It is unlike my mother to act purely out of sentiment," he said. "But that appears to be what has happened in this case. She has taken the girl out of her own proper milieu and has brought her to town to present to the *ton*. It is her intention to find the girl a respectable husband."

Lord Francis coughed delicately behind one lace-covered wrist.

"Oh, not you, old chap," his grace said hastily. "It is just that for all my mother's consequence and influence, I am still afraid Miss Downes will not take. It would be an embarrassment to her grace as well as to the girl herself, I daresay. And therefore to me."

"Her own proper milieu?" Lord Francis's curiosity was piqued. It seemed to him an eternity since he had felt anything as wildly exhilarating as curiosity.

"Her father could probably buy you and me up with the small change in his purse, Kneller," the duke said, "and still have enough left to jingle in his pocket. He is a merchant from Bristol. He has recently bought property and set up as a gentleman. I believe his son has been to all the right schools and has taken up the practice of law. But there is the taint, you know, the lack of birth."

"Ah," Lord Francis said and pictured himself dancing with the girl and having his ears murdered with an uncouth provincial accent. Even that prospect was not utterly displeasing. It would be *amusing*. How long it was since he had been amused! "And my dancing with her will help her to take, Bridgwater?"

"Undoubtedly," his grace said after letting his glass pause on Lady Augusta Haville before he lowered it and observed his surroundings with his naked eye. "Everyone knows that you commune only with the most fashionable and the most lovely ladies, Kneller. Your taste is legendary. You are a connoisseur of beauty, as you yourself just said. You have but to bow to a lady and a host of other men takes particular notice. If you tread a measure with Miss Downes, other gentlemen will flock to take your place. The girl will dance all night. She will be launched. Mama will be ecstatic. And I will be grateful."

Lord Francis sifted through the flattery and decided that somewhere at the core of it was a sincere compliment. Was the girl so very dreadful, then? She was a merchant's daughter? A merchant with pretensions to gentility? Was she ghastly and vulgar? Why had the very fastidious Duchess of Bridgwater taken her on? He decided to ask the question.

"She is your mother's protégée?" he said, phrasing the sentence politely as a question.

"She saved my nephew's life in Bath," his grace explained. "Jumped into the river when he was drowning and almost drowned herself while fishing him out. A damned heroic thing to do, actually. We will be eternally in her debt, and I feel the debt personally as head of the family even though Henry belongs to George. But this seems a foolish way of paying it. Ah."

His glass was to his eye again and directed at the doorway. Lord Francis glanced that way too and saw the Duchess of Bridgwater, her usual regal and beautiful self in purple, Lady Elizabeth Munro as beautiful and as aloof as ever, Lady Jane as small and sweet and innocent as she had looked last year during her first Season, and—and another young lady, who must be the protégée.

She was tall, large—he caught his mind in the act of using the latter word. She was not fat. Nothing like fat. But there was something large about her. *Voluptuous,* he thought, was a more accurate word. If she ever appeared on the stage, she would draw men to the green room like bees to a flower.

It was an unkind thought. She was dressed in virginal white, like Lady Jane—it was rather unfortunate that she stood next to the younger Munro sister—and the gown had been carefully designed to show somewhat less of her bosom than was fashionable. He suspected the restraining hand of the duchess. If the girl's gown had been designed according to strict fashion, cut lower—well, his temperature threatened to soar a couple of degrees at the very thought.

He found himself wondering what she must have looked like when she climbed out of the river in Bath after having saved Bridgwater's nephew. His temperature *did* rise at least one degree.

"The protégée?" he asked his grace.

"You see what I mean?" the duke asked, setting aside his quizzing glass and looking as if he were girding his loins for unpleasant action. "She looks for all the world as if she should be in a damned green room."

Their minds sometimes moved along strange parallels, Lord Francis thought.

"And my mother thinks to find her a respectable husband," the duke said with a sign. "Come along, Kneller. You did promise, did you not?"

She was not beautiful. Once the eye could be persuaded to rise above the level of the woman's neck, one could see that. Her features were too strong for true delicacy and her eyes were too wide-spaced and too candid to inspire lovelorn sighs. Her hair was unfortunately dressed. It was a rich chestnut color, it was true, and was abundant and shining and clean. But it was far *too* abundant for the curls and ringlets she wore. One found oneself picturing it worn down about her waist—with the bosom of her gown cut lower.

Lord Francis fingered his quizzing glass and raised his eyebrows.

And then she saw him coming. Her hand shot to her mouth, her eyes lit up with unholy amusement, and she half turned her head as if to whisper something to Lady Jane. Then she noticed Bridgwater, appeared to realize that the two of them were moving in her direction, and dropped her hand. She very noticeably blanked her eyes.

But there must have been a speck of dust on the floor in front of her, Lord Francis thought afterward. There must have been. Certainly there was nothing else. Nothing that was visible. So it must have been something invisible over which she tripped. She did so quite inelegantly—not that there was an elegant way to trip, Lord Francis might have realized if he had been at liberty to consider the matter—and with a little shriek.

Lord Francis quickened his pace sufficiently to leap forward and save her from quite upending herself on the floor. For one moment before he set her to rights and stepped back in order to regard her with eyebrows that were raised again in polite inquiry, he felt the full impact of that remarkable voluptuous bosom against his chest. And for the same moment it seemed somehow irrelevant that her chemise and gown, his coat and waistcoat and shirt all separated his bare flesh from her bare flesh.

Quite irrelevant indeed. Lord Francis wondered if Prinny was due at tonight's ball. If he was not, one was left to wonder why Lady Markley kept her ballroom so suffocatingly hot.

Miss Cora Downes, to whom the Duke of Bridgwater was proceeding to present him as if nothing untoward had happened, even though for a moment he had closed his eyes in pained acknowledgment of the fact that one-half of the gathered guests must have witnessed the un-couth debut of his mother's protégée and the other half would be told of it within the next five minutes—Miss Cora Downes blushed a shade brighter than scarlet and then giggled.

"Oops!" she said, interrupting his grace's opening re-marks. "I wonder if it is permitted to go back outside onto the staircase and try it all over again." She spoke rather too loudly and heartily and then giggled once more before suddenly sobering in order to pay attention to Lord Francis's name and to his request that he might lead her into the opening set.

What a deliciously frightful young lady, he thought, feeling genuinely diverted for the first time in two or three eternities.

2

SHE WAS FRANKLY TERRIFIED. AND SHE DESPISED HER-self for feeling so, since rationally speaking she did not consider herself inferior to anyone. Lady Markley's ballroom was stuffed full of the *ton* in all its jeweled splendor—all the *ton* and Cora Downes. The vast majority of those present were probably mere misters and misseses and misses, she reassured herself as she paused just inside the doorway with her three companions, surely the most conspicuous place of all to stand in any ballroom. She had to resist the urge to look down at herself to make sure she had remembered to put on her gown. The duchess would surely have thought before now of commenting on its absence if indeed she was clad in merely her shift.

Of course, there were undoubtedly several titled people present too. Cora felt a strange bonelessness in her knees—a most unfortunate part of the anatomy in which to feel it. Why be awed by titles? Jane had a title and was a very ordinary, pleasant young lady. And Papa always said that title and birth meant nothing but snobbery. It was wealth and property and the ability to acquire and manage both that really mattered. Cora herself was not really sure that even that was true, but it was a comforting thought to which to cling at the moment.

She tried to look about her at individual people to assure herself that really they were just people—each with two eyes, a nose, and a mouth, so to speak. She saw jewels and fans and feathers and fobs and quizzing glasses wherever she looked. Formidable ladies and even more formidable gentlemen. Many of the latter looked sober and immaculate—and formidable—in black coats and knee breeches, a fast-growing fashion that both her father and Edgar applauded as did all the men of their middle-class world. In fact, they often had unkind things to say about men who did not follow it.

And then her eyes lit on a gentleman who was so much the antithesis of that fashion that he stood out in the crowd like the proverbial sore thumb. He wore a bright turquoise satin coat with turquoise-and-silver striped waistcoat and silver knee breeches. His linen was sparkling white. There were copious amounts of lace at his wrists and half covering his hands. The knot of his neckcloth was a superior work of art. Edgar would have declared with some contempt that the man's valet must have sweated for several hours to create such perfection. The face above the startling clothes displayed a lazy kind of cynicism as if the man were bored with his very existence.

Cora thought immediately of a peacock, which was the first word Edgar would have used, she was sure. Remembering that only titters—and even those solely at appropriate moments—were allowed in her present surroundings, she clapped a hand to her mouth in order to thrust back the merriment that was in grave danger of bubbling out of her. Oh, if only Edgar were here to see—and to comment!

But Jane was here and Jane had a healthy sense of humor. Cora had half turned to share the glorious joke of the man's foppish appearance when she froze and humor died an instantaneous death. The man was moving in her direction. And at his side was another gentleman, elegant and handsome in varying shades of dark green. The Duke of Bridgwater.

Their destination was instantly apparent to Cora. *Heavenly days*, she thought, her mind robbed of coherence. *Oh, heavenly days.*

She had had a problem with clumsiness as a girl. Not as a child. It had come upon her at about the age of twelve and had dogged her footsteps—almost literally—for several years after that. Edgar had started to call her a walking disaster and her father's habitual expression when she was about had seemed to be one of resigned glumness, his eyes roiled ceiling- or skyward, as if he were sending up a fervent prayer, "Why me, Lord?"

Miss Graham, her governess, had always been kinder than either of the two men in her life. Miss Graham had always explained to her that she was growing into her body. Her brain had not quite got the message that she was no longer inside her dainty child's body but instead was in this girl's frame, which was developing in alarming ways—Cora's words, not Miss Graham's. Miss Graham had merely explained that the child in her was resisting the developing woman but that finally she would be comfortable with her femininity.

She was still waiting to grow comfortable, though she had outgrown the clumsiness. Almost.

On this occasion all she had to do was wait for the Duke of Bridgwater to come up and greet his mother and his sisters and her, Cora—and probably present the turquoise peacock to them. She did not even have to move. She did not know why she did so. Indeed, she did not even realize that she *had* moved until her cramped toes somehow did not advance with the rest of her and she stumbled—and shrieked—in surely the most embarrassing place possible in which to stumble and shriek.

Not that she ever *chose* to be clumsy.

She collided with a brick wall, which fortunately saved her from sprawling out flat on the floor and disgracing herself beyond measure. She righted herself, realized that the brick wall had been a gentleman's chest—the *turquoise* gentleman's chest—and disgraced herself after all.

She giggled.

It was not even honest-to-goodness laughter. It was unmistakably a giggle, occasioned by acute embarrassment. She wondered hopefully if she was exaggerating even ever-so slightly in believing that everyone was watching her. She did not think so.

"Oops!" she heard someone exclaim in her voice—how *many* times had Miss Graham told her that she must learn to wipe that word from her vocabulary? "I wonder if it is permitted to go back outside onto the staircase and try it all over again."

And the same person who spoke giggled—again—at the sadly unwitty joke. And sounded for all the world like a silly twelve-year-old.

It was only then she realized that his grace was speaking—quietly and courteously and quite as if she had not just held up him and his mother and his sisters to public ridicule. He was, she realized, the perfectly well-bred gentleman. He terrified her and had done so ever since Elizabeth and Jane had first started talking about him in Bath with mutual adoration. He was so perfectly handsome and elegant and gentlemanly and—ducal. If he had had DUKE written in black ink across his forehead, he could not be more obviously who he was.

She also realized—too late—that he had presented his companion to her and that she had missed his name. She could only smile with facial muscles that suddenly felt unaccountably stiff as he called her Miss Downes and took her hand in his and bowed over it.

He was taller than she was, she thought irrelevantly—

so many gentleman were not. He also did *not*—as so many gentlemen did—have a spot of thinning hair on the crown of his head. His brown hair was of a uniform thickness and was expertly cut so that even when it was windblown it would look just so, she guessed. She also guessed that he spent several hours of each week with his barber—and with a manicurist. She glanced at his perfect hands. It was rather sad that he was so far to the left of true masculinity. *Was* it sad? Perhaps it was not to him. Perhaps he enjoyed looking like a peacock.

She suffered from another affliction in addition to clumsiness—though she had not really suffered from that since girlhood. She suffered from the inability to be always present when it was essential that she be present. She had gone off now into her own distant world, thinking of trivialities like bald spots and peacocks, and as a consequence a few important details of the present moment had passed her by. Like the man's name. And the identity of the person whom her grace was describing as a great heroine to whom they would all be indebted for the rest of their lives.

"Yes, indeed," his grace said with a grave and elegant inclination of his head in Cora's direction.

"Oh, dear," she said, realizing they were talking about her. "All I did was leap into the river without pausing for thought. It was really quite unheroic. And I ruined a brand-new bonnet."

The anonymous gentleman—who would *not* be anonymous if she had only remained present long enough to hear what his grace had named him—pursed his lips and fingered his quizzing glass. It was studded with jewels that looked suspiciously like sapphires, Cora noticed when she glanced down at it. She would wager they were real gems and not merely paste. She wondered if he had a glass to match each of his outfits—and giggled yet again.

"A bona fide heroine indeed," the gentleman said in a voice that sounded as languid and bored as his face had appeared when she first looked into it. "One perhaps might find another lady willing to risk her life for a child, but I declare that nowhere would one find another willing to sacrifice her bonnet in the same cause."

Cora stared at him, fascinated. Was he *serious*? He probably was, she decided.

"Ma'am." He was bowing to the duchess. "With your permission, I would request the honor of leading Miss Downes in to the opening set."

Cora brightened instantly. Her great fear, she knew, though she despised herself for feeling it, was of being an utter and total wallflower. But very close behind that fear—and really she did not believe her grace would allow that first one to become reality—was the terror of being asked to dance by a gentleman so very elegant and proper and aristocratic that she would freeze into a block of ice that just happened to have two left feet attached to its base. His grace of Bridgwater himself, for example. She had found herself praying fervently last night—literally praying, with palms pressed together and eyes tightly scrunched shut—that he would not for his mother's sake feel obliged to lead her out. She would *die*.

The anonymous gentleman would not be threatening at all to dance with. Indeed, she would derive great amusement from the opportunity to observe him more closely for all of half an hour. But she almost absented herself too long again in these happy thoughts.

"Certainly, Lord Francis," the duchess was saying, inclining her head graciously and setting her plumes to dancing again. "I am sure Cora would be delighted."

Francis. The name suited him perfectly, being one of those that might belong to either a man or a woman—with a slight variation in the spelling, of course. But

Lord Francis? He was an aristocrat, then? But quite an unthreatening one, she told herself before panic could well into her nostrils. He was making her a half bow and asking her for the honor of leading her in to the set.

"Thank you, Lord Francis," she said, vaunting her new knowledge. She smiled dazzlingly at him. "It is a set of country dances? How wonderful! I *LOVE* the vigor of a country dance."

She could almost hear Elizabeth's voice as it had spoken just a few days ago, as soon as they knew they were to come to this ball. *One must always assume an attitude of ennui at such functions,* she had warned. *One must never be thought to enthuse.* Enthusiasm was something very far removed from true gentility. Her grace had nodded in agreement, though she had added with a smile that one need not go as far as to look downright bored. That might be somewhat insulting to both one's hosts and one's partners. Jane had added that one might smile and even look happy as long as one remained demure and did not *bubble.*

And she, Cora, had just said, *I LOVE the vigor of a country dance* with all the enthusiasm of her lack of gentility.

She thought she saw amusement for the merest moment in Lord Francis's eyes. Ridicule, no doubt. No matter. She was not at all intent on impressing Lord Francis Whoever-He-Was. She really should have listened to his full name.

They were blue eyes, she thought, apropos of nothing. She had always favored blue eyes in men. She had secretly thought that perhaps one of the reasons—though only a very minor one—she had been unable to feel affection for any of the three men who had offered for her was that they had not one blue eye among the three of them. But if that was true, then she was setting about choosing a lifelong mate according to very trivial criteria.

It was perhaps a shame that the first truly blue eyes she had encountered in a gentleman belonged to a peacock. And an aristocratic peacock at that.

A turquoise satin arm with an elegant, lace-bedecked hand at the end of it—on one of the fingers of which was a large square sapphire ring—was poised before Cora and she realized that she was being invited to join a set without further delay. The duke was already talking with another gentleman, who had come along with the obvious intention of dancing with Jane.

Cora set her arm along the turquoise one and repressed the very silly urge to giggle yet again. She had *never* been a giggler. She had no wish to acquire the nasty habit at this advanced stage of her life.

She wished with all the power of her being that she had bought her slippers in a larger size. There was plenty of room for her feet in these particular ones but very little left over for her toes.

She smiled hard, trying not to look gauche.

I LOVE THE *vigor of a country dance.* The words rang in Lord Francis's ears as he led Miss Cora Downes onto the floor. She was priceless. He felt marvelously diverted. *And I ruined a brand-new bonnet.* When she might have preened herself on her reputation as a heroine, someone who had risked her life in order to save that of a child, she had belittled herself with such an observation.

She was almost, though not quite, as tall as he, he noticed. And he prided himself on being considerably above the average in height. She was the possessor of truly glorious curves, which even the loose-fitting, high-waisted style of her fashionable gown could not hide. Of course, muslin was a notorious figure-hugger. She was looking all about her with her eager face and bold eyes, not even attempting to hide her interest and curiosity. She caught his eye and—grinned.

"I am so *glad* you asked me to dance," she said. "I had positive horrors that no one would. And I suppose her grace could not actually *coerce* anyone into it. I daresay his grace asked you to ask me, which was re- markably kind of him, considering the fact that I am no relative of his and I am not sure he even approves of me. And it was kind of you too to say yes to him."

Lord Francis supposed that most young ladies must experience such fears. But he had never before heard one candidly confess to them—in a voice slightly louder than was necessary to make herself heard above the hum of conversation and the sound of the orchestra tun- ing their instruments.

He thought of Samantha and the fact that she must never have felt the fear of being without a partner at a ball. She had always been besieged by admirers and suit- ors. Tiny, dainty, blond-haired, exquisitely lovely Sa- mantha. Just a few weeks ago he had been dancing with her himself, her most devoted suitor, though she had chosen to believe after betrothing herself to Carew that he had never been serious about her. His heart per- formed a series of painful somersaults and landed in the soles of his shoes again.

"Perhaps," he said, "I saw you and admired you as soon as you came into the ballroom, Miss Downes, and sought an introduction to you. Have you thought of that?"

She looked squarely at him and he could see that she *was* thinking about it. And then she laughed. It was not a giggle this time, he was happy to find. It was a laugh of unrestrained mirth, drawing to her the rather startled glances of the other couples who were forming their particular set.

"You saw me and admired me," she said. "Oh, that is a good one."

He was not at liberty to consider what the one was or what was good about it. The music had begun and Lady Markley's daughter and her newly betrothed were leading off the first set.

It was indeed a lively country dance, which the ladies performed with grace and precision and Miss Cora Downes performed with—enthusiasm. She danced with energetic vigor just as if there were not a whole eveningful of sets yet to be danced, and with a bright smile on her face.

She danced, Lord Francis decided, as if she should have the ribbon of a maypole in her hand and sunshine on her face and in her loosened chestnut hair and all the fresh beauty of a village green surrounding her.

He watched her with considerable amusement and not a little appreciation—in her own way she was rather magnificent, he decided. And other gentlemen watched her too. There was something about her even apart from her height and her curves that would inevitably draw male eyes. Something that was not quite vulgar—not at all vulgar, in fact. But something very different from what one expected to find in a fashionable ballroom in London. Some—well, some raw femininity.

Her grace of Bridgwater might well have problems marrying the girl off, Lord Francis thought. Not just because of her origins—indeed, if it was true that the father was almost indecently wealthy, there would be any number of impecunious gentlemen, and even a few moderately pecunious ones, who would be only too delighted to overlook the fact that he had made his fortune in trade. No, it was the woman's looks and manner that would discourage serious suitors. Any red-blooded male would immediately dream of setting a mattress at Miss Cora Downes's back, whereas precious few of them would indulge in any corresponding dream of leading her to the altar first.

It was unfortunate.

He rather suspected that before the Season was over—unless the considerable awe in which both Bridgwater and his mother were held by the *ton* acted as a restraining force—Miss Cora Downes would be offered more than one carte blanche.

She was breathless and flushed and bright-eyed when the set was over. Her bosom was heaving as she tried to replace the missing air in her lungs.

"Oh, that was wonderful," she said. "Far more fun than any of the assemblies in Bath. There the dancers are mostly elderly, you know, and so the music is slower. Thank you so very much, Lord Francis. You are very kind."

"Thank *you*," he said, taking her arm on his sleeve and leading her back toward the duchess. "It was my honor and my pleasure, Miss Downes."

"May I ask you something?" she said, looking sideways into his eyes. Her own were a dark gray, he saw. He had at first thought them to be black. "What is your *name*? I was woolgathering when his grace presented you to me—or perhaps I was still flustered over the fact that I had tripped over my own feet and would have disgraced myself utterly instead of only partially if you had not stepped smartly forward and grabbed me. I am *always* woolgathering when something important is being said. It drives my papa insane. It drove my governess to despair."

"Kneller," he said, repressing the urge to chuckle. "It is the family name of the Dukes of Fairhurst. My elder brother is the current holder of the title."

"Oh," she said with an openmouthed gasp, "you are the brother of a *duke*. I am so glad I did not know it when I danced with you." She laughed.

There was a quality of merriment in her that was almost unladylike and was quite infectious, Lord Francis thought. He would like to draw the cork of any man who offered her carte blanche during what remained of the Season.

Perhaps he would take her under his wing, he thought suddenly. Bridgwater would undoubtedly be relieved and the duchess would surely not be displeased. As for himself, he had perhaps a great deal of a leftover life to kill. He had no wish to spend it pining away to a mere shadow of his former self over a woman who was now in Yorkshire with her new husband, doubtless proceeding with the pleasant business of living happily ever after.

Taking Miss Cora Downes under his wing would amuse him. And perhaps it would protect her from harm. Perhaps too he could steer toward her some likely candidate for matrimony. It might be diverting to become a matchmaker for the few weeks that remained of the Season. It would be a new role for him, one he had never even in his wildest imaginings thought of for himself. It was a feminine role, one his elder sisters delighted in. She had been trying to do it to him for so long that it was a testament to her endurance that she had not long ago lost faith in her powers.

It would be an amusing role to assume—if anything in life could ever again be amusing.

He returned Cora Downes to her place, stayed to make himself agreeable to the duchess and Lady Jane—Lady Elizabeth was promenading about the room on the arm of her future sister-in-law—waited until Corsham paused at his side with significant looks and throat-clearing, in the obvious hope of being presented to Miss Downes, performed that office, and had the satisfaction of watching her being led out for a quadrille while her grace and Bridgwater were still marshaling their forces of prospective partners for the merchant's daughter.

Corsham, Lord Francis thought in some satisfaction, was in possession of property and ten thousand a year. His mother was a draper's daughter, his father a second son of a second son. Fortunately he had had a wealthy aunt who had doted on him and left him everything on her demise.

An eminently eligible match for Miss Cora Downes.

"My thanks, old chap," his grace said at his elbow. "I owe you a favor. Fortunately the girl seems not quite vulgar, would you not agree? *Rustic* might be more the word. One can only hope she will improve under my mother's guidance. Though one does hope too that she does not make a habit of tripping over her feet." He grimaced.

Lord Francis chuckled. The sound seemed strange to his own ears. He wondered when he had last laughed.

3

THE DUCHESS OF BRIDGWATER HAD ALREADY PRO-
nounced herself well satisfied. There was no question about her satisfaction with Elizabeth and Jane, of
course. Elizabeth had moved almost immediately into
the illustrious circle of her future in-laws and had stayed
there. Jane had been rediscovered by last year's admirers
and had been discovered by several more, who had been
properly presented to her by her brother. But then Jane,
even apart from her beauty and youth and sweetness,
was the daughter of a duke.

No, it was with Cora that her grace was really ex-
pressing satisfaction. Apart from the unfortunate fact
that she had tripped over her feet at the sight of Lord
Francis Kneller's turquoise splendor, and that one heavy
lock of her hair had fallen down about her shoulder during the third set, another round of vigorous country
dances, and that she had trodden on her own hem at the
end of the same set and ripped the stitching out of a
stretch of it—apart from those slight mishaps, of which
her grace made light, she had behaved quite becomingly.
And up to and including the supper dance, she had had
a partner for every set except the waltz, which she was
not allowed to dance because certain dragons—the pa-
tronesses of Almack's, apparently—had not yet given
her the nod of approval. Which was all a parcel of non-

sense, as far as Cora was concerned, but her grace looked faintly alarmed and very slightly haughty when she mentioned the fact.

It seemed that Cora had taken well.

She took none of the credit to herself. The ladies who spoke with her—there were several—were friends either of her grace or of one of the girls. The gentlemen who danced with her were presented to her by either his grace or Lord Francis Kneller. All of them, she suspected, had had their arms twisted up behind their backs—even if only figuratively speaking—as an incentive to oblige her.

And some of the credit too, she had to admit, was due to the extraordinary story that was circulating. She was a great heroine, it seemed. She had saved the life of Lord George Munro's son—the child was second in line to the Bridgwater title—at considerable risk to her own life. His grace was deeply in her debt. Everyone referred to the story. Everyone looked at her almost in awe—just as if she were someone special.

It was really rather embarrassing. Especially when she recalled how very foolishly stupid she had been to shriek out and plunge into the river the way she had. She had not been heroic at all—only brainless, as Edgar had pointed out afterward while she was mourning over the bedraggled remains of her bonnet. He had taken her and bought her a new one the following morning—before the duchess descended upon her and bore her away to find her a husband from among the ranks of the gentry as a reward for her heroism.

It had been a successful evening. Her grace said so and even Cora felt it. But the trouble was that the part of her that felt it the most acutely was her toes. She dared not take her slippers off to wiggle them or to assess them for damages. She needed no assessment of the eyes. She would be very surprised if there was not a blister on every single toe. She could even feel blisters on toes that were not there. It was very difficult to sit through supper and smile and converse with her partner, Mr. Pandry, and the other people at her table—one of the ladies asked her repeated questions about dear little Henry and his behavior throughout his watery ordeal in the river at Bath—it was difficult to be sociable when all ten of her toes in addition to the ghost ones were screeching for her attention.

To dance after supper was an impossibility. To refuse to dance was an equal impossibility. Half of her mind dealt with the conversation at hand while the other half considered her dilemma. She was ashamed to admit the truth to her grace. A real lady, she rather suspected, would dance even if all ten of her toes were broken and a couple of ankles to boot. A real lady . . . She had never—before the incident of little Henry, that was—even considered the fact that she was not a real lady. She had been very satisfied with who she was. She still was satisfied. She had no wish to start pretending to be anything she was not. She was her papa's daughter. Papa was not, according to strict definition, a gentleman. She loved her papa.

She told the duchess when they had returned to the ballroom that she needed to go to the ladies' withdrawing room and that she might be gone a little while—words uttered with some blushing embarrassment. She declined the offer to be accompanied.

She really did intend to go to the ladies' room, but she suddenly remembered from the time she had gone there with her grace earlier to have her hair pinned up again and her hem mended that it was crowded and noisy. If she sat there for any length of time the fact would surely be remarked upon. And she would feel the eyes of the maids stationed there upon her. She turned sharply instead and walked out through the open French doors onto the balcony outside.

It was all but deserted. After the supper break, everyone was ready to dance or to play cards again, she guessed. She discovered a vacant chair behind a large and dense potted plant. She sank gratefully onto it and tried wiggling her toes. The attempt did not help at all. She would not have thought it possible for slippers to cause such pain, but she supposed it made sense that they did so when they were a size too small.

She looked carefully to both sides and even over her shoulder. There was no one in sight. Everyone was in the ballroom. The music had struck up again. She lifted one foot onto the opposite knee, bending her leg outward, and cradled her foot in both hands. For a short while she resisted further temptation. But it was too insistent. She pulled off her slipper and tossed it to the balcony beside her other foot. The freedom, the rush of coolness, even the pain was exquisite. She closed her eyes and sighed.

"Trouble?" a languid, almost bored voice asked.

She snapped to attention, still clutching her foot. And then she breathed out through puffed cheeks in noisy relief when she saw who it was. It was only Lord Francis Kneller. She would have been horribly mortified if it had been any other gentleman. Lord Francis seemed almost like a woman friend. Not that she meant the thought at all unkindly. After an evening of observing him—she had found her eyes following him about the ballroom— and occasionally exchanging a few words with him and dancing with him that once, she had come to believe that he was happy with who he was. As any person should be, she firmly believed.

"Oh, it is just you," she said. Even so she edged down the hem of her gown, which had been up somewhere in the region of her knee. "Sore feet is all. I have slunk out here, where I thought to remain unobserved."

"Just sore?" he asked. "Or blistered?"

"Blistered," she admitted after a short pause. Now she did feel mortified after all. "My feet are too large, you see. I thought to reduce them to greater daintiness with slippers that are too small."

"Not a wise idea," he said and he seated himself on the stone bench that ran beneath the balustrade and took her foot onto his lap. He massaged it with his thumb, avoiding her toes. She was inclined to giggle and pull away at first, but the pressure of his thumb was too firm and too soothing to tickle.

"You are a tall lady," he said. "You would not be able to balance on tiny feet. I believe a certain incident earlier this evening proved that. Besides, you would look funny. Out of proportion."

She chuckled, pain forgotten for a moment. "Vanity is a dreadful thing," she said. She supposed that he would understand that himself.

"When it causes blisters, yes," he said. "I suppose the other foot is in just as bad a case?"

"Yes," she admitted ruefully.

He set her stockinged foot on the ground and lifted the other onto his lap, easing off the slipper and proceeding to massage the foot as he had the other.

"Not that it is any of my concern, Miss Downes," he said at last, "but where is your chaperon, pray?"

"Oh, what nonsense it is," she said, "this business of chaperons. I had a great deal more freedom before I became a *heroine,* I do assure you."

"Your parents allowed you to roam about unescorted?" he asked, raising his eyebrows. "Dear me."

"My mother is dead," she said. "Edgar—my brother—told me once, a long time ago, that she ventured one look at me after giving birth to me, took fright, and quit this world without further ado. But Papa scolded him for making light of so serious a matter and even thrashed him for it, I do believe, though I was sorry because it was said only as a joke even if it was in poor taste. No, Papa does not allow me to roam unescorted, as you put it. But now that I have become a heroine and a protégée, I may not move a muscle, it seems, without having a female companion accompany it."

"It is for your own protection, I do assure you," he said. "How do you know that I am not about to take great liberties with your person? Indeed, I have already taken liberties. Many ladies I know would faint dead away if they knew I had been fondling your feet for the past ten minutes or so."

Cora threw back her head and laughed. "Oh, I know I am safe with *you*," she said and then realized that perhaps her words were ill-bred even though she had not meant them unkindly. "You were presented to me by the Duke of Bridgwater himself," she added.

"Does her grace know you are out here?" he asked.

She smiled at him conspiratorially. "I told her I was going to the ladies' withdrawing room," she said. "But it is always so crowded there. It was cooler and quieter out here."

"Stay here." He got to his feet after setting her foot down beside the other. "I shall explain to the duchess that you are ready to go home and see to the ordering around of her carriage if Bridgwater is nowhere in sight. Then I shall come back and escort you to it."

"She will have to know about my blisters," she said. "It seems so ungenteel somehow."

"Even one of the royal princesses would develop blisters if she wore slippers of too small a size and then proceeded to dance for several hours in them with—ah—*vigor*," he said. "I shall return."

And he was gone.

She would be packed up and sent home to Bath, Cora thought. It must be disgraceful to have to leave one's very first *ton* ball early because one had blistered feet. Now her grace was going to have to leave early and Jane and Elizabeth too—and doubtless their dancing cards were full and they were going to have to excuse themselves to all the gentlemen with whom they were to dance. And they would be miserable at having to lose half an evening's entertainment but they would be too well mannered to blame her openly.

If only she had not jumped into that river. There was nothing callous in the thought. Little Henry's survival had not depended upon such theatrical heroics.

Well, she thought, stooping down to pick up her slippers and eyeing them with a grimace, if she was sent home in disgrace, she would not care. She really had not wanted to become the Duchess of Bridgwater's protégée in the first place. But her grace had been importunate and Lord George had been charmingly insistent—and Lady George too, though because of her confinement she had had to relay her pleas through her husband and one lengthy letter—and Papa had thought it a splendid opportunity for her. Even Edgar had told her she would be a fool to reject the chance that was being offered her.

But she had no wish for a genteel husband. Or for a husband at all, in fact. Though that was a bouncer, she admitted in all fairness. Of course she wanted a husband. And of course it would be pleasant to have one who was well set up and genteel in manner. But mostly she wanted a husband for affection and companionship and for—well, for the other. She had no particularly clear picture of what was involved in that other, but she was very convinced that she would like it excessively. Provided she felt an affection for her husband, that was. And she knew that she would like to have children.

Perhaps, she thought, she should merely have had

Lord Francis escort her back into the ballroom. She could have sat through the rest of the evening without disturbing anyone else. But it was too late now to think of that. She flexed her slippers in her hands as if she thought to enlarge them a whole size by doing so.

And then Lord Francis appeared again. Cora looked sheepishly beyond his shoulder, but it was just Betty who was standing there, the maid the duchess had brought with them.

"Her grace is making arrangements for Lady Elizabeth and Lady Jane to be chaperoned and fetched home by Lady Fuller," he said. "I shall escort you to the carriage, Miss Downes. I have brought Betty with me so that you will not be forced to the impropriety of moving a muscle without its being accompanied by a chaperon, you see."

Lady Fuller was sister to the Marquess of Hayden, Elizabeth's betrothed. Cora felt better knowing that the evening was not going to be ruined for Elizabeth and Jane.

"Was she very cross?" she asked.

"Her grace?" He raised his eyebrows. "Cross? I do not believe duchesses are ever *cross,* Miss Downes. Actually I believe she was more relieved than anything else. She was coming to the conclusion that you had vanished into the proverbial thin air. No, I would not advise trying to squeeze your toes back into the slippers."

She sighed. "I cannot walk back through the ballroom in my stockinged feet," she said. "Even merchants' daughters know that much about gentility, my lord."

"I would not have brought Betty if that had been my planned route," he said, "Come along. We shall avoid the ballroom altogether."

He took her slippers as she got to her feet, and handed them to Betty. Then he drew her arm through his and led her slowly toward the steps leading down into the garden. Betty followed silently behind. Cora hoped fervently that the few people who were strolling on the balcony would not look downward to notice that she was unshod.

"It is such a shame," she said with a sigh as they descended the steps, "to have to miss the rest of the ball. Just listen to that music. You are very kind, Lord Francis. Would you not prefer to be dancing?"

"When I might be escorting the loveliest lady among the guests to her carriage instead?" he said. "Absolutely not, ma'am."

Cora chuckled. "What a thorough bouncer," she said. "You will go straight to hell for that one, Lord Francis."

"Dear me," he said rather faintly.

They were to walk about the house to the front, it seemed. It also appeared that the house was surrounded on three sides by a cobbled walk.

"This is by far the best part," he said as they reached it, "and the reason I felt it wise to bring Betty along." And he disengaged his arm from hers, turned to her, and scooped her up into his arms.

Cora shrieked.

"It was definitely wise," he said. "Stay close, Betty, if you please."

"You cannot *carry* me," Cora said, feeling considerably flustered and doing with her arms the only thing that seemed possible to do with them—she set them about his shoulders. "I weigh a *ton*."

His voice, when he spoke, betrayed the truth of her words—he was breathless. "The merest feather, Miss Downes," he said, "I do assure you."

He was unexpectedly strong. Even Edgar, who was both tall and husky and who was also very, very masculine—she had seen the way women followed him with their eyes with expressions ranging from wistful to downright predatory—even Edgar had been red-faced and puffing a few weeks ago by the time he had hauled her, dripping, out of the river. And yet Lord Francis Kneller, whom she still could not resist comparing to a peacock, was carrying her along half the length of the back of the house, along its whole width, and then back along the front to her grace's waiting carriage. Cora hoped for the sake of his pride that he would not have to set her down in order to recover breath and muscle power before they reached their destination, but he did not.

There was no reason, she supposed, to believe that a man who dressed so and who spoke and moved with studied elegance and who appeared as a result to be somewhat—well, *effeminate* was not quite the word. It was too ruthless and unkind. She could not think of the word she meant if there were such a word. Anyway, there was no reason to believe that such a man was also a weakling. And yet that was just what she would have expected of Lord Francis Kneller. Nobody, she supposed, fit inside neat little boxes of expectation. Everyone was an individual and must be judged, if at all, on individual merits.

She was well satisfied with the profound insight into life that the evening had brought her. And what if he had been a weakling? Philosophical insights now bubbled up into her consciousness. Would that fact have diminished him as a person? She liked him. He had been kind to her. And at the basest level, he had provided her with amusement.

"Woolgathering again, Miss Downes?" he asked her, his voice still managing to sound languid despite the fact that he was definitely short of breath.

"What?" she said.

But they were at the carriage and he still had the strength left to swing her inside and deposit her on one of the seats instead of doing what would have been easier and simply dropping her so that she could climb the steps herself. He offered his hand to Betty, who bobbed a series of curtsies and allowed him to hand her inside.

"I asked," he said, leaning across the carriage seat and looking up at Cora, "if I might have the honor of driving you in the park tomorrow afternoon. My guess is that you will not be walking any great distance for the next couple of days at least."

"In the park?" she said. "*Hyde* Park?" It was the dream. It was the pinnacle. Everyone—even the merchant class of Bristol—knew all about Hyde Park in the afternoons during the Season.

"None other," he said. "At precisely five o'clock, ma'am. At precisely the time when there will be so many carriages and horsemen and pedestrians there that only a snail could be content with the speed of movement."

"How splendid!" Cora said, clasping her hands to her bosom. "And you want *me* to drive with you?"

"A simple yes or no would suffice, you know," he said.

She grinned at him and then remembered that ladies did not grin. She was reminded by the arrival of the Duchess of Bridgwater, whom Lord Francis handed into the carriage. The coachman put up the steps and began to close the door. But Cora leaned hastily forward.

"Yes, then," she said. "And thank you. You are very kind."

"THIS IS ELIZABETH's doing, at an educated guess," her grace said when they were finally on their way, her voice not unkind. "Elizabeth holds the strange and rather painful belief that feet must be made to appear as small as possible. I should have remembered that, dear, when I allowed her to accompany you to the shoemaker's. To-morrow, or as soon as your feet have healed, we must begin all over again. Betty, I believe, wears just the size of these slippers."

Betty brightened considerably.

"Lord Francis said that small feet on a large person would look silly," Cora said.

"And Lord Francis is an authority on feminine beauty and fashion," her grace said. "You would do well to pay him heed, Cora. But I would be willing to wager that he did not imply that you are *large*. Did he perhaps use the word *tall*? He is far too well-bred to have used the former."

She was not in disgrace after all, Cora thought. She sank back against the squabs and relaxed. It really was fun to be part of the *ton* for a short while. Tonight she had danced with numerous gentlemen and even with a duke's son—it did not matter that he dressed like a peacock. The blisters had been won in an almost worthwhile cause. She had enjoyed herself greatly. And tomorrow she was to drive in Hyde Park at five o'clock in the afternoon.

She closed her eyes and thought of the letter she would write to Papa and Edgar tomorrow morning.

LORD FRANCIS KNELLER was in the depths of gloom. He toyed with breakfast, pushing the kidneys into a neat triangle at one side of his plate and lining up the three sausages like soldiers at the other. One soldier was taller than the other two—he moved it to the middle for better symmetry. He could not decide at quite what angle to set his toast on the plate for best aesthetic effect.

His heart was squashed flat against the soles of his riding boots.

He had been feeling almost cheerful when he had got up after only a few hours of sleep following the Markley ball. All through his morning ride in the park he had felt almost cheerful. He had kept thinking about the rather odd Miss Cora Downes, and somehow every thought had brought amusement—and occasionally an actual chuckle—with it.

He had been somewhat exhilarated at his plan to bring her into fashion, perhaps even to find her the husband the Duchess of Bridgwater had brought her to London to find. He had thought that perhaps at last he would have something *amusing* on which to fix his mind and his energies. It might not be easy to bring Cora Downes into fashion—though none of her partners last evening had looked as if he had had to be coerced into dancing with her. There had been some lascivious glances, of course, especially when she had been dancing most vigorously.

By the time he had reached home and stabled his horse and walked back to his rooms for breakfast, he had still felt almost cheerful. There was always the qualification of the *almost,* of course. Always deep within, sometimes beyond the medium of conscious thought, was the awareness that today, no matter how much he was out and about in Society, he would not see Samantha.

He had been *almost* cheerful. This afternoon he would take Miss Downes up in his phaeton and would drive her in the park and see what amusement might be derived from doing so.

And then he had sat down to breakfast and his newspaper and his letters. And instead of reading the paper first and then tackling the post, he had thumbed through the letters and discovered one from Gabe—his close friend, the Earl of Thornhill. And because Gabe was his friend, and because he lived in Yorkshire on the estate adjoining Highmoor, the Marquess of Carew's seat, Lord Francis had opened and read the letter before anything else.

The crops were all planted and growing. The sheep

had all lambed, most of them successfully, and the cows had all calved. Everything, in fact, appeared to be going well with Gabe's life even though he pretended to complain about a projected visit to Harrogate with his wife and children in order to shop. Lord Francis knew that Gabe doted on his wife and family and would take them to Peking to shop if he thought it would give them pleasure. Though not at the present time, of course. Lady Thornhill was increasing—Lord Francis had known about that before—and Gabe was strict about the amount of traveling he would allow her to do at such times.

"And our neighbors, Frank," Gabe had written just when Lord Francis had been feeling elated and mortally depressed at the conviction that they were not going to be mentioned at all. "Nothing will do but Jennifer must call upon them almost every day when they are not calling upon us, and since I will not allow her far out of my sight when she is in such a delicate way, I call upon them almost every day too—except when they are with us. All is domestic bliss there. We have been delighted and a little surprised to find it, though in truth I am the only one surprised. Jennifer declares that Samantha would not have married for anything less than love (you know what incurable romantics women are and ought to know that Jennifer is perhaps the most incurable of all). But if you had any doubts, Frank, and I know you were a particular friend of Samantha's, then you may put them to rest. She did not marry Carew for his title and wealth. My wife was purple with indignation when I was unwise enough to suggest to her that such might be the case. And one more *on-dit*, Frank, before I take up the theme of the beginning of this letter and beg you to come and spend part of the summer with us—the children claim that summer will not be complete without the presence of Uncle Frank, who swam and climbed trees and played cricket with them last year. One more *on-dit*—Jennifer whispered to me and I am whispering to you, in the strictest confidence, of course, that our Marchioness of Carew is to present her marquess with an heir or—heaven forbid—a daughter sometime within the next nine months."

Lord Francis read the rest of the letter with eyes to which his mind was not attached.

So she was with child. It was hardly surprising when she had been married for longer than a month. Of course she was with child. It did not matter to him. He had lost her as soon as she betrothed herself to Carew. He had lost her utterly on her wedding day.

Now he lost her just a little more again.

4

I DO BELIEVE SHE IS ABOUT TO BECOME A NINE-DAYS wonder," the Duke of Bridgwater said to his mother after all her afternoon visitors—except him—had left. Although he lived alone in a large town house, his mother always chose to open her own house, left her as part of her legacy in her husband's will, whenever she came to town for longer than a week at a time. She was so accustomed to being mistress of her own house, she always said by way of explanation, that she would doubtless be an obnoxious, domineering mother if she lived with her son.

"It is very gratifying indeed, Alistair," the duchess replied. "One realized that Elizabeth's status as Hayden's betrothed would draw visitors and one hoped that Jane's eligibility would do likewise—do you not agree that she is in remarkable good looks this year? But one could only be anxious about Cora. I find her delightful, though I recognize that there is something about her that is not quite the thing. But one could not help but wonder if her origins would be too much of an impediment in town."

His grace withdrew an enameled snuffbox from a pocket, flicked it open with a practiced thumb, and proceeded to set a pinch of his favorite blend on the back of one hand.

"Instead of which," he said, "she very near outshone

Jane this afternoon. It is to be wondered, by the way, if Jane will find someone to her liking during what is left of the Season this year. It became tedious last year sending away all those suitors who came to me with their offers merely because she had assured me each time that she could not possibly, possibly marry so-and-so. I believe I acquired notoriety as an ogre of a brother."

"Jane is still very young," his mother said, "and very full of ideals. She still believes that somewhere out there is the person who was created with the sole purpose of being her mate. I believe, Alistair, that she is not alone among my children in harboring such a belief."

The duke sniffed a portion of the snuff up each nostril and paused for it to take effect. In doing so, he avoided responding to his mother's comment.

"It appears," he said when he was able, "that one does not even need to stress the fact that Miss Downes will undoubtedly be the recipient of a very large dowry indeed when she marries. At least, I have not stressed any such fact yet. Have you?"

"Not at all," his mother said. "People have chosen to take to her for a far more noble reason. She is the heroine of the hour. It is very gratifying."

"I have often wondered." His grace regarded his mother with lazy eyes, which perhaps held a modicum of humor. "*Would* Henry have drowned without Miss Downes's heroic act?"

The duchess looked shocked. "Of course he would have drowned," she said. "Cora saved his life at considerable risk to her own."

"Can Henry not swim?" his grace asked. He knew the answer. He had taught the child himself the previous summer.

"Alistair!" her grace exclaimed. "A five-year-old who takes a tumble fully clothed into a cold river is scarcely

likely to remember the skills taught him almost a year
ago."

"I suppose not." His grace returned his snuffbox to
his pocket. "And so a number of visitors called this afternoon for the express purpose of conversing with the
heroine and congratulating her. There were even one or
two eligibles among them. Did they come out of curiosity alone, do you think? Can any of them be brought to
the point?"

"I believe Mr. Corsham is a possibility," the duchess
said. "He danced with her last evening and you say he
inquired about her after I had fetched her home. He is
just the sort of young man who would be eager to marry
a fortune, Alistair. He has the one his aunt left him, but
he is still very much a younger son."

"I shall be sure to have a word with him at White's,"
his grace said, "and steer the conversation toward the
enormous wealth of Mr. Downes, in addition to his recent emergence as a man of property."

"Mr. Pandry might be brought around as well," the
duchess said. "Sir Robert Webster might not. He would
not wish to risk the reputation of a baronet's title by taking a bride of inferior rank. Lord Francis Kneller was
remarkably kind to her last evening, and he is to take
her driving in the park later. Did you know? He is out of
the question as a suitor, of course, but his notice can do
her nothing but good in the eyes of the *ton*."

"Yes," his grace agreed. "It is well known that Kneller
takes notice only of those ladies who are worth noticing.
He was obliging me last evening and clearly decided to
take my plea seriously enough to extend the invitation
for today. I shall encourage him to continue to take notice of her. He needs employment. He has recently suffered a severe disappointment."

"Miss Newman?" his mother asked. "I heard of her
recent marriage to your friend the Marquess of Carew. I

was surprised, I must confess. I thought Lord Francis to be the favorite among her suitors, and heaven knows he paid determined court to her for long enough."

"But Carew bore off the prize," his grace said, "and Kneller needs diversion while he looks about him for another Incomparable to whose court to attach himself—his words, not mine, I do assure you, Mama. He can do Miss Downes nothing but good. Perhaps he can teach her to be a little less—exuberant."

The duchess laughed. "I find her delightful, Alistair," she said. "But you are right, of course. She needs polish. I actually saw her throw back her head last evening and laugh. I was caught between horror and amusement."

"If it had been Lizzie or Jane," her son said, his eyebrows raised, "there would have been no question of amusement, Mama."

"Oh, no, indeed," she agreed fervently. "I do hope that between us, you and I—and perhaps Lord Francis, if he will be so obliging—will be able to smooth out some rough edges. Cora deserves a respectable husband after what she did for dear Henry, Alistair."

"We will try what we can do, Mama," he said. "But I hope for your sake she will not blame us at some future date for lifting her out of her own class and making her unhappy."

CORA COULD NOT remember a time when she had enjoyed herself more. All her anxieties of last night and this morning and the early part of this afternoon had been for naught. Not only was it not raining, but the sun shone down from a cloudless sky and the day was hot, though only pleasantly so by five o'clock in the afternoon. In addition to these happy circumstances was the fact that Lord Francis Kneller had not forgotten his appointment to take her driving in Hyde Park. He arrived punctually at half past four.

She was wearing her favorite of her new day clothes—a bright yellow muslin dress with blue sash and blue cornflowers embroidered about the scalloped hem, and a straw hat whose brim was trimmed with artificial cornflowers and which sported a wide yellow ribbon stretched over the brim of the hat and tied beneath her chin. She carried a blue parasol. She wore a pair of her old shoes, a regrettable fact, but better than wearing no shoes at all—which seemed the only alternative for today at least.

Cora was feeling very smart indeed. Her papa had given her a vast sum of money to bring with her to London, with the strict instructions that a certain specified amount of it was to be spent on fashionable clothes. And Edgar had made her a gift of another large sum with which to buy herself baubles and gewgaws, as he had phrased it. She had been happily obedient to the wishes of both.

Another fact was contributing to her happiness. She had had a dreadful thought sometime during the night, when she had woken to think back to the ball and to flex her stinging toes gingerly against the bandages a maid had swathed them in. And the thought had haunted her all day. What if Lord Francis Kneller's appearance last evening was uncharacteristic of him? What if he was not after all a rather foppish gentleman? What if he appeared today to take her driving, looking as forbiddingly masculine and aristocratic as the Duke of Bridgwater had looked in her grace's drawing room? She would die. He was *Lord* Francis Kneller, after all. His father had been a duke. His brother was a duke. Her tongue would tie itself into one giant knot and she would doubtless simper and stammer and blush her way through the ordeal of a drive in the park with him.

Not that a duke's son or even a duke was inherently superior to Papa and Edgar and the other men of their class with whom she was acquainted. But it was one thing for the head to know that. It was another for the body and the emotions to act in accordance with the belief.

She had longed for and dreaded the arrival of Lord Francis Kneller. She had bitten both cheeks to shreds.

Yet again all her fears had been for nothing. He was standing in the hall of her grace's house when she came downstairs at the summons of a footman, and she felt herself exhale in relief. His coat was not quite pink or quite a mulberry color. It was halfway between the two. She remembered Edgar's saying that some of the fops of the *ton* liked to appear as if they had been poured into their coats. Cora was reminded of those words as she looked at Lord Francis. And his pantaloons too. They were of fine gray leather and molded his form so tightly that she might have blushed if he had been anyone else. Certainly she was aware of splendid calf muscles—she had had the proof of their strength last evening when he had carried her all the way to the carriage. His Hessian boots were so glossy that she was convinced that if she bent over them she would be able to make sure that the bow of her hat was tied at just the right angle beneath her chin. And his neckcloth was as elaborately tied as the one he had worn last night. He carried his hat and whip in one hand.

His appearance, elegant and gorgeous, quite reassured her and made her joy complete. But the crowning glory was the high-perch phaeton into which he lifted her when he had escorted her outside. It was a splendid confection of a vehicle, all show and lack of practicality. It was painted a bright blue and yellow. How fortunate, she thought, that she had dressed to match it. Two almost identical chestnuts were harnessed to it.

"This," she said later, as they were turning into the park, "is surely the most exciting afternoon of my life." And then she turned her head in order to smile apologetically at him. "I am not to enthuse, am I? Lady Elizabeth has constantly to remind me of that. But no matter since it is only to you. I shall behave myself when we are among the crowds, I promise." She opened her parasol since she had just become aware that they were very close to being among the crowds, and gave it a vigorous twirl above her head.

"Just so," Lord Francis said, looking at her. "But why young ladies feel obliged to squash the natural exuberance of their spirits in order to appear *ton*nish escapes my understanding at the present moment."

"I believe it appears gauche," Cora said. "Or *rustic*. That is what Elizabeth says anyway. Oh, my!" Such a crush of vehicles and riders and walkers it had been impossible to imagine though she had been told about it. No one could possibly be out for the sole purpose of a drive or a ride. Or even a walk.

"It would be far more sensible," she said to Lord Francis, "for everyone to leave their carriages and horses at the gate and merely stroll here. It is obvious that everyone has come here to talk."

"Ah," he said, "but how would we impress one another, Miss Downes, if we could not be outdoing one another in the splendor of our carriages and the superiority of our cattle? We can observe one another's clothes and persons at any ball or concert. What would the day have to offer of novelty?"

"How absurd," she said.

"Quite so," he said agreeably. "Absurdity is amusing, Miss Downes. Endlessly entertaining."

She wondered if he ever dressed out of any sense of the absurd and decided that he probably did not. But there was no more time for private reflection or even for conversation tête-à-tête. They were among the throng and they were not being ignored.

Whatever he might be, Lord Francis was no outcast with the *ton,* Cora discovered now even if she had not noticed it the evening before. Gentlemen hailed him and very often stopped to exchange civilities. Ladies, both old and young, had their carriages stopped in order to converse with him. Old and young tittered at his practiced and smoothly flattering gallantries. Some, particularly the older ladies, gave as good as they received. Cora guessed that ladies felt it safe to flirt with someone like Lord Francis.

But it soon became obvious to her that she herself was not invisible. Several people merely nodded pleasantly to her when Lord Francis presented them to her and then continued their remarks to him. But far more people seemed to have approached him with the intention of making her acquaintance and commending her on the jolly good show of her heroism in the little Henry incident. Two of the gentlemen she had danced with last evening—Mr. Corsham and Mr. Pandry—rode up beside her and engaged her in conversation while Lord Francis chatted with other people. Mr. Corsham remarked with a smirk that now he knew the identity of the gentleman with whom she had told him earlier she was engaged to drive, he would likely slap a glove in the face of Lord Francis the next time he saw him alone. Mr. Pandry asked her if she was to attend a certain ball next week and hoped she would reserve a set for him.

It was all very flattering. So were the particular attentions of two or three gentlemen to whom Lord Francis presented her as the heroine they must have heard of by now, and daughter of the Mr. Downes who had recently purchased and rebuilt Mobley Abbey near Bristol. Cora had not even realized that Lord Francis knew those facts himself.

She was enjoying herself immensely.

But as usually happened, her mind wandered from the here and now after some time. There were just too many people at whom to smile and nod, too many names to remember, and too many faces to which to have to attach those names in the future. She withdrew a little into herself, became more of a spectator than a participant.

It was very clear that a number of people had come to the park neither to take the air nor to converse. Some had come merely to be seen and admired. The lady in pink, for example, who was walking her dogs, four tiny poodles, each on the end of a different-colored silk leash. An insignificant little maid moved along slightly behind her mistress. The pink plumes in the lady's pink bonnet must be at least four feet high, Cora thought. Her mind was occasionally prone to exaggerate. And she carried herself with great dignity, a proud, half contemptuous smile on her lips. The dogs were for picturesque effect, Cora decided. But poor little things—it had not been the wisest idea in the world to bring them into such a crush. They were in considerable danger of being trodden upon.

And then there was the gentleman in green and buff, who was riding a magnificent black horse, which was far too spirited for the crowded circumstances. He was a very proud and haughty gentleman too, Cora thought. He had a decidedly prominent nose but no chin at all. He had a quite fascinating profile.

They fancied each other, Cora suddenly realized. The lady was lifting her chin and her bosom and was tugging on the leashes entirely for the chinless gentleman's benefit, and he was prancing on his black horse for hers.

How very, very amusing. If only Lord Francis were not engaged in conversation with an elderly lady and gentleman who had finished congratulating her and were tackling the weather with him, she would be able to point out the scene to him. He would be entertained by it, she was sure.

But as the two approached each other, Cora became aware of something else. The trotting poodles and the prancing black were soon going to be trying to occupy the exact same spot of land. It did not take a vivid imagination to guess which animals were going to have the worst of it. There were going to be a couple of squashed poodles at the very least.

"Oh," she said in great agitation just as Lord Francis and the elderly couple took their leave of each other and he turned to her. "Oh, dear. Oh, dear."

There was time neither to explain the situation to him nor to shout out a warning, though she did the latter anyway. But at the same moment she hurled herself over the side of Lord Francis's high-perch phaeton.

DURING WHAT HAD remained of the morning after his ride and his nonbreakfast, Lord Francis had sat in White's, reading the papers and conversing with various acquaintances. Actually he had maneuvered the latter activity so that he spoke with the gentlemen he wished to speak with. It had not been difficult to steer the conversation to last evening's ball and the new arrivals—any new faces were to be remarked upon this late in the Season. And it had not been difficult to focus upon Miss Downes and her heroic deed. It had been, as Walter Parker remarked, "a demned fine show."

And it had not been difficult to drop the subtlest of hints about the father and Mobley Abbey and the splendid job he appeared to have done in restoring it to modern grandeur. It went without saying that the man must be enormously wealthy. It also went without saying that the daughter's dowry would in all probability be more than substantial.

Now Lord Francis had the satisfaction of seeing his hints begin to bear fruit. A number of the gentlemen he had spoken with this morning happened to be riding in the park this afternoon—he had, of course, mentioned the fact that he was to drive Miss Downes there at the fashionable hour—and deemed it a courtesy to stop to pay their respects to him and their gallantries to his companion.

Being a matchmaker, he was discovering, was providing definite amusement. And God knew, he was desperately in need of amusement.

She was looking really quite handsome this afternoon in yellow and pale blue. The vivid colors suited her far better than last night's virginal white. And her smiles, her sparkling eyes, and her general exuberance were a little less conspicuous in the outdoors. Not that he had any particular objection to them anywhere.

But he sensed her tiring after a while. She was a little quieter, a little more withdrawn. He supposed all this must be somewhat bewildering to a young lady who had not been brought up to it. He would maneuver his phaeton out of the crowds after this particular conversation, he thought—she had not participated in it beyond nodding and smiling in acknowledgment of the usual congratulations on her heroic deed. He would drive her through a quieter part of the park and then take her home. The afternoon had done well for her. He had hopes that with very little more effort today's admirers would turn into tomorrow's partners and escorts and the day after tomorrow's suitors—well, one or two of them anyway. Even one would be enough—only one of them could marry her, after all.

He would keep an eye out, of course, to make sure that no mere fortune hunter bore her off. Not that it was his responsibility to see to any such thing. There were the duchess and Bridgwater to look to her interests, not to mention her father and brother. Lord Francis had no doubt that the father at least was a shrewd judge of a man's character and motives.

He turned to her, his mouth opening to suggest that they move on. But several things happened in such close succession that he was never sure afterward if his mouth had been left hanging open to the breeze or if it had snapped shut. Her gaze was fixed on a point a little to one side, away from him, her whole manner was agitated, she muttered, "Oh, dear. Oh, dear," and with a shriek, she hurled herself over the side of his high-perch phaeton. To her certain death, it seemed. Only perhaps a fraction of a second passed before he went after her, abandoning his horses to their own devices, but in that split second he saw several things. He saw Lady Kellington walking her poodles and issuing come-hither glances to Lord Lanting, who was preening himself before her on his giant black and proceeding to come hither. He knew that the dogs were too accustomed to this sort of scene to be in any danger from the horse's hooves and that the horse was too well trained to trample them anyway.

He also saw that Miss Cora Downes, if she survived the descent from his phaeton, would be in considerable danger from those hooves.

He jumped.

Those close enough to observe what followed—and there were many—could not have found more thrilling entertainment even at Astley's, Lord Francis thought ruefully later, when he was at liberty to think. Lady Kellington's poodles yapped with sudden panic at the descent of a shrieking whirlwind into their ranks and tried to break loose in as many directions as there were dogs. The lady clung on to their leashes and screamed. Lord Lanting's black whinnied and reared. His lordship roared but displayed superb horsemanship in not being ignominiously tossed into the crowd. Cora Downes shrieked—or rather, she continued to shriek—and grabbed for poodles before the horse could plant all four feet back on earth, or on whatever happened to be between them and earth. Somehow she succeeded in gathering two of them under one arm and one under the other. Almost at the same moment Lord Francis himself, muttering what he hoped later had not been either obscenities or blasphemies, launched himself at her, grabbed her about the waist, spun her away from those dangerously flailing hooves, and landed heavily on the grass with her and an indeterminate number of poodles beneath him and colored leashes twined all about him.

Lord Francis's first sane thought since he had sat perched up in his phaeton was of the spectacle they were offering to the avidly curious eyes of the *ton*. To do him justice, it was of Cora he thought first. Before he rolled off her and released the furiously barking dogs, he checked hastily to make sure that her dress was decently down about her legs. It was.

But moving off was not simply a matter of rolling to one side. They were both entangled in leashes, and the dog that had remained free was now rushing in wild circles about its fallen comrades, making the tangle worse.

"The devil," Lord Francis muttered, struggling free with a superhuman effort.

Miss Cora Downes was laughing. "Ouch!" she said. "Are there supposed to be two suns up there? Are the dogs all safe?" Her face, he saw, was flushed. Her eyes were dazed—or rather her *eye*. Her hat had swiveled about her head so that it covered one side of her face. One of her short puffed sleeves had almost entirely parted company with the rest of her dress. Her bosom, decently covered, fortunately, was heaving.

"Lie still," he commanded her, sitting up and prepar-

ing to take inventory of his own various parts and garments. She must be suffering from a concussion.

But suddenly reality rushed in with considerable noise
and motion. The poodles were all free, though they were
hopelessly tangled together, and barking. Lady Kellington was on her knees in the midst of them, trying to hug
them all at once while they tried all at once to lick her
face. Lord Lanting was on his feet just behind her, a firm
hand on the bridle of his horse, which was still snorting
and rolling its eyes. A whole army of other people was
gathered about.

"My darlings, my darlings," Lady Kellington was
crooning. "You are all safe. You might all have been
killed."

"I say, Lucy," Lord Lanting said. "I say, I am most
awfully sorry, old girl. I do not know what got into Jet.
He don't usually behave like that."

Lord Francis could have given him an idea or two on
what had got into the black—she was currently lying
face up on the grass, gazing at two suns through one
eye.

But she was not to remain neglected for long. Lady
Kellington gently pushed away her poodles, having assured herself that they were all not only alive, but un-
harmed, and turned to grasp one of Cora's hands in
both of her own.

"Oh, my dear," she said. "My dear, you have saved
the lives of my darlings. How will I ever be able to thank
you?" And she raised Cora's hand to her face in order to
wash it with her tears.

"Oh, I say," Lord Lanting added, his eyes turning in
Cora's direction, "a splendid act of courage, m'dear."

"You might have killed yourself," Lady Kellington
said through her tears.

The crowd acted like a Greek chorus. There were
mutterings and murmurings and a few quite distinct

voices. All of them were singing the same tune. All of them were chanting the praises of Miss Cora Downes, who had saved the lives of Lady Kellington's poodles at considerable risk to her own life.

The leather of his new pantaloons was scuffed beyond repair, Lord Francis noticed with deep regret. So was one of his boots. One side and one sleeve of his coat were covered with dust. His white shirt cuff was stained green from the grass. So, he noticed with a grimace when he turned his arm, was the elbow of his coat. His hat was nowhere in sight.

"By Gad," someone said, "she is Miss Downes. The Duchess of Bridgwater's protégée. She was at Lady Markley's last evening."

"The one who saved Bridgwater's nephew by jumping into the river in Bath after him." Someone else had taken up the chorus.

"The heroine!" It was almost a communal whisper of awe.

5

$\mathcal{T}$T WAS A LITTLE MORTIFYING TO EMERGE FROM A DAZE to find oneself lying prostrate on a grass verge in Hyde Park, gazing up at a blue sky that was rimmed about like a fluted picture frame by the concerned faces of half the *ton*. It was even more mortifying to realize that one reason for the distortion of one's vision was the fact that one's new hat, which one had thought looked very fetching earlier in the afternoon, was now being worn sideways.

Cora dared not look down to observe the state of her dress.

She realized then what was being said. They were calling her a heroine—again. Because she had saved a poodle or two from extinction beneath a horse's hoof.

She laughed.

"If you please," someone said firmly as the picture frame moved in closer to the center of the sky, "it would be wiser to give her air. She is winded, I do believe, and perhaps suffering from a concussion as well."

Lord Francis Kneller's voice. She felt a rush of gladness when she recalled that it was with him she had been driving. She would have felt horribly embarrassed if it had been any other gentleman. Of course, she was feeling horribly embarrassed anyway. She laughed again.

Someone was weeping all over her hand. The lady in

pink—the owner of the poodles. The poodles! Were they all safe? But they must be if she was being hailed as a heroine. *Had* she been heroic this time? She rather thought she had.

And then Lord Francis was bending over her. His hair looked adorably rumpled. His coat was dusty. His elbow was grass-stained. Oh, dear, he would be dreadfully upset over that. The coat really was a gorgeous shade of pink.

"Miss Downes," he said, "are you all right?"

"Oh, perfectly," she said and sat up, lifting her arms at the same moment to straighten her hat and try to inject a little decorum into the scene. Her father, had he been present, would have been tossing his eyes skyward. Edgar would have been calling her a clumsy booby or something lowering to that effect. Sky and picture frame did a complete spin before slowing down. "Oops," she added.

There were murmurings of concern from the picture frame.

Lord Francis helped her to her feet and even brushed some grass from her dress. There was a swell of sound, almost like a cheer, from the gathered *ton*—presumably in congratulation over the fact that she was upright.

"No, no," Lord Francis was saying, "I shall convey Miss Downes home myself. If someone would just hold my horses' heads for a moment."

She leaned heavily against his arm—it was such a nicely solid arm—while the world about her made up its mind whether to stop completely or swing around again. She was not quite sure afterward how she got back up into the high seat of his phaeton. She rather believed that he climbed up there with her in his arms, though how that could have been accomplished was beyond her comprehension. Certain it was that he drove away— magically, a clear path, lined with spectators, opened for him—with her fitted tightly against his side, one of his arms about her to prevent her from toppling either forward or sideways, something she might well have done.

Something was bothering her—apart from the painful throbbing at the back of her head. She had not summoned up the courage to feel back there yet, but she suspected that she must have a goose egg sitting on the back of her skull. She frowned.

"You saved me," she said. "It was wonderfully courageous of you. You might have got hurt."

He looked down at her—somehow her head, hat and all, was nestled on his shoulder. "Miss Downes," he said dryly, "you render me speechless."

But that was not what had been really bothering her. She frowned again. "Lord Francis," she said, "were the dogs *really* in danger?"

Edgar would not have waited to be asked—he had not done so after the incident of little Henry. But then Edgar assumed all the annoying privileges of an older brother. Lord Francis Kneller was far more polite.

He did not answer for a while. During that while Cora realized how shockingly improper it was to be riding in the streets of London like this. She felt very thankful yet again that it was only Lord Francis. His arm and his shoulder really did feel remarkably comforting.

"The dogs certainly did panic," he said at last. "As did the horse. Someone or some creature might definitely have come to harm. I can only wish that I had been the one to land on the bottom so that it would have been my head that was banged. I wonder how I am to explain to her grace that you came to harm while under my protection."

"Oh," she said, trying to sit up and changing her mind hastily, "but you saved me from much worse harm, as I shall be sure to explain. There would have been no danger, would there, if I had not jumped down. The dogs

would not have panicked and neither would the horse."
It was a horrid admission to make even to herself. Honesty compelled her to admit it to him as well.

Surprisingly he chuckled. "It is a debatable point," he said. "But it would be as well to keep that fact between the two of us, Miss Downes. Your image as a heroine has swelled to twice its size this afternoon. That can do you no harm at all on the marriage mart."

"Oh," she said, mortified. "Does it push up my value?"

He chuckled again. He sounded genuinely amused, she was relieved to find. He was not unduly annoyed with her, then.

"Let us just say," he said, "that it will do you no harm to be seen as heroic. And there is no doubt at all that your actions with regard to Bridgwater's nephew truly were."

Cora grimaced. "You should talk with my brother about that," she said.

He looked down at her again. His way of guiding his horses with just one hand was remarkably impressive, she thought.

"They were not?" he asked her.

"Edgar says that the child would have swum to the bank without my assistance," she said. "He says that I almost drowned him."

Lord Francis's voice sounded amused when he spoke, but he did not laugh again. "That was remarkably unhandsome of him," he said.

"Well," she said, "he *is* my brother, you know. Do you have brothers or sisters, Lord Francis?" Then she remembered that he had a brother who was a duke.

"One brother and two sisters," he said. "Two of them older than me. I know what that can be like. But let us not disallow your image as a heroine, Miss Downes. The *beau monde* is enormously cheered by it. We are a jaded lot, you know. We must constantly seek novelty and entertainment. A female heroine is irresistible."

"So we must tell lies?" she asked him doubtfully.

"Not at all," he said. "We need say nothing. There were a dozen witnesses to this afternoon's heroic act, Miss Downes, and a hundred more who will convince themselves that they were witnesses. They will describe what they have seen, and each new teller will embellish the story told by the one before. You will find that single-handedly you have saved four innocent and lovable poodles from certain death—not to mention having saved Lady Kellington from an irreparably broken heart."

"Oh," she said. But her thoughts were diverted. "Why does the road keep rushing up toward me when I can feel that you are holding me securely in place?"

"Close your eyes," he said, his arm tightening about her.

She did not even realize until she was inside the hall of the Duchess of Bridgwater's town house that she had allowed him to carry her there. This was becoming something of a habit—an unfortunate one for him. She wondered what soap or cologne he used. It smelled good. It was subtle. Almost manly. Well, she thought, to be fair she must admit that on anyone else she would not have thought of qualifying that judgment. And she really did not care that Lord Francis Kneller favored bright, foppish colors and elegant manners. She liked him just as he was.

Edgar would have scolded her without stopping for endangering other lives as well as her own and for acting so brainlessly. He would have done so even knowing that she had banged her head and was not feeling quite the thing.

"She has had a slight accident," Lord Francis was explaining to her grace. "I believe it is altogether possible that she has a lump on the back of her head that will need attention. If you will allow me, ma'am, I will carry her up to her bed."

"Soames." Her grace's voice was one of calm command. "You will send for Sir Calvin Pennard and ask him to attend me without delay, if you please."

Sir Calvin, Cora guessed, must be the duchess's physician.

"Follow me, Lord Francis," her grace said, still in the same tone of voice. "I hope there is a good explanation for what happened."

"I do believe you will hear explanations in every drawing room and ballroom in town for the next several days, ma'am," he said. "Miss Downes was injured in the performance of an act of extraordinary courage."

Cora looked once into his face and held her peace. She really was feeling very dizzy indeed. And she remembered now that her toes were still rather sore too.

MISS CORA DOWNES was confined to her room for two days following the incident in the park. Sir Calvin Pennard, the Duchess of Bridgwater's physician, had insisted upon it, mainly for the sake of her head, but partly too for the sake of her feet.

She was allowed no visitors during those two days. Her grace and Elizabeth and Jane kept her company. The only exceptions to the prohibition were the Duke of Bridgwater, who made his bow to her one afternoon, inquired after her health, and congratulated her on her act of bravery, and Lord Francis Kneller, who paid a courtesy call and was invited to Miss Downes's boudoir, where her grace's maid played chaperon.

"I feel so *silly*," Cora said, stretching out her hands to Lord Francis and forcing him to cross the room to her when he had intended merely to stand inside the door for a few minutes. It was true that she was fully dressed and that her hair was up, though in a looser, more luxuriant style than he had seen before, but she was reclining on a daybed and he found himself having to suppress improper thoughts. "I am *never* ill and *never* bedridden. How kind of you to call. And how tiresome you must find me."

He squeezed her hands, released them, and seated himself on a stool beside her. She spoke with utter candor and no noticeable intent to draw a disclaimer or a compliment from him.

"On the contrary," he said anyway. "I am honored that you have admitted me when so many have been turned away after presenting their cards, Miss Downes."

"Everyone is *so* kind," she said. "Especially when I was so foolish. I have even been sent *flowers*. Look at them. My room looks like a *garden*."

She spoke with an enthusiasm and an emphasis on certain key words that were not at all ladylike. Most ladies of his acquaintance would behave with wilting grace under circumstances like these. Cora Downes was clearly fretting from the inactivity.

"You are," he said, "a heroine, ma'am. Every gentleman in town wishes to make his bow to you. Every lady wishes to kiss your cheek."

"How absurd." She laughed, throwing back her head and showing her very white teeth and making no attempt whatsoever to reduce her amusement to a mere simper. "Lady Kellington has called twice and sent a servant three other times to inquire after me."

"Lady Kellington," he said, "is rumored to love her poodles more than she has ever loved any person, including her late husband and her four children."

"That is because dogs are invariably affectionate to their owners," she surprised him by saying. He had expected a reaction of shocked disbelief or of riot-

ous amusement. "Sometimes when I want to wound
Edgar—it is usually when he has been scolding me for
something or other—I tell him that I love Papa's dogs
more than I love him. He tells me that is because the
dogs do not have enough brain power to recognize my
shortcomings."

"Older brothers and sisters," Lord Francis said, wonderfully diverted, "are a pestilential breed."

"Yes, they are," she said. "But I miss Edgar. And Papa.
I suggested to her grace this morning that she send me
home as soon as I am deemed well enough to travel. I
have been nothing but trouble and embarrassment to
her. But she says I must stay until she finds me a husband. I think it will be an impossibility. No man who is
a *gentleman* will want to marry *me*."

Lord Francis wondered if all young ladies who were
not quite ladies discussed such matters freely with near
strangers. But he would wager not. Miss Cora Downes
was one of a kind, he suspected.

"I believe you will be surprised, then," he said. "Perhaps you should be warned, Miss Downes, that you are
very much in fashion."

She fixed him with an intent stare. "In fashion?"

"Indeed yes," he said. It was quite true. He had
expected it, especially as it was late in the Season and
everyone was starved for novelty. But it had happened
even more forcefully than he had anticipated. "Drawing
room and ballroom and club conversations have cen-
tered about little else but you and your heroic deeds in
the past two days. And it is a veritable mountain of
cards that are piled on the table downstairs. I believe
that when you finally go out, Miss Downes, or even just
downstairs, you will find yourself besieged."

She paled. "I *hate* being conspicuous," she said.

Which, in light of her behavior in the park a few afternoons before, was a rather comical thing to say. He did not laugh.

"I believe," he said, "that her grace's wishes for you may well be fulfilled quite soon. And your own too. I assume you do want a husband?"

"Oh, yes," she said. "But not one who wants me only because he thinks I am a heroine, or because Papa is wealthy. Not one who will remind me every day for the rest of my life that he has elevated me on the social scale. Only one who will like me and perhaps love me as well. And one I can feel affection for. And respect. And not an old man. Not one above—oh, thirty at the most. And not an old poker face. I would like someone who knows how to laugh, someone with some sense of the absurd. Life is frequently absurd, you know. Why are you chuckling? What have I said?"

"Nothing," he assured her. But he was enjoying himself. He had woken this morning feeling mortally depressed again and had realized that he had been waltzing with Samantha in his dreams and she had been smiling at him and telling him that she was with child. Only as he woke up had he realized that it was not his child. Oh, yes, life was frequently absurd. Much as he had admired Samantha for the last several years, he would never have expected to feel like a sick and lovelorn boy at her marrying someone else. "I imagine, Miss Downes, that you will have your choice of several candidates. You must make a check list and interview each one."

"You are making fun of me." She looked sharply at him and then went off into peals of laughter again. "Now what I should do is marry *you*." She held up a staying hand even as he felt a slight stirring of alarm, and laughed merrily once more. "But I will not. You are *Lord* Francis Kneller and your brother is a duke. You are far too high on the social scale for my comfort. Besides—" She blushed, bit her lip, and smiled.

He waited with raised eyebrows for the completion of the sentence, but it did not come.

"I am devastated by your rejection, ma'am," he said. He got to his feet. It was time he took his leave. "I shall go elsewhere to nurse my broken heart."

"Oh, must you leave?" She looked suddenly wistful, but she smiled again. "Yes, I suppose you must. It was very kind of you to come and to take me driving the other afternoon—I did not have a chance to thank you at the time. And to dance with me that first evening. You are a very kind gentleman. I believe you must be a close friend of the Duke of Bridgwater and are obliging him. But you have made me happy too. Good afternoon, my lord." She offered her hand.

"It has been my pleasure," he said, bowing over it and even lifting it to his lips.

He liked her, he thought as he was descending the stairs a minute later and taking his hat and cane from her grace's butler. She interested him and amused him. He really must see to it that she was well married. There would be no lack of suitors. Already several would-be husbands were sounding him out on the subject of Miss Cora Downes and her prospects—and he was not even a relative or guardian. He had learned from Bridgwater at White's this morning that there were others. Both the duke and his mother had been approached by several interested parties.

She could be betrothed and married within the month if she chose to be. He would miss her—a strange thought when he had known her but a few days. But she was the only person he had found since the marriage of the Marquess and Marchioness of Carew who could take his mind off his own personal depression and even make him laugh.

It was strange, he thought as he wandered along the street—he had not brought a carriage with him. Different as the two women were—he would be hard put to it to discover one point of likeness between Samantha and Cora Downes—there was a certain similarity in his relationship with them. He and Samantha had teased each other a great deal. He had teased her earlier this year about being in her seventh Season. He had told her that if she was unmarried at the end of it, she must don caps and retire into spinsterhood. She had teased him about his appearance. He had dressed partly to amuse Samantha, though not entirely, he had to admit. He hated the swing to soberness in gentlemen's dress and fought the trend. He dressed to please himself.

Perhaps the reason Samantha had never taken his courtship or even his marriage offers seriously was that she did not take *him* seriously. A man who always teased and joked could be seen as a man without depths of feeling or character, he supposed. He could remember how alarmed Samantha had been at his first angry reaction to her telling him about her betrothal. And so he had retracted his words, assuring her with a smile that he had been merely trying to make her feel bad—and had succeeded.

Cora Downes did not take him seriously either. Why else would she have announced so boldly that she should marry *him*? Would she have said that to any other man in this world? And what was that "Besides—" that would keep her from marrying him? Besides, he was a shallow man who could never be taken seriously?

It was as well, of course, that Cora Downes felt that way. He wanted no more than a teasing relationship with her and she wanted no more with him—her ambitions were very modest. She had no aspirations to the aristocracy in her search for a husband.

But it was a disturbing insight into himself he had just had, for all that. Was he so cleverly masked that no one could see beyond the mask? Maybe that was as well too. Bridgwater had certainly known his feelings for Samantha—had even warned him not to wear them on his sleeve. But he doubted anyone else had known, and he doubted that even Bridgwater realized that he was still pining. It would not do at all for anyone to know how constantly he had loved a woman who had spurned him and recently married a man she had not even met six months ago.

The very thought of anyone knowing made him shudder.

IT WAS ALL unbelievably true, what Lord Francis had warned her about. She was in fashion, as he had phrased it. In her language that soon came to mean that she was very much on display.

Everyone wished to gawk at her. It was not a polite word to use of the *ton,* but Cora was learning something about the *ton.* Its members were very much like ordinary people except that they couched their behavior in somewhat greater elegance. Everyone gawked. And everyone wished to pay their respects to her and to congratulate her.

The story of the Hyde Park incident had crystallized by the time she made her appearance again. Lord Lanting, it appeared, had lost control of his mount, a fierce, unmanageable beast, which could—and would—squash a dozen poodles or half a dozen maidens underhoof without a qualm. Had not the animal been at Waterloo and learned its ferocity there? Lord Lanting had done his valiant best, poor man, but he had lost control.

Lady Kellington's poodles had been for it. There was no doubt in anyone's mind that there would not have been a single survivor if events had been left to take their natural course. Lady Kellington herself had already foreseen their imminent demise and had been in the hysterical stage of a first-class fit of the vapors. The scene had been set for a spectacular disaster.

Enter Miss Cora Downes, heroine of the Bath incident involving that poor dear infant, Lord George Munro's son, the Duke of Bridgwater's nephew. Miss Cora Downes, with no thought for her own life and safety, had launched herself from the high perch of Lord Francis Kneller's phaeton—she might easily have broken both ankles, not to mention her neck, in the process—and had thrown herself between the beast's flashing hooves and the innocent, shivering dogs and plucked them to safety in the nick of time.

Miss Cora Downes had survived the ordeal. But only just. Sir Clayton Pennard, the Duchess of Bridgwater's personal physician, had pronounced the young lady in grave danger. Only his skill and the devoted care of her grace and the indomitable will of the heroine herself had effected her miraculously speedy recovery.

A few times Cora tried to remind her admirers that it was Lord Francis who had really saved her life and that of a few of the dogs—just as she had tried to remind other people in Bath that it was her brother who had saved both her and little Henry. But Lord Francis, apart from being the owner of the phaeton, had no part in this story.

The duchess's town house was besieged with callers, just as Lord Francis had predicted. Cora would have felt even more embarrassed about it than she did if Elizabeth had not been off, out with her future in-laws a great deal of the time, and Jane had not had steady calls from the Earl of Greenwald, her favored suitor. Lady Kellington whisked Cora off two days in a row, for a picnic the first day and to dinner and the theater on the second. At her first ball after the incident, Cora might have filled her card up twice over and even more, so eager were gentlemen to dance with her. Fortunately, by the time the Duke of Bridgwater arrived and made his bow to his mother, there were no sets left to grant him, though he did ask her. Less fortunately, there were none to grant Lord Francis either. He grinned and winked at her when she told him so.

"That is such a lovely shade of lemon," she said kindly, referring to his coat. Her suspicions of an earlier occasion seemed to be correct. The handle of the quizzing glass he wore on a ribbon this evening was studded with topazes. He wore a topaz ring on one finger of his right hand.

"My dear Miss Downes," he said, fingering his glass and pursing his lips, "as usual you render me speechless. Now I may not compliment you on your gown without inducing you to say '*Touché*' in response."

Her grace pronounced the evening a marked success, and indeed Cora agreed. She had not missed any sets apart from the two waltzes—though late in the evening she had been brought the exciting news that she had been approved and might waltz to her heart's content at all future balls. And at the end of the evening, even though she was weary and footsore, there was not a single blister to be nursed.

Her grace was even more gratified the next morning when Mr. Bentley called privately on her and asked her to whom he must make application for the heroine's hand. Her grace replied that perhaps he should speak first with Miss Downes herself since she was of age. Cora, in the presence of her grace, refused Mr. Bentley— she had never been more surprised in her life—which the duchess said afterward was the right and proper thing to do since she certainly did not need to accept the very first offer she received. There might seem to be some desperation in such overeagerness. But it was extremely satisfying to know that Cora's matrimonial prospects were very bright indeed. Mr. Bentley was the third son of a baronet.

Cora was pleased. Certainly she had had no chance to be bored since she had emerged from her room with a lumpless head and rejuvenated toes—and larger slippers. And certainly too her dream of seeing London and participating in some of its most dazzling social events had come true. She had danced and danced at her second ball and enjoyed every moment of it. Some of the gentlemen she had met—even apart from Mr. Bentley—seemed interested in her as a person and were not at all daunted by the fact that her father was a merchant and her brother a lawyer.

She was very pleased indeed. She wrote and told her papa so.

And yet part of her was unaccountably lonely. She kept remembering telling Lord Francis Kneller what kind of husband she would like. She had never put it into words before, but she had spoken the truth to him. And she kept remembering telling him as a joke—which, of course, he had taken in good part—that she ought to marry him. And she kept thinking what a shame it was that he was quite disqualified as a prospective suitor. For the reason she had given him and for the reason she had only just stopped herself in time from giving.

How could one tell a gentleman—even such a kindly and good-natured gentleman as Lord Francis—that one could not marry him because he was not a masculine man? The very thought that she had almost said it aloud could turn her hot and cold at the same time.

She did not mind that fact about him. She really had admired his lemon satin coat. And she admired him for not being hypocritical, for dressing the way he wished to dress.

Now if only she could find all his other qualities in an eligible gentleman. Especially his ability to laugh.

She missed him, she thought when she had been back out in Society for a few days and had spoken with him only that once at the ball. But how absurd it was to think of missing someone one had met only three times before that.

It was her papa and Edgar she really missed, she decided. And her life with them—where she belonged.

But how ungrateful she was to think thus!

6

*B*Y THE END OF THE MORNING CORA HAD DECIDED
that she was not going to marry a gentleman.

The duchess was writing letters in her private sitting
room. Lady Elizabeth had taken the carriage to Lord
Fuller's on Grosvenor Square to assist Lady Fuller in the
final plans for her ball—one of the last the Season would
have to offer. Lady Jane had made a secret assignation
to meet the Earl of Greenwald quite accidentally either
in the park during a morning walk or at the library, de-
pending on the weather. It really was not an *assignation*,
Jane assured Cora, flushing with guilt. It was more that
he had said that he *might* ride in the park if the weather
was fine and she had commented on the strange coincidence that she might walk there—if the weather was
fine. Presumably they had made similar commitments to
the library if the weather was *not* fine.

And so Cora had agreed to accompany Jane. Indeed,
it was essential to the plan that she do so. Jane could not
possibly go alone to the park, even if a maid trailed
along behind her as she would do anyway if the two of
them went.

Cora never particularly enjoyed walking alone with
Jane, although she was excessively fond of her. Jane
was small and dainty and pretty and always behaved
with perfect decorum—except perhaps when she made

almost-assignations with earls who had not yet made any formal offers for her.

"Mama would lecture me for a month without pause if she thought I had arranged to meet his lordship in the park," Jane herself confessed. "Alistair would not need to lecture. He would merely have to look at me in a certain way and I would wither up and die. But of course I have made no such arrangement. If he happens to be riding in the park and I happen to be walking there and we happen to meet and stop to exchange civilities, that cannot be deemed an arranged meeting, can it?"

Cora was not quite sure what all the fuss was about. But she did know that Jane fancied herself in love and as a result had departed ever so slightly from strict propriety. The fact cheered Cora a little. But she still disliked walking out alone with Jane. She felt so very large and clumsy beside her. She always had to reduce her stride to about half its usual span and she always had to resist the urge to droop her shoulders in order to look shorter and less conspicuous. Miss Graham had told her she must never do that. Apart from the intrinsic virtue of good posture was the fact that a tall person who hunched over only succeeded in making herself appear taller and more conspicuous.

And so they walked in the park side by side, their maid a little distance behind them, and Cora soon forgot about the awkwardness of her person in her enjoyment of the morning. The sun was shining and the air promised heat later on. But this morning it was only comfortably warm with a stiff breeze to fan the face and make one imagine that one was almost in the country.

It was the perfect morning for a quiet walk. Of course, sooner or later the Earl of Greenwald would ride by and pause for a chat, but apart from that there were peace and a cozy chat with Jane to be enjoyed. The park was always pleasantly empty and quiet during the mornings.

And then Mr. Parker rode toward them—for one moment Jane thought he was the earl and had almost visible heart palpitations. Mr. Parker paused when he came up to them, inclined his head and touched his hat, reminded them that it was a fine day, and then invited himself to dismount and walk a little way with them since indeed it was such a fine day.

And then Mr. Pandry and Mr. Johnson appeared, walking briskly together, also in the opposite direction from that taken by the ladies. They too paused with the usual gallantries, decided that it was far too fine a day to hurry anywhere, and turned to stroll with the ladies and Mr. Parker.

Before their walk was half an hour old, they had gathered no fewer than eight fellow strollers and enjoyers of the weather—all male and all congratulating themselves with jocular good humor on their good fortune in being able to take a turn about the park with the heroine—and with Lady Jane Munro, of course.

All of them had either danced with her or applied to dance with her the evening before, Cora noted. Several of them had called upon her grace since she had emerged from her sick chamber. A few of them had sent bouquets or posies. One of them had kissed her hand last evening after she had danced a minuet with him. A few of them were handsome. Most of them were taller than she, and even one who was not was on an exact level with her when he wore riding boots. All of them were gentlemen. One of them was heir to a baronet—he had informed her of that last evening. Three of them had been presented to her by the duchess, four by the duke, and one by Lord Francis Kneller.

This, Cora supposed, giving her parasol a twirl, was what success felt like. She knew beyond a doubt that all these gentlemen were interested in her, even though all of them were scrupulous about dividing their attentions between her and Jane. For one thing, none of them were titled gentlemen. They had been presented to her because they were possible matches for her. None of them would be allowed within a mile of Jane as a suitor. But even apart from that practical fact, Cora knew with her woman's intuition that their interest was all in her.

Eight gentlemen—*gentlemen!*—strolled in the park when they might be off elsewhere about their more congenial masculine pursuits. Eight gentlemen hung on her every word, laughed at her every sally into wit, jostled with one another to be closest to her—though all were well-bred enough to keep a proper distance, of course. Eight gentlemen were giving serious consideration to making her their wife—subject to her acceptance. It was a good feeling.

It was success.

And it would be hasty success. The Season was almost over. There was no time for a leisurely courtship. She would receive a few more marriage offers before she returned to Bristol, she knew. Mr. Bentley already had offered—and had been refused. She had panicked when it came to the point, though she had no possible objection to him beyond the fact that he must be at least three inches shorter than she was—it might be four, but she could hardly ask him to stand back to back with her while someone measured merely to satisfy her curiosity.

She could be a married lady—with the key word being *lady*—before Christmas. Papa would be proud of her. Edgar would nod his approval. Her children would be assured a place in society. She would be able to sponsor Edgar's children. Not that they would need sponsorship—if he ever married and had them, that was. Edgar had been to good schools and he was successful and wealthy in his own right apart from being Papa's heir, and he was very gentlemanly. Besides, times were beginning to change, as Papa always said.

Cora had been woolgathering. At the same time she had had her arm linked with Jane's and had been occasionally patting her hand. Eight gentlemen and no sign of the very one they had come here to run into accidentally on purpose. But she felt Jane brighten suddenly, and sure enough, the Earl of Greenwald himself was cantering along the green, looking very dashing in clothes only Weston could have made. Even Cora was beginning to recognize the excellence of his tailoring.

The earl looked somewhat taken aback when he spotted the two ladies in the midst of a throng of gentlemen. One of those ladies—Jane—was busily conversing with one of the gentlemen. Cora raised a hand and waved to him, smiling gaily. Only then did Jane look up and appear surprised and prettily confused to see his lordship.

His lordship joined the parade.

Her grace's maid paced determinedly behind, though what she would have done if the gentlemen had all decided to pounce en masse on her two charges was not at all clear, especially to her own mind.

And then something happened to cause mass diversion and mass entertainment. A series of shrieks turned everyone's attention ahead along the way. But the immediate fear that someone was in distress was put to flight when it was seen that the screamer was a small hatless child who was chasing after his missing hat. The hat itself, a splendid confection in blue and white with ribbon streamers—all of which matched his outfit—was bowling merrily along in the breeze, pausing only long enough on the grass for the child to have it within a fingertip of his grasp before dancing gaily off again. A buxom woman—apparently the child's nurse—was puffing along behind him, alternately urging him to catch the hat when he was close to it, and pleading with him to let it go when it blew away again.

The scene afforded great merriment in Cora's group and inspired the gentlemen to elevated heights of wit.

Mr. Johnson whistled piercingly. "At it, lad!" he yelled.

The outfit and the hat were clearly new, Cora thought. She could imagine how very proud the boy must have felt this morning to don them and be taken into the park to display them for all to see. And now the hat with its gay streamers was in danger of being lost forever.

"Oh," she said, handing her parasol without thought to the nearest gentleman and grasping the sides of her skirt. "Oh, the poor child." And she was off and running.

The hat was bowling toward her group. But not quite in a straight line. If they stood still it would sail by yards away from them. The poor child would never catch it. And so Cora went streaking off to intercept the hat and left her admirers gawking after her and realizing too late that they had lost the chance to display superior gallantry in her eyes.

The trouble with wind, Cora thought, was that it never blew quite steadily. One could never predict with certain accuracy where it would blow a certain object by a certain moment. She made several grabs for the hat when it came close and each time it hopped when she lunged or came to a halt when she hesitated or changed direction when she had it for sure. But it was close. She would have it in just a moment.

This was *fun,* she thought, beginning to laugh and beginning to realize what a spectacle she must be making of herself for those who were watching. Coordination had never been her strong point.

She was laughing helplessly and with imminent triumph as her hand descended finally for the kill—only to find that the hat lifted itself straight upward and the top of her bonnet almost collided with a pair of muscular legs clad in black leather pantaloons and boots designed to accentuate their muscularity.

"Dear me," Lord Francis Kneller said, "fun and games, Miss Downes?" He was holding the hat between a thumb and forefinger.

She laughed at him. "You wretch!" she said. "It was mine. I had run it to earth."

He raised his eyebrows and she realized several things. He was standing beside his horse, which had lowered its head to munch at the grass. On the other side of his horse was another with a silent rider on its back—the Duke of Bridgwater. From some distance away there was a chorus of gentlemen's cheers. And from a very short distance behind there were the pantings of a winded child.

"My hat," he cried with a gasp. "Give me my hat."

"Dear me." Lord Francis raised it higher. "What do you say, sir?"

"Give me it," the child insisted, glaring.

"Not," Lord Francis said, sounding infinitely bored, "until I hear the magic word, my young sir."

"You must call me *your grace*," the child said with haughty command.

The Duke of Bridgwater coughed delicately. Lord Francis's arm stayed where it was. Cora's jaw dropped and she stared at the little boy.

"Oh, your grace, your grace." The nurse had come puffing into earshot. "You must not run off like that. It is only a hat. Make your bow and thank the lady and gentlemen."

"He has my hat," the child said, pointing.

The nurse looked helpless.

The Duke of Bridgwater's voice sounded even more bored than Lord Francis's had just done. "Even dukes say thank you for favors rendered, my lad," he said. "Take it from someone who knows. Miss Downes has done you a service even without being aware of your illustrious identity. Lord Francis Kneller has retrieved your hat and will be only too delighted to return it to you. It would not fit his own head after all, would it? Let us hear it now."

"Who are you?" The child frowned up at him.

"A fellow duke," his grace said with a sigh. "Who happens to be much larger and far better mannered than you are, lad. And who happens too to possess a far heavier hand, which at this moment is itching to be put to use. What do you have to say?"

"Thank you, ma'am," the child said, looking at Cora and inclining his head to her. "Thank you, my lord." He bowed to Lord Francis, who tossed him the hat, which he caught.

His nurse behind him was bobbing curtsies indiscriminately in all directions. She took the child's hand and hurried him away.

Cora looked into Lord Francis's face and exploded into laughter, though she would rather not have done so with the duke close by. It had been such a ridiculous incident.

"Finchley's brat," his grace said by way of explanation. "The *late* Finchley, that is. He was not much of an improvement on his son, it pains me to say."

Lord Francis was pursing his lips and Cora realized that her bonnet must have blown back on her head and that doubtless her hair beneath it resembled a tangled bush. Sometimes she wished her hair did not grow quite so thickly, but she could not bring herself to have it cut even though short hair was all the crack. Papa thought short hair on women was scandalous.

Cora lifted her arms and did some hasty repairs.

"Another heroic deed, Miss Downes?" Lord Francis asked her. His riding coat was a glorious shade of puce.

"Chasing after a child's hat?" she said. "Hardly."

But his grace was clearing his throat again. "Miss Downes," he asked, "is that by any chance my *sister* in the center of the group of cheering gentlemen?"

To be quite fair, they were no longer cheering, though several of them were grinning and one of them was laughing out loud. And another of them cried "Bravo!" as she looked toward them.

"Oh, dear, yes," Cora said. "We were walking here, your grace, for the air and the peace, and these gentlemen walked or rode by and were obliging enough to accompany us for a short distance."

His grace had a quizzing glass to his eye and was looking in some distaste at Jane and the nine gentlemen.

Lord Francis chuckled. "And your maid looks as if she is wondering how she may divide herself in two and chaperon both of you in order to keep all decent and proper," he said. "Do take my arm, Miss Downes. We will solve her problem by having you rejoin Lady Jane."

The duke stayed where he was, holding the reins of Lord Francis's horse as the two of them walked away.

"How glad I am that *you* arrived," Cora said gaily. "Without you—and his grace—I do believe the infant duke would have chewed me up and spat me out. I had sentimental images of a poor child who was about to lose his new hat and would cry all day and all night over its loss and never be able to afford one to replace it until next year at the very earliest."

"Doubtless," he said, "with so many witnesses, Miss Downes, you will find that this heroic act will be added to the other two in order to swell your fame."

She laughed. "Oh, what nonsense," she said. "If I had been a true lady, I would have fluttered my eyelashes at one of the gentlemen and he would have raced after the hat for me."

"And the incident would have lacked all sense of

drama," he said. "You are to be at Lady Fuller's ball tomorrow evening?"

"Yes, indeed," she said. "Lady Elizabeth is betrothed to her brother, you know. Will you be there too, Lord Francis? Will you come early enough to engage a set with me this time? I was sorry last evening to find that there were none left for you."

"I have noticed a tendency in you to take words from my mouth, Miss Downes," he said. "Will you do me the honor of reserving a set for me tomorrow evening?"

"Yes." She smiled dazzlingly at him. "Can you waltz? I have been *approved*, though I think it all a parcel of nonsense, and now may waltz myself."

"Then I will request that you write my name in your card next to the first waltz," he said.

They were almost up to the others, a fact that she found regretful. She would prefer a quiet stroll with Lord Francis. But a nasty thought struck her. "Oh, dear," she said, "I asked you to dance with me, did I not? That is something a lady *never* does. I gave you no choice but to be gallant, did I? And I dare not ask now if you really *wish* to dance with me because of course you would be gallant again and say that of course you do. I *do* apologize."

"Miss Downes," he said, "you do seem to have perfected the art of rendering me speechless."

"Well," she said, "no matter. It is only you and you do not mind if I occasionally ask you to dance with me, do you?"

He looked sidelong at her but did not reply. She found herself surrounded by laughing, admiring gentlemen, who congratulated her on her prompt action with regard to the young Duke of Finchley's hat.

"Well done, Miss Downes," Mr. Parker said.

"Jolly good show," Mr. Pandry agreed, returning her parasol to her.

"Miss Downes is tired," Lord Francis said, sounding bored again and faintly haughty. "She has wisely decided to return home with Lady Jane. Good morning, gentlemen." He made them all a slight bow.

The Earl of Greenwald was the first to leave after glancing across to the Duke of Bridgwater, who was still sitting on his motionless horse some distance away, observing the scene. The others wandered away too, one by one or two by two.

"Ladies?" Lord Francis bowed to both Jane and Cora before glancing at their maid—who was looking remarkably relieved. He turned and walked back to the duke and his horse without looking behind him.

"Cora." Jane grasped her arm and hurried her back in the direction from which they had come. "Do you think Alistair believed there was an assignation?"

"Goodness," Cora said, "I hope not. Why would any woman in her right mind make assignations to meet so many gentlemen at the same time and in the same place?" She laughed. "Unless it were because there is safety in numbers. Do you like puce, Jane?"

"Lord Francis always looks elegant," Jane said. "Do you believe Alistair *knew*?"

"I doubt it." Cora patted her hand reassuringly.

They lapsed into silence, each thinking her own thoughts about the eventfulness of their morning walk.

Cora's thoughts were quite decisive and rather disturbing. She was not going to marry a gentleman, she realized. Gentlemen were silly. Remarkably so. Mr. Bentley had proposed marriage to her when he scarcely knew her merely because she was in fashion and wealthier than he was—or such was her educated guess. All eight gentlemen this morning had been silly, preening themselves before her in the hope of winning her favor. *Her*—Cora Downes! All of them had thought the distress of a little child comical—though, as it had turned out, he had deserved a little distress in his life. None of them would have given a thought to rescuing the wretched hat themselves. And yet all of them pretended deep admiration for her mad and undignified dash after it.

And these were supposed to be her prospective *husbands*? She would lose patience with any one of them within a week—within a *day*. She would rather marry any of the men she had rejected at home. At least all of them were worthy men. She would rather marry someone of her own kind. Someone with a little sense between his two ears. What nonsense all this business of heroism was. She should have told her grace so before all this started. But of course the prospect of coming to London—and while the Season was still in progress—had been irresistible.

If there had been any doubt left in her mind about her decision not to marry a gentleman, it was put to rout as soon as she thought of Lord Francis. She had been so very glad to see him. She would have given anything to have walked off with him and forgotten about all her foolish suitors. And she was already warmed to exuberance at the thought of dancing with him again tomorrow—*waltzing* with him. And yet she was not thinking of Lord Francis in terms of marriage. How absurd! She felt a deep friendship for him, almost an affection—well, perhaps *quite* an affection.

If she could have felt so much more gladness to meet and walk with a friend, then, when eight prospective husbands had been waiting to receive her back into their admiring midst, how could she possibly take them seriously?

She would a hundred times rather spend a morning or afternoon with Edgar than with any of them. She would a thousand times rather spend them with Lord Francis. Lord Francis could make her relax and laugh. She could say anything she wished to say to him without fear of shocking him. Lord Francis liked her, she believed. She preferred to be liked than to be admired. Especially when she suspected—when she *knew*—that the admiration was all feigned. How could anyone possibly admire *her*? She looked down at Jane's bonnet and felt her own largeness again.

No, she was not going to marry a gentleman. She was going to go home to Bristol when she decently could and keep house for Papa until her ideal man came along. If he ever did. If he did not, well, then, she would remain a spinster for the rest of her life. There were worse fates—she could be a wife to one of this morning's eight gentlemen.

She hoped Lord Francis waltzed well. She would wager he did. He did everything else so elegantly. She had only ever waltzed with a dancing master. She looked forward with such eagerness to twirling about a London ballroom in the arms of a gentleman with whom she could relax and perform the steps without tripping all over his feet—or her own.

She hummed a waltz tune and Jane smiled at her.

"I have promised the first waltz tomorrow evening to Lord Greenwald," she said. "Is he not the most handsome gentleman you have ever seen in your life, Cora?"

Cora was feeling quite cheerful enough to concede the point, though she believed that to any impartial observer Edgar would have the edge.

"MUCH OBLIGED, KNELLER," the Duke of Bridgwater said as they resumed their morning ride. "My mother made a huge mistake, I believe."

"You believe so?" Lord Francis looked at him.

"You must confess," his grace said, "that there was

something perilously close to—vulgarity about that scene, Kneller."

Lord Francis chuckled. "I might have chosen the word *farce*," he said. "I am beginning to think that farcical situations find out Miss Downes wherever she goes in public. But she is not vulgar, Bridgwater. I must quarrel with you there."

His grace sighed. "No, I did not call her so," he said. "Strangely, one cannot help but like the girl. But I must admit to some uneasiness when I recall that Jane's chief companion here is a woman who vaults down from high-perch phaetons in the middle of Rotten Row in order to rescue a few miserable curs from a danger that was doubtless more apparent than real. And one who attracts admirers like bees to flowers and then leaves my sister in the midst of them while she dashes away, all bare ankles—and even one knee, I swear, Kneller—in order to catch a runaway hat." He sighed again, sounding considerably aggrieved.

Lord Francis could only continue to chuckle. "She showed them a thing or two, though, Bridgwater," he said. "Apart from the ankle and knee, I mean—I missed the knee, unfortunately. The ankles were well worth looking at, though. Come, you must admit that she is refreshing. I derive enormous amusement from her. And the admirers should please you. It was for the purpose of finding her a husband that her grace brought her here, was it not?"

"*A* husband," the duke said. "Singular, Kneller. I am beginning to lose sleep over the chit. She refused Bentley, you know."

"Good," Lord Francis said without hesitation. "The man has not enough humor with which to paint his little fingernail. He would not be amused by her at all. She can do better."

His grace sighed yet again. "I hope Greenwald comes

to the point this year," he said. "He had to leave in a hurry last year—sick aunt or some such thing. I believe Jane has a *tendre* for him. How thankful I am to have only two sisters. Perhaps I will be able to concentrate on my own life once they are both settled."

"Ah," Lord Francis said. "You are thinking about setting up your nursery, Bridgwater?"

His grace frowned. "I had in mind other, ah, pleasures to precede that particular one," he said, "though I suppose that is inevitable too. One tires a little of mistresses, do you not find?"

"I swore off them a year or more ago," Lord Francis said, feeling his mood slip.

"And there is something to be said for nurseries, I suppose," his grace said. "I never thought to see Carew so happy. Lady Carew is in a delicate way, so he informs me."

"Yes," Lord Francis said.

The duke looked at him sharply. "Oh, sorry, old chap," he said. "I was not thinking."

Lord Francis raised his eyebrows. "No harm done at all," he said with a wave of one hand. "Ancient history."

"Glad to hear it," the duke said. "You are going to Brighton for the summer? You have not attached yourself to Lady Augusta's court, I see. Maybe there will be some new beauties there."

But Lord Francis was too busy fighting a familiar drooping of the spirits to give the matter serious thought. He concentrated on images that would perhaps restore his humor. The image of Cora Downes, for example, her skirts hitched almost to her knees, dashing across the grass, flushed and windblown and laughing, in pursuit of a ridiculous little child's hat. Or the imagined picture of her waltzing with all her usual exuberance—in his arms.

Yes. He smiled. There was something about Cora Downes that would lift the lowest of spirits. Farce did follow her about. And a certain innocent charm. And of course she was deliciously lovely despite the bold face and tall stature. Perhaps because of them. And certainly because of the generous endowment of curves in all the right places.

"I have made no definite plans for the summer," he said.

7

LORD FRANCIS KNEW AS SOON AS HE ARRIVED AT LADY Fuller's ball that the Prince of Wales was expected. Not that one ever *expected* Prinny to honor any social invitation even if it had been duly accepted. He went where he wished to go, and no one, including the prince himself, ever knew quite where he wanted to go until the last possible moment. But at least if he had accepted an invitation, preparations were duly made.

It was clear that the Regent had accepted his invitation to Lady Fuller's ball.

How did he know? Lord Francis asked himself rhetorically. It was easy to know. Every window and French door in the ballroom was tightly shut even though it was a warm night outside. Already, although the dancing had not even begun and all the guests had not arrived, the air was heavy with the scents of flowers and perfumes. Soon, once the dancing was in progress, it would be unbearable.

The Prince of Wales was terrified of drafts. Coveted invitations to Carlton House and the Pavilion at Brighton were also dreaded invitations. It was a physical ordeal to be a guest of Prinny or to be a guest at a function he had decided he might favor—if he was in the mood.

Lord Francis looked about him, acknowledged a few friends and acquaintances with a nod or a discreet raising of the hand, and located the Duchess of Bridgwater and her party. Her grace, her usual elegant self in dark green, was looking rather pleased with herself. As a chaperon she had good reason to be pleased. At least the largest gathering in the whole room was clustered about the two young ladies in her charge. Those about Cora Downes were almost exclusively gentlemen.

Lord Francis fingered his quizzing glass and then raised it to his eye.

"Yes, all is as it should be," the Duke of Bridgwater said from beside him a few moments later. "He has come up to scratch."

"Pandry?" Lord Francis frowned. The man was shorter than she was by a good two inches and he was already, at the age of five- or six-and-twenty, showing signs of portliness to come. Not to mention incipient baldness. All of which were no rational disqualifications for him as her husband. But Lord Francis hoped she would have better taste.

"Greenwald," his grace said. "He called on me this morning and we came to a very amicable settlement. It seems the same can be said for his visit to Jane this afternoon. She is—glowing, would you not agree, Kneller?"

Lord Francis changed the direction of his glass. Yes, indeed. Lady Jane Munro was talking with Greenwald's mother while the earl stood beside them, looking a comic mixture of smugness and sheepishness. Lady Jane herself was glowing, as Bridgwater had just said.

"My congratulations," Lord Francis said. "Two sisters and both well settled."

"Johnson called too this morning," the duke said. "For Miss Downes, of course. I had to direct him to my mother since I have no authority to negotiate on her behalf. It could well be a memorable day for my mother."

"Johnson?" Lord Francis's brows snapped together

again. Johnson had a pea for a brain. And he was at least *three* inches shorter than she was.

"He has a very respectable property in Berkshire," the duke said, "and a tidy income. She will have done very well for herself if she has netted him. I had better pay my respects and kiss the bride-to-be yet again. Would you care to join me, Kneller?"

Lord Francis kissed the hand of Lady Jane a few moments later, shook the hand of Greenwald, and made his bow to the duchess. The betrothal had not been officially announced yet, but no secret was being made of it. The cluster of people about the couple was clear proof of that.

Cora Downes was in the center of a group of gentlemen—her usual court. His use of that word gave Lord Francis a mental jolt. Only the Incomparables of the *ton*'s beauties ever acquired courts that gathered about them wherever they went. Lady Augusta Haville was the queen of the Incomparables at this stage of the Season. Earlier she had been a mere shadow of a rival to Samantha Newman. He and Gabriel, Earl of Thornhill, had always teased Samantha about her court. And Gabe had teased *him* about his membership in that court—its most devoted member.

And now Cora Downes, the most unlikely candidate of all, had acquired her own court, all within two weeks. And in the midst of it she looked quite as comfortable and quite as animated as Samantha had ever looked.

The thought that he was after all attaching himself to someone else's court this year amused him as he wove his way to her side and smiled at her. Not that he was really a member, of course. Courting Miss Cora Downes was the very farthest thing from his mind. But he felt a certain protective instinct toward her, and some of the members of this court were not eligible suitors at all. There was one notorious fortune hunter among them, one inveterate gambler, and any number of fools. Of course, by now all his concerns might be academic. By now she might have betrothed herself to Johnson.

She tapped him on the arm with her fan and smiled brightly at him. "Pink," she said. "It is my very favorite shade of pink."

It was his favorite evening coat. Samantha had always teased him mercilessly about it, as had Gabe when he stayed at Chalcote just after Christmas—because Samantha had been there too, visiting her cousin, Gabe's wife. But Miss Downes, he believed, though she smiled, was not teasing. It seemed almost as if she were—being kind to him? He had no chance to ponder the strange thought.

"Have you *heard*?" she asked him, leaning toward him as if she thought thereby to give them some privacy. Her cheeks had flushed and her eyes had grown anxious. "The Prince of *Wales* may be coming here this evening."

"He does not always honor such commitments," he said "I would not get my hopes up too high if I were you, Miss Downes."

"My *hopes*?" Her voice was almost a squeak. "I shall die if he comes, Lord Francis. I shall just *die*."

But he was given no chance to deal with her fears himself. There was a chorus of protest and reassurance from her court, though for a while she kept her eyes fixed on him. How could a great *heroine*—who had saved the life of a child by plunging into an icy river and the lives of four poodles by diving beneath the flashing hooves of a fierce horse—how could a heroine be afraid of meeting Prinny? The group made much mirth out of the idea.

Lord Francis merely took her hand and patted it in avuncular fashion and asked her between the mirth and her departure with Mr. Dalman for the opening set of country dances if she had remembered to reserve the first waltz for him.

Her white gown, which was almost obligatory evening wear during her first Season in town, did not suit her, Lord Francis thought, watching her broodingly while he tapped his finger on the handle of his quizzing glass. She was far too vivid a creature for white. And the evening coiffure, all curls and ringlets piled high, did not suit either. It made her look too girlish, an impression that was incompatible with her height and her figure. He had preferred the looser style she had worn in her boudoir. He rather believed he would like it best unconfined down her back, but that was not a practical idea. Neither was it a wise idea in a room that was already quite stifling hot.

If she were an actress, he thought, or an opera singer—she could easily be an opera singer with that bosom—she would crowd a green room to overflowing every night, even without the attendant heroism. And he rather thought he might be one of the men crowding it.

It was a thought that was not worthy of him at all. And certainly not fair to her. There had been not the slightest hint of loose behavior in her since he had known her. He was ashamed of himself. Damnation, but he *liked* her. He had no wish to be also lusting after her. He had been without a woman for too long, he thought ruefully. It had seemed somehow disloyal to his broken heart to go seeking out a willing bedfellow for mere sexual satisfaction.

"Not dancing, old chap?" his grace asked. "Are you for the card room?"

"No, I think not," Lord Francis said. "I am engaged for the first waltz." She was twirling down the set with Dalman with such enthusiasm that if he should happen to release her hand by some chance, she would go spinning off into space—doubtless with a shriek. His lips twitched. He could almost wish it would happen. Farce had not touched upon her tonight yet.

The duke cleared his throat. "It would not do at all, you know," he said. "Fairhurst would have your head."

His brother? Lord Francis turned sharply and looked, startled, at his recently acquired friend. "*What* would not do?" he asked.

"She is a merchant's daughter," his grace said, picking at an invisible speck of lint on his sleeve. "And you are a duke's son and brother. Not that it is any of my concern, Kneller, but I have heard a few murmurings. And I *was* the one who asked you to take notice of the girl and help bring her into fashion."

Lord Francis was not normally given to extremes of emotion. Perhaps that was why he was having such difficulty coping with an unexpectedly broken heart. But he felt a sudden blazing of anger.

"A few murmurings," he said, his voice as icy as his heart was fiery. "My brother would have my head. It seems to me, Bridgwater, that you do your fair share of being your brother's keeper. Except that you are not my brother or even any kin of mine."

The duke took a snuffbox from a pocket, snapped the lid open, seemed to decide that the taking of snuff in a ballroom was not quite the thing, closed the lid, and put the box away again.

Bridgwater had advised him not to wear his heart on his sleeve over Samantha, Lord Francis remembered, still steaming. And now he was advising him against lusting after a merchant's daughter. God damn it all to hell! Bridgwater had been a mere passing acquaintance until a few weeks ago, before his friend, that damned Carew, decided to play Romeo to Samantha's Juliet.

For two pins he would pop Bridgwater a good one right here. Serve him right too.

"You are quite right, my good fellow," his grace said and left without another word or glance.

And damn him to hell and back again, Lord Francis thought. He did not even have the decency to know when a quarrel was being picked with him. The cowardly scoundrel had walked away.

She was weaving in and out of a line of gentlemen in her set, her eyes sparkling, her lips smiling, her feet moving with surprisingly light grace. Those murmurers were damned wrong. So was Bridgwater if he believed them. Never more wrong in their lives. Devil take it, he knew what he must look for in a bride when the time came. The time had not come and perhaps never would. The only woman he had ever loved was married to someone else and was in a delicate way.

His heart weighed down the soles of his dancing shoes again.

"OH," CORA SAID, "how *hot* it is in here. I shall *expire* from lack of air." But despite her discomfort she smiled. She could not remember being happier in her life, which was surely an absurd thought when all she was doing was dancing with Lord Francis Kneller. Waltzing with him. As she had suspected, he waltzed superbly.

"Do you wish to stop and rest?" he asked her. He had watched her all through the dance but he had spoken little and had not smiled a great deal.

"No," she said. "Oh, please no. This is so *very* wonderful. I have never been happier in my life."

"Have you not?"

He smiled then, gently with his eyes, and she felt a rush of intense feeling for him. A protective, warm, maternal affection. She almost wished that someone would comment—with a sneer—on his pink evening coat, which she really did think rather splendid. She would give that person such a length of her tongue that he would slink away as if whipped and bruised.

"I am so happy that my first waltz is with *you*," she said, smiling warmly at him. "It is such an intimate dance, is it not? I would be mortally embarrassed with anyone else and would be treading all over his feet. I can relax with you. I know you are skilled enough to keep your feet from beneath mine."

"You do yourself an injustice," he said. "You are an excellent dancer, Miss Downes."

She felt herself glow at the compliment. Lord Francis was so very graceful himself. "Thank you," she said.

He was looking at her again in that quiet, unsmiling way. She smiled at him.

"What is wrong?" she asked.

"Nothing," he said. "I rather believe something might be very right, in fact. Are congratulations in order, by any chance?"

She looked at him blankly for a moment and then threw back her head and laughed aloud before she remembered where she was. "You are referring to Mr. Johnson," she said. "Oh, I ought not to laugh, Lord Francis. He came calling this afternoon and stammered his way through a very earnest speech. I do assure you I did not laugh at him. Indeed, I was much obliged to him. I let him down quite gently. I did not hurt him, you know. He is not in love with me, only with what I have become for this fleeting moment, poor man."

"And you are not in love with him?" he said.

"Oh, goodness, no," she said. "Or with any of them, I am sad to say. Sad for her grace's sake, that is. She was kind enough to bring me here to find a husband for me and it must seem to her that she has achieved undreamed-of success. Several more of them are going to offer within the next week or so, you see. But I cannot take any of them seriously. I realized that yesterday morning when they were all so silly in the park and all made fun of that poor child and his hat—though he was not a poor child as it turned out, was he? Was he not a horrid little brat? Anyway, I realized as soon as I ran into you—I almost did so literally, did I not?—that I could not care for any of *them*. I would as soon stroll in the park with just you than with twenty of them put together. So that is telling me something, is it not?" She grinned at him, remembered their surroundings, and reduced the grin to a smile.

"Yes, indeed," he said.

She waited for him to make his own comments on the absurdity of the events in the park the day before, but he said nothing. The heat was affecting him, she guessed. And really it was quite overpowering. She looked away from him in order to drink in the splendor of her surroundings. In a few weeks she was going to be back home again, where she belonged and where she wanted to be. But she knew too that she would always remember these weeks and the wonder of the fact that for a short time she had been accepted by the *ton* and even fêted by the *ton*. And she would always remember Lord Francis Kneller and his pink and lemon and turquoise coats—and his kindness.

She was about to turn her head to smile at him again when she suddenly froze. A group of gentlemen had appeared in the ballroom doorway. Lord and Lady Fuller were hurrying across the room toward them. The music stopped abruptly. There was a buzz of well-bred excitement.

And then the gentlemen parted so that another could step into the doorway and pause to observe the scene. An enormously large gentleman. A gentleman larger than any other Cora had ever seen in her life, she would swear.

"Oh, dear. Oh, dear," she muttered and wondered what had happened to all the air in the room—and where she had misplaced her knees.

"There is nothing to fear," Lord Francis had drawn her arm firmly through his and held it now against his side. "He is only a man, Miss Downes."

Which was about the stupidest thing anyone had ever said to her in her life. She could hear the sound of teeth clattering and drowning out all other sounds. Only a man! He was the Prince of *Wales*.

And then she wished she had not verbalized his name in her mind.

All the dancers had retreated to the edge of the ballroom and waited in anticipation of His Highness's finishing with greeting his hosts and proceeding deeper into the room.

Cora tugged on Lord Francis's arm. "I have to leave," she told him. "I have to go." But she knew even as she said it that in order to leave she was going to have to skirt about that huge mound of royalty standing in the doorway. "Oh, dear. Oh, dear. Let us hide. Find somewhere to hide."

She thought she saw amusement in his eyes for a moment and felt horribly betrayed—her only friend was turning against her. But it was gentle concern, she saw when she looked closer.

"He is going to promenade about the room," he said, "and stop to exchange civilities with the chosen few. There are several hundred here who are only too eager for that honor, Miss Downes. We will skulk in the background here and merely bow and curtsy when everyone else does. I can assure you that the royal eyes will not even alight on you. But you will be able to go home afterward to boast that you have been within arm's length of the Prince Regent himself."

His voice was calm, matter of fact, almost bored—but

a little too kindly to be entirely so. He spoke that way only to reassure her, she knew. She was reassured though her heart thumped and she felt as if she had just run five miles uphill against a stiff wind. Why did someone not pump air into the room?

A great dense mass of persons began to move slowly clockwise about the ballroom. The Prince of Wales was hidden somewhere among them, Cora tried not to tell herself. A wave of bowing gentlemen and deeply curtsying ladies preceded their progress, though every few moments all came to a halt as the hidden prince presumably favored some poor soul with his notice.

Cora cowered back against the wall as they drew closer and tried to worm her way slightly behind Lord Francis while clinging to his arm at the same time. She distorted her face and nibbled furiously at one cheek. If only she could suddenly discover a door at her back. If only she were four feet tall instead of being far closer to six.

And how foolish she was being. She was Cora Downes. If everyone in this room were to line up in order of rank, she would be at the very back of the line. Dead last. She was a nobody. A nothing. The realization was enormously reassuring. She relaxed marginally, though the thought did touch the edge of her consciousness that it would not take a great deal to cause her to vomit. The thought was pushed aside with haste.

"Oh, dear. Oh, dear," she muttered as the cavalcade drew closer. The Duke of Bridgwater was part of it. In fact, he appeared to have the royal ear. The royal ear and the enormous person to which it was attached hove into sight. A slight tightening on her arm reminded her to sink into a curtsy. Horror of horrors, she had almost been left standing upright five feet above all the persons who surrounded her. As it was, she crouched low and looked down hopefully for trapdoors.

One more moment and they would pass.

"Ah," the haughty and languid voice of the Duke of Bridgwater said quite distinctly. "Here she is, sir."

"Where, Bridgwater?" the man mountain asked, and Cora emerged from her curtsy to find a million eyes riveted to her person—at least that many.

"Curtsy again," Lord Francis muttered to her as a path opened magically in front of them and he led her forward.

She curtsied as he led and almost had her arm yanked from its socket. Fortunately Lord Francis seemed far more in control of his faculties than she and allowed her to dip down where she was before taking her forward to stand before the Illustrious Presence.

She would die. There was nothing left in life to do now but die. Preferably now or sooner. Before the agony could be prolonged.

Everyone was still looking at her. Everyone was also smiling at her. From some distance away there was the faint smattering of applause. She felt the hysterical urge to giggle.

"My dear Miss Downes." Her *hand* was in the Prince of Wales's *two hands*. He was drawing her to her feet. She had curtsied again. She had lost the support of Lord Francis's arm. She looked about her wildly, but he was there at her side. "I beg leave to offer you my own personal thanks as well as those of the nation for your act of extreme bravery in saving the life of the Duke of Bridgwater's nephew."

"Oh, it was really nothing at all, Your Majesty," someone said. "I-I mean, your gr—. Oh dear, I do not know what I mean."

There was a burst of laughter from everyone within earshot and the prince himself shook alarmingly with it.

"Your modesty becomes you, my dear," he said. "His

Majesty and I need more subjects like you. Enjoy the ball."

And the procession moved on. The dipping and bowing proceeded to Cora's left.

The people about her were nodding and smiling and murmuring their own congratulations—though whether for her supposed heroism or for the honor that had just been accorded her Cora neither knew nor cared. She grabbed for Lord Francis's arm

"I am going to faint," she told him. "Or vomit."

"Come." He led her back behind the crowds, who were still standing and watching the royal progress and craning their necks to see whom else he would favor with his personal notice. Cora was gasping. She was in deep distress.

And then blessedly there *was* a door and he was opening it just wide enough to usher her through and follow himself before closing it behind them.

Fresh air. And darkness. And privacy.

Cora drew a deep breath and then really did faint.

8

$\mathcal{F}$ORTUNATELY SHE HAD WARNED HIM. AND FORTU-
nately too it was the first of her predictions of what
was about to happen to her, rather than the second,
which came true. He caught her sagging body in his
arms, looked hastily about in the darkness, to which
his eyes had not yet accustomed themselves, spotted a
wrought-iron seat not far away on the balcony, and carried her toward it.

Carrying Cora Downes about in his arms was becoming a habit, he thought. An uncomfortable habit, for
more than one reason.

He set her down on the seat and took the empty place
beside her. He set one hand at the back of her head and
eased it downward almost to her knees. He should, he
thought belatedly, have spoken with someone before
stepping out of doors, and sent a message to the Duchess of Bridgwater. It was not at all the thing to be out
here alone like this with a single young lady.

If that damned Prinny had not decided to put in an
appearance, of course, all the French doors would have
been wide open all evening and lamps lit on the balcony.
There would have been guests strolling out here and his
being with Miss Downes would have been almost
proper.

But then if Prinny had not come, she would not have

fainted. The waltz would have been at an end by now and she would have been dancing with her next partner. He would have been on his way elsewhere. Oh, yes, indeed he would.

"Oh, dear," she said, addressing her knees, "did I faint?"

"Take some deep slow breaths," he advised her. "The air is cooler out here. You will feel better in a moment."

"How very foolish of me," she said after following his directions. "Thank heaven it was only you who saw me have a fit of the vapors. I *never* have fits of the vapors, you know. But then I have never been in the presence of royalty before."

He felt uncomfortable again. As he had while they had waltzed. She had misinterpreted his attentions to her. She was falling in love with him—had perhaps already fallen. Almost every time she spoke to him she expressed a preference for him. But only tonight, after Bridgwater's words, had he noted the fact. He did not believe she was setting her cap at him. She was far too open and candid for that. Yet she was not even trying to hide her feelings. She must assume that he shared them.

Bridgwater had been right. He had been amusing himself bringing the woman into fashion, introducing her to eligible gentlemen, playing matchmaker, and all the while he had been giving the impression that he was taken with her himself. He had given her the same impression.

What a coil! He had been so preoccupied by his feelings for Samantha that it had not struck him anyone could possibly think him interested in any other woman. And yet he had been at pains to hide his broken heart.

"You acquitted yourself very well," he said. "The aftermath will be our little secret, Miss Downes."

She sat up and looked at him. He could not tell in the

darkness if she had recovered her color, but he set a steadying arm about her shoulders just in case.

"He actually spoke to me." She set her palms against her cheeks. "He actually took my hand in his. And *I spoke to him.* What did I say? Did I make an utter cake of myself?"

"Not at all," he said.

"Yes, I did." Her eyes, fixed on his, widened in horror. "I called him 'Your Majesty.' And then I remembered that only the king is called that, but I could not remember what I should call him—and *I told him so.* Ohh!" She wailed out her distress and hid her face on his shoulder.

He wished she would not. She had a physical presence it was difficult to be unaware of when she was close. He wished he had not set his arm about her shoulders. It appeared she had recovered from her faint even if not from her mortification.

"He was charmed," he said.

She started to laugh then, her head still against his shoulder. At first it was silent laughter and he thought in some alarm that she was shaking with grief. But soon she was chuckling softly and then laughing helplessly.

Even when one had entirely missed a joke, Lord Francis had learned in the course of his life, it was sometimes impossible to remain serious in the presence of someone else's mirth. He found himself chuckling along with her.

"I was bobbing like a cork in the ocean," she said. "And I swear there were no bones at all in my knees. It is amazing I did not fall flat at his feet." She succeeded in delivering this speech only after several pauses for merriment en route.

"He would have been even further charmed if you had," Lord Francis said. "He likes nothing more than to see people prostrated by his majestic presence."

They both found this little conversational exchange irresistibly hilarious.

"He is e-enormous," she said. "If I *had* fallen and he had trodden on me, I would be as flat as a piece of paper. You would be able to write a letter on me."

"Yes," he agreed. "There is a great deal of visible majesty there, is there not?"

She set her arm about his neck, presumably to steady herself, while they bellowed with unholy—and quite unkind—glee.

"Oh," she said. "Oh, my chest hurts. Would we be charged with treason if we could be heard saying such disrespectful things?"

"We would have our heads chopped off in the Tower," he said. "With a giant ax by a hooded headman."

They found the prospect of such a gory fate enormously tickling. They clung to each other, snorting and wheezing, absorbed by silliness—as Lord Francis reflected afterward when it was too late to go back and behave with more dignity and more decorum. He could not remember any other occasion when he had so abandoned himself to uncontrolled foolishness.

The Prince of Wales had not come to Lady Fuller's ball to dance. He had come to receive the homage of the *ton* and play the part of grand, majestic gentleman. Having received the one and acted out the other, he took his leave, and the ball resumed. But before the excitement had quite died down and before the music had struck up once more, there was something imperative to be done. Lady Fuller had the message taken to several footmen, and her guests, seeing their intent, followed them gratefully to the French doors and prepared to spill out onto the balcony for fresh air and blessed coolness before the serious business of enjoying themselves began again.

That, at least, was the scene as Lord Francis re-created

it for himself in his imagination much later. He was not inside the ballroom to observe for himself, of course.

He was outside.

Sitting on a wrought-iron seat like an actor on stage, invisible to the audience until the curtains were swept back and all eyes focused on him. Or, in his case, until the doors were thrown open and the light of hundreds of candles streamed outward to illuminate him to the interested gaze of several dozen members of the *beau monde,* among whom was the Duke of Bridgwater.

Sitting on a wrought-iron seat, apparently in close embrace with Miss Cora Downes. With nary a chaperon in sight.

"Oops," Cora Downes said, startled out of her laughter and dropping her arm from about his neck with what could only be interpreted as guilty haste. "Oh, dear."

Lord Francis behaved even more foolishly. He lugged his arm awkwardly from about her, smiled idiotically at no one in particular, and muttered to no one in particular, "I escorted Miss Downes outside for some air and privacy."

Well! He recovered both his famous ennui and the handle of his quizzing glass a moment later and got to his feet with his usual elegance to bow over Miss Downes's hand and inform her that he would escort her to her grace's side.

But it was very much too late, he feared.

"Hayden is returning from Vienna in September," Elizabeth announced calmly at the breakfast table just as if the fact did not concern her personally. "Lady Fuller received a letter from him yesterday. He hopes to celebrate our nuptials before Christmas."

Jane sighed and looked back at the announcement in the *Morning Post* for surely the two dozenth time since they had sat down. "I do hope so, Lizzie," she said. "I cannot marry before you, but Charles would marry by special license if he had his way. He is that impatient."

"Special licenses are vulgar," Elizabeth said. "And so is calling your betrothed by his given name, Jane. I would not dream of addressing Hayden by his even after our marriage."

"But then Charles and I *love* each other, Lizzie," Jane said gently.

Which was a decided hit, Cora thought. She sighed inwardly. She wished that one day she would be able to say that too. *But then So-and-so and I love each other. So-and-so would marry by special license if he had his way. He is that impatient.*

She was envious of Jane. Not jealous—the Earl of Greenwald was a gentle young man, a type she could never fall in love with herself even if he was in her own social milieu. But she wished she could fall in love too. She was beginning to despair of ever doing so. There had been those three worthies at home. There had been Mr. Bentley and Mr. Johnson here and she knew without conceit that there would be others. She could feel nothing except gratitude and a little irritability for any of them. But she was one-and-twenty already. She was on the shelf.

She sighed again and smiled.

The duchess was smiling too—at her daughters. She must be well pleased. Both of them settled and so well settled, Elizabeth with a marquess and Jane with an earl. Neither was married yet, of course, but then a betrothal was as binding as a marriage, especially when settlements had been carefully drawn up and signed by each of the prospective grooms and the Duke of Bridgwater.

How pleased Papa would be to draw up such a settlement for her, Cora thought. Perhaps she would never be able to give him that pleasure.

The duchess was looking at her. "Have you finished your breakfast, Cora?" she asked. "I would like a word with you in my sitting room if you have."

Not another marriage offer already, Cora thought in dismay. She always found it so painful to say no even when she knew that it was only Papa's wealth that had provoked the proposal—though one of her suitors in Bristol had been a very wealthy man in his own right, she must admit.

"Yes, your grace," she said, getting to her feet.

But it was a scold she was being taken aside for. Very gently expressed, but a scold nonetheless. They had been very late home last night—or this morning rather—and they had all been very tired. Jane had been marvelously happy over her betrothal, and all of them had been abuzz with the brief appearance of the Regent and his kind condescension in speaking with Cora and congratulating her on her bravery in saving little Henry's life.

Her grace had left any unpleasantness for this morning, Cora guessed now.

"It is of course quite understandable that you would be overcome with awe at being singled out by the prince," her grace said when Cora had made her explanations. "I can see that you would want to escape for a while to collect yourself. But you really should have sent for me, my dear. Or Lord Francis should have done so. I find it strange that he would have behaved so thoughtlessly."

"It was really not his fault," Cora said, hastening to his defense. "I told him I was going to faint or *vomit*. He acted promptly. It would have been unspeakably embarrassing if I had done either in public. Especially with the Prince of Wales *still there*."

The duchess smiled for a moment. But only for a moment.

"Cora," she said, looking closely at her charge. "You

have not developed a *tendre* for Lord Francis, my dear? He is the brother of the Duke of Fairhurst, and while you are very ladylike and your father owns Mobley Abbey and you are an acknowledged heroine, we must still be realistic. It would be unwise—"

But Cora interrupted her with a merry laugh. "Have a *tendre* for Lord Francis?" she said. "Oh, no, your grace. That would be remarkably foolish." Did not her grace *know*? "I like him excessively but there can be no possible thought of anything else."

The duchess looked at her in silence for a moment and then nodded. "And what about him?" she asked. "He could never think of you in terms of matrimony, Cora, brutal as I might seem in putting it to you thus baldly. I have never known him to behave improperly—quite the contrary, in fact. But you are extraordinarily attractive even if your face is not classically pretty. I do hope—"

But Cora's eyes had widened. Her grace did *not* know. How droll. "Lord Francis is quite unaffected by my charms, I do assure you, ma'am," she said—though of course she had no charms for him to be affected by even if he were so inclined, despite what her grace had just said out of her kindness. "And he has been nothing but a perfect gentleman to me."

"And yet," the duchess said gently, "you were seen to be in close embrace with him out on a dark and deserted balcony, Cora."

Cora giggled despite herself. "We were laughing," she said. "I had been badly frightened and then I had fainted. I reacted by making a joke of it all and Lord Francis found it funny too. We were merely laughing and holding each other up."

It sounded remarkably foolish in the retelling. But shared laughter was a wonderful thing. She and Papa and Edgar sometimes did it, all three of them together. Not often, it was true, because Papa was a sober businessman and Edgar was a dignified lawyer. But when they were alone together and got started on some topic that amused them all, they could work it and tease it and exaggerate it until they were all holding their sides and wiping the tears from their eyes.

It had never happened with anyone else—anyone outside her own family. Until last night with Lord Francis. She felt an enormous affection for him. She would never see him again after the next week or so. How she wished he were her brother too. He and Edgar both. She pictured herself tripping along a street in Bristol or Bath between the two of them, an arm linked through each of one of theirs. Edgar and Lord Francis would like each other, she believed. Though perhaps not. Men like Edgar did not always approve of men like Lord Francis. The thought saddened her.

"I believe you, dear," the duchess said. "But perhaps it should be remembered that decorum dictates that one should carefully avoid even the appearance of impropriety. When a man and a woman are discovered alone together and in each other's arms, it is unlikely that most people will conclude they are merely sharing a joke."

"Yes, ma'am." Cora could appreciate the truth of that. "Have I disgraced you? I am so very sorry. And sorry too if I have compromised Lord Francis. Though I do believe that most people will not misconstrue his behavior." Surely most people must know.

Her grace smiled. "Gentlemen are not compromised, dear," she said. "Only ladies. This can be smoothed over, I am quite sure. After all, everyone was very sensible of the fact that you had just been singled out for congratulations by the Prince Regent himself. And even apart from that you are riding high in the esteem of the *ton* at present. But you must be careful, Cora. The *ton* is a fickle body."

"Yes, ma'am," Cora said.

"You are to go to the library with Jane this morning?" her grace said with a smile. "I do believe there is to be an accidental meeting there with Greenwald. Run along then, dear. And do stay by her side, will you not? You will not chase after windblown hats and leave her alone?"

Cora flushed. It seemed that her grace saw and knew far more than was apparent to either her daughters or her protégée.

"No, ma'am," she said and fled the room.

She had been indiscreet. She would never understand the world of gentility, she thought. But then it did not matter. She would not be in that world for much longer. Soon she would be back in her own, where the rules and expectations were not quite so strict and where people did not spy on one another in such gleeful expectation of catching one another in some misdemeanor. But for the sake of the Duchess of Bridgwater, who had been kind to her, she would be careful of her behavior for as long as they remained in town.

She was longing to see Lord Francis again, though. She wanted to tell him what people thought and what her grace had said. He would appreciate the joke no end. They would have a good laugh over it.

Oh, dear, she thought, she was going to miss him dreadfully when she left town and returned home.

LORD FRANCIS KNELLER called upon the Duke of Bridgwater when the latter was still at breakfast. He was shown into the breakfast parlor and invited to partake of the contents of the dishes displayed on a sideboard. He grimaced slightly and seated himself empty-handed at the table.

His grace set aside the *Morning Post*, which was opened to the page of announcements, looked shrewdly at his guest, and nodded to his butler, who quietly left the room.

"Well," Lord Francis said, picking up the napkin the butler had set beside his empty place and tapping the silver holder with one fingernail, "give me your candid opinion, Bridge." It was the first time he had used the shortened form of the duke's title that his closer friends used. But he did so unconsciously. "Do I owe her an offer?"

"Good Lord," his grace said, his fork suspended midway between his plate and his mouth.

"You are not her father or her brother or in any way her guardian," Lord Francis said. "And I believe she is of age anyway. But you have chosen to take on some responsibility for her. Well, then, do I owe her an offer?"

The duke set his fork down, the food impaled on its tines untasted. "It had not occurred to me that you would even consider making one," he said. "You have *not* given the matter serious consideration, have you?"

"I had her alone," Lord Francis said. "In a dark place where there was no one else to lend even the semblance of propriety. I had my arms about her. She had hers about me. We were seen by a shudderingly large number of the *ton,* yourself included. I certainly cannot blame anyone for concluding that we were embracing, especially in light of the first asinine words I uttered."

"Were you *not* embracing?" his grace asked faintly.

"We were *laughing,*" Lord Francis said. "But that seems woefully irrelevant at the moment. I believe I owe her the protection of my name."

"Good Lord," the duke said. "I was coming to see you after breakfast, Kneller. To instruct you in no uncertain terms that I would not have my mother's protégée offered carte blanche. I assumed that was your intention, perhaps even already your expressed intention. She is after all extremely—well, beddable. But my business this morning was to tell you that it just would not do, that you would have to go through me before effecting it."

Lord Francis scraped back his chair with his knees as he stood abruptly. He felt a return of last evening's fury. "Carte blanche?" he said. "Me to Miss Downes? Are you out of your mind, Bridgwater? She is a lady."

"Ah," his grace said quietly, "but she is not, is she?"

Lord Francis had never seen red. But he knew now what was meant by the expression. "I could call you out for that," he said through his teeth.

The duke looked at him, raised his eyebrows, and laid his napkin unhurriedly on the table. He set a finger and thumb on either side of the bridge of his nose. "Sit down, Kneller," he said. "Let us not become farcical."

"There is nothing farcical about suggesting that Miss Downes is the sort of woman to whom one might offer carte blanche," Lord Francis said. But he sat down again when the duke merely closed his eyes and rested his elbow on the table.

"Good Lord," his grace said, "you are in love with her, Kneller."

"Nonsense," Lord Kneller said. "Stuff and nonsense. But she has character and charm and courage, Bridge, and does not deserve to be discussed between us as someone who might or might not agree to be my mistress. The very thought!"

"I would certainly meet *you* before I would allow such a thing," his grace said. "Her father allowed her to come here under my mother's sponsorship and protection. Under *my* protection, in other words. You cannot marry her, Kneller. It would be a disaster for both of you."

"Yes," Lord Francis agreed after thinking about it for a moment. Though he had thought of nothing else all night. He had tried to imagine the interview he would have with his brother after making the announcement and had succeeded all too well. Besides, she would never be comfortable in his world. Look what had happened last evening when old Prinny had put in an appearance. "But what will happen to her if I do *not* offer? Was she irrevocably compromised?"

"By no means," his grace said with a sigh. "I will spend my day wandering from drawing room to drawing room. I shall call on my mother first and make sure that she does the same. We will both be amused by the terror with which our sweet, innocent heroine greeted her moment of fame with Prinny. And amused too by the way she took to her heels afterward and clung to you in fear and trembling when you went after her to console her and bring her back. No one will dare contradict me, and no one will even think of disbelieving my mother when she is at her most gracious."

"And the story would be almost entirely true," Lord Francis said. "Except that we were *laughing*. Relief on her part that it was all over, I suppose, and genuine amusement on my part. She has a way of amusing me." He spoke rather sadly. He would not be able to allow himself to be amused by her ever again.

"Yes, well, it will be done," his grace said, reaching for his snuffbox even though he had not quite finished his breakfast. "And no more nonsense about offering for her, Kneller."

Lord Francis got to his feet again, pushed his chair under the table, and grasped the back of it. "I am much obliged to you, Bridge," he said, "for her sake. If there is any scandal, it is entirely my fault. She is far more innocent than her years would lead one to expect. I believe she had no notion at the time that there was anything worse in the situation than a measure of embarrassment. If there is no way of smoothing all over, you will make sure that I know?"

"Indeed," his grace said, his snuff-bedecked hand poised before his face. "But if that happens, Kneller, we will send her quietly home. Scandal would not follow her there into her own world, you know."

Lord Francis drummed the fingers of one hand against the chair for a moment before nodding curtly and taking his leave.

He felt considerably better, he thought as he hurried away down the street on foot. He had been very much afraid that Bridgwater would have a marriage contract all drawn up to wave beneath his nose as soon as they met. Not that Bridgwater had any authority to draw up any such document, of course. But even so . . .

Perhaps he had escaped. Perhaps she had escaped.

But one thing was sure. He was not going to be seen within half a mile of Miss Cora Downes for what remained of the Season.

The thought was strangely depressing.

For the first time in several weeks Lord Francis quite deliberately conjured up a mental image of Samantha Newman, now Samantha Wade, Marchioness of Carew. Quite deliberately he tortured himself with images of her walking hand in hand with Carew about Highmoor Park in Yorkshire. Quite deliberately he reminded himself that she was increasing.

Quite deliberately he forced himself into an agony of loneliness and self-pity.

His heart no longer felt as if it were in the soles of his boots. It felt as if it were six feet beneath the ground.

Damnation, but life was an unpleasant business these days.

9

THERE WAS, OF COURSE, NO SCANDAL. CORA HAD NOT expected there would be. How foolish! All that had happened was that she had been seen laughing helplessly in Lord Francis Kneller's arms—Lord Francis of all people. It had been embarrassing to be so caught, but nothing else. No one with any sense would have suspected anything else. And apparently no one did.

For the next week she was besieged by admirers, both old and new. She had two marriage offers and declined them both. None of her gentlemen admirers referred to the incident at the Fuller ball—at least not to *that* incident. A few were dazzled by the fact that the Prince of Wales had actually spoken with her.

A few of her lady acquaintances made oblique reference to *the* incident, it was true. One of them told her she was fortunate indeed to have Lord Francis Kneller as part of her court. Apparently he added something called *tone* to it. With Lord Francis as a member of one's court, it seemed, one was assured of attracting many more members. If that was true, Cora thought, then he had been extraordinarily successful. Of course he was not really paying court to her, but perhaps he had intended to bring her to the attention of other gentlemen. She must remember to ask him about it the next time she saw him. They would have a laugh over it.

The Honorable Miss Pamela Fletcher—who had not taken well at all this year, largely because of a nasty disposition, in Cora's estimation—was a little less kind.

"Lord Francis Kneller has attached himself to Miss Downes's court," she explained kindly to one young lady, "because he is so accustomed to being part of *someone's* court, poor gentleman." She sighed.

No one then present cared to feed her the lines that would enable her to enlarge on the observation. But neither did anyone start talking furiously about the weather or any other innocuous subject. Everyone looked mildly embarrassed, except for Cora, who looked mildly interested. And so Miss Fletcher continued uninvited.

"Lord Francis was a part of Samantha Newman's court for *years*, you know," she said, speaking to Cora, though it was obvious she thought Cora did not know. "He was devoted to her. It was rumored that he was heartbroken when she married the Marquess of Carew earlier this Season. But who could blame her?" She looked about the group with a smile, inviting agreement. "The marquess is lamentably lacking in good looks and he is a *cripple*, though one does not like to use such a vulgar word aloud, but he is said to be worth more than fifty thousand a year. I might have been tempted to marry him myself if he had asked." She tittered merrily.

Miss Fletcher, Cora concluded, was seriously deficient in brain power. If Lord Francis had been a member of a lady's court for *years*, was not that indication enough that he had had no real romantic interest in her? Lord Francis heartbroken because his lady love had married another man for his fortune? What nonsense. She stored up this little tidbit of gossip to share with him too. She was going to tease him about Samantha Whatever-her-name-was, now the Marchioness of Wherever.

But the trouble was, even though the week following

Lady Fuller's ball was an extremely busy one, and even though there were more gentlemen than enough to dance with Cora and drive with her and walk with her and converse with her, there was never the only one with whom she could *enjoy* doing those things. During the whole week she did not exchange a single word with Lord Francis Kneller. She saw him only twice—once at the theater when she was there with a party made up by the Earl of Greenwald, and once when she was shopping on Oxford Street. On neither occasion were they close enough to each other to exchange more than a distant and cheerful wave.

It was most provoking and most dreary. She had decided she wanted nothing to do with suitors, yet she dealt with nothing but suitors all day and every day. She wanted only a friend for the final two weeks she was to spend in London—a friend with whom she could relax and chat and laugh. She saw nothing of the only real friend she had in London—though that seemed an absurd and disloyal thought when she had Jane and even Elizabeth to be her friends.

She had known she was going to miss Lord Francis when she returned to Bristol. But she had not expected to have to start missing him so soon. Of course, he owed her nothing. He had been far kinder than could have been expected of a gentleman of his rank. He had tired of taking notice of her. He did not even think of her as a friend. How could she even have thought he might? The realization was a little humiliating.

There was just a week left in London. Apart from the usual daily rounds of entertainments, there was one in particular to which she looked forward. She was to go to Vauxhall Gardens one evening, again as part of the Earl of Greenwald's party. She had not been there before and was excited at the prospect of seeing the famous pleasure gardens at night, when they were reputed to be magical with their lamp-laden trees and shady walks and pavilion and music and food and fireworks.

It would be one last thrilling memory to store away before she went home again. How she longed to be at home! How she longed to boast to Papa and Edgar about all she had seen and done. How she longed to tell them about meeting the prince. She had mentioned in her letter only that he had attended the Fuller ball, at which she had been a guest. She had hugged to herself the main detail—*that he had spoken to her personally*—to tell them face-to-face. She wanted to watch their expressions when they heard it.

Oh, yes, she longed to be home. But first there were Vauxhall and a final week of merrymaking.

HE DID NOT know quite what he was doing still in London. There was no real reason to stay and the Season was all but at an end. Several people had already left. But where would he go? He had an estate of his own in Wiltshire, left him by his mother, but he always felt restless, even lonely there unless he took a house party with him. He did not feel like organizing a house party. He could go to his brother's for a few weeks—there was always a standing invitation for him there, and the children would be delirious with joy. Or he could go to either of his sisters'. Both of them would go into instant action trotting out before him all the local eligible hopefuls. No, he was not in the mood for family, especially the matchmaking members of the family—and even his sister-in-law was not entirely blameless in that department. He could go to Brighton, where the entertainments of the Season would continue almost unabated in new surroundings. But he did not feel like more of the same. He could go to Chalcote in Yorkshire to visit Gabe and Lady Thornhill . . .

No, he could not. Highmoor adjoined Chalcote and they visited back and forth almost every day, Gabe had written. He could never go back to Chalcote—not for a long, long time, anyway, until he could be sure of doing so without making an ass of himself. He certainly did not want to see her with a growing womb. The very thought invited something near panic.

And so he stayed on in London simply because there was nowhere else he fancied going. Besides, for a few days he was not certain that scandal had been averted in that unfortunate affair at Lady Fuller's ball. He could not understand what had got into him on that occasion. He could not recall laughing helplessly over nothing since he was a boy, and he certainly could not recall ever clinging to a female while he did so. And they had been seen. It was alarmingly humiliating. He was not at all sure that Bridgwater and his mother, even with all their consequence and influence, would be able to persuade the *ton* that what had been witnessed by so many had not been a passionate embrace.

He stayed so that he might offer for the woman if worse came to worst. It was another alarming thought. Fairhurst would have his head, Bridgwater had said. It was perfectly true—but his head would be had by chewing more than by chopping. Even a younger son of a Duke of Fairhurst was expected to be rather high in the instep. Even Samantha would have been somewhat frowned upon as his bride.

Samantha—he wished he could stop thinking about her. He was weary of doing so. He was tired of nursing a broken heart.

There was no scandal. Either the *ton* was far more sensible than it usually was—surely no one would seriously believe that he had been either courting or dallying with Miss Downes—or it was so dazzled by the honor Prinny had just paid her inside the ballroom that it readily forgave her minor indiscretion in celebrating her victory with an exuberant hug with her partner of the moment. Or Bridge and his mother had accomplished a very good day's work in deadening the growing gossip.

Lord Francis did his part by staying in case he was needed, but by keeping his distance from the dangerous person of Miss Cora Downes. It meant ducking out of ballrooms whenever he saw her in them and scooting down streets when he spotted her, so that they would not meet face-to-face, and doing an about-face with his horse in Hyde Park one afternoon, leaving the park only a few moments after entering it because she was there driving with Pandry. It meant being watchful and devious.

It meant being a little depressed.

He was missing her bright chatter and gay laughter. He was missing the expectation of farce in her company. There had been something farcical even in the fact that rollicking laughter had almost precipitated them into scandal and a forced union. He had to admit to himself at the end of one week that the high points of the week had been the two occasions when he had been unable to duck out of her sight and had been forced to lift a hand in acknowledgment of her. Both times she had smiled brightly and waved gaily.

Just as if she really cared. He remembered his discomfort at the ball and his growing conviction that she had allowed her feelings for him to grow too warm. He hoped she was not in love with him. But he had to confess on both occasions that she did not look quite like a woman who was pining over an elusive lover.

He danced with Lady Augusta Haville once during the week—the first time he had done so, even though he had been thinking about it for some time and she had been signaling her willingness for an even longer time. The morning after, he received an unexpected invitation from Lady Augusta's mama to make one of an evening party to Vauxhall. *Why not?* he thought with a shrug, the invitation still in his hand after he had already decided to refuse. *Why not?* He had been to Vauxhall only once this year. It was always worth a visit. And if there was any lingering gossip about Miss Downes and him, then he would put it finally to rest by appearing in public with Lady Augusta and her party.

He penned an acceptance.

VAUXHALL WAS INDEED magical. As soon as they entered it from the river entrance, Cora knew that it would be this place above all others she had seen in London that would remain in her memory and in her dreams. It had been a hot day and the evening was still warm, with just enough of a breeze to set the lamps to swaying in the branches of the trees, sending their colored circles of light dancing over the paths beneath.

An orchestra played in the pavilion and a few couples were already dancing in the space before it. Vauxhall was the place for lovers, Jane had said earlier, blushing and making sure that she was out of earshot of her mother—and even of Elizabeth. There were broad paths for strolling and there were a few narrower, darker paths along which a couple might lose themselves for a few minutes if they were clever enough to arrange it and discreet enough not to be gone long enough to be missed.

Perhaps, Jane had said, her hands clasped to her bosom and her eyes closed, so that Cora knew that really she was thinking aloud—perhaps at Vauxhall she would be kissed for the first time. Jane and the Earl of Greenwald, Cora guessed, were hotly in love and were finding irksome the fact that their wedding must wait until after her elder sister's.

It must feel good, Cora had thought, *to be hotly in love.* She thought so even more when they arrived at Vauxhall. Although they sat down first in their reserved box to eat supper, she longed to dance and to walk along the shady paths. She wished there were someone a little more romantic than Mr. Corsham with whom to do both—she wished there were someone with whom *she* would wish to steal a kiss. But she intended to enjoy herself anyway.

Her spirits were dampened somewhat when she spotted Lord Francis Kneller in another box not far distant from her own. He had not seen her yet. He was with a party that included the very lovely Lady Augusta Haville and several other ladies and gentlemen, all of whom, Cora realized, had titles. Just a few weeks ago she would have been terrified of all of them just on that count alone.

He was seated next to Lady Augusta and was deep in conversation with her. He looked his usual elegant, just slightly to-the-left-of-masculinity self. His coat was lavender, his waistcoat silver.

In fact Cora's spirits were a little more than dampened. She felt downright depressed, if the truth were to be told. She was not jealous—Lord Francis would not flirt with Lady Augusta any more than he would flirt with her or any other lady. But she was envious. She wanted him to be seated next to her, looking at her, deep in conversation with her. Oh, dear, she thought, she *was* jealous. She wanted him for *her* friend. She did not want to share him.

Share? She almost laughed aloud even though Mr. Corsham was in the middle of a very serious description of a pair of grays he had almost bid upon at Tattersall's this very week. There was no question of sharing Lord Francis. He was not interested in her any longer. He had not spoken to her in a week. He might have come to

Lord Greenwald's box at the theater during the intermission to pay his respects to her. He might have hurried down Oxford Street to greet her. But he had kept his distance both times. Now tonight he had not even noticed her though she had already stolen at least twenty glances at him.

Supper was over finally and she danced, first with Mr. Corsham and then with a viscount who was the unfortunate possessor of two left feet and the inability to feel rhythm. Then she walked with Mr. Corsham and two other couples, including Jane and her earl. The duchess and the earl's mama stayed in the box.

It was all so very beautiful, Cora thought as they strolled. She tried to imagine that she was walking with someone very special. Though it did not really matter that she was not. The place and the evening were lovely in their own right. Peaceful. Soothing. She tipped her head back and tried to see the sky and the stars beyond the lamps and the swaying branches of the trees.

Lord Francis had also walked along this way. He had had Lady Augusta on his arm and another couple had gone with them. They had not yet returned. Perhaps, Cora thought, they would meet farther along the path. Perhaps they would stop and converse. Though she did not really want to do that. She knew now that he had been deliberately avoiding her during the past week. She would not force him into a meeting. And she would not be able to talk or laugh with him, anyway, when he had Lady Augusta on his arm and she was on Mr. Corsham's.

No, she hoped they would not meet.

Jane and the earl had slipped to the back of the group. Soon enough, Cora noticed, they disappeared altogether. She smiled to herself. They would as quietly reappear after a few minutes, she was sure. They were ever discreet, those two. The other couple had got a little way ahead.

And then there was a distraction, just at the moment when Cora thought she saw Lord Francis and his group approaching from a distance. A rather poorly dressed woman—anyone who could pay the admission fee could get into Vauxhall and perhaps there were ways of getting in without even having to pay—said something to Mr. Corsham and caught at his sleeve. He spoke gruffly to her and tried to shrug off her hold, but she clung tenaciously and launched into a tale of woe that would doubtless have caught Cora's interest and sympathy if she had been at leisure to listen. But she was not.

A young child darted out of the trees to her left and wailed at her, clinging to her evening gown as he did so. He was a thin, ragged, barefooted little urchin. Cora bent to listen to him, all frowning concern.

"Me bruvver," he said with a gasp. "He's stuck up a tree, missus. He's too scared to come down. An' we'll be whipped for sure if we gets caught in 'ere." Having delivered this pathetic speech without pause, he resumed the wailing, and the clinging turned to tugging.

Cora spared one fraction of a moment—no longer—to glance in Mr. Corsham's direction. But he was still engaged in trying to detach the woman from his arm and apparently had not noticed the child. Yet somewhere to Cora's left, among the dark trees, a child was caught in a tree and might fall out of it at any moment, and both boys would be in trouble if caught. Without a doubt they had sneaked into the pleasure gardens, hoping to observe all the splendor of the proceedings from the branches of a tree. Poor little mites.

Without even a word to Mr. Corsham, Cora grasped the child's thin hand and sallied off with him into the darkness. It did not even enter her mind that it was a strange coincidence for both her escort and her to be accosted with woeful stories almost at the same moment.

"Do not be afraid," she instructed the little boy in her most reassuringly maternal voice. "We will have your brother down from his tree in no time at all. I am an expert tree climber. The secret is never to look down—*never*. And as for being whipped, I shall see that no harm comes to either of you. Doubtless it was naughty of you to sneak in without paying, but everyone knows that boys will be boys."

The child trotted and panted at her side.

"Now," Cora said when they were deep along surely the narrowest, darkest path in Vauxhall, "where is he? I do not hear him crying. He must be a brave lad." Or one so petrified by terror that he could not even utter a sound.

"'Ere, missus," the child said, speaking quietly and tonelessly and coming to an abrupt halt.

Cora stopped too and peered upward. And felt an arm come about her waist from behind and another about her neck. And smelled the disgusting odor of onions and garlic and rotten teeth and sweat. A hand found its way over her mouth while she stood in mute surprise.

"Quiet, my luverly lydy," a hoarse male voice advised her, "an' nobody will come to no 'arm. Tyke 'er bracelet, Jemmie, an' be quick about it. Oi'll get this."

Jemmie, the pathetic little urchin with the brother up a tree, set about trying to relieve Cora not only of her bracelet—an extremely expensive gift Edgar had given her for her last birthday—but also of her wrist. The male of the disgustingly bad breath and body odor raised the hand of the arm that was about her waist and grabbed the pearls that Papa had given her mother on their fifth wedding anniversary, only months before her death.

Cora bit his hand, stamped on his foot, and back-handed the boy simultaneously. It was an extremely un-clean hand, and it was against her principles to strike a child. But she was very angry indeed. She had come into this dark thicket to risk her own safety and one of her favorite gowns in climbing a tree to rescue a petrified infant—and as a reward she was being manhandled and robbed.

It was marginally satisfying to hear the man yelp and the boy screech.

If she could only turn, she thought, she would be able to deliver her finest blow, the one Edgar had instructed her to deliver if ever she found herself in a tight corner— this corner felt about as tight as a corner could get. Edgar had actually blushed when teaching her, but he had been quite adamant about it.

The trouble was she could not turn.

But suddenly the child seemed to be levitated straight up into the air and then went flying through it to land sprawling several feet away—fortunately he released his hold on both Cora's wrist and her bracelet before he began the flight. At the same moment the unwashed man released his hold on her person and her property, roaring as he did so.

Cora whirled about, making the instantaneous decision to use her *right* knee as her right leg was perhaps a little stronger than the left. But she had no chance to use either. She was forced to stand and watch like a helpless female as someone else grappled with the robber— someone who looked suspiciously in the darkness as if he might be wearing a lavender evening coat.

The boy fled quietly into the night.

Cora clasped both hands over her mouth. He would be slaughtered. Oh, the dear gallant man. He knew nothing about thugs and ruffians as did she, who had lived in Bristol for most of her childhood and had frequently been taken to the docks by her father.

He was going to be killed at the very least.

She waited for an opening to come to his assistance.

It came quite soon, when the ruffian came staggering backward. Fortunately, he must have tripped over a tree root. Cora steadied him with both hands from behind for a moment and then allowed him to continue his fall. She kicked him in the side with her slippered foot when he was down, doing marvelous damage to her recently healed toes.

"There," she said crossly, setting her hands firmly on her hips and glaring down at him, "take that!"

Obviously the thief knew when he had met his match. He pressed the heel of one hand against his jaw, grimacing and working it from side to side, and then scrambled in ungainly haste to his feet and disappeared into the darkness after his young accomplice.

"Well," Cora said, peering after him, "we certainly taught *him* a lesson."

But then she whirled about, in sudden mortal fear lest before his flight her assailant had murdered Lord Francis Kneller.

10

HE HAD SEEN HER AS SOON AS SHE ARRIVED AT VAUX-hall, one of a party of ten, which included Green-wald and Lady Jane Munro and the mothers of the newly betrothed couple. They had taken a box quite close to the one he occupied with Lady Augusta and her party.

It would have been the easiest thing in the world to have caught her eye and smiled and nodded. Indeed, several times he had felt her eyes on him. He could have strolled across to the other box to pay his respects. He need have stayed only a few moments. Instead, he had pretended not to notice her. He had ignored her alto-gether.

It had been a gauche and inexplicable thing to do. He could not understand why he had done it. It was not as if he had quarreled with the woman. Far from it. The last time they had been together they had laughed so hard that they had had to hold each other up. And it was not as if she had ever meant anything to him. Good Lord, he had not avoided even Samantha after she had announced her betrothal. He had been a guest at her wedding. It had been foolish to behave as he had to-night.

But the trouble was that with every minute that passed, it had become more difficult suddenly to notice that she was there at Vauxhall, in full view, a mere few yards from the box he occupied. He had even looked away from her when she danced. He had been very relieved when someone suggested a walk.

He would put matters right when they returned, he had decided. He would hand Lady Augusta back into the box and stroll across to Greenwald's, pretending that he had just noticed them. Not that it would sound very convincing. Even the Duchess of Bridgwater and Lady Jane must be wondering why he had suddenly become so blind. Cora Downes must be feeling quite upset with him. Lord, he hoped she did not fancy herself in love with him.

But it had seemed that he would not have to wait until the return to the pavilion. He had walked the length of the main path with Lady Augusta and another couple, deftly turning aside the former's hints that they explore one of the darker side paths. They had been strolling back again, enjoying the warmth of the evening, admiring the lanterns and the dancing colored lights they created on the path, nodding at acquaintances who passed them.

And then in the distance he had seen the unmistakable tall figure of Cora Downes approaching on Corsham's arm. For some reason he could not fathom, Lord Francis had felt jittery and breathless at the prospect of meeting her. He had considered after all drawing Lady Augusta off the path. He had not done so because he knew that the woman wanted to be kissed, and that after she was kissed she would as like as not expect him to call upon her papa tomorrow morning to discuss marriage settlements. He had become adept over the years at avoiding such situations.

Perhaps, he had thought fleetingly—but he had dismissed the thought as absurd—that was why he had attached himself to Samantha Newman's court for so long. Samantha had never been in search of a husband. And though he had loved her and offered for her several times, he had never really expected her to have him. There had been deep shock in discovering that she *would* have someone else and in haste too. Shock and humiliation. And heartbreak.

What would he do? he had wondered now. Nod pleasantly to Cora Downes and walk on by? Stop to converse with her and Corsham? Normally he did not have to think consciously about such matters. Normally he acted from instinct. What would instinct have him do, then? Stop and talk, of course. It would be the polite thing to do.

But before he had been able to do it—before he had been anywhere close to doing it—he had seen Miss Downes and Corsham fall prey to one of the oldest tricks in the book of thieves. A woman had approached Corsham from his side of the path and caught at his arm. Doubtless she would be spinning him a tale of poverty and starving children. As soon as his attention was engaged, a pathetic little urchin had approached Miss Downes from her side of the path and clutched at her gown. His tale would be even more heartrending and of course it would be falling on the most fertile ears in London. She had disappeared with the child almost immediately. Corsham and the other couple with them had not even seen her go.

There would be one more in the trees, of course. A man, in all probability, someone strong enough to relieve her of her jewels and valuables. And perhaps too—though not likely in the presence of the lad and with the woman not far away—of her virtue and even her life.

"Pardon me," Lord Francis had said hastily to Lady Augusta, who had had her head turned back over her shoulder while she addressed some remark to the couple who were strolling with them. "Someone to whom I must pay my respects." And he had gone hurrying down the path in unseemly haste and crashing into the trees after Miss Downes and the boy—Corsham had still been demanding that the woman unhand him.

Lord Francis had lost a few moments trying to force a path among dark trees before he realized that a few steps to his left there was a ready-made path, albeit a narrow one. But he had been quite right. Even in the darkness he had been able to see that there were now three figures ahead of him, a man and a boy dealing with a struggling woman. Both the man and the boy had let out sounds of pain just before Lord Francis launched himself at them, mindless with fury.

The boy had been easy to deal with. Lord Francis had merely lifted him from the ground with one hand on the collar of his ragged coat, and flung him. At the same moment he had got his arm about the man's neck, just as the man had his about Miss Downes's. The element of surprise had been on Lord Francis's side. The man had released his prey with a roar of mingled surprise and rage, and had spun about.

Lord Francis had not spent several mornings of each week for several years past at Jackson's boxing saloon for nothing. He was fit and he was competent, even skilled, with his fists. Jackson had always told him that he could be one of his star pupils if only he had a little more desire. Desire tonight was no problem at all. A few preparatory punches gave him the opening he needed and he landed a right upper cut to the man's chin with a satisfying crunching of bone and snapping of teeth. The villain reeled and in the natural course of things would have crashed to the ground within another second or two.

Nothing ever followed its natural course when Cora Downes was involved, of course. Somehow she had got herself behind the tottering rogue and reached out her hands to steady him. For one moment Lord Francis thought she was holding the man up so that he could deliver another blow. For the same moment he was terrified that she would be taken down with the man and squashed beneath him. But she stepped deftly aside, let him fall, and then kicked him in the side.

"There," she said fiercely, planting both hands on her hips, "take that!"

She probably hurt her foot more than she hurt the thief's side, Lord Francis thought. The man scrambled to his feet almost immediately and made off into the darkness. It was probably as well to let him go rather than try to confine him and take him into custody. Lord Francis made no move to pursue him. Miss Downes stood looking after him.

"Well," she said, "we certainly taught *him* a lesson."

Bless her heart, Lord Francis thought, relief beginning to replace his rage, she had restored the sanity of farce to a potentially nasty situation. He almost grinned at her when she spun around to face him.

"Lord Francis?" she said. "Oh, it *is* you. Did he hurt you? How foolish of you to come up on him like that. He might have *killed* you." She took a couple of steps toward him.

"I suppose," he said, trying to set his coat and sleeves to rights on his shoulders and arms, "you had the situation quite under control, Miss Downes?"

"No." The confidence went from her voice and one of her hands crept up to clutch her pearls. "No, I was deceived. The child said he had a brother stuck up a tree. They had crept in here just to watch the festivities, he told me, and would be whipped if they were caught. But he had that—ruffian waiting here."

"You are all right?" Lord Francis asked her, trying to see her expression in the darkness. "No real harm has been done? They picked a perfect victim, of course, although I am sure it was accidental on their part. You never could pass by anyone in trouble, could you?"

"I am all right," she said. But he watched her shudder. "He was dirty. He smelled dirty. He touched me. He had a hand over my mouth. They were going to take Mama's pearls and my bracelet from Edgar. I feel—I feel dirty too."

The intrepid Miss Cora Downes was beginning to suffer from delayed shock. She was beginning to come to pieces. Lord Francis took a step toward her.

"They are gone now," he said, making his voice as soothing as he was able. "You are quite safe. I will not allow them to come back and harm you."

She closed the gap between them in sudden haste and grabbed for the lapels of his coat. Her face came burrowing into the folds of his neckcloth that had taken his valet half an hour to perfect a few hours before. But that appeared not to be close enough. She straightened up, hid her face against his shoulder, wrapped her arms tightly about his neck, and pressed her body against his from shoulders to knees. Lord Francis was given the distinct impression that she would have climbed right inside him if it had been possible to do so.

"Hold me," she commanded him.

He held her. Tightly. And felt as if someone had moved the sun a few million miles closer to the earth and was beaming its heat directly at him. Good Lord—oh, devil take it! He furiously ignored his body's interest—a euphemistic word if ever he had thought of one—and concentrated all the power of his mind on giving her comfort.

"Shh," he told her softly, though she was making no noise. "I have you. You are quite safe, Cora."

He wished her bosom would not heave against his chest as if she had just run a mile or more.

"Ah." She sighed deeply into his shoulder. "You smell

so good." Perhaps she needed to say it again in case he had not heard it the first time. Perhaps she merely needed to look into his face to make sure that she really was with someone with whom she could feel safe. She lifted her head and looked into his eyes—their noses and mouths were almost touching. "You smell so very good."

No one had ever before told him that he smelled good. Somehow Miss Cora Downes made the words sound quite blisteringly erotic. He tipped his head slightly to one side so that their noses would not collide, focused his eyes on her lips, muttered "Cora" from somewhere deep in his throat, and had his mouth perhaps a quarter of an inch from hers when hell broke loose.

"Well!"

That was the start of it. The word was uttered in the shocked, outraged, haughty voice of Lady Augusta Haville.

She had brought a whole army with her—or so it seemed in the dark, close confines of the path. The couple they had been walking with was there, as was the couple Miss Downes had been with—as well as Greenwald and Lady Jane Munro and Corsham himself. There were a few other people too, people Lord Francis suspected he might know if only someone would come along with a branch of candles so that he could see better.

Apparently not one of the lot of them needed a branch of candles or even a single candle to know very well what he was up to. And of course they were very nearly right. Another quarter of a second and another quarter of an inch and he would have had no cause for outrage at all.

"Well, Kneller," Mr. Corsham said stiffly, "it is plain to see that they were right all along."

No one needed to be told who *they* were or what it was they had been right about all along.

"No sooner do I turn my back for the merest moment . . ." Mr. Corsham did not finish his sentence, but turned his back once more and stalked away.

"Cora," Lady Jane said, sounding tearful.

"Come, my love," her betrothed said. "This is none of our concern, I believe."

Except that Miss Cora Downes was his invited guest and might have been robbed and ravished and murdered, Lord Francis thought.

"And I thought to give you the benefit of the doubt," Lady Augusta said, a universe of scorn in her voice. She was presumably addressing herself to Lord Francis. "But you could not wait for the opportunity to rush to the arms of that *slut*."

"Oh," Cora Downes said, sounding more interested than shocked, "is that *me* she is talking about?"

"If the glove fits, wear it." Lady Augusta spat out the triumphant cliché with an equally clichéd toss of the head and turned to march away, taking the other couple from her party with her.

"I was almost *robbed*," Cora Downes said. "Lord Francis came to *rescue* me."

But they appeared to have lost the bulk of their audience except for a now sobbing Jane, an embarrassed-looking Greenwald—Lord Francis suspected that the two of them had been up to clandestine business in the woods when they should have been walking with Miss Downes and Corsham and keeping an eye on them—and the sheepish-looking couple who were members of the same party.

The rest of the audience were doubtless breaking speed records in their haste to get back to the pavilion and the crowds in order to spread the glad tidings.

"Hush," Lord Francis said, setting an arm about Miss

Downes's waist and drawing her against his side. "Come, I will escort you back to Greenwald's box. Her grace will take you home."

"They thought we were having a *tryst* here," she said, sounding dazed. "Did they not realize it was only me—and only you?"

Lord Francis suspected that they—every last one of the spectators—had known those facts very well indeed. They were the same couple who had been discovered in close embrace out on the deserted balcony of Lady Fuller's ballroom.

"Come," he said quietly. "Take my arm."

She took it. "This is ridiculous," she said. Her voice had gained strength. "How very foolish people are. Yes, take me back to the pavilion, Lord Francis, and we will tell everyone exactly what happened. Will they not be embarrassed to have so misjudged the situation?" She laughed suddenly and sounded genuinely amused. "You and I enjoying a secret tryst—what a delightful joke! Can they not see it?"

Probably not, Lord Francis thought, patting her hand soothingly. He could not see it himself. In fact, he felt about as far removed from laughter and jokes as he had ever felt in his life.

CORA HAD BEEN shut up inside the Duchess of Bridgwater's house for four whole days, even though the sun had shone brightly from a cloudless sky for all of those days and summer was upon them. And even though there had been plans and engagements for every morning and afternoon and evening of those days.

No one had called. She had been nowhere.

It seemed that she was in something of a scrape. Her grace and Jane and even Elizabeth were very kind about it, but they made no attempt to tell the world how ridiculous the situation was. And they did not encourage Cora to brazen it out by keeping her engagements.

It was definitely ridiculous. It had been from the start. When they had arrived back at the pavilion after that dreadful incident with the thieves—the woman must have been an accomplice too, Cora had realized in a moment of inspiration—it had appeared that everyone was looking at them and that an unnatural hush had fallen over the gathered revelers. Cora was not given to conceit. She was not one to imagine that everyone was looking at her when in fact everyone was not.

Cora would have stood in the middle of the dancing area before the pavilion and addressed the mob since she obviously had their attention anyway. She would have told what had happened. She would have explained how clever the woman and the boy had been and how evil-smelling the man had been. She would have described her struggles and told about how she and Lord Francis between them had vanquished the foe. She would even—since she was not conceited—have admitted to that moment of weakness when she had felt suddenly dirty and violated though no serious harm had been done and had needed the comfort of Lord Francis's arms.

She would have made them all lower their eyes in embarrassment at their mistake. And then she would have made them laugh and everything would have returned to normal. Not that she would ever again admit Mr. Corsham to her smiles and her conversation and her company. He had behaved with a shocking lack of gallantry. Good heavens, he had fallen into the trap quite as much as she had. And it had certainly not been he who had come galloping to her rescue.

But she had been given no chance to tell her story, and to her chagrin Lord Francis had made no attempt to tell it either—except in a hushed voice and in the barest of details to her grace, to whose side he had escorted her without pause. He had ended his explanation with the advice that her grace take Miss Downes home immediately and keep her there until he called the next morning.

And so Cora had known all the indignation and all the ignominy of being hustled out of Vauxhall, Lord Greenwald's party all behind her like silent whipped dogs, feeling as if somehow she was in deep disgrace.

She had been brought home—though it was not home at all, she had been only too aware for four whole days—and kept there. And Lord Francis had *not* come the day after Vauxhall or any day since. No one had come.

She wanted to go home, Cora decided. She wanted Papa and Edgar and her familiar world. A world that was ruled by sane laws of common sense. She wanted to have done with this world. It had been an exciting world and a gratifying world—she was not going to pretend that it had not been fun to be a heroine. But it was a silly world.

She had asked her grace if she might go home. She was only an embarrassment now to the family that had brought her here. Elizabeth and Jane still had commitments to honor and naturally enough the duchess must wish to concentrate on the progress of her daughters' betrothals. But the duchess was being gracious about the whole thing. Cora must stay and relax, she said. All would be well. She was very sorry that she had been the cause of all this unpleasantness. She should have found Cora a husband in Bath.

Cora felt like a nuisance even though she could feel no guilt over anything that had happened. *Nothing* had happened. She could not understand how anyone could have imagined that anything had—especially with Lord Francis Kneller, of all people. But she felt a nuisance. She felt in the way. All she could do, she supposed, was to stay quietly here until everyone returned to the country next week and she could go home to Mobley Abbey. There would still be plenty of summer left.

Lady Augusta Haville had called her a *slut,* she kept thinking. Oh, how she would dearly love to slap that young lady's face for her. In *her* world, in Cora's world, women did not go about being so vulgarly insulting to one another. And this was supposed to be the genteel world? Ha, Cora thought.

Lord Francis had been about to *kiss* her, she kept thinking. On the lips. Papa and Edgar often kissed her— they were an openly affectionate family. They kissed her on birthdays and when one or other of them was coming or going. Always on the forehead or one of her cheeks. Sometimes she felt a little weak-kneed when she remembered that Lord Francis had been about to kiss her on the lips. And she wondered what it would have felt like. She smiled to herself when she caught herself in such wonderings. Like a brother's kiss, that was what. It would have been comforting just as his arms had been and his body had been—she had been a little surprised to find that there had been nothing at all soft or effeminate about either, though her eyes had given her the same message before. And he had been able to *carry* her before.

He had called her Cora. Her name had sounded softly feminine on his lips. She had always thought that her name had an unfortunate resemblance to the cawing of crows.

She was bored. For four whole days she was so bored she could have screamed. But even in Bristol and at Mobley she had learned that it was ungenteel for a lady to scream except in some dire emergency, like the sudden appearance of a mouse, for example. But whenever

Cora saw a mouse, she forgot all about screaming in her curiosity to get closer to observe the little creature.

On the fifth day there was finally a diversion. Elizabeth and Jane were both at a garden party that Cora herself had been looking forward to. They were under the chaperonage of Lady Fuller. Her grace and Cora sat at their embroidery until the former was summoned to the downstairs salon by the arrival of a visitor.

Cora felt as if she were in quarantine for some deadly disease. The visitor would not be brought up to the drawing room, of course. She stitched on.

But then the butler returned with the request that Miss Downes join her grace in the lower salon. Cora put aside her embroidery and got to her feet with an eagerness that she despised. Someone had called and was willing to say how-d'ye-do to her? What a miracle!

She stepped through the salon door, which a footman had opened for her, and felt her spirits soar even higher. She beamed at Lord Francis Kneller as her grace got to her feet and came toward the door.

"Lord Francis wishes to have a word alone with you, Cora," she said. "I shall be upstairs, dear, if you need me." She left the room.

Cora scarcely heard her. She hurried across the room, both hands outstretched, and smiled brightly at her visitor.

"Oh, Lord Francis," she said. "How *happy* I am to see you."

She could see immediately, even before he had clasped both her hands in his, why he had not called before. The poor man had been ill. He was deathly pale.

11

*H*ER FACE HAD LIT UP WITH SUCH TOTAL DELIGHT THAT for the moment she seemed startlingly, vividly beautiful. For a moment he felt dazzled.

The past four days must have been dreadful for her. She had not been out of the house, her grace had just told him, or received any visitors. Even his own visit here, the morning after Vauxhall, had not been made to her. And Bridgwater had not called on her either. The girl was in awe of him, he had told Lord Francis with a grimace just an hour ago. He had thought it better to stay away.

But Bridge felt terribly guilty about the whole thing. It was his mother who had brought her to town, his mother who had undertaken to introduce her to the *ton* and to find her a husband not too far above her in station. And he, Bridgwater, was the head of the family. Ultimately the girl's safety and reputation were his responsibility. And, to add to his guilt, there was the fact that it was *he* who had asked Kneller to dance with her at that first ball, to bring her into fashion.

But here she was, after four lonely days spent indoors, looking far more blooming than he felt. And as soon as the duchess left the room, she came hurrying toward him, her hands outstretched, and spoke as she always spoke—quite openly and without artifice. Cora Downes, he suspected, was incapable of calling a spade anything but a spade.

"Oh, Lord Francis," she said as he took her hands in his and clasped them tightly. "How *happy* I am to see you."

He felt doubly wretched, if that were possible.

She should have been pale and quiet. She should have hovered at the door, eyes downcast. But he realized something, and the realization amazed him. She had no idea why he was here. She had no idea what he had been doing for the past four days. She had no idea!

"I am so *glad* you have come." She rushed onward with further speech before he could properly marshal his thoughts. "I am so desperately in need of a good laugh. You would not believe how dreary it has been here for the past four days. I have been advised not to go out, not to see anyone. I am sure her grace and the girls mean well, but really it is so ridiculous. Do you know what is being *said*? It was being said that evening, of course, but to have had the myth continued with since then is the outside of enough. Tell me how foolish you think it all is, and we will have a good laugh together."

Her bright smile, delivered only inches away from his face, would have seemed coquettish with anyone else. With her, it was quite without guile. It was merely a bright smile.

He clasped her hands a little more tightly. "I am afraid," he said, "you are in something of a scrape, Miss Downes."

"Oh," she said, and her smile faded instantly. "That is just the word her grace used. Is it true, then, that everyone really believes that we slunk away together for a *tryst*? I have never known any more stupid body of people than the *ton*. And that is what has made you ill, is it not? You are dreadfully pale, you know. Because you are a member of the *ton*, it has bothered you. You do not want to have the reputation of being a gentleman who seduces ladies. But no matter. The *ton* will forget. I will be going home to Mobley Abbey at the end of this week and in another week I will have been forgotten about here. You need not worry. But I am sorry that I have made you ill. You came to rescue me in Vauxhall, which was extraordinarily brave of you when you might have been killed. But instead of being hailed as a hero, you have landed yourself in a *scrape*. It is very unfair."

She was looking at him with earnest sympathy. Good Lord, *she* was the one trying to get *him* out of the scrape.

"Miss Downes," he said, "I must apologize for keeping you waiting here for all of four days. I have not been ill in my bed, you know. I have just returned from a visit to Bristol and one to my brother."

Her eyes opened wide with amazement. "*Bristol*?" she said. "Oh, if only I had known you were going there. Mobley Abbey is only just outside Bristol, you know. I would have asked you to call on my father." But she flushed suddenly and bit her lip. "No, that would not have done, would it? A duke's son to call on a Bristol merchant. Perhaps it is as well I did not know. I would—"

"Miss Downes," he said firmly. "It was to Mobley Abbey I went, not to Bristol."

At last she was at a loss. "Oh," she said.

"I went to speak with your father," he said. "To offer for you. He approved my suit. A marriage contract, mutually agreeable to both of us, was drawn up. It will be signed as soon as I have had your consent. *If* I have your consent. Will you do me the honor of marrying me?"

Any other woman but Cora Downes would have been expecting this, he thought. Or desperately hoping for it. Or dreading that it might not happen. Any other woman would have realized that there could be only disgrace ahead of her if this did not happen. But Cora Downes stared at him for several silent moments with blank eyes and a slightly hanging jaw.

Then she threw back her head and laughed so merrily that he almost found himself joining her.

"Oh, that is priceless," she said when she finally sobered. "It is marvelous. I just *knew* that if only I could see you again I would laugh again. You are so *funny*. I almost believed you for a moment. Now, would not you have been surprised if my eyes had become starry and I had said yes? *Then* you would have known what it was to be in a scrape. Oh, I wish I had thought fast enough and done it." She bit her lower lip and looked at him with sparkling eyes.

"It is no joke," he said quietly.

He watched her smile fade very gradually and her eyes become wary. She continued to clamp her teeth onto her lower lip.

"No," she whispered after a long while, and she drew her hands away from his. "Oh, no." She shook her head slowly from side to side. "You are being *gallant*. How foolish the *ton* is. How criminally foolish. But I am not a member of the *ton*, Lord Francis. I will not force you into anything so abhorrent to you."

It was tempting. So very tempting.

"You have been compromised twice in the last week and a half, Miss Downes," he said. "Both times by me. It will be better if we set it right—better for both of us. But let us not make it a negative thing. There are positives, are there not? I believe we like each other. We never seem to lack for conversation, and we are comfortable together. We seem to have the ability to make each other laugh. Will it be so bad for us to be married? I think it might be rather pleasant."

He had convinced himself that it would. Surely friendship was an important ingredient of marriage.

"Pleasant," she said. "You think no such thing. You cannot possibly wish to *marry*."

"I am thirty years old," he said. "A dreadful age to be, is it not? It is high time I was married. I can think of no one else I would rather marry." No one else who was not already married, that was. Oh, Samantha!

"You would hate it," she said. She was looking sympathetic again. "Marriage, I mean. And to me, of all people. I am not even a lady, Lord Francis. My father is not a gentleman. He is very wealthy, but he made his money in trade. You are more than a gentleman. You are a duke's son, a duke's brother. Good heavens, you have a *title*. I would be Lady Cora if I married you. That is absurd."

"You would be Lady Francis Kneller," he said, smiling, "not Lady Cora. Is it such a very daunting title?"

"You went to visit your brother," she said. "What did *he* say? I will wager he was not pleased."

That would be an understatement. Fairhurst had grown purple in the face. He had bellowed. He had reasoned and argued and cajoled and grown belligerent and thoroughly obnoxious. He had tried to lay down the law when there was no law to lay. He had stopped just short of disowning his brother, but he had made it perfectly clear that he would receive Lady Francis only with the greatest reluctance if she was not even a lady to start with.

"My brother is not my keeper," he said.

"You see?" Her voice was accusing. "You cannot say that he liked it, can you? You cannot say that he gave his blessing. What did *Papa* say?"

Her father had surprised him—pleasantly. He was not in any way vulgar. On the other hand, despite his wealth and his newly won status as a landowner, he was not pretentious. He was candid, down-to-earth, forceful. After a very brief acquaintance with the father, it had been easy for Lord Francis to know why the daughter was as she was. The brother had been a little trickier to deal with. Also a man without pretensions, he was indistinguishable in manner and appearance from a born gentleman. He was a handsome devil, Lord Francis had noticed, and also a rather hostile one. He had not thought that marriage into the aristocracy would suit his sister.

"Corey does not take well to rules and restrictions," he had said with eyes that had the same directness as his sister's. "If she has fallen afoul of the *ton* this time, it will happen again. I will wager she does not even know that it has happened. She will never know because she does not deal in petty intrigues or gossip. It will happen over and over again. Corey is a walking disaster."

Lord Francis had been unable to stop himself from grinning. "I have noticed," he had said, "that farce seems to dog her footsteps."

Rather than offending the younger Downes, he had seemed somehow to have pleased him. Relations between them had thawed somewhat after that.

"She needs someone who can find humor in her disasters," Edgar Downes had said. "My father and I can—usually. We are extremely fond of her, you know."

It had been both statement and warning. If he ever treated Cora badly, Lord Francis had understood, he could expect to be squashed to a pulp between the two of them. The father had questioned him just as closely about his means and prospects and had driven as hard a bargain on the marriage settlement as if he had been any Tom, Dick, or Harry who had stepped in off the street demanding to marry his daughter. He had not given his blessing lightly.

"He interrogated me for all of an hour," Lord Francis told Cora now, "and then agreed to give his blessing to our union—*if* you would agree to it. He warned me that you would be in no way influenced by the fact that you could become *Lady* Francis. Your brother looked as if he was about to hoist me with one hand and squeeze all the air out of me until I promised always to laugh at your disasters."

"You saw Edgar too?" she said. Then she bristled. "He has called me a walking disaster ever since I was a girl. That is most unfair. How dare he say it to you? What will you think of me?"

He leaned down slightly until his eyes were on a level with hers. "Do you care what I think of you, Cora?" he asked. "I will tell you if you like. I think you are a woman who has been unspoiled by life—by your father's wealth, by your privileged upbringing, by your unexpected fame as a heroine, by your introduction to the *créme de la créme* of society, even by the chance that has presented itself this morning to elevate yourself permanently to almost its highest ranks. I think you are a woman who thinks her own thoughts and is unafraid to be herself no matter what society demands of her. You are a woman I like, Cora Downes, a woman I respect."

He was rather surprised to realize that he meant what he said. He had never really considered what he thought of her until this moment.

"Oh," she said. She looked unusually forlorn. And even as he watched, her eyes filled with tears. "Please, will you go away now? I will always be grateful to you. I want you to believe that. This is the greatest kindness of all, what you have done during the last four days, what you are doing now. But I cannot marry you. I could not do that to you. You are too kind." She lifted a hand that was noticeably shaking and set her palm lightly against his cheek. "Thank you."

He should have left at a run. He should not have stopped running until he had put the breadth of London between them. Instead he stood where he was and felt very like crying himself.

"And what about you?" he asked. "You have not said that I could not do that to you. Would marriage to me be quite abhorrent to you?"

"No," she said softly. Her fingertips were caressing his cheek. She was going to say it in a moment, he thought in something of a panic, and then he would be forced to say it too and lie to her for the first time. *Don't say it.* "No, not abhorrent. I like you excessively. But—" She bit her lip for a moment. "But I am a romantic, you see. I have always thought that when I married, it would be for love. I want more than companionship and laughter. I want—oh, togetherness. I want children. Half a dozen children. Don't laugh." He was very far from laughing. "I want—well, the moon and every one of the stars. We could never have that, you and I, because we only like each other. I have always thought that I would not settle for less than my dream. But I suppose it is too much of a dream. It is too unrealistic."

What he felt mostly was relief. She was not in love with him, then? But it was too late to feel relief about such a thing. She must marry him, and it would be desirable that she love him, would it not?

He covered her hand against his cheek and turned his head to set his lips against her palm. There was nothing dainty about her hand, he thought irrelevantly. Although smooth and well manicured, it was a hand that looked capable of doing a good day's work.

"Let us settle for as much of the dream as we can make come true, then, shall we?" he asked her. "Marry me, Cora, will you?"

"I cannot see the need," she said. "They were such stupid incidents, both of them—the one at Lady Fuller's ball and the one at Vauxhall. Good heavens, did no one else but you and me *see* that child? Why should we let them force us into a marriage neither of us wants?"

"Why?" he asked. "Because something like this has the unfortunate habit of following one about, Miss Downes. Not so much me. Doubtless I will be seen as one devil of a fellow for a while. It is not an image of myself I cultivate, but it will do my reputation no real harm. But you may find that even in Bristol and Bath society there will be whispers to the effect that you are *fast*. It is not a pleasant word for a lady to have attached to her name."

"It is a silly word," she said.

"Silly and unpleasant," he said.

There was a light knock on the door and it opened almost immediately. The Duchess of Bridgwater stepped inside without hesitation, though she looked rather apologetic.

"This interview is still in progress?" she asked, her eyebrows raised.

Lord Francis frowned. Was Cora Downes a green girl that she could not be left alone with him for longer than the ten or fifteen minutes they had been allowed? Had her grace feared that she would find them locked in a lascivious embrace?

"Yes," he said.

"I shall take Mr. Downes and Mr. Edgar Downes upstairs to the drawing room, then," she said. "You will find us there when you are finished."

Ah, yes. They had said they would follow him to London. He had not expected they would come before hearing from Cora. But he had understood from his meeting with them that they were very fond of her indeed.

"Papa?" She was close enough for her shriek to feel as if it was doing damage to Lord Francis's eardrums. "And Edgar? Here? Now? *Where?*"

They would have had to be stone deaf not to have

heard her even if they had been waiting in the attic. They appeared in the doorway behind the duchess, and her grace had to step smartly out of the way to avoid being bowled over by Cora Downes, who hurtled past her, still shrieking. Her father caught her in a bear hug that would surely have crushed every bone in the body of a lesser woman. Her brother did likewise when her father was finished with her, but he also lifted her off the floor and swung her in a complete circle.

The duchess looked vaguely amused. Lord Francis's nerves were too taut for humor.

"Well?" the elder Mr. Downes asked, looking from his prospective son-in-law to his daughter and back again.

SHE HAD BEEN missing them dreadfully. She had not known quite how dreadfully until she heard they were just outside the door. Seeing their dear faces and the blessedly solid bulk of each of them—Papa and Edgar could actually make her feel *petite*—made Cora almost delirious with happiness.

All would be well now. They had come.

And then Papa asked the single word question— "Well?"

They had come to see if she would have Lord Francis. They had come for the wedding. She understood suddenly that if there was a wedding, it would be soon. There was a scandal to be squashed in the bud. They had come to buy her bride clothes and to give her their love and support. Papa had come to lead her tottering form down the aisle of some church so that she would reach the altar in time to say *I do* or *I will* or whatever it was a bride said to change her life forevermore.

It all seemed very real suddenly. *They expected her to marry Lord Francis.* Papa and Edgar avoided London whenever they could. It was not a place they would visit purely for pleasure. They had come for a wedding.

Her eyes focused on Lord Francis from across the room, where she stood with Edgar's arm about her waist. And she tried to see him through their eyes. She was surprised that they had approved his suit—especially Edgar. Edgar had one weakness if he had any at all. He could be rather cutting about men whom he deemed less than fully masculine. Edgar, unlike herself, could not adopt the philosophy of live and let live.

What she saw surprised her a little. Lord Francis was, as usual, dressed quite immaculately. He must have gone home after his long journey to bathe and change his clothes before paying this call. But he was dressed uncharacteristically in a dark green superfine coat with buff breeches and sparkling Hessians. His neckcloth was tied neatly, with no suggestion of flamboyance. Suddenly he looked a fine figure of a man by anyone's standards. And handsome. Except for his blue eyes, she had never really thought of him before as handsome. Or ugly either. She just had not passed any particular judgment on his face or his dark hair.

If he had dressed like this at Mobley, Papa and Edgar would have had no reason to *know*.

She felt something else too as she gazed at him in the few seconds that elapsed between Papa's question and Lord Francis's answer. She felt a sudden and unexpected and almost fierce protectiveness. She did not *want* them to know and sneer. He was a very precious person. If he chose to wear pink or lavender or turquoise coats at a time when most men were turning to more sober black, then that was his concern. Personally, she found black rather tedious and hoped that the fashion would not last long.

Lord Francis smiled at her and then looked at Papa.

"You were quite right, sir," he said. "She is by no

means easy to persuade. I was almost at the point of trying a little arm-twisting when you arrived."

Good heavens! Papa and Lord Francis had become well enough acquainted to *joke* with each other? For Papa threw back his head and uttered a short bark of laughter.

"She has not been dazzled by the prospect of a title, then, has she?" he said. "Well, I warned you she may not have you. She has not been willing to have anyone else yet, including a few eligible men at home and a few more here, I have heard."

"You do not have to have anyone you do not want, Corey," Edgar said, giving her waist a little squeeze.

"I think perhaps she wants to devote herself to her father in his old age," Papa said, chuckling. "But we are much obliged to you, my lord, for being willing to do the decent thing by my daughter. We will look after her from this point on."

"We certainly will," Edgar said. "We will take you home tomorrow, Corey."

There were several points about the conversation that unexpectedly irritated Cora. For one thing, she was being spoken of in the third person—by three *men*. As soon as two or more men got together, of course, the superiority of their gender made a woman quite insignificant. Even if they loved and cherished her, she was merely a fragile toy to be protected. For another thing, she did not like to hear Lord Francis being lumped with all those other silly suitors whom she had rejected. There was no comparison whatsoever. And for another thing, much as she loved her father, there was something distinctly chilling about the prospect of devoting herself to him in his old age—no romantic love, no marriage, no home of her own, no children, none of *that other,* about which she was avidly and embarrassedly curious.

Of course, even if she married Lord Francis she would

never know most of those things. But *some* of them—surely she would be able to expect some of them. Would *some* be enough? How much physical aversion did he feel for women? She squashed the very improper thought.

Oh, dear, she was so confused.

"Miss Downes?" Lord Francis was addressing her, ignoring Papa and Edgar for the moment, though in their usual manner they were proceeding to take charge. "You have not given me a final answer. Can you give it now? Or would you prefer that I return—perhaps tomorrow? Will you marry me?"

"Yes," she said. As meekly as that.

And *that* was that, she thought a few moments later while she was being subjected to hugs again—including one from the Duchess of Bridgwater.

Gracious heaven, what had she done?

Papa was slapping Lord Francis on the shoulder and pumping his hand at the same time.

And if his paleness had not been occasioned by illness, she thought suddenly when it was far too late to think at all, what *had* it been caused by? By the fact that he felt compelled to marry her?

Oh, the poor gentleman. The poor, dear man.

12

IT WAS A SURPRISINGLY LARGE WEDDING, CONSIDERING the fact that it took place only two weeks after the incident in Vauxhall that had precipitated it.

The Duke of Fairhurst surprised Lord Francis by arriving in London two days before the event and bringing his wife with him. It was as well that they had opened the Fairhurst town house. The following day Lord Francis's sisters both arrived from the country with their husbands.

The groom gave them no chance to express to him their opinions of his marriage. He paid them only a brief call and took Cora with him. He did not suppose afterward that she had made a particularly good impression on any of them—she sat stiff and almost mute throughout tea, ate only half a scone, and took only one sip of tea. Lord Francis realized that she could drink no more as her hand was shaking. It amused him that a woman who was so bold and fearless in almost any situation that presented itself could be reduced to shivering terror in the presence of aristocracy.

She did not make a good impression on them, perhaps, but neither did she make a bad impression. She was dressed elegantly and fortunately had left farce at home behind her for once.

Of course, his family did not approve. He did not

need private words with any of them to confirm that impression. The other three had all made excellent matches. They had expected as much of him. At the very least they had expected him to marry a lady. But they were family, when all was said and done. They were not prepared to turn him off merely because he was insisting on marrying far beneath him.

Mr. Downes had a brother and numerous nephews and nieces living in Canterbury. All of them were prosperous businessmen or married to successful men. All of them were summoned to London for the wedding and all of them came except for one niece, who was in imminent expectation of a confinement. They took up collective residence in the Pulteney Hotel. Lord Francis and Cora took a second tea with them there after leaving Fairhurst's. This time Cora ate heartily and drank two cups of tea. She talked and joked and laughed.

And of course the Duke of Bridgwater, with his mother and his two sisters, attended the wedding. Indeed, her grace offered to have the wedding breakfast prepared at her town house, but she had two rivals. Fairhurst offered to host it. Mr. Downes did not *offer* to have it at the Pulteney—he insisted. And so a private banqueting room was reserved and a private banquet ordered.

Bridgwater had agreed to be Lord Francis's best man. He seemed rather abjectly apologetic about the whole thing, as if it had all been his fault.

"This is the devil of a thing, Kneller," he said. "It makes one realize how fragile a thing one's freedom is and how unexpectedly limited one can suddenly be in one's choices. It gives me the jitters, to be quite frank with you." He took snuff with slow deliberation. "After this and after I have got Lizzie and Jane safely wed, I am going to retire from the world and become a recluse. No marriage is better than a forced marriage, after all. I am most terribly sorry for my part in this, old chap."

Lord Francis felt compelled to assure his grace that this marriage *was* of his own choosing, though perhaps the timing was not. He felt compelled to declare that he was fond of Miss Downes—"damned fond," as he put it, not to appear too lukewarm.

But his grace went away still declaring that never, *never* would he risk matrimony or the danger of matrimony himself. No more looking about him in the hope that his eye would suddenly alight on that one woman who had been created for his eternal delight. No looking about him at all from this moment on. No eye contact with any single female below the age of forty or with the mama of any single female.

The Earl of Greenwald attended the wedding with Lady Jane. Lord Francis had also invited a few of his friends as well as his young cousin, Lord Hawthorne. Lady Kellington, who still declared she would be eternally grateful to Cora for snatching her dogs from the clutches of death, more or less invited herself. Lord Francis had written to the Earl of Thornhill to announce his coming nuptials, but there would be no time for his friend to come from Yorkshire. Besides, Lady Thornhill was with child, and Gabe was strict about not allowing her to travel at such times. They had not even come for Samantha's wedding for that reason, though Samantha was more like a sister than a cousin to Lady Thornhill.

Even in the days leading up to his wedding Lord Francis could not stop thinking of Samantha. If someone could have told him at her wedding to Carew that he himself would be marrying a mere few weeks later, he would have . . . Well, he did not care to think of it. It seemed disloyal to his love for Samantha to be marrying so soon after losing her. And yet it *was* disloyal to Cora to be thinking such thoughts.

Cora was blameless in this whole mess. So was he. But mess there was, and there was only one way in which to set all to rights. At least he did not dislike the woman. Quite the contrary. And at least he did not find her unattractive. If anything, he found her too attractive. No gentleman, he thought, should have such lustful thoughts about the woman he was about to marry. Not, at least, when he did not love her. Not when he loved another woman.

He was going to have to try, at least, he decided, to grow fond of Cora. It should not be impossible. Indeed, he already was fond of her to a certain degree. And he was going to be faithful to her. Not just in body—although he had kept his fair share of mistresses, he had never approved of married men doing so. He was going to have to be faithful to Cora in mind too. That meant forgetting that his heart had been broken, forgetting that he was being forced into marrying the wrong woman.

Yet even as he made the decision, he wondered how soon it would be before Samantha heard the news from Thornhill—or from Bridgwater. And how she would feel about it. Or if she would feel anything at all.

His wedding was not at the fashionable St. George's with half the *ton* in attendance. It was at a smaller church with his family and hers and some of their friends. Larger than might have been expected, yes, but still a far more intimate wedding than Samantha's had been. It was very sweet and very solemn and very, very real.

Cora was dressed in spring green muslin and looked rather like an earth goddess, he thought. He was glad she had not dressed in white, as most brides did. White did not suit her. In her own way, he thought, taking her hand in his when the vicar instructed him to do so—in her own way, despite her bold features and heavy hair and overgenerous figure and unusual height, she was beautiful. Or perhaps it was because of those attributes. Cora Downes was very much her own person, in both appearance and behavior.

Cora Downes. He repeated words after the vicar when instructed to do so, and she repeated words. He took the ring from Bridgwater and slid it onto her finger. And then strangely, mysteriously, irrevocably, she was no longer Cora Downes. She was Lady Francis Kneller.

She was his wife.

He remembered to smile at her.

And so it was done. He was a married man. The register duly signed, he led her outside into the heat and the sunshine and paused on the church steps with her so that they could be greeted by their guests before driving away in his carriage. In the course of just a very few minutes, his life had been changed into a course that was so new and so unknown that he was bewildered by the prospect of proceeding with it at all.

"Lord Francis," she said, squeezing his arm. "You do look splendid. That is a lovely pale shade of green. It makes my dress seem almost garish."

She had saved him from meaningless panic by bringing him laughter instead. It had been *his* place to compliment *her* on her appearance and give her that little reassuring squeeze of the arm.

"Cora," he said, chuckling, "as usual, you render me speechless. But not garish, my dear. Glorious, vivid, like spring turning to summer. But then perhaps I mean the woman inside the dress more than just the dress itself."

She laughed merrily. "Oh," she said, "you are so *good* with words. You make me feel almost beautiful."

They were the last private words they exchanged until they were alone together after the wedding breakfast, on their way to Sidley, his estate in Wiltshire.

ALL DAY, SINCE the moment she woke up to find the Duchess of Bridgwater's maid drawing back the curtains at her window, she had pretended to herself that this was the wedding day she had always dreamed of.

It had not been so very difficult. As soon as the curtains were back, she had seen that yet again the sky was cloudless. And as soon as she had set foot inside her dressing room she had seen the wedding dress spread out there that she had insisted upon even though her grace and Jane had tried gently to persuade her to choose white, since white was what most brides were now wearing. But she loved her dress. To her, green was the perfect color for a bride, suggestive as it was of life and warmth and energy—and springtime.

Then downstairs in the breakfast room and later back in her dressing room, her grace and Elizabeth and Jane had all been determinedly gay. Dressing for her wedding had been a communal exercise, involving the three of them and two maids—and involving too a great deal of chatter and laughter.

And then Papa and Edgar had arrived—Edgar had insisted on coming too rather than proceeding to the church alone—to take her to her wedding and had aroused both excitement and nervousness in her—and even tears.

Inside the church, while her papa had escorted her to the altar rail, she had noticed immediately the contrast between the sober colors worn by her male relatives—solid middle-class citizens all—and even of the other male guests, including the Duke of Bridgwater, who was the best man, and the light green worn by Lord Francis. And fixing her eyes on him as he stood waiting for her and watching her, she had felt again that rush of protectiveness for him. Let her hear or see just one suggestion of a sneer over him for the rest of this morning and she would make her feelings known and no mistake about it.

He also had copious amounts of lace at his wrists and

throat and his neckcloth was a work of art to surpass all others.

And then there had been the wedding service itself. She had listened to every word, watched every gesture, felt every nuance of atmosphere. It had been her wedding—her wonderful wedding, her dream wedding— and she had been determined to commit every detail of it to memory. Including the paleness of her groom's face and the nervousness in his voice and the slight trembling in his hand as he put her ring on her finger and the same slight tremble in his lips when he kissed her. And his smile afterward, telling her that he did not blame her for all this, that together they would make the best of it.

In his own way, she had thought, he was very handsome, and she would take on anyone who dared to hint otherwise. Even Edgar. It would not be the first time she had gone at Edgar with her fists—she had always scorned to use her fingernails—and their battles had never been as uneven as they might have been because he never felt at liberty to come back at her with *his* fists. She would black both of his eyes if he ever so much as pursed his lips in criticism of Lord Francis.

Her husband.

Despite the close attention she had paid the wedding service, the realization had still jolted her with surprise.

He was her husband. She was Lady Francis Kneller.

And then, outside the church and at the Pulteney, she had been hugged and kissed to death—her uncle and her male cousins and even the female cousins' husbands all seemed to be large men like Papa and Edgar. Even the Duke of Fairhurst had hugged her, and her new sisters-in-law had pecked her cheeks, though Cora suspected that none of them really liked her at all. The duchess of Bridgwater had been kind enough to shed tears over her and Jane might have crushed every bone in her body had she only been a little larger and a great deal stronger.

Oh, yes, it had not been so very difficult to imagine that this was the wedding day of her dreams. In many ways it really had been wonderful. Lord Francis had kept her at his side at the Pulteney and had refused to allow either her family to pry her away from him or his family to do the like for him. He had behaved as if they were any normal bride and groom—unwilling to be parted for a moment. It had been easy to believe that it was so.

But finally, after another round of hugs and kisses and handshakes and back slappings, they were in his carriage, alone this time—the Duke and Duchess of Bridgwater had ridden with them from the church to the Pulteney. They were on their way to Wiltshire, to Sidley, his home there. They would arrive before dark, he had assured her.

They were alone together, and she had to admit to herself finally that this was no normal marriage after all. Was it?

Her grace had had a talk with her last evening after ascertaining that her Aunt Downes from Canterbury had not already done so. She had tried her best to sound reassuring, though there really had been no need. Cora had already known or guessed most of what she had had to say, but the knowing had never frightened her, as it was perhaps supposed to do. It had only aroused her curiosity to experience it for herself. And a little more than curiosity. She had always *wanted* it and was unable to imagine how any woman could cringe from the very thought of it.

But the trouble was that she was not going to have it with this marriage. Was she? She was really not at all sure, but she rather thought not. And she would prefer not to expect it rather than be disappointed over the coming days and weeks. But if she was not to experience it in her marriage, then she was never going to experience it at all. The thought saddened her immensely. Even apart from the loss of her half a dozen children, she was sad.

But it was not his fault. She was never going to blame him.

She turned to him. But he had turned to her at the same moment and was taking her hand and lacing his fingers with hers and smiling at her.

"Well, Cora," he said, "the deed is done and we have survived it. Do you think we can rub along together tolerably well?"

"I think so," she said. She squared her shoulders and found that her left shoulder was now touching his right one. Neither of them sprang away from the contact. "I daresay your home is large and splendid and has a whole army of servants, but you will find that I will not be at a loss. I have managed Mobley Abbey for a few years and have been Papa's hostess on a number of occasions. I will not shame you before your servants and neighbors, I can assure you. And I am quite prepared to take on my responsibilities on the estate and in the parish. I will do all that is expected of any wife. I will not shame you. And I—"

He was laughing softly. What had she said wrong?

"Cora," he said, "you are not about to go into battle, dear. You need not look quite so determinedly belligerent. And what about me? Will your busy schedule allow you to grant me any of your time?"

"When you wish it, of course," she said. "But I shall not expect to live in your pocket, you may rest assured. I know that ladies are not expected to cling to their husbands. Even in *my* world that is so. Men think they have to spend their time about the important things in this world. They are quite misguided, of course. They look after only the mundane matters, like the making of money, while the women look after the really important things, like the well-being of people. But women have learned to pamper men and make them feel important even when they are not particularly so. I will not interfere with your life."

He was shaking with laughter now.

"Cora," he said, "you never fail me. What a delight you are. You have just dealt me the most excruciatingly cutting set-down of my life, and you do not even realize you have done so, do you?"

The trouble was that she did not think of him as an ordinary man. But she had just implied that she would leave him alone to his useless, self-important life of business while she looked after the truly important things.

She bit her lip and looked at him—and exploded into laughter. They leaned against each other's shoulder and indulged their amusement far longer than was necessary.

If she had said such a thing to Edgar—and she sometimes did, when goaded—she would have had a blistering argument on her hands. There would have been no glimmering of humor in the matter.

"Will I have to plead for some of your time?" Lord Francis asked.

"No," she said, her laughter fading. "But what I meant to say is that you must not feel obliged to entertain me. I will soon learn to entertain myself. I am not a cowering, helpless person."

"Only when you are in the presence of princes and dukes," he said.

"That was unkind," she told him. "You would too if you had never met any before in your life. But really you must feel no responsibility toward me. I know this marriage was not of your choosing. I know that left to yourself, you would not have chosen marriage at all. Well, if you *had* to marry, perhaps it is as well you married me. I will be quite happy to allow you to be free, you see. I will be quite happy to be free myself."

She felt more miserable saying so than she cared to admit to herself. Was that what she had undertaken by marrying Lord Francis? Was she going to lead a lonely life?

He clasped her hand a little more tightly. There was no laughter in his face now, she saw when she glanced at him. "What are you saying, Cora?" he asked. "Are you saying that you married me because you saw the necessity of doing so, but that you would rather it be a marriage in name only? That perhaps it would even be better for us to live apart?"

Oh, no, she would not *rather* it be any such thing. And live apart? She had not expected this. Oh, not quite this. They were going to live apart? Panic made the air in her nostrils feel icy.

"If you wish it," she said.

"I do not wish it." His words were curt. There was coldness, even anger, in his voice. "And I will tell you now, Cora, that if it is what you wish, if it is what you think to insist upon, then you may find yourself in for a shock. I may not be the husband of your choice and you may not be the wife of mine—I will pay you the respect of being honest with you, you see—but we are husband and wife. I intend that we remain so—for the rest of our lives. Fight me if you wish. I promise you it will be a fight you cannot and will not win."

She should be feeling outrage at this blatant evidence that even Lord Francis Kneller could play at being lord and master when he thought he was being challenged. She waited for the familiar fury against *those males*. But all she could feel was something quite unfamiliar. Not anger. Certainly not meekness or fear. Desire? If that was really what she was feeling, she had better squash it without further ado. She could not possibly feel desire for Lord Francis. It would be emotional suicide to feel any such thing.

But what did he mean? *What did he mean?*

"Capitulation, Cora?" he asked. "Without a shot fired? You disappoint me." The anger—if that was what it had been—had gone from his voice. "Come, talk to me."

"I really did not want us to live apart," she said. "That was not what I meant. I merely meant . . . Oh, it does not matter."

"I know what you meant," he said. The familiar amusement was back. "You meant that you did not want me to feel the burden of having been forced into offering for you and marrying you. You were being *noble,* Cora. You were being *gallant.* You do like to turn our roles upside down and inside out, do you not, dear? I am supposed to be the noble one. I am supposed to be the one reassuring *you.* Instead of which I have been ripping up at you. I *never* rip up at people. You see what an effect you have on me?"

She looked at him sideways. His eyes were smiling.

"I suspect that after a week of marriage to you, I will not know whether I am on my head or my feet," he said. "And I will predict now, Cora, that life with you is not going to be dull."

"I do hope not, Lord Francis," she said. "I cannot abide a dull life."

"Cora," he said, "since you live in terror of lordships, would it be wise to drop mine? Shall I be plain Francis?"

"I am not terrified," she said indignantly. "Merely—"

"—terrified," he said when she was unwise enough to pause to seek for the best word. "Call me Francis."

"Francis," she said.

They lapsed into silence. He wriggled a little lower on the seat and set one foot on the opposite seat. Before many minutes had passed, she knew that he was sleeping. He was breathing deeply and evenly. Her fingers were still laced firmly with his.

What had he meant? The question turned itself over and over in her mind without bringing any answers along behind it. What had he meant when he said that they were husband and wife and would remain so for the rest of their lives?

What had he meant?

13

SHE STARED OUT INTO DARKNESS, THOUGH IN HER mind's eye she could see the cobbled terrace below her window and the sharply sloping terraced bank of shrubs and flowers beyond it. At the foot of the slope there were formal gardens with grass, low box hedges, and gravel arranged into immaculately kept geometric shapes. There was a fountain at the center, with jets of water spouting from the mouth of a winged cherub.

She had fallen in love with the park and the gardens even before noticing the house, neat and solid and classical in design. She was so very glad he did not intend that they live apart. Her heart had gone out to her new home from the start. Though he had told her he did not spend a great deal of time here. Perhaps she could change that now that she was with him to give him some companionship.

Would they be able to rub along together tolerably well? he had asked her in the carriage. Oh, she really thought they might. After all the fuss of their arrival and her presentation to the staff, who had been lined up rather dauntingly in the hall, and after the housekeeper had shown her to her apartments and she had bathed and changed and had her hair dressed—after it all they had sat down together for dinner and then had gone together to the drawing room. They had not stopped talking except when the need to laugh had given them pause. They had laughed a great deal. She had told him some stories from her childhood and he had reciprocated with tales from his. They had both chosen amusing stories that they knew would tickle the other.

He *did* like her, she thought, as she liked him. She liked him exceedingly well. She drew her single braid over her shoulder and ran her fingers absently along it. He had been very kind to marry her. She was going to make sure that he never regretted doing so. He did not dislike her—else he would have jumped at the chance for near-freedom she had offered him in the carriage. Instead he had appeared quite offended.

And would she ever regret it? She drew a slow breath and let it out just as slowly. She thought of all her dreams of marriage and of the men she had refused because none of them had fit the dream. She thought of what the Duchess of Bridgwater had told her yesterday, expecting that she was putting fear into Cora, assuring her that it was really not so fearsome after all, that once she grew accustomed to it she might even come to like it. Cora had always expected to like it—in her dream marriage. And she thought of today and the way she had deliberately tried to enjoy her wedding day. She *had* enjoyed it. Right up until the moment when Lord Francis—she must remember to drop the *Lord*—had escorted her upstairs and paused outside her dressing room to kiss her hand and open the door for her.

She had felt lonely since then. There was no reason to feel lonely. Every night since her infancy she had gone to bed alone, and she had frequently stayed alone in strange houses. There was nothing different from usual about tonight. Except that it was her wedding night and it should—if this had been a normal marriage—have been gloriously different from any other that had gone before it.

She wondered if companionship was going to be enough. Not that she had any choice in the matter now. The deed, as Francis had put it, was done.

And then there was a tap on the door of her bedchamber and the door opened almost before she could spin about and long before she could think of calling to whoever it was to come in.

It was Francis, looking very gorgeous indeed in a scarlet silk dressing gown.

"Oh, Francis," she said, smiling brightly, wondering why she sounded breathless, "did you want something?"

He paused with his hand still on the knob of the door after closing it. He looked at her with raised eyebrows. "Cora, my dear," he said, "you leave me near speechless, as usual." He relinquished his hold of the knob and came toward her. "Now what could I possibly want with my wife on my wedding night?"

Her knees almost buckled. Certainly her stomach performed a headstand and then rolled into a tumble toss.

"Oh," she said, gripping her braid as if only by doing so could she keep herself upright. "Oh, Francis, how kind of you. But there is really no need, you know. You must not feel you *have* to, just for my sake. I shall be quite content . . ." She swallowed. He had come close and had set his hands on her shoulders. He was looking into her eyes.

"Kind?" he said. "I must not feel I have to? That is remarkably generous of you, Cora. Are you frightened, by any chance?"

"Frightened? Me?" she said. "No, of course not." They were going to have a *wedding night*? "I just meant that you must not feel obliged to do this if it is distasteful to you. I will understand. I did not expect it." She should not be too persuasive, she thought. She did not want him to go away. If she could experience this—even just once in her life—she would be content. Even if it must be with a man she did not love. She *liked* him enormously. That would suffice.

One of his hands was cupping her cheek. His eyes really were decidedly blue, she thought. They were not the sort of gray that wishful thinking pretended was blue. "Because we married in haste and under some compulsion?" he said. "You expected I would think all my obligations to you fulfilled once I had given you the protection of my name, Cora? No, dear, we will be man and wife in more than just name."

Her knees really did go then and he had to catch her in his arms.

"Oops," she said and laughed. Suddenly she really did feel both nervous and self-conscious. She was so very unattractive. She was so very large. He was both elegant and graceful. And she had not thought of wearing a dressing gown over her nightgown. She had *braided* her hair. She must look like an overgrown twelve-year-old.

"Cora." His voice was very low. "It is just me, dear. We have talked and laughed and been comfortable together all afternoon and evening. And I am not one of those nasty princes or dukes or marquesses to terrify you."

"I am not terrified of them," she said, "or of you. I am not, Francis."

He smiled and loosened his hold of her. "Unbraid your hair for me, if you please," he said. "I have always wondered what it looks like down."

"Just as unruly as it looks when it is up," she said, lifting her arms to comply with his request. "I should have had it cut. I know short hair is all the crack. But I keep thinking that if I do not like it short I will have to wait years before it is long again. Besides, Papa thinks there is something rather sinful about short hair on women. If God had wanted them with short hair, he always says, he would have made it so that it would not grow. But he never thinks that the same argument could be used of men. And of men's beards, too."

She was prattling. She wished now she had not persuaded herself that he would not come. She wished she had prepared her mind, planned what she would say.

He took her hands away from her hair when she had unbraided it and was combing through it with her fingers. He did it himself. She could feel herself blushing. She had never thought to blush before Francis.

"Oh, Cora," he said, "it is beautiful. It is a shame you cannot always wear it down. Though I must admit I feel smug at the thought that only I will see it thus. I can sympathize with sultans and their harems. Don't ever have it cut. If you ever do, I shall take you over my knee and beat you for gross disobedience."

She threw back her head and laughed merrily. "You may try it if you fancy the idea of two black eyes and a broken nose and smashed teeth," she said.

He was grinning too and then chuckling. "This is better," he said. "I thought your eyes were about to start from your head, Cora, and your cheeks were about to burst into flame. Come to bed."

It was a good antidote to laughter, that last sentence. She wondered if he really wanted her or if this was very much a matter of duty to him. It made little difference, she supposed. It was something he had decided to do and she was not going to argue further. She was going to enjoy the experience while it was being offered. Perhaps this would be the one and only time. She climbed into bed while he removed his dressing gown and blew out the candles.

This was her wedding night, she thought. She set herself deliberately to enjoy it, as she had set herself earlier to enjoy her wedding day.

* * *

IT WAS A necessity to desire her enough to consummate their marriage. He had married her that day and owed her certain duties. He owed her his body and his seed. It was necessary that he make love to her often enough to enable her to perform *her* duty of filling his nursery and getting his heir.

But he felt almost ashamed of the extent of his desire for her. She was—or had been—Cora Downes, he reminded himself when he entered her room and saw her standing at the window, dressed only in a thin cotton nightgown. She was the woman he had agreed to bring into fashion, the woman for whom he had set himself to find a husband. She was the woman whom farce followed closely. The woman he had been forced, much against his inclination, into marrying because twice he had inadvertently compromised her. She was *not* the woman he loved.

And yet, as he dealt with her nervousness, he found himself wanting her very much indeed. And as he watched her unbraid her hair and then pushed aside her hands so that he could smooth it out with his own fingers, he felt himself harden into arousal far sooner than he would have wanted to do so. Her long, loose hair was the one extra ingredient, missing until now, that made her finally and magnificently beautiful. Not in any remotely delicate way. He found himself thinking of Amazons—and then she was threatening to black his eyes and break his nose and his teeth in response to his teasing threat to spank her.

She was wonderful.

She was also a virgin and very, very innocent, he suspected. His mind went to determined war with his body as he climbed into bed beside her and slid one arm beneath her neck to turn her against him. He must be gentle with her. He must not frighten or disgust her. He must hurt her as little as he possibly could. He must be patient.

He did not kiss her. With his free hand he caressed her face and her neck.

"Mm," she said, and she put her arm about his waist and wriggled closer to him. He paused and drew a few deep breaths. His mind was threatening to lose the battle.

He slid his hand down her back, pausing at her waist, continuing more lightly to her buttocks, moving up over her hip to her breast. She moved back a little from him not to impede his progress.

He felt as if he had been plunged into a bath of steam. She was warm and shapely, generously curved in all the right places, soft where she was supposed to be soft, firm where she was supposed to be firm. Her breasts were large and youthfully firm. He cupped one in his hand, tested the nipple with the pad of his thumb. It hardened under his touch.

"Oh," she said and she started panting quite audibly.

He opened the buttons of her nightgown, going slowly in order to give himself a chance to impose control on himself and to give her a chance to know what he was about to do. He fondled her other breast beneath the fabric of her gown.

"Ah," she said. "Ah."

She had forgotten her nervousness. He moved his hand down inside the gown, flat over her stomach, down over the warm hair to curl into warmer depths. He did not attempt any more intimate exploration. She was breathing in gasps against his shoulder.

It was time, he thought. He could teach her gradually over time more about foreplay. But he would not frighten her again tonight. He removed his hand and reached down to draw up her nightgown—up over her legs to her hips. He paused there, but he gave in to desire and raised it up over her breasts and turned her onto her back.

He could hear the blood thundering in his ears. He could not remember a time when he had been so hotly aroused—not that he spent a great deal of time trying to remember such an occasion.

She was all magnificent, warm woman, he thought as he came on top of her, nudged his knees between hers, and spread her legs wide. There was no resistance. He gritted his teeth, pressed his eyes shut, and imposed iron control on himself as he slid his hands beneath her to hold her firm while he mounted her. He moved slowly, pushing inward to the barrier and slowly yet firmly beyond it to embed himself deeply in her. She whimpered once, quietly. He lifted some of his weight onto his forearms so that she would be able to breathe beneath him. He waited, gathering his breath and control.

And then she took charge.

He felt her legs slide up the outsides of his own—long, slim, smooth legs, which raised his temperature as they moved. And then she lifted them to twine about his own. And tilted her hips and pushed against him so that he seemed even deeper. He was alarmed at the sensations she aroused in him. He raised his head and looked down at her. His eyes had accustomed themselves enough to the darkness that he could see her head thrown back on the pillow, her eyes closed, her hair all about her face and shoulders. Her mouth was open. Even as he watched she pressed her shoulders back into the pillow and thrust up her bosom to touch his chest with her hardened nipples.

Something snapped in him—his control. His body had won the war.

"Cora," he said with a groan, lowering his face into her hair, gritting his teeth again, shutting his eyes tightly again. But nothing helped. His hands came beneath her once again and he moved in her with deep, convulsive, swift strokes.

It was all over in moments. He thrust deeply and spilled and gushed into her.

Like a schoolboy with his first woman, he thought when thought returned after a few seconds of oblivion. No, that was insulting to schoolboys. His first woman had had to coax him, gauche and terrified, to climax.

He felt deeply ashamed. He disengaged from her, lifted himself off her to lie beside her. He rested one arm across his eyes and tried to stop panting.

"I am sorry," he said. "I am so very sorry, Cora."

He hoped he had not hurt her badly or shocked her too deeply. But he must have done both. At the age of thirty he had been gauchely excited by a woman's well-endowed body. His wife's. He had had women who were marvelously skilled at their profession, and had never relinquished his control. No, he had had to reserve that ignominy for his wife's bed. On their wedding night. While he was in the process of taking her virginity.

Her hand burrowed its way into his. "It is all right, Francis," she said. "Don't distress yourself. I understand. I do." She lifted his hand and held it against her cheek. She turned her head and kissed the back of it. "I do understand," she said. "And I do not mind at all. You must not think I do. I am very fond of you just as you are of me. You do not have to pretend for me. I understand."

He was not sure he understood what it was *she* understood or what it was he need not pretend to. Sexual expertise? Well, he had just proved that he was sadly lacking on that score. He could not reply immediately. He merely squeezed her hand slightly.

She was quite magnificent, he thought. If only he could get his desire for such a sexual feast under control, he would be the most fortunate of husbands. This was his for a lifetime. *She* was his for a lifetime. It somehow did not seem right that he did not love her. He thought fleetingly of Samantha, but ruthlessly suppressed the thought. It was certainly not right to think about *her*. He would be far better employed cultivating an affection for his wife to match his physical desire for her. He already was fond of her. He had never been in any doubt about that.

He did not want to come to crave her only like this. He had never wanted a marriage of just this. He wanted friendship and emotional intimacy and partnership and parenthood as well as sexual satisfaction. None of which was impossible with Cora, except perhaps the second. He must work on the second.

He should have left her bed and returned to his own, he thought when it was too late to act on the thought. He was warm and comfortable and very close to sleep.

What was it that she understood? What was it that she did not mind? What was it he need not pretend to?

Lord Francis slept, his one arm still over his eyes, his other hand held against Cora's cheek.

FOR A FEW minutes she was horribly disappointed. It was all over—so soon. Almost before she had started to enjoy it. And it might never happen again. He would not wish to do it with her ever again.

She had been too eager, perhaps. She had scared him, disgusted him. But she had not been able to help herself. He had lain down beside her and set his arm about her and she had been instantly aware of his warmth and his firmly muscled, splendidly proportioned body. He had felt so very masculine. And his hand, moving first over her face, and then over her body, and finally over the most private parts beneath her nightgown had excited her almost beyond thought. She had forgotten entirely that he was—well, that he was not as other men were.

She had wanted the rest of it so eagerly, so hungrily. When he had lifted her nightgown and come on top of her, she had hardly waited, as any modest bride would, for him to part her legs. She had opened for him. What had followed had been indescribably wonderful. She had expected it to feel good. But she had never imagined the sensation of stretching, as if she was really too narrow but he would forge a passage anyway. The pain she had expected. But it had been over in a moment almost before she had been able to feel it as pain. And he had come deeper. That had been the most wonderful part of all. She had never imagined such depth. She really had not dreamed there could be that much room inside her. But there was—she had even coaxed him deeper.

She had been so very excited. She had known there was more to come. She had known there was ecstasy to come. From sheer instinct she had moved her body into position to feel the ecstasy. She had expected it to take a long time. She had heard that men derived great pleasure from this. There had been little time for much pleasure yet.

Then he had started to move, again with unimagined force. But before she had even begun to enjoy it or to somehow fit herself to it so that she could partake of the pleasure, it was all over. He had stopped suddenly, pushing even more deeply into her, she had felt increased heat deep inside, and he had gradually relaxed on top of her.

It had all been over. She had felt deeply disappointed.

Until she had heard his apology. Until she remembered. It had not been possible to remember while it was happening. He had such a very masculine body—not that she had any with which to compare it.

She pushed disappointment aside in her concern for his feelings. She felt a welling of the now-familiar tenderness and protectiveness. He had done this for her. All of it. He had married her and brought her here and done this to her all because he wanted to protect her from disgrace with the *ton*. Really, it had been all her fault. If she had not been so foolishly terrified at meeting the Prince of Wales, Francis would not have had to take her out onto that balcony when there was no one out there to act as chaperon. If she had not so foolishly fallen for that little boy's pathetic story at Vauxhall, he would not have had to come after her and comfort her and be caught with his arms about her.

It was all her fault.

And through it all he had acted as the perfect gentleman. Not only for the sake of society, but for her sake too. He had known that without a consummated marriage she would feel less of a woman and a failure as a wife. And so he had consummated it. And had hated every moment of it.

She was so very unattractive. She was too tall and too large everywhere. It was no wonder . . . But then even an attractive woman would not appeal to Francis.

She would not allow it to happen again. She would somehow convince him that it really did not matter to her. But the very thought brought unexpected tears welling to her eyes. Just a matter of minutes ago she had told herself that if she could experience this but once in her life she would be contented. But she knew now how wrong she had been to think that. It had been so wonderful, so very, very wonderful even if it had ended in disappointment. The prospect of never experiencing it again made her feel dreadfully bleak. She sighed aloud and turned her head to lay her lips against Francis's hand again.

She could not sleep. And she could not get comfortable. She turned onto her side facing him and onto her back again. And again onto her side, all the while holding his hand. And then the thought came to her in a flash of unwelcome insight—the thought that would doom her to an entirely sleepless night, she knew.

She had fallen in love with him.

All this time she had been telling herself that she enjoyed his company, that he was easy to talk with and laugh with, that she was a little fond of him. And all the while she had been falling in love with him.

But being in love under the circumstances was a little painful.

No, really it was quite, quite painful.

What a stupid, brainless thing to have allowed herself to do.

Cora sighed once more and tried to find comfort for her cheek against his hand.

14

LORD FRANCIS WOKE UP WHEN A SUNBEAM AND HIS right eye decided to occupy the same spot on the bed. He blinked and moved his head—and realized with a start that he was at Sidley and, more specifically, in his wife's bed. At surely a far later hour than the one at which he usually got up. He was surprised to find that he had slept deeply through the night.

He turned his head gingerly, hoping that his sudden movement had not woken Cora. Perhaps he could get himself out of her bed and out of her room without disturbing her.

She was not there.

He sat up, feeling remarkably foolish. His wife had got up on the morning after her wedding, leaving him to sleep on? Was not the situation usually reversed? But he might have known that Cora would turn the tables on him. She was probably out and about by now, running the estate.

He hated the thought of meeting her face-to-face this morning.

She had had an early breakfast, he discovered when he had dressed and went downstairs. She had eaten just toast and coffee—she had been unwilling to wait for anything to be cooked. They just had not expected her ladyship to be down so early this morning, the butler said, sounding almost aggrieved. And was he looking reproachfully at his master? Lord Francis wondered, hoping that he was not blushing. As if to ask what on earth a bride was doing up early on the morning after her wedding night.

The whole thing seemed about to become a public as well as a private disaster.

She had spoken with the housekeeper and made arrangements to consult with her and to examine the household accounts later in the morning. She had appeared in the kitchen—a domain on which he had never trespassed since he knew it to be ruled by a somewhat tyrannical cook—in order to bid everyone a sunny good morning and ask Alice how her cold was healing. Alice had been unfortunate enough to sneeze while standing in line for inspection in the hall yesterday afternoon. Cora had suggested coming back later to discuss the day's menu since Cook was busy getting his lordship's breakfast.

The devil. Cook would not like that, Lord Francis thought, almost nervously.

And then she had taken herself outside to enjoy the morning air and to explore the gardens. That was what she had told the butler, anyway. She was nowhere to be seen by the time Lord Francis went out there, breakfastless.

He found her in the stables, bent over the raised hoof of one of his carriage horses with his head groom. She was wearing a simple cotton morning gown. Her hair was up but dressed loosely and simply. He guessed that she had dressed without benefit of her maid. She wore neither shawl nor bonnet.

She turned her head and smiled brightly when he appeared. No blushes at the sight of him—and no grimace of distaste either.

"You suspected yesterday that one of the horses was

not quite fit, did you not, Francis?" she said. "It is this one. I mentioned it to Mr. Latterly and he looked and sure enough there was a stone and it has chafed the poor horse's hoof. It is a good thing we do not plan to travel today."

She had mentioned it to Latterly. Not either he or his coachman. Lady Francis Kneller, he thought, was going to take some careful handling. But he could not stop himself from seeing the humor of the situation. His bride had been out and busy while the exhausted bridegroom had kept to his bed in order to sleep off the effects of his wedding night. He grinned.

"Good morning, my dear," he said. "Good morning, Latterly." He too bent over the horse's hoof attentively in order to confirm with his own eyes what he had already been told.

A few minutes later he was leading his wife from the stables, her arm linked through his. She was chattering to him about horses. She had learned to ride as a child, but there had not been nearly enough opportunity to practice her skills until the move to Mobley Abbey. She loved riding. There was no exercise quite so exhilarating. She was talking very brightly, he noticed. Too brightly? She was looking ahead instead of at him.

"I hear that you have a busy morning planned," he said. "Can you spare half an hour for a mere husband, my dear?" It would have been easier to have gone inside for breakfast and to have allowed her to disappear with the housekeeper. But he had the feeling that if he did not talk to her now, they might never talk again. Not really talk, that was. And he might turn forever craven.

"Of course." She smiled quickly at him, turning her head and lifting her eyes to his chin before looking ahead again. "What a foolish question, Francis. I will always have time for you. You are my husband."

"There is a scenic walk," he said, pointing to the trees

at the far side of the terrace. "A planned route that circles up behind the house and comes out close to the stables again. It was created for maximum picturesque effect and to give the illusion of peace and seclusion. The whole park has been very carefully designed."

"And yet you have spent little of your time here," she said. "Perhaps things will change, Francis, now that you have me as a companion."

A companion. Not a wife. She even seemed to throw special emphasis on the word. The subject had to be dealt with.

"Cora." He covered her hand on his arm and patted it. "I must apologize for last night. It must have been a less than pleasant experience for you."

"It was not unpleasant," she said briskly, "and I thank you for it. It was extremely kind of you. But it is over now. We can put it behind us. It was not necessary, but I was and am grateful."

Had he understood her correctly? Was she saying that the sexual aspect of their marriage was unnecessary? Had he been that bad? He winced inwardly.

"*What* was extremely kind of me?" he asked. "Hurting you and then leaving you wanting, Cora? It was unpardonable."

Her cheeks were rosy, he saw. She walked onto the path between rhododendron trees without looking to the right or to the left.

"You knew," she said, her voice trembling slightly, "that it was something I wished to experience at least once in my life, and so you made an effort for my sake. I am very grateful to you. My curiosity has been satisfied and it was—well, really it was pleasant even though it ended sooner than I hoped. It is something I will always remember. But it is not something you need feel duty-bound to repeat. I understand. I truly do. And it will never make me think any the less of you. I like you and I respect you just as you are."

He felt the insane urge to laugh. Her voice had become so very earnest as she had proceeded in her speech. They were approaching a marble statute of Pan blowing his pipes, but she had not even glanced at it. She was staring determinedly into the middle distance.

"Cora." He drew her to a halt with a hand over hers. They had been moving along almost at a run. "I am relieved to hear that I did not utterly shock you last night. But are you assuming that I have no wish to repeat what we did together? Do you not think I would wish to redeem myself by doing better tonight and in the coming nights? Do you not think perhaps it will be a matter of pride with me to see to it that it does not end sooner than you hoped tonight?"

"Oh, Francis." She caught at his hands and leaned toward him, looking so directly into his eyes that he felt robbed of breath. "No. No, really you must not. I understood even before we married, before I agreed to marry you. I accepted it then. It is all right. I will find plenty with which to fill my life and give it happiness. I want you to relax now and find happiness in your own way. You owe me nothing—except perhaps a little companionship. But that will not be difficult, will it? I think you like me." She smiled at him.

She kept saying that. She had said it last night. He frowned, feeling as if she were privy to some secret that had been withheld from him.

"Cora," he said, "*what* is it that you understand, pray? I must confess myself mystified."

Her face, which had recovered its normal color a few minutes before, flushed crimson again. Even her ears were red-tipped. "*You* know," she said.

"No." Even her neck was red. "I am afraid I do not,

dear. Why do you believe so earnestly that I do not wish to make love to my own wife?"

"*Because,*" she said.

"Which is a marvelously eloquent reason," he said, "to someone who can read minds."

But she would say no more. She stared at him, clinging to his hands, as though it were impossible to look away or to move at all. She had said nothing intelligible to give him an inkling of her meaning. But it flashed on him suddenly anyway. He stared back.

"Cora," he said, "do you believe that I prefer—men to women?"

Her continued silence gave him his answer.

Good Lord! Whatever had given her . . . ? What the deuce?

He should have felt anger, outrage. It was not a tolerant age in which they lived. What she suggested was a capital offense. He should have been white with fury.

Only Cora could possibly have come up with such a preposterous theory. And she had married him believing it.

The thought saved him. Only Cora!

He threw back his head and shouted with laughter. He roared with it. He dropped her hands, turned away from her, and doubled over with it, clutching an aching side.

"Oops," she said from behind him at just the moment he had decided to turn to find out why she was not laughing with him, as she usually was. She sounded quite sober. "Have I been mistaken? Have I made an utter cake of myself?"

He turned to look at her. She was standing very still, one hand over her mouth. Her eyes were as wide as saucers and were filled with dismay.

"One might say that," he said, "if one wished to be unkind. Cora, whatever gave you that ridiculous idea?

Why would I have married you? Why would I have—consummated our marriage?"

"I thought you were being kind," she said. "You said yourself that I was in something of a scrape."

"Kind indeed," he said, tipping back his head and laughing again. "But what made you think it?"

"Well, your coa— Your app—" She bit her upper lip. She was looking very unhappy. That fact only added to his amusement. "Papa and Edgar and all the men with whom they associate always dress in the soberest of dark colors. They never wear lace or fancy knots in their neckcloths or a great deal of jewels, even in their *quizzing* glasses. Edgar always says that men who wear bright colors are . . . Well, Francis, you *do* wear turquoise coats, you must confess. And lavender ones. And *pink*. I do not mind at all. I like to see you dressed that way. Fashions for men are becoming all too sober. But . . ." Her voice trailed away.

"Cora." He set his head to one side and looked at her. He was still brimming with laughter. "I wear pink coats and you *think*. Merely because your brother *said*. It is my experience that people are not so easily classified. A man who prefers men is just as likely to be large and brawny and dressed all in sober black as to wear pink coats and lace. More so. Most men would not be eager to advertise such a preference. It would be dangerous. And you have thought this of me from the start? But why did you marry me? Your father and brother, I remember, were quite willing to take you home with them and look after you. They were exerting no pressure on you to have me. Why did you?"

Unexpectedly her eyes filled with tears and he felt sorry for his laughter. "Because," she whispered. Then she caught at her skirts with both hands. "I have never been so mortified in my life. I wish I could *die*. I will never *ever* be able to look you in the eye again. Excuse me. I have appointments I must keep at the house. I must be busy. I have a home to run."

And she was gone, flying down the path the way they had come, all pretty ankles and shapely derrière and hair falling out of its loose knot.

He did not try to stop her or go after her. He stayed where he was, feeling sorry that he had laughed so hard and humiliated her so deeply. And yet he continued to feel amused. He had been teased mercilessly enough over the years about his preference for bright colors and pastel shades in his clothing. But he had always felt secure enough in his masculinity to follow his own inclination. He had even done so deliberately to amuse others. He could remember choosing his pink coat with the conscious thought that it would amuse Samantha.

But Cora came from a middle-class world, where men were perhaps not so free to display their individuality. Not if they wanted to rise in the world, anyway. She had seen him through middle-class eyes and had judged him accordingly. And yet she had liked him. And she had married him.

That last thought sobered him finally. Why had she married him, thinking what she had thought? She had not really needed to do so. Although there had been scandal and doubtless it would have clung to her for a long time if she were really a lady of *ton,* her father had not seemed to feel that it was imperative for her to marry. She was part of a close and loving family, and they had been quite prepared to take her home with them. The compulsion on her to accept him had not been as strong as it had been on him to offer.

Why had she married him, then? He thought now of the impression he had once had that she loved him. It was an amusing memory, considering what she had believed of him, or would have been amusing if he were still in the mood to be amused. Obviously *that* had not been the reason.

There could be only one. She had wanted a home of her own, a world of her own in which she was mistress. She had wanted companionship with him, some conversation, some laughter. She had been content to enter a marriage that she had expected not to be a marriage at all.

She did not really want him. Not in that way. And yet she had thanked him for what had happened last night, fumbling and gauche a performance as it had been. He wondered if she *wanted* it again. Perhaps not. Perhaps her assurances that she really did not mind the situation as it was—or as she had perceived it to be—also expressed her preference.

But it was out of the question. He did not love her and she was not the bride of his choice. But she was his wife and he had discovered last night the full power of his sexual attraction to her. He had not wanted to marry her, but the fact was that he *was* married to her. She would have to grow accustomed to a marriage far different from the one she had expected. Even if she did not like it.

It was a chilling thought to have less than twenty-four hours after they had been irrevocably bound together for life.

IT WAS AN extremely busy day. She had scarcely a moment to herself. After coming back into the house from her walk with Francis, she went down to the kitchen and chatted with the cook. Her first impression that Cook was not pleased to see her quickly dissolved as she listened to the woman's plans for the day's menu and showed admiring interest in the recipes for various dishes and told Cook about some of her favorite recipes and offered to write them out and bring them down one day. She found herself within half an hour seated at the large wooden work table, eating a hearty cooked breakfast merely because she had breathed in deeply and made appreciative comments on the appetizing smells.

By the time she left the kitchen, having discussed at satisfying length all the various herbs known to man and all the familiar and unfamiliar remedies for every ailment either of them had ever encountered or treated, Cora had the impression that she had won the approval of her cook.

And then she spent several hours with the housekeeper, looking at every room in the house, commenting on how neat and clean everything appeared even though Lord Francis was not a great deal at home. She pored over the household accounts and commended the housekeeper on her management and bookkeeping skills. She gave her approval of the purchase of new bed linens, which was apparently long overdue. She checked carefully first in the books to see that the housekeeping budget would stretch to such an expense.

Then she went walking with her maid into the village of Sidley Bank, having discovered with some relief that her husband was busy with his steward. She went to look at the church and there met the rector, who bowed and rubbed his hands together as if washing them and murmured about the honor her ladyship was doing him and his humble church. He took her into the rectory to meet his wife and she stayed to take tea with the two of them. Then the rector's wife took her to call on the late rector's widow and on two spinster sisters, who were clearly gentlewomen living on limited means. She took more tea at each visit.

It was only at a late dinner that she was finally forced to be with Francis again. She recounted at tedious length every minute detail of her day for his entertainment and was quite prepared to begin all over again if necessary. She did not allow even the smallest moment of silence. She did not once look him in the eye.

She looked regretfully at the pianoforte when they retired to the drawing room, but even Miss Graham, who had been the most patient and persistent governess ever to be born, had been forced to admit many years ago that Cora had been gifted with ten thumbs instead of only the usual two and eight nimble fingers. It seemed that conversation must be engaged in again. But she made the amazing discovery that *Francis* played. He played very well. He played all evening at her request and sang too with a very pleasing tenor voice. She joined him in a few songs since the musical ineptness of her fingers did not extend to her voice as well.

Finally the day was over. She had lived through it without having to do any thinking at all. Though that was a lie, she thought as she got into bed and raised the bedclothes up over her head and hoped that she could be alone with her shame until tomorrow. Of course it was a lie. The truth was she had done nothing but think all day.

She wished she could die.

How could she *possibly* have made such a ghastly, ghastly error? And how could she have let him *know* what she suspected? She admitted, now that it was far too late, that she had had no evidence at all—none whatsoever—for thinking what she had thought except for the pathetically unconvincing fact that he wore pretty coats. There had been nothing in his behavior, nothing in the behavior of anyone else toward him. Only that silly fact that she had seen him at her first ball dressed in turquoise and had immediately thought of peacocks. Her mind had been made up and firmly closed from that moment on.

Oh, the humiliation was too much to bear. She burrowed farther beneath the bedclothes.

She cringed into total immobility when she heard the same tap on the door she had heard last night and the door opened.

And now to cap everything she had been caught hiding beneath the bedclothes. She was too mortified to come out. She listened to the silence until she felt a weight depress the mattress close to her head and felt a hand come to rest on her rump.

"Cora," he said quietly, "it is just me, dear."

Which was an extremely foolish thing for an intelligent man to say. Did he not realize that that was the whole trouble?

"There is no need to hide from me," he said. "I am not going to ridicule you or tell anyone else about your error. It really does not matter. I am sorry I laughed. It struck me as funny, but I know it was humiliating for you."

"I am not hiding," she said. "I am cold." On a night so warm that all the windows had been left wide open in the hope of catching some cooling breeze.

"Then come out and let me warm you," he said.

She felt a stabbing of longing, of desire. But she wished he would go away and never come back.

"Cora." He was patting his hand on her derrière. "Come, my dear. We cannot go on like this for the next forty or fifty years."

There was laughter in his voice again. Oh, how dare he! She threw back the covers and looked deliberately into his eyes. It was, she thought, as difficult to do as it must be to persuade oneself to jump off a cliff. His blue eyes were twinkling.

"Well, it was all your fault," she said, glaring at him. "Turquoise coat, lace everywhere, a work of art at your neck, a sapphire ring on your finger, sapphires all over your quizzing glass, such elegant manners. What was I *supposed* to think?"

"That is the spirit," he said. "Rip up at me if doing so will make you feel better." He bent his head and kissed her.

She turned to jelly all the way down to her toes. His lips were not even *closed*. "And leather pantaloons," she said when she had her mouth back to herself, "and a dark pink coat."

"Quite so." He had stood up to remove his dressing gown, and then he sat down again and was opening the buttons at the front of her nightgown. With the candles still burning. And he was looking at what he was doing.

Her insides were performing intricate acrobatic feats.

"And a blue-and-yellow phaeton," she said. "What kind of man drives around in a blue-and-yellow phaeton?"

"This kind, apparently," he said. He opened back her gown so that she was exposed to below the waist. He looked at her and then he lowered his head to feather kisses over her breasts. He opened his mouth over the peak of one of them, licked at it, and then closed his lips over it and sucked.

There was such an ache in the place he had been last night that it was indistinguishable from pain. And then his hand was down there, inside her nightgown, and his fingers were doing something that should have been horribly embarrassing. But the ache and the pain and the sharp longing drowned out the embarrassment.

"You dressed soberly for Papa and Edgar," she said. "That was not fair. Not fair at all. Ooh!"

"Life is not always fair," he said. He had taken her nightgown by the shoulders and was stripping it right off her, down over her feet. And the bedclothes were right off her too. And the candles were still burning.

"You should have *told* me," she said. "You might

have guessed what I thought. But you kept quiet. Just so that I would make a thorough cake of myself and you could laugh your head off."

He grinned at her as he stood again to pull his nightshirt off over his head. Now if only she had *seen* him, she thought, gulping, she would surely have known herself. Though she had always known that he had a magnificent body. She had fallen against it, had she not, that very first evening?

"Francis," she said, "do not *laugh* at me. I cannot abide being laughed at when I am feeling so very mortified. Especially when it is all your fault."

He was coming on top of her as he had last night. He was pushing her legs wide as he had then. She looked down and marveled anew that there was room enough inside her. It was going to happen again, she thought. Oh, she was so *glad* it was going to happen again.

"It is all my fault," he said. "Let me see if I can do better than last night, dear. Let me see if I can prevent it ending too soon for you."

She closed her eyes and bit hard on her lower lip as he came inside. There was no pain tonight. There was all the marvelous stretching and all the deep penetration, but none of the pain.

Let there be time, she thought as he began to move— slowly, quite unlike the hurried pounding of last night. *Please let there be time.*

There was all the time in the world. It was gloriously, deliriously wonderful. She twined herself about him, lifted herself against him, moved with him, experimented with muscles she had not known she had, ached her way toward what must surely be unbearable pain, and then eased her way beyond it to total pleasure and relaxation.

When she finally relaxed, she felt him quicken as he had at the start last night. And she felt again that increased heat deep within just before he relaxed his weight on top of her.

Oh, thank you. Thank you. Thank you.

Thank you, Francis, she told him silently when he had moved off her and was tucking the upper sheet about her.

Don't leave. Please don't leave.

He had got out of bed, but he was just blowing out the candles. He climbed in beside her again and took her hand in his.

Good night, Francis. Thank you.

"You are so very beautiful," he said softly to her. "Thank you, dear."

But she was fast asleep.

15

$\mathcal{H}$E NEED NOT HAVE WORRIED, AS HE HAD DONE BRIEFLY
that first morning in the stables, that she would
turn out to be such a managing female that she would
try to run the estate for him. She did not.

She turned out to be an extremely busy and efficient
mistress of Sidley. There was no doubt in anyone's mind
after the first two or three days who was in charge of the
household. And yet she was surprisingly well-liked. One
might have expected that servants who had run the
house without any interference for years would resent a
mistress who insisted on having a finger in every pie. But
they did not.

His wife had a way about her, Lord Francis discovered. She was never overfamiliar with the servants—
there was never any doubt that she was the mistress and
they were the employees. And yet she talked with them,
smiled with them, joked with them, advised them, listened to their advice. He was amazed one day when he
sent his compliments to the cook on the new and delicious dessert that had been served to discover that it had
been made from a recipe given Cook by Cora.

Cook had allowed his wife to supply her with a recipe? *And had used it?*

His wife never trespassed on his domain—with the
possible exception of that morning in the stables. But

she took charge of her own with a competence that could only have come from training and long experience.

Lord Francis began to feel very comfortable in his home.

She spent almost all of every afternoon visiting or being visited. She visited laborers' cottages and tenants' homes alone. He usually accompanied her when she called upon the neighboring gentry and attended her in the drawing room when she was entertaining them. She was at ease and friendly without being in any way vulgar. Not that he looked for vulgarity in her. He had never seen any.

In the evenings they often visited or entertained. Sometimes they stayed home alone and whiled away the time with music or with reading. She liked to have him read aloud to her while she stitched away at her embroidery. She was not a particularly skilled needlewoman, but as she herself said, she could hardly sit and twiddle her thumbs when she was at leisure, could she?

At night they made love. Only once each night. It seemed somehow distasteful to him to think of doing it more frequently. Perhaps if his appetite for her had been less voracious, he would have allowed himself to have her more often. Or if he had loved her. As it was, he did not wish to use her as he would use a mistress, merely to satisfy his lust. He had too great a respect for her.

Not that she showed any distaste for what they did together in her bed each night, despite his fears that first morning. Quite the contrary. She was a willing and eager participant in what happened. She never spoke her satisfaction, but her actions spoke it for her as well as the little sigh of completion with which her own participation always ended—the signal for him finally to let go of the control he had never lost involuntarily since their wedding night.

They had a good marriage, he decided after three weeks. Far better than he could possibly have expected. They had settled into a comfortable routine at Sidley. They were firm friends. They laughed together frequently. They were good together in bed.

It was a good marriage. What more could a man ask for?

Unfortunately, it was a question he kept asking himself. A question he could not stop asking himself. For there was something—an indefinable something—that prevented them from relaxing into true happiness. Both of them.

From the beginning he had been startlingly aware of Cora's openness and candor. He could remember thinking that it would be impossible for her to call a spade anything but a spade. And it was still true. She still looked him more directly in the eye when she spoke to him than anyone else he had ever known. And she still spoke to him freely on any topic he cared to introduce. There was no evidence whatsoever that she kept anything from him or harbored any dark secrets.

And yet . . .

And yet there was something. He could not put a finger on it or even begin to grasp it with his mind. It was nothing he felt he could ask her about. It was nothing.

But he knew it was something. There was *something*.

Just as there was with him, of course. He could not help sometimes looking at her—often at moments of deepest contentment—and remembering that she was not the woman of his choice. He could not help remembering the dream he had had of love and the sort of marriage that would grow out of a mutual love. The dream had gone and he was settling for contentment, it seemed. Was that what happened to most people, if not all? Did dreams always give place to reality?

And yet he *was* content. He had a good life, one about

which it would be wicked to complain. But he felt as if he were waiting. As if there were a completion that had not yet come.

This could not be all, he sometimes thought. And it saddened him to know that he could not be thoroughly happy with contentment. Or with a wife who was good to him.

He kept remembering the dream and wondering if even that was illusory. *Had* it been so very wonderful? Had he loved Samantha as deeply as he had thought? Was she as beautiful and as perfect as he remembered her? Would he have lived happily ever after with her if she had only returned his love, or if she had not met Carew?

He did not want to think of her or of his love for her. He did not want to be disloyal to Cora even in his thoughts. She deserved better. She was a very likable person and she was a very good wife to him.

Contentment could have kept him at home for the rest of their lives. Sidley had never been a more pleasant place to live. And yet contentment itself became suspect. Was he going to settle for this for the rest of his life? Was there nothing more?

And so he stared at his letter at the breakfast table one morning long after he had finished reading it, feeling tempted.

"What is it?" she asked. Her hand came across the table to touch his arm. "Bad news, Francis?"

And he knew that he had hoped she would ask just such questions, and was ashamed of himself.

"No, not at all." He smiled at her. He always thought her most beautiful in the mornings—if he discounted the nights—when her hair was looped loosely over her ears and knotted simply at her neck. "It is from Gabe."

"The Earl of Thornhill?" she said. "Your friend from Yorkshire?"

"They want us to come for a few weeks," he said. "I have been a regular visitor there since their marriage six years ago. They were expecting me this summer."

She did not respond as he knew he hoped she would. She said nothing at all, but merely looked at him.

"What do you think?" he asked.

He had seen that pale, trapped look a few times before and knew what it meant. "Francis," she said almost in a whisper, "he is an *earl*."

"And so he is." He could not resist teasing her. "You would be in illustrious company, dear. Going to visit an earl and a countess in company with a duke's son and brother. As the wife of the said duke's son and brother." It always amused him that she had never been terrified of his own title.

"They must disapprove of me," she said. "They must have been disappointed for you, Francis. They must have thought, as your brother and sisters did, that you married far beneath yourself. And they were right. We should never have married. I would not have done so if I had known . . ."

He smiled at her confusion and covered her hand with his on the table. "I doubt they think any such thing, Cora," he said. "And if they do, the problem is theirs. You are my wife and I am not sorry I married you. You are in no way my inferior. In no way that matters even one iota."

"That is all very well to say as long as we stay here," she said, drawing her hand from his and getting to her feet. "But as soon as we leave here, you will realize that in everyone else's eyes I *am* inferior, Francis. I want to stay here, please. I am happy here."

And yet she looked anything but happy as she hurried from the breakfast parlor, muttering something about an appointment with Cook. Was that the problem? Was that what was between them on her part? She felt that the social differences between them would cause only problems for them as the future unfolded?

They would stay home, he thought with both regret and relief. She had saved him from temptation. He would stay home and carefully build on the contentment they had found in three weeks of marriage and residence at Sidley.

It was Cora, after all, who came first in his life. Before even himself.

SHE HURRIED INTO the scenic walk, the one Francis had introduced her to on the first morning. She pulled her shawl more tightly about her. It had rained during the night and the clouds were still low and threatening. There was a chill breeze. Summer seemed temporarily to have deserted them.

She had just been very selfish.

She had vowed to herself when she married him to devote herself wholly to his contentment, to forget about herself. To deny herself, as the Bible would have it. It was a horridly difficult thing to do.

And now she had disappointed him. The Earl of Thornhill, she understood, was his closest friend but they lived far apart. He must have been very happy to read that invitation this morning. He must have expected that she would be delighted by the prospect of traveling into Yorkshire.

Instead of which she had been peevish and self-pitying and selfish. If truth were known, she did not care the snap of two fingers what people said of her. But she did care what they said of him. She did not want his closest friend to censure or pity him because he had married her. He was probably doing so anyway, but if he saw her it would be worse. She was such a large *lump*.

She sat down on a wrought-iron bench beneath a

beech tree after first making sure that the seat was not wet. She drew her shawl close.

She *wished* she could be attractive for him. It had not mattered so very much when she had believed—she still grew hot and uncomfortable when she remembered that she had believed it—that he was not attracted to women. But it had mattered very much since. If only she could be a little smaller. If only her breasts were not so embarrassingly large. If only her face were pretty. If only her hair were fine and wavy. If only . . .

She wanted desperately to be beautiful for Francis.

She tried to compensate for her ugliness and her ungainliness by making his life comfortable. When she was busy making his home more cozy and livable, when she was visiting his people, seeing to their contentment, when she was visiting his neighbors or entertaining them, then she was almost happy. She convinced herself that she was being a good wife to him.

She tried to be a good wife in bed. Sometimes—most times—she lost herself in her own pleasure. It was difficult not to. He was so very—beautiful, so very masculine and virile. But she always determined not to lose herself but to lie still and passive for his pleasure. She had never yet succeeded.

She thought he enjoyed being in bed with her. But that was no occasion for pride. Men always enjoyed being in bed with a woman. She had heard that somewhere, though she could not for the life of her remember where—it was not a typical drawing room conversational topic. She had heard that sentiment did not matter to men as it did to women, that physical satisfaction was everything. She satisfied Francis physically, she believed.

But oh, she wished she could be beautiful for him. How he must wish he had a beautiful woman with whom to do that each night.

At first, once she had recovered from her embarrassment at discovering her error—not that she would *ever* fully recover—she had been overjoyed. It was to be a real marriage. She had physical closeness and intimacy to look forward to for a lifetime, or at least until they grew old. She could look forward to having children. She might be a *mother*. But her elation had not lasted long.

All too soon she had realized with cruel clarity exactly what she had done. She had married him and forever deprived him of the chance to marry a woman of his choice. She could not even comfort herself with the realization that he had done the same to her. There was a difference. He had been honor-bound to offer for her. As a gentleman—there was no truer gentleman than Francis—he had had no choice whatsoever. She had. Papa and Edgar had not thought it so imperative for her to marry him. It was unlikely that the scandal would have followed her so ruthlessly into her own world that it would have ruined her life.

He had had to offer for her. She had not had to accept. But she had.

And now he was trapped in a marriage that would never bring him true happiness. Or her either. If she had not loved him so painfully, perhaps she could have concentrated on making him comfortable and could have found contentment for herself. But she did love him.

And she had remembered something she would sooner not have remembered at all. That horrid woman in London—the Honorable Miss Pamela Fletcher—had said that he had loved some other woman who had married earlier in the Season. She had said that he was thought to be nursing a broken heart. Cora had dismissed the idea at the time as rather hilarious. But now . . .

Was it true? Had Francis loved another woman such a

short while ago? Had she broken his heart? Was it still broken? Cora frowned and bit the inside of her cheek and thought and thought, but she could not remember the woman's name or the name of the man she had married. Perhaps it was as well. She would always dread meeting the woman and seeing a confirmation in Francis's eyes that it was all true.

Was the other woman beautiful? she wondered. She would wager a quarter's allowance that she was.

And he was stuck with her, Cora.

She got to her feet and hurried back to the house. He was with his steward in the office wing, the butler told her after she had asked if his new, wider shoes were helping his bunion.

The steward himself answered her tap on his door, but Francis was visible beyond his shoulder. He came striding toward her and took her hands.

"What is it, dear?" he asked her. "Do you need me?" He stepped outside the door and closed it behind him after she had nodded.

"Francis," she said, "do reply to the Earl of Thornhill's letter and say we will come."

He bent his head to look more closely into her eyes. "But you do not wish to go," he said. "You want to stay here. Your wishes are mine, Cora."

She shook her head and smiled determinedly. "It was as you thought," she said. "I am terrified of his title. But that is ridiculous, is it not? You are better born than he since his father must have been an earl and yours was a duke. And I am not terrified of you. It is something I am determined to fight. I am no cringing creature."

He chuckled. "I had noticed," he said.

"Then we will go," she said briskly. "Write and tell him so."

"You are sure?" He searched her eyes with his own.

She nodded again. "What is the countess like?" she asked.

"She is very sweet and very amiable," he said. "You will like her, Cora."

She very much doubted it. And the countess would not like her either. "Yes," she said, "of course I will."

"They have two young children," he said. She could tell he was pleased, happy. "I always play with them. I like children."

It was something she had not known about him. Something that made her fall a little deeper still in love with him.

"We will go soon?" she said. "I will give instructions now, without further delay. I am looking forward to it, Francis."

"Liar," he said, his expression softening. "But you *will* like them. And thank you, dear."

She felt a silly rush of tears to her eyes and did what she had never done outside of her bed. She lifted her chin and kissed him on the mouth. And felt herself blush—after three weeks of intimacies at night. What sort of chucklehead would he think her?

He smiled and squeezed her hands.

HE KNEW THAT she was very nervous. As was he. Nervous and guilty. He would have wanted to come to visit Gabe and Lady Thornhill even without other inducement. He had always enjoyed visiting them. He would have wanted them to meet Cora, since she was now such an intimate part of his life. He had kept telling himself these things ever since she had come to him in his steward's office almost a week ago.

He would have wanted to come regardless.

But of course there had been that other reason. He knew that for a fleeting moment fifteen minutes or so before they reached Chalcote, there would be a view of Highmoor Abbey from the road. He knew exactly between which hedgerows he would have to look, though he was surprised by his own knowledge since he had never before had any particular reason to look at the house from the road. The last time he had driven this route, back in the early spring, she had not even met Carew.

They would be passing that gap in the hedgerows in about five minutes' time. His heart thumped dully against his chest and in his ears. He tightened his hold on Cora's hand.

"They married out of necessity, you know," he said. He had been talking about Gabe and his wife, trying to distract both her attention and his own. "Their marriage had an inauspicious beginning too." *Too*. Had he had to add that word?

"What happened?" She turned her head to look directly into his eyes.

And so he told her how six years ago Gabe had returned from the Continent, where he had left his stepmother, and had sought revenge against the man who had ruined her. The man to whom Miss Jennifer Winwood, now the Countess of Thornhill, had been betrothed. He had tried to get at his enemy through her, wooing her himself. But the villain had been only too eager to rid himself of her and had plotted quite ruthlessly to make it appear as if she were having a clandestine affair with Thornhill. He had succeeded all too well—a forged letter purportedly from Thornhill to Miss Winwood was read aloud to the whole *ton* assembled for her betrothal ball. Thornhill had been forced to rush her into marriage.

"A very inauspicious beginning," Lord Francis said now. "She hated him and he had meant only to use her.

For a while our friendship was on very shaky ground. Gabe had not behaved admirably."

"No," she said. "What happened to the other man?"

The other man had been exiled when his father had discovered the truth. He had returned this spring and tried to seduce Samantha. Until Carew had found out and challenged him and beaten him to a pulp at Jackson's boxing saloon despite a deformed hand and foot. Lord Francis had not experienced anything quite so satisfying in a long while. He had been one of Carew's seconds. Bridgwater had been the other.

"He has left England for good," he said. "And good riddance to him. You will see soon, Cora, that bad beginnings sometimes have happy endings. There is a close attachment between Gabe and his lady."

He did not know whether he was trying to tell her that the same thing could happen with their marriage. But then their marriage had not had a *bad* beginning exactly. He deliberately did not turn his head to see the distant prospect of Highmoor Abbey. He watched his wife instead. She was biting the inside of her cheek, a habit with her that made him wince. It seemed such a painful habit.

The Earl and Countess of Thornhill were out on the terrace with their two children. It looked as if they had been out walking, Lord Francis thought, and had seen the carriage approaching. Gabe and his wife spent far more time with their children than was fashionable. Lady Thornhill, he noticed as the steps were put down and the door opened, was quite noticeably rounded with child again.

"Oh dear," Cora muttered to herself, sounding quite breathless.

He threw her a reassuring smile as he vaulted out of the carriage. He directed a quick grin at Gabe and the others and turned to hand her out. She need not worry, he thought. She was looking very smart indeed in a spring green carriage dress and straw bonnet. They would love her.

He did not know quite what happened—whether she stepped on the hem of her dress or whether her foot skidded on the wooden step or whether it was one of those invisible specks of dust that had brought her to grief at the Markley ball. However it was, she stumbled awkwardly, shrieked, and came tumbling forward to land in his arms, sending him staggering backward while breath whooshed audibly out of his lungs. Only by some superhuman effort did he succeed in keeping his footing.

"Oops!" she said loudly. And giggled.

"Oh, dear me," Lady Thornhill said, hurrying forward. "Did you hurt yourself?"

Gabe hung back, looking embarrassed. Lord Francis met his eyes over the top of Cora's bonnet. He grinned. He might have known that once they left the sanctuary of Sidley farce would catch up to her.

Cora was straightening her bonnet, which had skidded round to half cover one eye. She had flushed scarlet and was looking acutely uncomfortable.

"I wish I could do this all over again," she said. And giggled once more.

Lord Francis set an arm about her waist, something he would not normally have done in public. "Cora," he said, "meet Lady Thornhill. And the Earl of Thornhill. Gabriel. Gabe. This is Cora, my wife." He felt an unexpected, almost fierce protectiveness for her. If they wished to continue the friendship, let there not be even a suggestion now of laughter or contempt.

Of course there was not. *Of course* there was not.

"I am so pleased to meet you." Lady Thornhill clasped her hands to her bosom and smiled warmly at Cora. "We have scarce been able to wait, have we, Gabriel? I thought you might arrive yesterday, though Gabriel said it could not possibly be until today."

"Jennifer made every excuse she could muster yesterday," the earl said, chuckling, "to be at the front of the house, looking out the windows just in case. Lady Francis"—he held out his right hand—"welcome to our home. We will do our best to make your stay here a pleasant one."

"I am not normally so clumsy, my lord," Cora said, placing her hand on his. "Am I, Francis? Oh dear. But I tripped and fell—over *nothing*—the very first time I saw you, did I not?"

The earl smiled kindly and held on to her hand. "You fell for Frank at first sight, did you?" he said and laughed.

"I believe," Lord Francis said, "it was the effect of seeing my turquoise coat, Gabe."

Lady Thornhill laughed. "That must be a new one," she said. "Turquoise? Dear me. I do not blame you, Lady Francis. Though they are always very gorgeous coats, of course."

Fortunately Cora found the remark funny and they all had a good laugh. *Good old Gabe and his wife,* Lord Francis thought. They had worked hard, seemingly without effort, to take Cora's mind off her embarrassing entry into their lives.

"Uncle Frank." An insistent little hand was pulling at his coattail. "Uncle Frank, I bowled Papa out in cricket this morning. The wickets went *crash*."

"That's the boy, Michael," Lord Francis said. "You must try me tomorrow. I shall see if I can guard my wickets better than your papa can."

"Uncle Frank." Another little hand was patting one leg of his pantaloons. "Uncle Frank, may I sit up there?"

"Certainly, Mary," he said and swung the child up to sit on one of his shoulders. He set one hand on the little boy's head. "Meet your new honorary aunt. Aunt Cora."

"Aunt Cora," Mary said and reached for a handhold on one of Lord Francis's ears.

"Mary trips and falls lots too," Michael said, looking up at Cora. "Papa says she has two left feet and twenty toes on each one."

"Which is a matter entirely between Mary and me, my lad," his father said hastily.

"Lady Francis"—the countess took her arm—"do come inside. You will want to freshen up before tea. Let me show you your room. Your husband can find his own way. He knows it well enough. How *pleased* I am at the prospect of having your company for a few weeks."

"Well, Frank." The earl was holding out his right hand again. "Congratulations. There is nothing so satisfying as the married state. You will discover the truth of that for yourself soon enough if you have not already done so. She will soon be less nervous about being here. Jennifer will see to that."

Lord Francis could think of only one thing now that his wife had gone inside. He tried to suppress the thought but it was impossible. She was only a few miles away, he thought. No more than three or four as the crow flies.

And she was on close visiting terms with her cousin, the Countess of Thornhill.

16

At first Cora was intimidated. The Earl of Thornhill was a tall, darkly handsome man. The countess was tall by any normal standard, though not nearly as tall as Cora, with silky dark red hair. She was elegant and slender—at least her frame suggested slenderness even though she was quite noticeably with child.

They were the perfect couple, perfectly well-bred, perfectly devoted to each other and their children.

But they were perfect in another way too. They were perfectly amiable and kind. Cora knew very well that they must have been dismayed to hear that Francis had been forced into a marriage with a merchant's daughter. She knew that her appearance could have done nothing to reassure them—she was the ugly smudge among three beautiful people, five if she counted the children. And she knew that her shudderingly embarrassing descent from the carriage must have confirmed them in all their worst expectations.

But the countess spoke with her as if she were an eagerly anticipated, newly acquired friend. Before they came downstairs for tea on that first day, Lady Francis was Cora and the countess was Jennifer. And before tea was over Francis had been assured that after six years he must finally capitulate and drop the formality with which he had always insisted on addressing the countess. Whether he would or no, *she* was going to call him Francis. And then suddenly Cora was Cora and the earl was Gabriel.

Before the day was over Cora had relaxed. They really were very pleasant people. She told Francis so when they were in bed together that night, before they got too mindlessly involved in lovemaking.

"They are just like normal people," she said.

He chuckled. "I shall pass the compliment on to them tomorrow at breakfast," he said.

"Don't you dare!" she said in horror.

He chuckled again and kissed her. She shivered with pleasurable anticipation when he rubbed the tip of his tongue lightly back and forth across her upper lip.

"I was not even wearing shoes that were too small for me," she said, wincing again at the memory that had plagued her all evening. "Oh, Francis, I could have *died*. Why do things like that always happen to me?"

"I think perhaps for my eternal delight, dear," he said.

Which was a remarkably gallant thing to say when he must have been *so* ashamed of her.

The following morning they all went riding. Even the children went, young Michael on his own pony, Mary up before her father on his horse. And then the men played cricket with Michael while the ladies rolled a ball with Mary and Cora helped her make a daisy chain. Cora paid some afternoon calls with Jennifer while Gabriel took Francis to see some new development on one of his farms. In the evening they played cards after the children were in bed.

It was all very pleasant. A very enjoyable holiday. Francis did not seem unhappy—but then he had not seemed so at Sidley either. Perhaps, Cora thought, she had been foolish not to allow herself to be fully happy. Perhaps it did not matter that she had not been his choice, that he did not love her. Perhaps love was not as important to men as it was to women.

Perhaps the same would happen with her marriage as had happened with Gabriel and Jennifer's. If Francis had not told her, she would never have guessed that their marriage had had an inauspicious beginning. They were very well-bred. They did not embarrass their guests with any show of public affection. But they did not need to do so. It was there for all to see in the faces and manner of both—the fact that there was a deep emotional attachment between them.

Perhaps . . .

But she would not hope for something that would probably never happen. She would merely learn to accept and appreciate what she had. What she had was not so very bad at all.

But what if it was not acceptable to Francis? What if time only made him less and less happy?

Ah, life was a hard business, she thought, full of ifs, ands, and buts to distract one just when one thought one had it all figured out.

And something else worried her. There was another large estate adjoining Chalcote. Highmoor Abbey was only a few miles away, the seat of the Marquess of Carew. The marchioness was Jennifer's cousin and the two families frequently visited. At the moment they were in Harrogate for a few days, but they were expected home.

"We will be able to offer you a little more company, Cora," Jennifer said with a smile. "You will like Sam, I believe. She is more like a sister than a cousin to me. We were brought up together after the death of my aunt and uncle, her parents. Can you imagine how delighted I was when she married Hartley just this year and came to live close to me?"

The prospect of meeting them made Cora feel slightly

sick even though she told herself that by now she should be quite blasé about meeting members of the aristocracy. She was even one of them now, she reminded herself. She was Lady Francis Kneller, sister-in-law of the Duke of Fairhurst. She did not feel a great deal better.

She thought at first that she must have met the Marquess of Carew. The name sounded familiar. But think as she would, she could not put a face to the name or remember where she might have met him. And then she discovered that he and the marchioness had married early in June, when she was still in Bath, and had returned home soon after.

No, clearly she was mistaken.

AT FIRST HE thought he had been saved from himself. They were in Harrogate. But not for long, it seemed. They were expected back every day.

"They cannot be separated from Highmoor for too long, those two," the earl told Lord Francis. "They are having a bridge built across the narrow end of the lake there and must supervise the laying of every stone. Carew is widely renowned as a landscape gardener, as you are probably aware, and Samantha has embraced his interest with enthusiasm. An unlikelier pair you never saw, Frank, but you can tell that for each of them the world only really contains the other."

"You mean they do not hide it as well as you and Jennifer?" Lord Francis asked dryly. But in reality his stomach was churning and his heart was thumping and he wished fervently that Cora had not persuaded him to come here. Which was being grossly unfair to his wife, of course.

They came on the fourth day, unexpectedly, quite early in the afternoon just as the earl and countess with their children and guests were about to begin a walk to the lake. Indeed, they would have been on the way if Cora had not discovered as they stepped out onto the terrace that she had forgotten her parasol. Lord Francis ran upstairs to fetch it for her. When he came back down, he found her standing in the middle of the hall looking round-eyed and white-faced—a familiar look. He half guessed even before she spoke.

"Francis," she said in a loud whisper as if she were afraid her voice would carry to the outside, "there is a carriage coming. Jennifer said it is the Marquess of Carew's."

If she had slammed her fist into his stomach he could not have felt more robbed of breath. He smiled at her. "Cora," he said, "you found the courage to meet and to speak with Prinny himself. This is a mere marquess. You will find him quite unthreatening, I promise you."

"Oh," she said, "you think I am foolish and you are quite right. But you do not understand, Francis. You were born to all this."

He set his hands on her shoulders and drew her against him despite the presence of a footman in the hall. He wished he could take her back to their room and close the door. He wanted this meeting as little as she did.

"Come," he said. "I will be there beside you, dear."

She looked up at him. "Francis," she said, "do not let me fall down the steps. There are four of them—or is it five? Oh, I cannot remember whether there are four or five steps. What if I think there are four and there turn out to be five?"

"Your eyes would see the fifth," he said, tucking her arm through his. "But there are only four."

He could hear her drawing a deep breath and releasing it slowly.

The carriage was already being drawn away in the direction of the stables. Carew was saying something to

Gabe. Samantha was bent over Mary, listening and smiling at her.

God!

And then she looked up and spotted them coming down the steps. Her eyes lit up as only Samantha's could and she straightened up. There was no outer sign yet of her condition, he half noticed. She was dressed all in pale blue. Small and dainty and blond, she was all delicate beauty and light.

"Francis!" she said. "Oh, we knew you might come, but we did not know for sure. We did not know you had come. Hartley, look who is here."

"I see, my love," Carew said. "Good to see you, Kneller."

But Lord Francis only half noticed him. Samantha was hurrying toward him with eager light steps and a brightly smiling face, and both her hands were stretched toward him. He was saved from making an utter fool of himself only by the fact that though her hands came to rest in his, her smile was for Cora, who was still clinging to his arm.

"Cora, dear," he said and then wished he had not added the *dear*—it sounded affected. "Meet the Marchioness of Carew. And the marquess."

He had a chance to complete only half the introduction. Samantha dropped his hands and took Cora's.

"I have been so eager to meet you," she said. "Francis has been a dear friend for a long time. I take it unkindly that he married in such eager haste that Hartley and I could not even attend. He attended our wedding, you know."

"It was rather hasty," Cora said.

Carew had come limping up to them. He bowed to Cora and smiled. "Lady Francis," he said, "I am happy to make your acquaintance. We were delighted to learn of your nuptials from Bridgwater and Gabriel. Now tell me what you think of Yorkshire."

Samantha laughed. "Hartley swears that there is nowhere on earth to compete with it for beauty and the freshness of its air," she said. "You must be careful to give the correct answer, Lady Francis. Though you must not let him bully you. Francis, lemon yellow for the afternoon? You match your wife's dress almost exactly. I am delighted to discover that you have not become a *sober* married man."

They decided to join the walk to the lake. Carew's disability never stopped him from doing almost all that other men did, Lord Francis had discovered—even challenging far larger men to fisticuffs. Carew offered his arm to Cora, who appeared to have mastered her terror, perhaps at the sight of a very ordinary-looking marquess who was no taller than she and who could very easily pass for the landscape gardener he loved to be.

Gabe swung his daughter up onto his shoulder and took a hand of his son. Jennifer took the other.

Lord Francis offered his arm to Samantha.

She was very tiny. The top of her head reached barely to his chin. There was a familiar feel about her on his arm, a familiar fragrance. He marveled that for six years he had been part of her court. He had danced with her, walked with her, ridden with her, driven her, talked and flirted with her, even offered her marriage. And yet never had he felt the trembling awareness of her that he felt now. He did not like the feeling at all.

She talked to him about Highmoor, about the building of the bridge, which she had planned with Carew after she had first met him, when she had not even realized that he was Carew but had mistaken him for the landscaper, she told him now with a laugh. She told him about the little pavilion, the rain house as she called it, that they planned to build next year at the far side of the bridge. She asked him about Cora, and he found himself telling her about his wife's fame as a heroine. He told her with some amusement about her encounter with Lady Kellington's poodles and about her chase after the Duke of Finchley's hat.

"Do you wonder that I was enchanted with her?" he asked and was surprised to find that the words had come without conscious thought. Cora *had* enchanted him. She still did. He thought with some affection of her recent terror, when she had realized that the Marquess and Marchioness of Carew were approaching.

"No, I do not wonder at all, Francis," Samantha said. "Oh dear, she is so wonderfully tall and elegant. I am mortally jealous. When I reached my twenty-first birthday, I do believe I was still persuading myself that eventually I would grow up. With the emphasis on the *up,* that is."

Cora did indeed look very fetching today. She was wearing the yellow dress with blue accessories that she had worn in the park the first time he drove her there. Somehow the clothes had not been permanently damaged as his own had been. Someone had sewn the sleeve back into the bodice. She was talking to Carew and laughing at the same time. His usual sunny Cora.

"Hartley and I are going to have a child," Samantha said. "Did you know? I am very proud of the fact that it does not show yet, but Hartley cannot wait for it to do so. I am not putting you to the blush, am I, Francis? I have never thanked you, by the way, for what you did for him that morning at Jackson's. Though I am still ready to do murder over the fact that you allowed him to fight. You and the Duke of Bridgwater both. Oh, his poor face. It took weeks to heal."

She did not monopolize the conversation. She listened to him and led him on to tell her more about himself and Cora and their wedding. But when she did talk about other things, he noticed, it was Carew who was at the center of everything. The focus of her life. The center of her universe.

It never ceased to surprise Lord Francis that of all the men who had courted her over the years—and they were legion—she had chosen Carew. Carew was, of course, the wealthiest man of his acquaintance. But he knew it was not that. Hers was a love match. The realization had never brought Lord Francis a great deal of comfort.

"If it is any consolation," he said, "I daresay Rushford's face is still healing and never will entirely heal, Samantha."

"That name." She shuddered. "Please do not mention it. Tell me how Lady Francis likes Sidley. Has she made any changes yet? Has she gone to war with your cook? You were always shamefully in awe of the woman."

"They are the best of friends," Lord Francis said. "They have exchanged recipes. Cora gets fed in the kitchen. I still do not dare set a foot inside it."

She laughed. "Lady Francis is a woman of character," she said. "I saw it in her face when I first looked into it and everything you have said about her confirms me in that impression. You are a very fortunate man. I am delighted for you. I have wished for your happiness more than for anyone else's I know." She squeezed his arm a little more tightly. "You need a woman of character, Francis, because you have so much of your own."

Yes, it was true, he thought, looking at his wife. She was still laughing gaily with Carew. She had a great deal of character. Delightful character. Even her weaknesses were utterly endearing. She was terrified of aristocracy but of almost nothing else that he had discovered. Yes, he was a fortunate man. He felt a sudden and totally unexpected rush of nostalgia for Sidley and the weeks he had spent there with Cora, getting to know her in every way a man can know his wife, learning to adjust his ways to hers, accepting the comfort she had brought into his life.

He longed to be back there. They would spend most of their time there, he thought, rather than moving restlessly between London and Brighton and other spas in search of entertainment. They would make a home of Sidley. They would bring their children up there and spend time with them, as Gabe and Jennifer did with theirs. She had told him once that she wanted half a dozen children. He hoped he could keep himself from burdening her with quite so many. But he had the feeling that Cora would never do anything by half measures. He smiled.

"Francis." Samantha squeezed his arm again. She was looking closely at him. "You are fond of her. Jennifer told us what happened and I was so afraid for you. Ask Hartley if I was not. But I was hopeful too. You had written to Gabriel that the first time you were caught together you were both laughing so hard that you had to cling to each other. And the other time you were rescuing her because she had been duped into going to the rescue of a child who was supposed to be stuck in a tree. She sounded so nice—what a lame word. I did not believe you could help being fond of such a woman. And you are. I can see it in your face. I am so glad."

He was exceedingly fond of her, he thought. Exceedingly. He could not quite imagine his life without her now. He tried to imagine being here alone, unmarried, unattached, free. He tried to imagine having taken his leave of Cora at the end of the Season if they had not been forced on each other. He tried to imagine her at home with her family in Bristol and himself here alone at Chalcote.

He would be missing her. He would be lonely without her. The laughter would have gone out of his life.

In fact, he thought, he doubted he would have stayed

here. He would have seen, as he was seeing now, that his friends, though undoubtedly fond of him, had lives of their own, Gabe's entwined with Jennifer's, Samantha's with Carew's. As they should be. He would be the outsider, the one who did not quite belong despite the warm hospitality with which he would have been treated. He would have been lonely.

And he would have remembered Cora. He would have missed her. Dreadfully. He would have gone after her. He was sure suddenly that he would have gone after her.

Why? Just because he would have been lonely? Just because she made him laugh?

"Yes," he said, "I am fond of her, Samantha."

"I am so relieved," she said. "I really feared that— that I had hurt you. I would have hated that more than anything in the world."

"I told you at the time," he said, covering her hand with his own for a moment, "that I had been teasing, Samantha, that I had been trying to punish you for deserting your court by so suddenly announcing your betrothal to a man we did not even realize you knew."

He had told her in a rash moment that he loved her and had then had to spend days retracting his words, convincing her that he had not spoken the truth.

Had he spoken the truth? Had he loved her? Did he love her? She was a beautiful woman who had been his friend for years. She was married to a man she loved. There was no place for him in her life. He was married to a woman of whom he was exceedingly fond, a woman he might well have married, he realized now, even if circumstances had not forced him into doing so. There was no room for Samantha in his life. Marriage, he realized now, was a very private business. A universe of two that would expand only with the birth of children.

Yes, perhaps he had spoken the truth. Certainly there

had been enough pain. But that was the past. This was the present. His future was walking on the arm of Carew.

"Well, I am very glad, Francis," Samantha said, sounding as enormously relieved as he was feeling. "Now we can resume a friendship that I feared might be broken."

THEY WERE ALL inside the boathouse looking at the boats. All except the children, who had grown tired of standing still, especially when Gabriel had told them that it was a little too windy today to take the boats out. They had gone outside to play. Cora wandered out too after a while. She had done nothing but chatter and laugh ever since they had begun this walk. She was tired of chattering and laughing.

Her heart was bleeding. She examined the words in her mind for theatricality. But she could not persuade herself that she was exaggerating her pain and her misery. Her heart *was* bleeding.

There had been that familiarity again when the Marquess of Carew's name had been spoken. But she knew as soon as she saw him that she had never met him before. Even if she had forgotten his face, she would not have forgotten his severe limp and his twisted right hand, which he tended to hold against his hip. And then the marchioness's name had been mentioned—Samantha. Jennifer had only ever referred to her as Sam. Samantha—the name had sounded so familiar, but Cora did not know this lady and she could not think of anyone else she knew with that name. They had been married quite recently, just a few months ago.

And then suddenly, out of nowhere, it seemed, as she had walked from the terrace on the arm of Lord Carew, it had hit her like a hammer over the head. She could almost hear Pamela Fletcher's voice. *Lord Francis was a part of Samantha Newman's court for years, you know . . . He was devoted to her . . . It was rumored that he was heartbroken when she married the Marquess of Carew earlier this Season . . . He is a cripple.*

Samantha, Lady Carew, was exquisitely beautiful. She was everything Cora would most like to be. She was small, dainty, blond, pretty. And she had walked to the lake on Francis's arm and had glowed at him while he had kept his head bent toward hers and the whole of his attention fixed on her. They had looked quite gorgeous together.

He was devoted to her . . . he was heartbroken.

Cora had walked all the way to the lake with Lord Carew, who was a kind and an unassuming gentleman, making gay conversation, laughing, having a merry time, and every step of the way she had been aware of Francis walking with the woman he loved. And yet he was stuck with her, Cora, for the rest of his life.

She walked along the bank beside the lake, not seeing anything, feeling about as miserable as it was possible to feel. How he must *hate* being married to her when he loved Samantha, who was the embodiment of female perfection. How could she have done this to him? How could she have allowed herself to be drawn into accepting his very gallant proposal? It was to Samantha, or someone beautiful like Samantha, that he should be married.

She wanted her papa. She wanted Edgar. But even the realization of how self-pitying and how childish she was being did not help.

"Papa," she whispered.

"Papa!" a voice shrieked and Michael hurtled head-first into her.

"What is it?" She caught at his arms and looked down into a frightened little face.

"Mary," he said, gasping. "She is stuck up that tree." He made a sweeping gesture behind him with one arm. "She will not come down. She is going to fall. And I am for it. I called her a scaredy and she went up. Now Papa will spank me." He began to wail.

A child stuck up a tree. Cora winced for a moment, but this was no ruse. There were no thugs with stinking breath attached to this plea for help.

"Come along," she said, taking the little boy's hand. "We will rescue Mary together. I am a famous tree climber. I have a brother too, you know, and had to keep pace with him while we were growing up. Your papa will not even need to know. It will be our secret."

She marched along the bank, forgetting all about self-pity and misery. There was a child in difficulties, even perhaps in danger. An infant who was sitting on a branch of an old oak tree, clinging to it with both hands while her feet dangled over the water of the lake. An infant who was too terrified even to cry.

"Hold tight, Mary," Cora called cheerfully, pulling off her hat and tossing it to the grass, and hitching her dress above her ankles with one hand. "I am coming for you. You are going to be quite safe."

"Aunt Cora, do be careful," Michael said as she set off on her ascent.

17

HE HAD NOTICED HER LEAVING THE BOATHOUSE BUT had not immediately followed her. Perhaps after all she was overwhelmed with the company, he thought, and would welcome a few minutes to herself. But after a while he left quietly and looked in both directions for her. The others followed him outside.

There was no sign of her. Only of young Michael, who was standing beneath a distant tree, hopping from one foot to the other, or so it seemed, until he spotted them. Then he raced toward them, waving his arms wildly.

"No. Go back," he could be heard to be yelling when he got a little closer. "Go back inside."

"Mischief," the Earl of Thornhill murmured in Lord Francis's ear. "They are up to something and do not want us to know. It doubtless involves getting their good clothes either wet or dirty or torn or all three." He raised his voice. "What is it, Michael?"

"Where is Mary?" the countess was asking.

Where was Cora?

Michael burst into tears. "It was all my fault, Papa," he said. "I am owning up, as you said I should always do."

"Where is Mary?" The countess asked a little more sharply.

"I called her a scaredy," Michael said with fresh wails.

"And she went up the tree. She cannot get down. She is going to fall."

"The devil!" the earl muttered, striding toward the tree his son had indicated. "*What* have I told you about leading Mary into danger? She is little more than a baby."

Michael trotted along at his side. "But she will be quite all right, Papa," he said. "Aunt Cora has gone up to rescue her."

Lord Francis had not needed to hear it. When his eyes had gone to the tree Michael had pointed to, he had seen something alien among its branches. Something yellow with a blue sash. Something with very visibly bare ankles.

Of course Aunt Cora had gone to the rescue.

He would have grinned if he had not also been able to see Mary, a tiny infant perched out on a tree branch that overhung the lake. Jennifer, both hands over her mouth, had seen the child too and was making noises of acute distress. Samantha was setting an arm about her shoulders and making soothing noises.

Lord Francis and the Marquess of Carew hurried after the earl to the base of the tree.

"Stay very still, Mary," the earl said in a voice of dreadful calm, "and do not look down. Aunt Cora and Papa will get you down in no time at all."

It was plain to see that Gabe had not lost any boyhood skill at climbing trees, Lord Francis thought. Cora was already at the inside end of the branch on which Mary sat. She was chatting to the child as if they were both sitting on the nursery floor whiling away an idle hour. She was also showing a delicious expanse of leg—or not so delicious, perhaps, when he remembered that she was showing it to two other men as well as to him.

"Let me, Cora," the earl said when he had climbed up

close to her. "You go on down. Be careful. Frank is down there to catch you."

But she was already seating herself on the branch and sliding very carefully along it toward Mary. It creaked and Jennifer, somewhere behind Lord Francis, stifled a moan with both hands.

"You would not be able to reach her from the trunk," Cora said, sounding very calm, "and this branch is not particularly strong. It will bear my weight, I believe, but not yours. I will hand her back to you."

The branch groaned again. So did Jennifer. Samantha gasped.

"You are over water," Lord Carew called up, all calm practicality. "It will be a soft landing at least if the branch does not hold. Can you swim, Lady Francis?"

"Of course she can swim," Lord Francis said. "She saved a child's life in the river in Bath earlier this year." He raised his voice. "Be careful, dear."

She was sitting beside Mary, smiling at her. Her dress was up almost to her knees. Gabe was leaning out from the trunk, stretching out a hand, which was at the end of an arm approximately three feet too short to pluck his daughter off her perch.

She really was a cool one, Lord Francis thought, staring appreciatively, wishing that Carew would have the decency to lower his eyes.

"Mary," she was saying conversationally, though her words carried quite distinctly to the ground, "I am going to pick you up. I want you to pretend that I am Mama or Nurse lifting you from your cot. You must not fight me. I am going to hand you to Papa, and Papa is going to carry you down to Mama. All right?"

Mary did not reply. But she played her part to perfection. Perhaps she was too petrified by terror even to fight when she was lifted away from the illusory safety of the branch, Lord Francis thought. Cora lifted her slowly across her own body and set her down again on the branch, where Gabe could reach her. He scooped her up with one hand and swung her in to safety, between his body and the trunk of the tree.

"There," Cora said briskly, smiling brightly. "That was not so difficult, was it? There really was no danger at all."

The tree branch disagreed. It creaked and groaned. And then with a crack that would have put a pistol shot to shame, it snapped free of the trunk and plunged into the water below, taking its shrieking occupant with it.

Jennifer was at the foot of the tree, arms reaching upward. But she turned her head and screamed. So did Samantha. Carew yelled. So did Gabe, who came down the tree with Mary with reckless speed. Michael whooped. Mary was crying loudly.

Lord Francis, having assured himself that the branch had not hit his wife on the way down, knelt on the bank and reached out an arm toward her. He was grinning. If everyone else only knew her better, they would all be doing likewise. Only Cora, he thought.

"Come on, Cora," he said, when she came up gasping and sputtering. "Grasp my hand."

Her scream was cut short by a watery glug. But her head shot up again almost immediately to reveal to him two panic-stricken eyes.

"I-CAN-NOT-SW—"

She was under again, but Lord Francis had not waited to hear even the half-completed final word. He had dived in to the accompaniment of more screams and bellows from the bank.

She fought him like a wild thing. He had to confine her arms with one of his own, turn her over onto her back, and clamp his free arm beneath her chin before he could swim the six feet to the reaching hands that extended from the bank. But he ignored them and hauled her out himself.

She acted as if she had swallowed half the lake. She knelt on all fours, coughing and heaving and wheezing, gripping the grass with clawed fingers. Her ruined dress clung to her like a second skin. Her hair, still partly caught up in its pins, hung about her face in an enviable imitation of rats' tails.

Lord Francis knelt beside her, leaning over her, thumping her on the back. "Don't fight it, Cora," he said. "The breath will come. Try to relax."

Finally she was only gasping. "Oh," she said, staring down at the grass, "I want to die."

"I think you have cheated death for this afternoon at least, dear," he said. He caught sight of the sleeve of his lemon coat and grimaced inwardly. He was beginning to feel the reality of the breeze that had kept Gabe from taking out the boats.

"I want to die," she repeated.

"Towels," Jennifer said. "There are towels and blankets in the boathouse."

"I will fetch them, Jenny," Samantha said and went racing off along the bank. Carew went after her.

Lord Francis patted his wife's back as reassuringly as he could. He had understood her wish to slip quietly out of this world. She did not want to straighten up and have to look anyone in the eye.

"Here, Cora." The earl knelt down at the other side of her and set his coat over her back and about her shoulders. "Sam and Hartley will have towels and blankets here in a few moments. My dear, how very brave you were. You must have known that branch would go as soon as you made the exertion of lifting Mary. I do not know how we will ever be able to thank you."

Mary was crying quietly in her mother's arms. Jennifer's voice was tearful too when she spoke. "To me you will always be the heroine who saved Mary's life, Cora," she said. "You risked your own doing it and very nearly lost it. How very wonderful you are. How very fortunate Francis was to find you."

"It was all my fault." Michael began to wail. "I nearly killed Mary and Aunt Cora. It will be quite all right if you spank me, Papa."

"That is extraordinarily magnanimous of you, son," his father said dryly. "My guess is that your punishment has been ghastly enough. But on the way back to the house you and I will have a little chat about the care we owe the ladies who have been placed under our protection. And although gentlemen are allowed to cry when there is good reason, as Mama and I have told you before, they are not well advised to wail in prolonged self-pity."

Michael was quiet again.

Samantha and Carew were back with an armful each of towels and blankets. Enough to dry and warm a whole pack of drowned rats.

"Wrap yourselves up, both of you," Carew said, "and hurry back to the house. Samantha and I will go ahead as fast as we can, if we may, Jennifer, to order water to be heated. At least it is a warm day, though I do not imagine either of you can feel the truth of that at the moment."

But Cora was still on her hands and knees, observing the grass a few inches from her face. "I want to die," she muttered.

"I think it would be best if you all left us here," Lord Francis said, taking one of the blankets and draping it over his wife after first removing the earl's coat. "We can get out of our wet clothes. And Cora needs a little time to recover."

He could see at a glance about the group that they all

understood. Cora was huddled under her blanket like a lopsided tent, her bottom elevated higher than her head.

"Come when you are ready, then," the earl said. "We will have hot drinks ready for both of you and enough water for two baths. Take my hand, Michael. We will stride on ahead. Is Mary too heavy for you, Jennifer?"

"I will help with her," Samantha said. But before she left with Jennifer and the child, she knelt down and set her hand lightly on Cora's head. "You were wonderfully brave, Lady Francis," she said. "How I admire your fearlessness."

"Bravo!" the marquess added quietly. "It is one thing to look up at a height and think it is nothing at all. It is another to be up there looking down and knowing that there is a very real danger of falling. My congratulations on your courage, ma'am."

"Oh, Francis," Samantha said, "your poor coat. And it was so splendid."

And finally they were gone.

SHE COULD HEAR that they were gone. She knew that he had not. She wished he had. She wanted to be alone. She wanted to be a million miles away. Preferably dead.

"Get out of your wet things, Cora," he said. His teeth were chattering. His voice came from somewhere above her and then she felt a dull thump close beside her. He had thrown down his coat. His poor ruined coat. It was the second coat of his she had caused to be ruined. Something else fell on top of it. He was undressing.

"There is no one here," he said, "and no one will come back here. You will feel better when you have taken off your wet things and dried yourself and wrapped yourself in a blanket. I will spread our clothes out in the sun. They will dry in no time at all."

What he said made sense. But there *was* someone

there. He was there. She did not want him to see her. She was so very *ugly*. She wriggled out of her dress under the protective covering of the blanket and then, after a little hesitation, out of her chemise. She hauled off her silk stockings. One shoe had still been attached to her foot. The other was not. It was probably resting on the bottom of the lake. She teased the pins out of her hair and pulled at the matted mess. It was hopeless.

"Here," he said. "Take a towel."

"The blanket has dried me," she said. "Francis, I have never been so mortified in my life."

He was silent for all of two minutes. She suspected he had walked a little distance away to spread their wet clothes on the grass. Then he was sitting beside her, wrapped in another blanket she saw a few moments later. He somehow knocked her off balance and then caught hold of her and turned her so that she was sitting beside him. It was very deftly done. She clutched the blanket closer and tried to hide her head beneath it— without much success.

"There really is no need to feel embarrassment, dear," he said, freeing one bare arm and setting it about her shoulders. "What you did really was very brave. I do not know how Gabe would have got Mary down without you."

"Probably with great speed and dignity," she said.

"No." His fingers were combing through her hair, easing their way patiently through the matted knots. But his hand stilled suddenly and he fell silent. Cora could see it coming as if it were a mile away and galloping inexorably toward her. She hunched her shoulders and braced herself. "Cora, you *cannot swim*?"

"I never could learn the trick," she said. "Edgar tried to convince me that water is heavier than I am, but I have never been able to believe it. I expect to sink like a stone when I lift my feet from the bottom, and I always do."

"Then how in thunder," he asked, "did you save Bridge's young nephew?"

It was too embarrassing for words. She had tried to *tell* everyone at the time, but no one had been willing to listen.

"I jumped in without thinking," she said. "And I caught hold of him and tried to save him. But I was only dragging him under with me. Fortunately we were right beside the bank and Edgar reached out and grabbed us both. He told me afterward that it was obvious little Henry *could* swim and that he was in the process of doing so when I dived in. Left to myself, I would have *drowned* him. Edgar said I was brainless—he is forever saying that—and I was. And so I became a great heroine while Edgar was censured for cowardice because he did not jump in. He said it was unnecessary because little Henry was so *close*."

It was a lengthy, horrible tale. And now Francis too would know just how great a fraud she was.

He threw back his head and shouted with laughter while her stomach contracted with humiliation.

"Cora," he said when he had finally brought his glee under control, "you are priceless. Only you! You truly are the delight of my life."

She finally succeeded in burrowing her head beneath the blanket. She set her forehead on her knees and clasped her arms tightly about them.

"I want to go home," she said.

His hand stilled again on the back of her neck. "No, dear," he said. "There is no need. Truly there is not. What was embarrassing to you was proof of your great courage to everyone who watched. They will be waiting for you at the house, Cora, to thank you again. Believe

me, they were all overcome with admiration and gratitude for what you did."

The thought of going back to Chalcote was frankly
terrifying. But she had not meant that. "I want to go
home," she said.

His voice sounded sad. "We will go then, dear," he
said. "Tomorrow morning. I have been missing Sidley
too. We will go home and spend what remains of the
summer there."

"To Bristol, not to Sidley," she said. "I want to go
home to Papa, Francis. Where I belong. You must stay
here with your friends. You will be happier when I am
gone. We will both be happier."

She was on her back on the grass then, the blanket
stripped right away from her face. And he was looming
over her, a frown on his face while his eyes searched
hers.

"Cora," he said, "what is this? I have hurt you? But I
did not laugh in derision. I laughed because I was
amused by your peculiar form of intrepidity. You act
first and think later when you perceive that someone is
in danger, do you not? It is a delightful aspect of your
character. But I ought not to have laughed. I am so sorry,
dear. You needed comfort and I laughed at you. Please
forgive me."

His face blurred before her vision. "I am so *ugly*," she
said. Ugly inside and out. She was so abject and cringing
and self-pitying. She had never been like this before *not*
rescuing little Henry and before being taken off to London to meet the *ton*. Before meeting Francis and being
stupid enough to fall in love with him. She had had some
dignity once upon a time.

"Ugly." He repeated the word without expression.
"Ugly, Cora? You?"

"I am as tall as a man," she said. "I have large feet and
hands. And I am—I am a *lump*. I have a coarse face and

a bramble bush for hair. I am *ugly* and you must *hate* me." There. How was that for groveling, sniveling self-flagellation? And she hated herself too at that moment. And hated herself for hating herself.

"Cora." There was amazement in his eyes. She blinked her own and saw it there. "I can remember your concern about the size of your feet, though they have never looked noticeably large to me. I had no idea that you perceived yourself as ugly. I am amazed. Almost speech-less again. How can you not have realized how very beautiful you are?"

"Ha!" She would have been proud of the world of scorn she threw into the single syllable if she had not been feeling quite so wretched.

"Cora." He wrestled with her for a moment, but he won—of course. Her blanket parted down the middle and she lay fully exposed to his view in bright, sunny daylight. And view her he did, moving his gaze slowly down the full length of her body to her toes. "You are quite out of the common way, dear. I think I would have to agree that your face is not pretty in any accepted way. It has far too much character for bland prettiness. Your hair is—glorious. I have been selfishly glad since our marriage that only I am permitted to see it at its most glorious, when it is down. Your body—well, perhaps I had better bring up the memory of my humiliation on our wedding night. I—ended it all far too fast because I had lost control. Because of your—beauty, Cora. You are truly—magnificent. You see how tongue-tied you al-ways succeed in making me?"

Francis. Always so very gallant. She reached up an arm to touch his face but let it drop to the grass again.

"I wish I could be beautiful for you," she whispered, "as she is beautiful."

"She?" His eyes snapped to hers.

"She is so small and dainty and pretty and blond-haired," she said. "And so sweet too. I wish I could be those things for you, Francis. Or better still, I wish I had said no when you asked me. I meant to say no, but when I opened my mouth to say it, yes came out instead. She is as lovely as I have always longed to be."

"My God." He lowered his head to rest his forehead beneath her chin. "You are talking about Samantha. You know! Ah, Cora, I had no idea you knew."

She threaded her fingers through his hair. "It is all right," she said. "You said yourself I was not the woman of your choice. But you have always been good to me, Francis. I think I would like to go home, though. Home to Papa."

"Ah, Cora," he said, lifting his head and looking down into her eyes. "I would not have had you know for worlds, dear. If there were someone with whom you had been infatuated not long before our marriage—and indeed, perhaps there is—I would not want to know. I would feel inferior, insecure. I would know that you did not marry me for love and I would imagine that you did love him—that you still do. I wish you did not know about Samantha."

She smoothed her hands through his hair.

"I must admit," he said, "that despite the great contentment I have found with you in the month of our marriage, I was a little apprehensive about seeing her again. I need not have been. I walked to the lake with her earlier and all I could see was you—your tall elegance as Samantha described it *with envy in her voice*. All I could think about was you and how I wished we were at home alone together in our own haven of domesticity. All I could think about was being with you and talking with you and laughing with you and loving you. Perhaps for me it is as well I came here. I have discovered just how deep my feelings are for you. But it has been a less pleasant experience for you. Don't leave me.

Please don't leave me. Give me a chance to make you as happy as you can possibly be with me. To make you love me as I have come to love you."

"Francis." She smoothed her fingers over his temples and through his hair. "I really am brainless. I fell in love with you even when I still thought—oh, *you know*." She could feel herself flushing.

He smiled slowly at her.

"Besides," she said with a sigh, "I could not really go back to Papa to stay, Francis. At least I do not think so. I knew it all along but ignored it. I have to stay with you. I think we are going to have a child. Nothing has happened since our marriage and something should have happened more than a week ago."

He lowered his head again to rest between her breasts. He said nothing. But she could hear him drawing in slow, deep breaths.

"Francis," she said wistfully after a while, looking up at tree branches and fluffy little clouds and blue sky, "do you really not mind that I am so large? Do you really think me a little bit beautiful?"

He groaned.

"My breas— My bosom is not too large, Francis?" she asked him anxiously. "My hips are not too wide?"

He was grinning when he lifted his head. He was also flushed and there was a certain look in his eyes. "Shall I prove to you just how very beautiful and attractive you are to me, dear?" he asked.

"Here?" Her voice had gone up a few tones in pitch. "Now? But would it not be dreadfully improper, Francis?"

"Dreadfully, dreadfully so," he said. But one of his thumbs was already feathering over one of her nipples.

"Francis," she said, "you *never* behave improperly."

"Shall I stop, then?" he asked into her mouth without removing his own first.

"No," she said hastily. "No, I will never tell anyone. I promise. Oh, what are you doing now?"

But what he was doing was so very pleasurable that she gave no more thought to daylight or sunshine or impropriety. At least not for a long, long time.

THEY WERE LYING side by side and hand in hand on the grass, gazing up at the sky. He thought he had probably been sleeping for a few minutes. He had never before made love in the outdoors. It was an experience well worth repeating and one he certainly would repeat since he appeared to have a very willing partner in impropriety. He squeezed her hand.

"They will be wondering back at the house where on earth we are," he said. "Perhaps we should begin to think of going back."

"I shall die," she said, but she sounded reasonably cheerful at the prospect of her own demise.

He could not resist. "They probably all know very well what we have been up to," he said. "They will greet us with rosy faces and shifty eyes." He had no doubt that it was the truth too.

"I shall die!" she said with considerably more conviction.

"And they will all be purple with envy," he said. "Doubtless none of them have ever had the courage to do what we have just done."

"Someone might have *come,* Francis," she said. "I would have died."

"Actually," he said, "while you were panting and mindless with passion, a dozen or so gardeners did emerge from the trees. They did not stay long, though. They were very discreet."

She shrieked and he threw his free hand over his eyes while he laughed.

"You are horrid," she said, having realized too late that he teased. "Francis, I am just *cringing* when I remember. I cannot stop remembering."

"Now to which of your most embarrassing moments are you referring, dear?" he asked.

"I sat on that branch," she said, "after handing Mary to Gabriel. I was a quivering jelly of terror because I have always been afraid of heights. Do not laugh, Francis. That is most unkind. But I could not merely *say* so, could I? I could not warn you to be on the alert because I could not swim. Oh no. I could not even just keep my mouth shut. I had to call out gaily and with *stupid* bravado. What did I say?"

"'There. That was not so difficult, was it?'" Lord Francis said. "'There really was no danger at all.'"

"Word perfect," she said with a groan. "But my question was rhetorical. *Don't laugh.*"

Lord Francis laughed.

"And the branch chose that very moment to break off," she said. "It would have been perfect if I had been acting out a farce. I must have looked so *inelegant,* Francis. All arms and legs and shrieking panic."

He laughed. "I can assure you," he said, "that we were not all lined up on the bank assessing the elegance of your fall, Cora." He could not stop laughing.

"It will head the list of topics for my nightmares for the next ten years," she said. She giggled.

"Oh, I hope not," he said. "No, no, dear, I have every confidence in you. You will find something else to replace that particular embarrassing memory before another month has passed."

She was laughing at the sky with open and loud merriment.

"How horrid you are," she said. "Do you mean what I think you mean, Francis?"

"I most certainly do." He paused for a hearty laugh.

"You will continue to be the delight of my life, Cora, for the rest of my days. I feel it in my bones."

They both roared with hilarity.

"And I shall continue to ruin your most splendid coats for the rest of mine," she said. "I feel it in my bones."

They rolled onto their sides to face each other and clutched each other as they bellowed with mirth.

"P-p-prinny—" he managed to get out. But more words were impossible.

If they had been standing they would have had to hold each other up. Fortunately for both, they were not standing.

The Plumed Bonnet

1

SHE WAS TRUDGING ALONG THE EDGE OF A NARROW roadway somewhere north of London—a long way north of London, though she was not at all sure exactly where, the fuchsia color of her cloak and her pink bonnet with its deeper pink, fuchsia, and purple plumes making her look like some flamboyant and exotic yet bedraggled bird that had landed on the dusty road. Anyone passing by—though so *few* vehicles seemed to pass by, and those that did were invariably traveling in the opposite direction—would surely just keep on passing when they saw her. Her half boots were the only colorless part of her apparel, being as gray as the road, though they were actually black beneath the dust, an old and shabby black. She clutched a creased and worn reticule, which contained her pathetically small and much depleted store of coins—frighteningly small, frighteningly depleted. It was no longer even plural, in fact. There was one coin left.

Anyone seeing her now—and anyone within five unobstructed miles could not fail to see her and even be blinded by the sight of her, she thought with a grimace—would never guess that she was an eminently respectable young woman and, in addition, a very wealthy one. She chuckled with a humor that only succeeded in frightening her more when she heard the sound of it. By her reckoning, it was going to take her days, perhaps even weeks to walk to Hampshire—she could not be more precise than that. But by her far more precise reckoning, she had enough money left in her reticule to buy one loaf of bread—one small loaf.

Could one loaf of bread sustain her through many days of walking? What would happen if it could not? She pushed the thought firmly aside and quickened her pace. It would simply have to do, that was all. When there was no food left, she would have to go on without it. Water would sustain her. There was always plenty of that to be had. She just hoped that the weather would stay fine and would not turn too cold at night. It was early May, after all. But she shuddered anew at the thought of having to face yet another night out of doors. Last night, even before she had had cause to do so, she had felt distinct unease. She had huddled on the field-ward side of a hedge. She had had no idea that a night could be so dark or so filled with unidentifiable noises—every one of them starkly terrifying. Later, of course, there had been real terror, from which she had been saved in the nick of time.

She could not believe this, she thought, stopping briefly to look back along the road. She just could not believe it. It could not be happening. Not to her. She had lived the most dull, the most drab, the most blameless of lives. Nothing even remotely resembling an adventure had ever come within hailing distance of her. Now she despised herself for ever longing for one. Beware of making wishes, someone had said—she could not remember who—for they might come true. The trouble with dream adventures was that they were always happy and jolly affairs. This one was anything but those things. Indeed, she would be fortunate to survive it.

The thought was so horrifying and yet so very realistic that she chuckled again. She had always accused the children of being melodramatic. She had always advised them not to exaggerate in the stories they told of their escapades.

Did nothing ever travel along this road? It was a main thoroughfare between north and south, was it not? But all she had seen all day—and it must be noon already—was a farmer's cart laden with manure. It had been traveling hardly any faster than she, and it had stunk terribly, but nevertheless she had begged for a ride. Strange how easily one could take to begging when the need arose. She wondered if she would beg for bread when her one remaining coin was spent. It was a ghastly thought. But the farmer, black teeth interspersed with gaps, had gawped at her as if she were some strange bird indeed, and had muttered something totally unintelligible before driving on a few yards and then turning into a field.

And of course both a stage and a mail coach had gone by. They did not count. One could hardly beg a ride on a public vehicle. Of course there had been whistles and catcalls from drivers and male passengers alike, all dreadfully mortifying for a woman who was accustomed to being invisible.

She turned to walk determinedly on again. Perhaps it was as well that her valise had been stolen and did not therefore have to be carried, she thought briefly, until she remembered that if it had not been stolen, she would be on a stagecoach right now, considerably closer to her destination than she was. She could still hardly believe how stupid she had been to keep her traveling money and her tickets in her valise and to entrust that valise to the care of a friendly, stout, seemingly respectable country woman who had traveled the first leg of the journey with her, talking to her in most amiable fashion all the way. All she had wanted to do was go inside the inn before the stage drew up in order to use the necessary. She had been gone for five minutes at the outside. When she had returned, the stout woman had gone. And so had her valise, and her money, and her tickets.

The stagecoach driver had refused to take her. The innkeeper had refused to call a constable and had looked at her as if she were a worm—a gray worm. She had still been wearing her own gray cloak and bonnet at that time.

Something was coming at last—something a little larger than a cart. It must be another stagecoach or post chaise, she thought with a sigh. But she stopped walking. She moved right off the road to press herself against the hedgerow. She did not want to be bowled over by a coachman who believed he owned the road.

It was a private vehicle—a plain coach drawn by four rather splendidly matched horses. The coachman and a footman were seated up on the box, both dressed in blue uniform. Obviously someone grand was riding inside, someone who would not only look at her as if she were a worm, but also tread her underfoot or under wheel without sparing her a thought—especially considering her present appearance.

Nevertheless, as the carriage drew closer, she held up one hand, at first tentatively, and then more boldly, reaching out her arm into the road. Panic welled into her throat and her nostrils. She did not think she had ever felt lonelier in her life—and she was an expert on loneliness.

The carriage swept past without slowing. The two servants did not even deign to turn their heads to glance at her, though the eyes of both swiveled in her direction, and they were nudging each other with their elbows and grinning before they passed from her sight. She bit her lower lip. But suddenly, a little ahead of her, the carriage not only slowed, but actually stopped. The coachman turned, somewhat startled, and looked back at her with a face that had lost its grin. She hurried forward.

Oh, please. Please, God. Dear, dear God.

A passenger was pulling down the window on the side closest to her. A hand, expensively gloved in cream leather, rested on top of it. Someone leaned forward to look at her as she approached. A man. He had a haughty, bored, handsome face topped by thick, carefully disheveled brown hair. His voice, when he spoke, matched his expression.

"A bird of bright plumage painting the landscape gay," he said. "Whatever is it that you want?"

Had she not been feeling so weary and so hungry, not to mention footsore and dusty and frightened—and embarrassed, she might have answered tartly. What on earth did he *think* she wanted, out here in the middle of a roadway, miles from anywhere?

"Please, sir," she said, lowering her eyes to her reticule, which she clutched with both hands as if to make sure that that too would not be snatched away from her, "would you allow me to ride up with your servants for a few miles?" She did not fancy riding up between those nudging, grinning two, but doing so was certainly preferable to the alternative.

"Where are you going?" She was aware of his gloved fingers drumming on the top of the glass. She could tell from his voice that he was frowning.

"Begging your pardon . . ." the coachman said with a respectful clearing of the throat.

"For coughing in my hearing?" the gentleman said, sounding even more bored than before. "Certainly, Bates. Where are you going, woman?"

"To Hampshire, sir," she said.

"To Hampshire?" She could hear the surprise in his voice, though she did not look up. "That is rather a distant destination for an afternoon's stroll, is it not?"

"Please." She raised her eyes to his. As she had suspected, he was frowning. His fingers were still drumming on the top of the window. He looked toplofty, arrogant. This looked like an impossibility. "Just for a few miles. Just to the next town or village."

The coachman cleared his throat again.

"We really must get you to an apothecary, Bates," the gentleman said impatiently.

And with that he opened the door and jumped down to the road without first putting down the steps. She took an involuntary step back, aware suddenly of the emptiness of the road to left and right and of the fact that there were only three strange men confronting her. He was a large gentleman, not so much in girth as in height. He was a whole head taller than she, and she was no midget. She was horribly reminded of last night.

"Well," the gentleman said, turning and bending to let down the steps himself, though the footman had vaulted hastily from his perch, "to the next village or town it is, Miss . . . ?" He turned back to look at her, his eyebrows raised.

"Gray," she said.

One eyebrow stayed up when the other came down. "Miss Gray," he repeated, reaching out a hand for hers. She had the impression that he was mentally naming off all the bright colors of her attire and considering the incongruity of her name. Belatedly, she wondered why she had not thought of pulling the plumes from her bonnet this morning and tossing them into the nearest hedgerow.

He expected her to ride *inside* the carriage with him? Did he not know how very improper . . . ? But clinging to propriety seemed absurd under the circumstances. And the prospect of being inside any structure, even if only a carriage, was dizzying.

"I did not expect to ride inside, sir," she said.

"Did you not?" He made an impatient gesture with his hand. "Come, come, Miss Gray. I shall try to curb my appetite for dining on tropical birds until after we have reached the next village."

She set her hand in his and immediately noticed the hole worn in the thumb of her glove, twisted around and perfectly visible. "Thank you," she said, feeling horribly mortified. And then as she settled herself on one of the seats, her back to the horses, and felt the warmth and softness of the blue velvet, she had to swallow several times to save herself from a despicable show of self-pity. She twisted the thumb of her glove inward in the hope that he had not noticed its shabbiness.

The gentleman closed the door again and seated himself opposite her, and the carriage lurched into well-sprung motion. She smiled at him a little uncertainly and tried not to blush. She could not remember another time when she had been quite alone with a gentleman.

ALISTAIR MUNRO, DUKE of Bridgwater, was on his way to London to take in the Season. His mother was already there, as was his sister-in-law, Lady George Munro. George was there too, of course, but his presence was without threat. And both of his sisters were there with their respective husbands. Bridgwater knew perfectly well what the presence of his female relatives in town during the Season was going to mean for him. He was going to be paraded to every ball, concert, soirée, and whatever other entertainment the *ton* could invent for its collective amusement, the ostensible reason being that they could not function without his escort—though presumably they had done very well for themselves during the first part of the Season, and all of them had husbands to be dragged about with them except his mother, who needed no escort at all. The real reason, of course, would be to expose him to the view of all the young beauties who were fresh on the market this year and of their mamas. His mother and his sisters—and his sister-in-law too—were determined to marry him off. He was, after all, four-and-thirty years old—alarmingly old for a duke with no heir of his own line.

The trouble was, he had been thinking gloomily before his thoughts had been happily diverted by the sight of a brightly flamboyant ladybird standing beside the road, one arm outstretched—the trouble was that he was beginning to lose his resistance. He was very much afraid that he might allow himself to be married off soon. For no other reason than that he was filled to the brim with a huge ennui, a massive boredom with life. Why not get married if his mother was so set on his doing so? It was something that must be done sooner or later, he supposed. There was that dratted matter of a nursery to be set up.

He was horribly bored—and restless—and depressed by the knowledge that life and love were passing him by. He had used to be a romantic. He had dreamed of finding that one woman who had been created for him from the beginning of the world. He had not found her all through his hopeful twenties. And then he had become nervous. Some of his closest friends had been tricked or forced into marriages not of their choosing, and he had panicked. What if the same thing should happen to him? There was Gabriel, Earl of Thornhill, for example, who had become involved in a reckless scheme of revenge and had ended up snaring an unwanted bride for himself. There was his closest friend, Hartley, Marquess of Carew, reclusive and unsure of himself, who had married for love one of the loveliest ladies in the land and had then discovered that she had married him under false pretenses. And there was Francis Kneller, who had kindly taken the gauche and alarmingly reckless Miss Cora Downes under his wing despite her being a merchant's daughter, and had ended up having to marry her after he had inadvertently compromised her. That last disaster had happened six years ago. Bridgwater had avoided any possible romantic entanglement since then.

And so he was bored and restless and none too happy. He had taken to staying away from home at Wightwick Hall in Gloucestershire, which could only remind him of the domestic bliss he had once dreamed of and never found, and instead wandered about the country, going from one house party to another, from one pleasure spa to another, in search of that elusive something that would spark his interest again.

He was coming now from Yorkshire, from an extended Easter visit with Carew and his lady at Highmoor Abbey. He had also seen a great deal of the Earl of Thornhill, whose estate adjoined Carew's. And as fate would have it, Lord Francis Kneller had been staying there for a visit, though he and his family had returned home a few weeks ago. Three couples, three marriages, all of which had frightened the duke out of his dreams of love and romance and happily ever afters. Three couples who were ironically proceeding to do what he had once dreamed of doing himself. Three happy and prolific couples. The two estates had seemed to teem with noisy, unruly, exuberant, strangely lovable children— Thornhill's three, Carew's two, and Kneller's four.

Bridgwater had never felt more alone than he had for the last several weeks. He had been a valued friend of everyone, a spouse and a lover of no one. He had been a favored uncle to nine children, a father to none.

He was desperate for diversion. So desperate, in fact, that he rapped on the front panel almost without hesitation as a signal for his carriage to stop when he spotted the little ladybird who was standing out in the middle of nowhere begging a ride when no respectable woman had any business doing either. Of course she was no respectable woman. She looked ludicrously out of place in her surroundings. She looked as if she might have just stepped out of a particularly lurid bawdy house—or out of a second- or third-rate theater.

Well, he thought, if love and romance had passed him by, there were other pleasures that assuredly had not—though he preferred to draw his mistresses and even his casual amours from the ranks of the rather more respectable.

She was disconcertingly dusty and shabby and wrinkled despite the splendor and gaudiness of the garments she wore. She was unconvincingly meek and mild, clutching at her shabby reticule with both hands as she stood beside his carriage and directing her eyes downward at it as if she expected him to wrest the wretched item from her grasp and give Bates the order to spring the horses. He was sorry in his heart that he had stopped. He was really not in the mood for the kind of gallantry that her type called for. And one never quite knew how dangerous it was to dally with total strangers. He felt irritable. But he had stopped. It would be cruel to drive on again and leave her standing there just because he was bored and not really in the mood, after all. Someone else had obviously kicked her out of another carriage and abandoned her, creating a rather nasty situation for her.

He just wished she would not play the part of demure maiden. It was rather like an exotic parrot masquerading as a gray squirrel.

But then she raised her eyes and looked full at him, and he saw that they were fine eyes—hazel with golden lights. They were large and clear and intelligent. They coolly assessed him. He sighed and hopped out to hand her in. He could not, after all, allow her to squeeze in between Bates and Hollander and distract them from the serious business of conveying him a certain number of miles before nightfall without overturning him into a ditch. Perhaps it would relieve his boredom somewhat to discover between here and the next village why she was in the process of walking all the way to Hampshire with only a small and shabby reticule for company.

Miss Gray. Miss *Gray*. It was too laughably inappropriate to be real. Miss Whatever-Her-Name-Was was also traveling incognito, he thought. Well, let her keep her real name to herself if she so chose. It mattered not one iota to him.

In addition to the fine eyes, he noticed, studying her at his leisure after his carriage was in motion again, she had a pretty face, which he was surprised to see was free of paint. Her auburn hair, just visible beneath the appallingly vulgar bonnet, clashed unfortunately with everything she wore—except for the gray dress he could glimpse beneath the cloak. She was younger than he had at first thought. She was not above five-and-twenty at a guess.

Her eyes, which had been directed at her lap, now lifted and focused on his. Oh, yes indeed, very fine eyes, and she was experienced at using them to maximum effect. He resisted the impulse to press his shoulders back against the cushions in order to put more distance between them and his own. He raised his eyebrows instead.

"Well, Miss *Gray*," he said, putting a slight emphasis on her name to show her that he did not for one moment believe that it was real, "might one be permitted to know why you are going to Hampshire?"

It was an impertinent question. But then she was no lady, and he had a right to expect some diversion as payment for conveying her a few miles along her way.

"I am going to take up my inheritance there," she said. "And I am going to make an advantageous marriage."

He folded his arms across his chest and felt eternally

grateful to the fates that had arranged for him to spot her beside the road as his carriage sped past her, though he had been dozing a mere five minutes before. He was not to be disappointed in her. She was going to regale him with a wonderfully diverting and extremely tall story. As tall as Jack's beanstalk, perhaps? She also, he noticed, spoke with a refined accent. Someone had invested in elocution lessons for her.

"Indeed?" he said encouragingly. "Your inheritance?" Having made such a bold and vivid start, surely she would need only a very little prodding to continue. He would explore the inheritance story first. When they had exhausted that, he would prompt her on the advantageous match story. If she was very inventive, he might even agree to take her on to the next village but one.

"My grandfather recently died," she said, "and left his home and his fortune to me. It is rather large, I believe. The house, I mean. Though the fortune is too, for that matter, or so I have been informed. It was a great surprise. I never knew him, you see. He was my mother's father, but he turned her off when she married my father and never saw her again."

He would wager half his fortune that the father would be a country vicar when she got around to describing him. It was the old cliché story—the great heiress marrying the poor country curate for love and living happily and poorly ever after. Bridgwater had hoped she would be more original. But perhaps she would improve once she had warmed to her story.

"Your father?" he asked.

"My father was a clergyman," she said. "He was neither wealthy nor wanted to be. But he and my mother loved each other and were happy together."

They would both be deceased, of course. Now what would Miss Gray have done when they died? She would have taken employment, of course, rather than go begging to her mother's wealthy father. Of course. Nobility and pride would have conquered greed. Employment as what, though? Something suitably genteel. Not a chambermaid. Never a whore. A lady's companion? A governess? The latter at a guess. Yes, he would wager she would decide on the governess's fate. But no, that would be impossible. She would not be able to choose the governess's role convincingly when she was dressed as she was. He wondered if she would think of that in time.

"They are both deceased?" He made his voice quiet and sympathetic.

"Yes."

He was pleased to see that she did not draw a handkerchief out of the reticule to dab at her eyes. She would have lost him as an audience if she had done so. Abjectness, even as an act, merely irritated him. More important, she would have doomed herself to getting down at the very next village. He wondered who had booted her out of his carriage a few miles back and why. His eyes moved down her body. The cloak was rather voluminous, but he guessed that it hid a figure that was perhaps less voluptuous than he had first thought.

"I took a position as a governess when Papa died," she said. "In the north of England." She gestured vaguely in his direction.

A very strange and eccentric governess she would have made. He amused himself with images of her in a schoolroom. He would wager that she would hold the fascinated attention of children far more easily than the gray, mouse-like creatures who normally fulfilled the role. The mistress of the house might have an apoplexy at the sight of her, of course. The master of the house, on the other hand . . .

"And then," he said, "just when you thought you were doomed forever to that life of lonely drudgery, you received word of the demise of your grandfather and his unexpected bequest."

"It *was* unexpected," she said, looking at him with an admirable imitation of candor. "He did not even reply to Papa's letter telling him of Mama's passing, you see. Besides, my mother had a brother. I suppose he must have died without issue. And so my grandfather left everything to me."

"Your grandfather lived in Hampshire?" he asked.

She nodded. She looked at him with eager innocence. With a butter-would-not-melt-in-my-mouth look. He wondered where she had slept last night. Her cloak looked distinctly as if it might have been slept in. The dreadful plumes in her bonnet looked rather sorry for themselves. And he wondered too how much money her reticule held. Certainly not enough to buy her a stage ticket to wherever it was she was going. Unless, of course, she disdained to spend money so senselessly when she could cajole bored travelers like himself into giving her carriage room in exchange for stories—and perhaps, if not probably, in exchange for something else. Perhaps if he asked her given name, she would call herself Scheherazade. Scheherazade Gray. Yes, it would suit her. Was she hungry?

But he did not want to feel pity for her. He wanted to be amused. And so far she was marvelously diverting. He had cheered up considerably.

"And so," he said, "having discovered what a great heiress you had become, you were so filled with excitement and the desire to exchange one sort of life for the other that you rushed from your employer's home in the north of England, carrying only the clothes on your back and a reticule, in order to walk to your new home in Hampshire. You are an impetuous young lady. But then, who on hearing of such a reversal in fortune would not be?"

She flushed and leaned back in her seat. "It was not quite as you imagine," she said. "But close enough to be embarrassing." She smiled at him to reveal a dimple in her left cheek—not to mention white and even teeth. Her eyes sparkled with merriment and with mischief. Yes, definitely. And he would wager that she knew the effect of that smile on her male victims. On his guard as he was, he felt his stomach attempt a creditable imitation of a headstand. Yes, indeed—an accomplished lady-bird.

"They were to send a carriage for me," she said, "and servants. I was very tempted to wait for them and to tell my employers of my good fortune. They had not been kind to me, you see, though the children were dears most of the time. They made pretensions of being grander than they were and treated me as if I had been born of a lesser breed. I know that they would have turned instantly and despicably obsequious if they had found out. They would have fawned on me. I would suddenly have become their dearest friend in all the world, one whom they had always loved as if I were truly a member of their family. It was tempting. But it was also sickening. I did not wish to see it. So I did not wait for the carriage to arrive. I left very early one morning without giving notice—though that did not matter since I had not been paid for the last quarter anyway."

He pursed his lips. He had to admit it was an amusing story. He could almost picture her mythical governess self striding down the driveway of the home of her erstwhile employers, not looking back, her plumes nodding gaily in the breeze.

"And so," he said, "you left without even enough money in your reticule to get you to Hampshire—unless you either walked or begged rides."

She flushed again, more deeply than before, and he felt almost sorry for his unmannerly words.

"Oh, I had enough," she said. "Just. I bought my tickets for the stage and still had enough with which to buy refreshments on the way and even a night or two of lodging if necessary. Unfortunately, I put both the money and the tickets in my valise for safekeeping."

And the valise had been stolen. It was priceless. Actually, the predictability of her story was proving more amusing after all than originality might have been.

"My valise was stolen," she said, "while I was changing stages. I left it for no longer than five minutes in the care of a woman with whom I had been traveling. She seemed so very kind and respectable."

"I suppose," he said, "no thief worth his salt would advertise his profession by appearing unkind and unrespectable and expect naive travelers to entrust property to his care."

"No, I suppose not," she said, looking up at him again. She smiled fleetingly. "I was very foolish. It is too embarrassing to talk about."

And yet she had talked about it to a complete stranger.

"And so," he said, "you have been reduced to walking."

"Yes." She laughed softly, though she was clever enough to make the laughter sound rueful rather than amused.

"And do you," he asked, "have enough money in your reticule to feed yourself as you walk?"

"Oh yes." Her eyes widened and the flush returned. "Yes, indeed. Of course I do."

A nice little display of confusion and pride. But really, how much money *was* in her reticule?

He had not noticed the approach of the village—a strange fact since it was the approach of villages and towns and inns with which he had attempted to relieve his boredom during his journey. The carriage was slowing and then turning into an inn yard. It was a posting inn, he guessed. Time to change the horses and have something substantial to eat.

"Oh." His companion turned her head to look out the window. She too seemed surprised—and a little disappointed. "Oh, here we are. I do thank you, sir. It was kind of you to take me up and save me a few miles of walking."

But he had not yet heard about the advantageous marriage. Besides, perhaps she was hungry. No, *probably* she was hungry. And besides again, only the very smallest of dents had yet been made in his massive boredom.

"Miss Gray," he said, "will you give me the pleasure of your company at dinner?"

"Oh." Her eyes grew larger, and he read unmistakable hunger in their depths. For a moment she was forgetting to act a part. "Oh, there is no need, sir. I can buy my own dinner. Though at the moment I am not hungry. I will walk to the next village before stopping, I believe. But thank you."

"Miss Gray," he said, "I will take you on to the next village. But first I must dine. I am hungry, you see. And if you are to sit and watch me eat, I shall be self-conscious. Do force yourself to take a bite with me."

"Oh." He knew suddenly for a certainty that she had not eaten that day and perhaps not yesterday either. It must have been yesterday, not today, that she had been tossed out of that other carriage. "You will take me one village farther? How kind of you. Very well, then. Perhaps I can eat just a little." She laughed. "Though I did have rather a large breakfast."

He raised his eyebrows as he vaulted from the carriage and handed her down the steps. He escorted her toward the private dining room that Hollander had already bespoken for his use. A gentleman and his ladybird. He read that interpretation in the eyes of the ostlers in the yard and in the eyes of the innkeeper when they went in and in those of the barmaid they passed inside.

Well, let them think what they would. Even gentlemen had to be amused at times. And even ladybirds suffered from hunger when they had been abandoned by their protectors and had not eaten for a day or longer.

2

SHE WAS SORRY SHE HAD ACCEPTED THE INVITATION TO dine with him. She was sorry she had been tempted by his offer to take her just one town farther along her way. Her legs were shaking so badly by the time she stepped inside the private dining room he had bespoken—he must be *very* wealthy—that she wondered they still held her upright. Her hands shook so badly that she would not for the moment try raising them in order to untie the ribbons of her bonnet.

She was so very accustomed to being invisible. Well, almost so anyway. It was true that the male guests Mr. Burnaby had brought to the house far too frequently for Mrs. Burnaby's liking—he was a gentleman who enjoyed shooting and hunting and used them as an excuse for having company and carousing for days and nights on end—it was true that those guests sometimes noticed her. It was true too that she had sometimes had difficulty in shaking off their attentions. But on the whole she had crept about the house in her gray garments and been invisible to both the servants, of whom she had not been quite one, and the master and mistress of the house. Mrs. Burnaby had even insisted that she wear a cap in order to douse the one splash of color she might have carried about with her—her hair.

She was certainly not accustomed to being looked

upon as if she were an actress—ironical that, really—or a wh—. But even in her mind she could not fully verbalize the word. Her hands developed pins and needles as well as the shakes. And yet that was exactly how everyone outside and inside the inn had just looked at her.

"Miss Gray," the gentleman said from behind her in his characteristic voice of hauteur—and yet it was a light and pleasant voice, she thought— "do please take a seat and make yourself at home."

"Thank you." She collapsed in a rather inelegant heap onto the nearest chair and reached for her bonnet ribbons. But no, it just could not be done. The offending monstrosity must remain where it was for a while longer.

And then she realized another cause of her distress, which had been drowned out so far by the looks she had been given as she entered the inn. There were strong smells of cooking food in the air. Her stomach clenched involuntarily, and she swallowed convulsively. She drew her gloves off one at a time, holding her hands in her lap so that she could control their shaking. And then her stomach protested with a loud and deep and prolonged growl.

"The horses will be changed here," the gentleman said, not waiting for the room to grow silent again. "I wish to press on as far as possible until nightfall. I find travel somewhat tedious. Would you not agree, Miss Gray?"

He was making an attempt to save her from embarrassment. She wondered if he knew she had lied about the large breakfast. She liked him. It was true that he was handsome and elegant and looked more than a little haughty and even bored, but he had been kind to her. It seemed such an age, an eternity, since anyone had been kind—or courteous. He had shown her courtesy despite her appearance and circumstances. She had almost forgotten what her own voice sounded like, except as she used it with the children during their lessons. But he had listened to her story and prompted her with questions and had seemed genuinely interested in her answers.

And now he was going to buy her dinner and take her a little farther on her way.

"Yes, I do, sir," she said in answer to his question, and she smiled at him.

His eyes dropped a fraction from hers. She had the feeling that he was looking at her dimple. Her dimple always embarrassed her. It seemed somehow childish. And Mrs. Burnaby had once told her she must bring it under control or else cease to smile at all. She had ceased to smile.

He sat down on the chair opposite hers, the table between them. The door opened again at the same moment, and the innkeeper himself came in carrying a tray from which rose steam and a smell that set her stomach to clenching again. The innkeeper set a bowl of oxtail soup before each of them, and a basket of fresh rolls on the table between them.

She swallowed and tested her hands in her lap, squeezing each in turn. Yes, the shaking had gone. She would be able to pick up her spoon and eat. She tried not to rush and waited for the gentleman to pick up his first.

"Miss Gray," he said as he did so, "do you have another name to go with the surname?"

She stared at him for a moment, desperate though she was to eat. No one had used her name, her given name, for so long that she no longer thought of it as public property. It was her own, private to herself, as certain parts of her body were. But there was no impertinent familiarity in his manner. He was looking at her in polite inquiry. His gray eyes, she thought irrelevantly, were so light that they might almost be described as silver. They were keen and rather lovely eyes. She wondered briefly if he was married. How fortunate his wife was to have such a handsome and such a gentlemanly husband.

"Stephanie," she said.

For a moment his eyes appeared to smile. She had noticed a similar expression a few times in the carriage as she talked.

"Alistair Munro at your service, Miss Stephanie Gray," he said and lifted his spoon to his mouth.

She did likewise and immediately thought that the idea of swooning with ecstasy was not quite as silly a one as she had always thought it.

"Ah," he said. "A cook of indifferent skills. A pity."

She looked at him in surprise. Food had never tasted even half as good as this soup did—and as the rolls did when she tried one, though it was true that it was a trifle doughy in the center.

"It is obvious, Mr. Munro," she said in the sort of voice she had sometimes used on the children, "that you have never had to go hungry."

His spoon paused halfway between his mouth and his bowl, and his face became coldly haughty. Then he half smiled at her.

"You are quite right," he said. "For a moment, Miss Gray, you sounded far more like a governess than a, ah, an heiress."

She laughed. "I have not become at all accustomed to the knowledge that I am wealthy," she said. She really had not. The reality of it still amazed her. She still expected to be able to pinch herself and wake up. "But I hope I will never cease to be grateful for my good fortune. I hope I will never squander my wealth or hoard it all selfishly to myself."

"Or complain about food that is indifferently prepared," he said.

She felt herself flushing. She had scolded him even though he was showing her incredible generosity.

"One has a right to an opinion," she said. "You are paying for my meal, sir. Perhaps that gives you a right to complain about your own."

The innkeeper returned with two plates piled with hefty portions of steak and kidney pie and with potatoes and vegetables. He removed their empty soup bowls and bowed himself out of the room. If she could only eat every mouthful of the dinner, Stephanie thought, it would surely fortify her for the rest of today and even tomorrow.

"And what *do* you plan to do with your riches, Miss Gray?" Mr. Munro asked. "Perform philanthropic good deeds for the rest of your life?"

She had a thought, suddenly. She flashed him a smile of bright amusement and noticed that his eyes stayed on her face even though he had already taken up his knife and fork.

"What I should do," she said, leaning slightly toward him, "is offer you a large sum to take me all the way to Hampshire. To be paid after I have been safely delivered, of course, since I am unable to pay in advance."

She was instantly sorry that she had spoken. It had been meant as a joke, of course. But he looked at her so intently and so haughtily, his eyes roaming her face and moving upward so that she was reminded of the ridiculous bonnet, which she never had taken off—she almost squirmed. She had been a mouse for so long a time. Was it possible that she had actually suggested something so very brazen and improper even as a joke?

"And *are* you offering, Miss Gray?" he asked.

He was undoubtedly a wealthy man. He must be hugely offended.

"No." She laughed again. "It was a joke, sir. No, of course not."

"Of course not," he repeated quietly, and then unexpectedly his eyes had that half-amused expression again. "But you have not told me of the advantageous match."

She wished she had not mentioned it to him in the carriage. He had been wonderfully polite and kind, listening to her story when it could be of no interest whatsoever to him. And yet she had never been much of a talker, even when she had lived at home with her parents. Certainly she had never talked on and on about herself. She had always been too conscious of the fact that she must be of no particular interest to anyone except herself. And marriage she knew was a subject that fascinated women far more than it did men. Mr. Munro could not really wish to hear about hers. He was just being polite again.

"You would not really wish to hear about it, sir," she said. "I must have bored you dreadfully in the carriage with the other details of my story."

"On the contrary, Miss Gray." When he raised his eyebrows, he looked downright arrogant, she thought. "You have saved me from a few hours of dreadful tedium. I will feel cheated if I do not hear about the advantageous match."

She chewed on a mouthful of pie. He was the complete gentleman, it seemed. He knew how to listen and appeared genuinely interested. She liked him a great deal despite his general air of lofty grandeur. Had she seen him from afar in other circumstances, at Mr. Burnaby's, for example—though she could not quite imagine him as a participant in any of Mr. Burnaby's rowdy gatherings—she would have disliked him on sight, seeing him as cold and arrogant and insufferably high in the instep. How looks could deceive!

"I am to be married," she said, "within four months. Actually, it was six months. That was what my grandfather stated in his will. But it took them two months to find me."

Mr. Munro pursed his lips. "Let me guess," he said. "You inherit from your grandfather only on condition that you marry within six months of his death. Otherwise the inheritance will pass to someone else."

How had he guessed? She nodded.

"To a distant relative?" he asked, his voice quietly sympathetic. "There always seems to be a distant relative waiting in the wings to seize one's property at the first glimmering of an opportunity—usually a *wicked* distant relative."

"I do not know him," she said. "I know none of Mama's family. But I doubt he is wicked. Very few people are in reality, you know. Only in fairy tales or Gothic stories. Most of us are a bewildering mixture of near-goodness and near-badness."

"But usually one of the two predominates," he said, smiling and revealing himself as a man who was purely handsome with the layers of aloof pride stripped away. "And who is the fortunate bridegroom?"

"Actually," she said, "my grandfather's will did not state who he must be. After all, I might have been married already, might I not? I am six-and-twenty, you see. All he did state was that I must be married within six months, and that if I was not already married before his death, my choice must be approved by both his solicitor and his nephew on my grandmother's side. The nephew apparently has a nephew of his own who is prepared to marry me. He is a man of substance and impeccable reputation and has not yet passed his fortieth birthday. I suppose I will have him. I will not have a great deal of time to find someone of my own choosing, will I?"

She smiled. In truth, she was somewhat elated at the prospect of marrying, even though she had not yet met the man and knew about him only what her grandfather's solicitor had written. All she had ever really dreamed of achieving in life was marriage and a home and a family. She had ached for all three since her father died when she was twenty. For six years she had lived a life of loneliness and invisibility as a governess. She had long ago given up the dream and adjusted her expectations. She was to be a spinster for life. All she could hope for was a post someday that would give her more satisfaction and that would bolster her self-esteem better than the first.

Yet, now suddenly she was wealthy and independent, and would remain so, provided she married soon. It was no difficult condition. Indeed, the prospect of being married lifted her spirits even more than the wealth and the independence did—both would pass into her husband's hands once she was married anyway. It was true, perhaps, that she would have liked to choose her own husband. It was true that deep within that original dream had been the hope that she would marry for love as her parents had. But this was the real world. In reality many people—*most* people—married for reasons other than love. And most marriages were to a greater or lesser degree arranged.

Mr. Munro had finished his dinner—he had eaten everything on his plate. He set his napkin on the table and leaned back in his chair. "You would cheerfully enter into an arranged marriage?" he asked. "When for twenty-six years you have preserved your independence?"

Ah, he had a man's blindness to some of the more bitter realities of life for a woman.

"I believe that marriage, sir, even an arranged marriage, is preferable to a life of independence as a governess," she said.

His eyes gazed deeply into hers. "Of course," he said, his voice sympathetic. His eyes looked above her head to the gaudy plumes of her bonnet. "But do you not dream of a love match, Miss Gray?"

"Dreams have no part to play in the waking world, sir," she said. "Besides, love can grow where there is respect to begin with. Or if not love, then at least companionship and affection."

"A life without dreams," he said so quietly that it seemed he was talking to himself more than to her. "Ah, yes, it is a lesson one learns with the experience of years, is it not? Have all your dreams been destroyed, Miss Gray?"

"If they have," she said, "I have not allowed their destruction also to destroy me, sir. There is always some satisfaction to be drawn from life. And there is always the future and always hope, even if there are not dreams."

"And yet," he said, looking fully into her eyes again, the half smile back in his, "some of your dreams—or perhaps they seemed too impossible even to be dreams— must have come true for you recently."

"Yes, indeed," she said. "My point is proved, you see."

"If you have finished," he said, "we should be on our way. I hope to be considerably closer to London before nightfall forces me to stop."

She had been unable to finish everything on her plate, much to her regret. She knew that even before the day was out she would look back with longing on the abandoned food, but she could hardly ask the innkeeper if he would wrap it up for her so that she might take it with her. She got to her feet.

"Yes, of course," she said. "It is kind of you to be willing to take me on to the next village."

"It is my pleasure, Miss Gray," he said. "We will while away the time in conversation. You must tell me about your life as a governess. Did you have just one charge or several? Were they eager to learn? What did you teach? Did you have influence over the formation of their characters as well as their minds? I shall be interested in hearing what you have to say."

He looked interested—almost amused. She could not imagine why he would be interested except that he was kind despite appearances, and he was a gentleman. And of course it would be very embarrassing to occupy the confined space of a carriage together if they had nothing to say to each other. She would talk to him, then. She was finding it strangely exhilarating to tell someone about her life and her good fortune. The telling was helping her forget the ill fortune of the day before—and of the night. And somehow it helped her to regain the identity she had submerged six years before in order to make her fate as a governess bearable.

She smiled and preceded Mr. Munro through the door. But the smile quickly faded. She had to walk the gauntlet of insolently staring guests and servants again in order to reach the haven of the waiting carriage.

She regretted the loss of her gray cloak and bonnet perhaps more than that of her valise. And she marveled at the respect Mr. Munro showed her. He was the only one.

HE COULD NOT quite make up his mind about her. What was she, exactly? An actress? She was certainly able to play a part. Sometimes she spoke so earnestly about her prospects and about her past life that he was almost convinced. But then she would flash him that smile, and his insides would turn over before he could catch himself. She must never lack for male admirers and protectors. It was difficult not to be drawn by the practiced mixture of innocence and artlessness on the one hand and the bright invitation of her eyes and her smile—and her dimple—on the other. And there was her beauty, of course. She was extremely pretty, despite the bright clothes, which if she only knew it, detracted from rather than enhanced her beauty. He would love to see her hair without the bonnet and without the pins.

Or was she merely an adventuress, setting out for the south, where she expected life to be more lively and more lucrative? Had she dressed this way on the mistaken assumption that she would look more fashionable? Or had she come north with a protector who had abandoned her? That was the interpretation he rather favored. But why would any man abandon her in the middle of nowhere? What had she done to displease?

She was clearly in search of another protector; there was no doubt about that. Her invitation to him to take her all the way to Hampshire and be paid after she was safely delivered there had been artfully done, but she had used every weapon in her considerable arsenal before withdrawing and pretending that it had all been a joke.

He was half inclined to take her up on her offer. She sat now on the seat opposite him, her head turned so that she could gaze through the window, though she was occasionally dozing. She had stopped talking, and he had stopped asking questions just for the amusement of discovering how inventive she could be. They had passed through several villages since they had stopped for a meal. At the first she had looked inquiringly at him and sat forward in her seat. Since then she had almost visibly held her breath every time a cluster of buildings appeared through the carriage windows.

Soon he must stop for the night. The landscape was growing gray with dusk. He could not quite decide what to do about her, Miss Stephanie Gray. She must have regretted the very dull surname she had given herself and had made up for it with the Christian name. Should he let her down and forget about her? Give her some money, maybe, so that if she was serious about going to

Hampshire, she could take herself there on a stage-coach? Or should he keep her with him?

He was surprised and somewhat alarmed at the tightening in the groin he felt at the latter thought. He always chose his bedfellows with meticulous care—never as the result of a simple flaring of lust. But it had been a long time. And she was both pretty and attractive—and willing. Doubtless she would be delighted to provide him with a couple of nights of pleasure in exchange for a ride to wherever she was going and food along the way. And a bed in which to sleep even if she must work first in order to earn that sleep. Not that he would make the work unpleasant for her. He liked to pleasure the women who pleasured him.

But she was a stranger with vulgar appearance and refined tongue. And she was the most accomplished liar it had ever been his privilege to encounter. Some other man had recently abandoned her for offenses unknown.

It would be better to set her down and give her money—and sleep alone.

And then her head jerked forward with such force that it brought her whole body with it. He had to lunge with both hands in order to save her from falling right off the seat.

"Oh." She looked up at him with blank eyes from a pale face. He kept his hands on her upper arms until awareness came back into her eyes and she sat up and leaned back again. "I am so sorry. I must have fallen asleep."

Deeply asleep. He did not believe it had been an act this time, a plea perhaps to give her a bed for the night.

"How much sleep did you have last night?" he asked her.

"Not a great deal." She bit her lower lip. "It was the only night I have ever spent out of doors. I did not sleep a great deal. I am sure I will sleep better tonight. I am more tired."

She smiled at him rather wanly. It was a masterful expression. He would have had to be a monster not to respond to it. Especially as he believed this one part of her story. She had spent last night alone out of doors and she had been terrified.

"I will be stopping at the next inn and taking a room for the night," he said, his mind made up at last—but what choice did he have, really? "You will stay there too, Miss Gray. And perhaps I will take you a little farther tomorrow. I still have not heard about your life at the parsonage."

He was alarmed and even a little embarrassed to see her bite hard on her upper lip while tears sprang to her eyes. Her face even crumpled for a moment before she brought herself under control.

"Oh," she whispered. "Thank you. You are the kindest person I have ever met. How will I ever repay you? Money will not do it, I know. You must tell me how I can show you my gratitude."

Shortly, Miss Stephanie Gray, he told her silently with his eyes. *But I doubt I will have to tell you how.* He was glad suddenly that her genuine distress and her ability to turn that distress to her own advantage had made his decision so easy to make.

He wanted her.

"Ah," he said, looking up as the carriage made a sudden turn to the left. "It appears that we have arrived."

3

$\mathcal{A}$ SERVANT SHOWED HER TO HER ROOM WHILE MR. Munro went back outside on some errand. The maid was obsequious while he was still in sight, and almost insolently abrupt once they were at the top of the stairs. She tossed her head before going back down and looked Stephanie over as if she were a sideshow at a summer fair.

Stephanie was too tired to care a great deal—and too relieved. She still felt on the verge of tears. The terrifying prospect of having to spend another night out of doors had been hammering at her brain for the last several hours. She stepped inside the inn room and stood against the door, her hands clasping the handle behind her back. Her own room. Four walls and a floor and a ceiling and privacy. She closed her eyes and allowed herself to feel the luxury of safety.

It was a large room with sofas and chairs and a table as well as a large bed and the usual furnishings of a bed-chamber. He need not have been so generous. A tiny attic would have sufficed. She felt a rush of gratitude. How would she ever repay him?

He had not said anything about another meal tonight, though it was hours since they had eaten. But she was not really hungry. Only a little thirsty. It did not matter. Surely there would be breakfast in the morning before they left. That would fortify her for the day. How far would he take her tomorrow? She thought of the blessed miles they must have covered today. It would have taken her a few days to walk as far.

She crossed the room to set her reticule down on the dressing table and caught sight of herself in the looking glass. She felt a shock of horror. The bonnet looked even more gaudy and vulgar on her head than it had looked in her hands. Perhaps the way its colors clashed with her hair had something to do with it. And the cloak looked garish, to say the least. Was it any wonder that everyone who had seen her today had looked at her askance? The horrified face in the mirror changed expression and registered amusement despite herself.

Oh, she looked quite, quite dreadful. Though of course *he* had not looked askance at her. He had been unfailingly courteous and kind.

She undid the ribbons with some haste and pulled off the offending bonnet. She plucked at the plumes, twisted them, pulled them. But whoever had put them there had intended that they stay there. With a sigh she set the bonnet down on one end of the dressing table. She unbuttoned the cloak and draped it over a chair. There, she thought, looking back at her image. Now she looked like herself again. Except that her hair was hopelessly flattened and tangled.

She drew out the pins. Ah, it felt so good to shake her hair free and to feel it loose and light against her back. It looked wild and curly, of course—its natural state, alas. It would take her all of five or ten minutes to tease a comb through it. She was just too tired. She took the few steps to the bed, sat on the edge of it, kicked off her half boots, spread her hands on the bed slightly behind her, and leaned back, bracing herself on her arms. She tipped back her head and shook her hair from side to side, her eyes closed. She sighed with contentment.

Something made her open her eyes and lift her head again, though she had not been conscious of any particular sound.

He was standing in the doorway, holding the door open, watching her. Had he knocked and she had not heard? She came to her feet and took a few hurried steps toward him. He came inside and closed the door and took a few steps toward her after setting down a valise.

"I am sorry," she said. "I did not hear—"

"It is beautiful," he said. His voice sounded husky, as if perhaps he had caught a chill. He was looking at her hair. "But I guessed that it would be."

She felt horribly mortified. She felt almost naked. No one ever saw her with her hair down.

"I am sorry," she said again. "I did not know—"

But he had taken several more steps toward her, and he had lifted one hand and was running the backs of his fingers lightly down her hair.

Gentlemen were very easily tempted, Mama had always said. It was a lady's responsibility to make sure that she never *ever* teased.

"Your beauty does not need to be enhanced with bright clothes," he said. "It speaks for itself. The gray dress, now, is a very clever touch."

"Oh, well," she said, horribly embarrassed. She wanted to take a step back, but it seemed unmannerly. "That cloak and that bonnet, you know . . ." And then with the corner of her eye she saw his valise again. And the ghastliest of ghastly certainties struck her.

"What is it?" he asked. His eyes, which had been on her mouth, lifted to hers. They really were quite silver, she thought irrelevantly, but they were saved from fading into insignificance by the dark outer lines—almost as if someone had taken a stick of very dark charcoal and outlined the irises.

"Oh," she said, closing her eyes tightly. "This is *your*

room, is it not?" How could she have believed even for a moment that such opulence was intended for her? Doubtless her room really was an attic. That malicious servant girl!

"Yes," he said softly. "This is my room."

"Oh, I am so *sorry*," she said. "The maid brought me here. Perhaps she did not realize . . . Though I am sure she did."

She felt the fingers of both his hands against her wrists and then moving up her arms until his hands came to rest on her shoulders. She was not conscious of either moving or being moved, but she could feel suddenly the tips of her breasts brushing against his coat.

"She was insolent?" he said. "Well. We will forget about her, Miss Stephanie Gray. She is of no significance."

His lips touched hers.

Her eyes snapped open, and her head jerked back. She had come to the wrong room, and she had let down her hair, and now look what had happened. Gentleman though he was, he was losing control. Mama had been right. Gentlemen—even the best of them—were weak creatures.

And then another thought struck her—ten times worse than the last. Perhaps he thought she had come *deliberately*. Perhaps he thought that when she had spoken in the carriage about repayment for his generosity, she had meant . . .

"No," she said. The word came out as a thin, wavering whisper of sound. It did not sound at all convincing even to her own ears.

"No?" His haughty, rather cold look was back.

One of his arms, she realized, was about her waist, and her waist and her abdomen were pressed to him. He seemed alarmingly muscular and masculine. And yet she was not frightened—not of him—only distressed by the misunderstanding that she had caused, or that the chambermaid had caused.

"No," she said more firmly.

She was not surprised when his arms fell away from her, and he took a step back. He was quite different, after all, from those other men with whom she had occasionally scuffled at Mr. Burnaby's. She had known that all day, and she knew it now too. She felt no fear, only embarrassment and regret that she had inadvertently tempted him. He was looking at her, eyebrows raised, waiting for an explanation.

"I *am* grateful," she said, forcing herself to look into his eyes. She clasped her hands at her bosom. "Believe me, I am, sir. More than I could possibly put into words. One day I will repay you."

"One day," he said very softly, and that gleam almost of amusement was back in his eyes.

"I think," she said, "I should like to go to my own room now, Mr. Munro. Can you direct me, or shall I ask the maid to do so?"

"Ah," he said, clasping his hands behind his back, "but I believe it is agreed that the chambermaid is unreliable, Miss Gray, if not downright malicious. It will be better if you stay here and I take the room that was intended for you."

"Oh, no," she protested as he turned toward the door and bent to take up his valise. "Oh, no, please. I could not allow—"

"Miss Gray," he said, and he spoke in a voice that she guessed his servants were accustomed to hearing and obeying, though he did not raise it at all, "I must insist. You will give me the honor of your company for breakfast—at eight?"

"Oh, please," she said, "I feel dreadful. This is *your* room. It is so very splendid."

He looked around him and then at her. "Indifferently

pleasant," he said. "I assure you that the one intended for your use is in no way inferior to this."

He spoke to make her feel better. She did not believe him for a moment. But there was no point in arguing further. He was determined to be the gentleman.

"Thank you," she said. "You are so very kind."

And then, before turning and leaving the room and closing the door behind him, he did what no one had ever done to her before. He took her right hand in his, raised it to his lips, and kissed the backs of her fingers.

"Good night, Miss Gray," he said. "Have pleasant dreams."

She closed her eyes and set her fingertips to her lips, prayer fashion, after he had gone. Oh, how dreadfully embarrassing. How would she ever face him tomorrow morning? She had come to his room and taken the pins from her hair. She had been on the bed when he arrived. And naturally he had thought . . . And yet, as soon as she had said no, he had let her go. Not only that, he had left her in possession of his room and asked for the *honor* of her company at breakfast tomorrow.

If she had lost faith in the male species during the past six years—and sometimes it had been difficult to believe that there were other men like Papa in the world— then that faith had been restored today. Oh, how *fortunate* his wife was, if he had a wife.

But perhaps not either. Stephanie was not naive enough to believe that he had intended only kisses a few minutes ago. He had intended— Well, he had intended to do *that* to her. Not that she could really blame him. It must have appeared as if she were offering a quite blatant invitation, and being a man—as Mama would have said—it had not occurred to him to resist it. But surely he *would* have resisted if he had a wife. Surely he would. He must be a single man.

She was glad he was a gentleman. She shivered when

she remembered the very real danger she had just been in. She had been alone in a bedchamber with him. She had inadvertently inflamed his passions. And she had felt two things during the brief moments when he had held her against him. She had felt his strength, against which she would have been powerless had he chosen to exert it. And she had felt something else. She swallowed and would not verbalize in her mind what that something else was.

She felt grubby and stale, she thought, turning her mind determinedly from the disturbing images. She needed to wash. She was going to take all her clothes off and wash all over. She was going to wash out some of her undergarments and trust that they would dry by the morning. And she was tired. So tired that both her mind and her limbs felt sluggish. She was going to lie down once she was clean, and sleep and sleep and sleep.

But half an hour later, before she had had a chance to lie down, a knock on the door heralded the arrival of a servant—not the chambermaid who had misdirected her—bearing a tray laden with food and a steaming teapot.

She bit her lip and wondered if this was perhaps Mr. Munro's dinner. But no.

"With the compliments of the gentleman, ma'am," the servant said with considerably more respect than anyone else had shown her today—except for Mr. Munro himself, of course.

HE WAS LYING on a narrow, lumpy bed in a little box of an attic room, his hands linked behind his head, staring up at a water-stained ceiling. Surprisingly, he was feeling amusement.

The landlord had been deeply apologetic that there was no other room available. He had even offered to turn some lesser mortal out of another room so that His Grace might pass the night in more pleasant surroundings. Bridgwater had declined the offer. He was only thankful that he was not doomed to spend the night on a wooden settle in the taproom.

Of course, the servants were all probably making delighted sport of the fact that he had been kicked out of the best room at the inn by the brazen whore he had brought there with him. Well, let them enjoy their amusement. The duke had never cared a great deal what servants thought or said of him. There were more important things in life on which to fix his thoughts and emotions.

He chuckled. She really was quite priceless. It was a long time since he had been so vastly entertained. He should be feeling both angry and sexually frustrated, of course. She had outmaneuvered him. She had teased him dangerously—but then he supposed she would not have been *very* upset if he had insisted on taking what she had been so artfully offering when he had opened the door to the room.

He felt an unwelcome tightening of the groin again when he remembered how she had looked on that bed, her slender body arched back against her supporting arms, her gorgeous mane of hair swaying from side to side behind her, her face lifted to the ceiling, as if in sexual ecstasy. He wondered how many hours she had spent before a looking glass before she had perfected the posture. And then she had affected surprise and confusion to find that he was standing in the doorway, watching her.

He chuckled again.

The gray dress really was a masterpiece. It complemented the glorious auburn of her hair to perfection, and its simplicity somehow enhanced her long-limbed, slender beauty. She did not have a voluptuous figure, but he had no doubt at all that she knew exactly how to make the most of what she had. Certainly she had succeeded in bringing him to painful arousal even before he had touched her.

He was not sorry she had said no. Well, perhaps that was not strictly true. He still felt uncomfortably warm as his mind touched on the imagined picture of that wavy, tangled hair spread on a pillow beneath him and of those long slim legs twined about his as he worked his pleasure on her. No, he could not pretend that he had not really wanted her. He had and he did.

But he was not sorry even so. One did not know with whom she had been last or with how many she had recently been. The mistake he had made, of course—but perhaps after all it was a fortunate one—was in offering her lodging for the night and in taking the room and sending her to it before agreeing to terms. He had been given the impression that she had enjoyed enormously evicting him while pretending to wish to evict herself. He wondered again if she really was an actress. She seemed almost too good. For there had been nothing melodramatic in her performance. It had been neither understated nor overstated. It had been almost convincing.

He smiled again. She was wonderful, he thought. A woman who lived by her wits and who knew how to use them to her own best advantage. What intelligent woman, after all, would willingly give herself an hour or so's strenuous work in bed when the bed might be had without the work? She had maneuvered him into offering the one without first extracting an agreement about the other. Very wise of her. Undoubtedly she was very tired. She needed to sleep tonight, not to work.

He wondered if she was sleeping peacefully. He would wager she was. And he wondered too if tomorrow night he would plan more carefully and make his conditions clearer. But he doubted it. It amused him to allow her to play out her hand.

Tomorrow night? Was he planning to have her with him again tomorrow night, then? Was it not time to set her down somewhere along the way? With the wherewithal to continue her journey in comfort, of course.

No, he knew he would not set her down. Neither would he go directly to London, he realized. He would take her to Hampshire, if that indeed was her destination. He would take her to the exact place she was going, if she did have an exact place in mind. He was curious to know where it was and why she was going there. And he looked forward to seeing her try to worm her way out of allowing him to travel the whole distance. She would not want to have all her lies exposed, after all.

So they would have a battle of wits. But this was one he intended to win. A night of sexual frustration notwithstanding, he had had more enjoyment out of today, and he had a brighter anticipation of the morrow than he had felt for a long, long time. It was a thought that made him feel a twinge of guilt when he remembered how eagerly and kindly Carew and his wife had entertained him for the past few weeks.

Miss Stephanie Gray—or whatever her name was—had succeeded where they had failed.

It was raining heavily when she got up the following morning. She looked out the window of her luxurious inn room and imagined the misery, as well as the terror, she would have lived through last night if it had not been for the generosity of Mr. Munro.

The rain eased up by midmorning, but it drizzled all day long, and the treetops were tossed about in a fitful and gusty wind. Even inside the carriage, which traveled more slowly than it had the day before because of the state of the roads, the air felt chill and slightly damp.

Through most of the morning she sat tensely in her seat. The tension was caused partly by embarrassment, although he was gentleman enough to make no mention of last evening's misunderstandings. She could not help remembering, though, that she had let her hair down and that he had touched it and called it beautiful—and that he had touched *her* and even kissed her. She could not help remembering that the bed had been behind her and that he had thought she was inviting him to take her there and— Well, she did not need to let her thoughts stray further.

But mostly she was tense because at every village and town she expected him to announce that he had brought her far enough. The long, comfortable journey with him had made her a dreadful coward. The prospect of being alone and destitute again was a terror she could not face, even in her mind. She thought of begging when he finally made his announcement and knew that perhaps she really would.

But so far it had been unnecessary. He had said nothing all morning or into the afternoon, when they had stopped for a meal and a change of horses. And he had handed her back into the carriage afterward, as if he had not even considered leaving her behind. Perhaps he no longer liked to suggest that she leave. Perhaps he expected her to broach the subject. But she would not do so, unmannerly as it might seem.

Please God, let him take her farther. Just a little farther.

He kept her talking all day. She told him about her childhood and her girlhood, about her mother and father. And in the telling, she found herself remembering details and events she had not thought of in years. She found herself becoming more animated, more relaxed, more prone to smiles and even laughter. And then she would remember where she was and glance at him anxiously and suggest that she was boring him. But he always urged her to continue.

She discussed plays with him—those of Mr. Shakespeare and Mr. Sheridan and Mr. Goldsmith. But when he asked her about her experiences with the theater, she had to confess to him that she had never seen a play performed on stage, though she had dreamed of doing so in London, where plays were surely performed at their best. Her only contact with the theater and actors had been a very recent one, but he had not asked about that, and it was something she tried not to remember, though they had been kind to her, of course.

He smiled when she told him she had only read plays, not seen them performed. He would think her impossibly rustic, of course. And he would be right. She *was* rustic. She would not pretend otherwise just in order to appear sophisticated in his eyes. He seemed to like her well enough as she was anyway. He did very little of the talking himself. Yet he appeared interested in everything she said. His eyes smiled frequently.

He had told her nothing of himself, she realized.

"Well, Miss Gray," he said finally when she was trying not to notice that afternoon had long ago turned to evening and evening was threatening to turn to night. "Another night is upon us."

"Yes, sir." She looked at him and kept her eyes on his. She knew that she was gazing pleadingly at him, but she could not muster up enough pride to look at him any other way.

"My coachman will stop at the next inn," he said.

"Yes, sir." She closed her eyes tightly suddenly and lost the final shreds of her dignity. "Please. Oh, please let me stay with you. I . . . It is raining and it is going to be very dark. There will be no moon. I . . . Oh, please."

"Miss Gray," he said, his voice sounding surprised, "I thought it would have been obvious to you by—"

"Please." She would beg and grovel if necessary. "I will do anything. I will repay you in any way you choose." She knew the implication of her words even as she spoke them, though she had not realized it in advance. But she did not care. She would not recall the words or qualify them in any way. She would do anything not to have to face the terrors of the darkness again.

There was a lengthy silence, during which she kept her eyes closed and held her breath.

"No," he said finally. "I think not, Miss Gray, though it is magnanimous of you to offer. Your pleas and your offers are unnecessary anyway." The bottom fell out of her stomach, but fortunately he continued. "I thought it would have been obvious to you by now that I am taking you to your grandfather's home, now yours, in Hampshire. I believe we will reach it tomorrow if the roads do not prove to be quite impassable and if you can tell me exactly what house I am looking for."

He was going to— "You are going to take me all the way?" She opened her eyes and stared at him uncomprehendingly. "All the way there?"

He smiled. "I am afraid so, Miss Gray," he said.

She was glad she was sitting down. Her legs would not have supported her. Her hands shook in her lap. Even so, she had to raise them quickly to cover her face before she lost control of every muscle in it. She swallowed repeatedly, intent on not bawling like a baby.

"Yes," he said. She did not even notice the thread of humor in his voice. "I thought you might be affected by the announcement, Miss Gray."

"Thank you," she whispered. "Thank you. Oh, thank you."

4

SINDON PARK—HE HAD HEARD OF IT. IT WAS SAID TO BE one of the grander manors in the south of England. The park, with its rhododendron groves and rose arbors and formal parterres, was said to draw visitors throughout the summer months.

At least, he thought, she was willing to practice deception on a grand scale. He wondered what she would do when she realized that there would be no getting rid of him, when she knew that he intended to escort her right to the main doors of Sindon and even within the doors—if she was allowed within them herself. But she would be—she was with him.

He wondered if she would turn her marvelous inventive skills on the poor unsuspecting inhabitants of the house. Would she claim to be a long-lost relative? He sincerely hoped so. He hoped she would not crumble at the grand scale awkwardness of it all. He would be disappointed in her.

He watched her with appreciation throughout the day. They did not do much talking. She watched the scenery through the window with eager—and with slightly anxious?—eyes. And he watched her.

He was a fool, he thought. He could have had her last night. She had offered herself. Had he accepted, there was no way she could have wormed out of the commit-

ment as she had done the night before. And he had
wanted her. He still wanted her. But he had decided not
to take on such an entanglement. Or perhaps it had
seemed distasteful to him to accept an offer that had
been made out of some desperation. He had no doubt
that she really had been alarmed at the prospect of having to spend the night out of doors. Somehow he liked
to sleep with women who wanted to sleep with him.

Perhaps, he thought, he would take her back to London with him once this charade played itself out to a
suitable denouement. Perhaps he would set her up somewhere and keep her for a while, until she found her feet
and could make her own way in the metropolis. He had
no doubt that that would not take her long at all. Perhaps he would buy her new clothes, ones that were
more . . . seemly for a mistress of his. Though he could
appreciate the humorous contrast between the flamboyant cloak and bonnet on the one hand and the demure
simplicity of the gray dress on the other.

He wondered for how long she would amuse him.
Would she succeed in pushing back the massive boredom from his life? She had succeeded admirably for longer than two days. But could she continue to do so? He
felt such a deep longing suddenly that he almost sighed
aloud.

He waited for her to speak. He knew that she would
do so quite soon now. They must, after all, be within ten
miles of Sindon. She could not wait much longer.

She was blushing when she looked at him—and biting
at her lower lip. Yes, she was setting up the situation
very well. He could almost hear already the words that
would follow. He was not disappointed.

"Are we close, sir?" she asked him. "Is Sindon Park
far off? Do you know?"

"Less than ten miles at a guess," he said, containing
his amusement. "Just relax, Miss Gray. I am not about

to abandon you now. We will be there in time for tea, I daresay."

Her eyes dropped from his again for a moment, and she played with the shabby glove of one hand, twisting the hole out of sight. "I have been thinking," she said.

He did not doubt it. The workings of her mind had been almost visible to his amused eye throughout the day.

She looked back up into his eyes. She was good with her eyes. They looked purely guileless—and purely beautiful, of course.

"I cannot arrive with you," she said.

He raised his eyebrows and resisted the urge to grin.

"You have been so very kind," she said earnestly. "And it seems so very ungrateful of me. But don't you see? I have no chaperone or even a maid. They will want to know how far you have brought me. I have been alone with you in this carriage for almost three days. I have stayed with you—in separate rooms, of course." She paused to sit back in the seat and to blush with maidenly modesty. "I have stayed with you for two nights. It will be impossible to explain and to make it appear as innocent as it has been." She flushed an even deeper shade.

He would not help her out. He was enjoying this too much. He kept his eyes on her and waited for her to continue.

"And I cannot lie about it," she said. "I am not good at lying."

He felt his lips twitch, but he would not spoil things. "What would you suggest?" he asked.

"I did think at first," she said, "that you might set me down at the gates of Sindon and I would walk the rest of the way. Though it would seem horridly inhospitable of me when you have come so far out of your way and the house is mine, after all. But that whole idea would not do. They would want to know where I came from, and perhaps there would have been no stage or mail coach anywhere near the time I would arrive. I would have to tell the truth after all, and if I were going to do that anyway, then you might as well take me all the way."

"I can see," he said, "that you might be no better off with that solution, Miss Gray."

"And so," she said, "I think it would be best, sir, if you set me down in the next town. I can take the stage from there and arrive properly just as if I had traveled by stage all the way." She blushed deeply again. "Though I will have to beg money to pay the fare. I daresay it will not be much. I will insist on sending it back to you if you will give me your direction in London."

He watched her closely. He was enjoying himself vastly. "I have developed a deep concern for your safety and well-being during the past few days, Miss Gray," he said. "I do not believe that in all conscience I can abandon you now. I would worry too much that after all something had gone awry, and you had not arrived safely to claim your inheritance."

She tipped her head slightly to one side. "How kind you are," she said. "But really—"

"You must remember, Miss Gray"—he gazed benignly at her—"you must remember that you are no longer either a clergyman's daughter or a governess. You are a great heiress. You have a certain degree of power. If you arrive at Sindon timid and cringing and expecting censure for the manner of your arrival, you will find that there will always be men—and women—willing to rule you and control your life. You and I have done nothing improper, apart from indulging in one small kiss, for which I am deeply sorry. *You* have done nothing improper. It would be far better for you to arrive in my carriage with my escort and prove to whoever is waiting to receive you that you are a woman of independent mind as well as means."

"Oh, but—" she said. She stopped to bite her lip once more. "Are you sure it will not appear very improper, sir? I have not really thought a great deal until now about the impropriety of having traveled alone with you because I have been in such desperate circumstances and have been so grateful for your help. But will it not appear improper to others? Will not my reputation be damaged? And perhaps yours too, sir? I should regret that of all things."

"I think not, Miss Gray," he said. "Sit back and relax. I insist on taking you to the door of Sindon Park and delivering you personally into the hands of your grandfather's solicitor and of your grandmother's cousin. I shall not abandon you. I shall see you inside the house, where you will be safe at last. And home at last." He finally allowed himself a reassuring smile.

She said no more, though he could see unease in her face and in her posture. He could almost see her mind racing over the possibilities of last-minute escape.

Think all you like, Stephanie Gray, he told her silently. *And squirm all you like. I have earned this pleasure.* The social events of the Season were going to seem tame indeed when he finally got to town. But then perhaps he would have a new mistress to brighten life for a few weeks or months. Eventually, he would surely tire of her ever fertile imagination. But perhaps not for a while.

She squirmed in good earnest when the carriage finally turned between two stone gateposts and proceeded along an elegant driveway lined with lime trees. He heard her draw a deep breath, which she let out raggedly through her mouth.

"Oh dear," she said, "my heart is pounding and my palms are clammy—and shaking." She held up both hands to prove her point. He had no doubt that she was not acting. "What will they think of me, dressed like this? And arriving with you instead of in the carriage that they have probably sent by now? Will they believe it is me, do you suppose? And what if it is all a hoax after all? What if none of it is real? What if they look at me as if they had never heard of me or anybody of my name?"

Ah, she had been using her time well. She had been thinking of a way out of her dilemma. She was paving the way.

"Relax," he told her soothingly.

"Oh," she said, "that is all very well for you to say. Ohh!"

The last exclamation came out on a note of agony. The house had come into view. It was a house of gray stone and indeterminate architectural design. There were turrets and gables and pillars, all somehow combining to create a surprisingly pleasing effect. The house was larger than he had expected, and the parterre gardens before it were magnificently kept. When he glanced at Stephanie Gray, he saw stark terror in her eyes.

He almost relented. He almost suggested rapping on the front panel and giving his coachman the order to turn around. He would get her to tell him her real destination. And then he would make his proposition to her. They could consummate their agreement tonight before returning to London. There was something distinctly exhilarating in the thought.

But no. He must see this to an end. And, indeed, it was too late to turn back without incident. The double doors at the top of the horseshoe steps had opened, and three people had stepped out to watch the approach of the carriage—two men and one woman, all of middle years and of thoroughly respectable appearance.

"Oh dear," Stephanie Gray said. Her voice was all breath. "What shall I do? What shall I say?"

"I am sure," he said, his mouth quirking again, "that you will think of just the right words."

"Do you think so?" she asked doubtfully. "You are so kind. But I am not good with words."

And she had just claimed to be a poor liar?

The carriage drew to a halt.

SHE HAD NOT expected to feel such terror. After all, there was no reason for it. She was not coming as a supplicant or as an employee. She had not come to make a favorable impression on anyone. She had come because all this was now hers.

But the thought brought only a renewed wave of fright.

It was *enormous*. And it was *magnificent*. She had somehow pictured Sindon Park as a larger version of some of the prettier, more prosperous country cottages she had seen. She had pictured the park itself as a large country garden. She had expected to feel very grand as the owner of such opulence.

But this . . .

Well, this would dwarf Mr. Burnaby's estate. His house and garden would fit into a corner of this property and not even be noticed. This was a house and a park fit for a king.

She had known that her grandfather was wealthy. But she had no real conception of wealth. To her, the Burnabys had appeared enormously wealthy. Was she now wealthier than they?

The thought that she owned all this seemed absurd to her, and she was quite serious when she suggested to Mr. Munro that perhaps everything had been a hoax. Surely, it could not be real. She felt at a terrible disadvantage. How could she arrive like this, a woman without baggage, without servants, without even her own clothes, except for her dress? There were *holes* in her gloves. And how could she arrive in Mr. Munro's carriage with Mr. Munro for escort?

It was an impossibility. She was on the verge of leaning forward and begging him—as she had begged him for a different reason last night—to direct his coachman to turn back, to take her somewhere else. Anywhere else.

But of course there was nowhere else to go.

Besides, it was too late. They had been seen. There were people coming out of the house. She could only go forward. And why should she not? She remembered Mr. Munro's words. She was no longer just a vicar's daughter or just a governess—not that there was anything demeaning in either identity. She was an heiress, a wealthy woman, the owner of Sindon Park, the granddaughter of the previous owner.

If she was cringing and timid, he had said, there would always be people willing and eager to rule her. She had had to be timid—and even a little cringing sometimes—for too long. She would be neither ever again. She squared her shoulders and lifted her chin. Mr. Munro had jumped out of the carriage and set down the steps himself. He turned now to hand her down and smiled encouragingly at her. There seemed to be almost mischief in his smile as if he were telling her that this was a new adventure and he looked forward to seeing how well she would acquit herself.

Well, she would not disappoint him.

The three people who had emerged from the house had come to the bottom of the horseshoe steps by the time she had descended from the carriage. She lifted her head to look at them and saw their smiles of welcome fade in perfect unison with one another. Oh dear, her wretched bonnet. The plumes had stubbornly refused to be detached from it, though she had tried again last night. But she kept her chin high and took a step forward, lest she give in to the temptation to hide behind Mr. Munro. This had nothing to do with him. This was her concern entirely.

She curtsied and smiled at them one at a time. "Good afternoon," she said. "I am Stephanie Gray."

They all succeeded in looking simultaneously aghast. Their eyes all swiveled to Mr. Munro. But clearly they got no encouragement from that direction. They all looked back at her.

"Mr. Watkins?" she said, looking from one of the men to the other.

One of them half raised a hand, seemed to think twice about acknowledging his identity, and scratched the side of his nose with it. Stephanie smiled at him.

"After I had your letter, sir," she said, "I decided not to wait for the carriage you offered to send for me. It was foolish of me, as matters turned out." But no, she would not be abjectly apologetic. "I took the stage, but at the first change from one to the other, I succeeded in having my valise and my tickets and almost all of my money stolen. I had to spend a whole night in a hedgerow beside the road, and during that night I was robbed of almost everything I had left. Fortunately, those assailants were frightened off by the approach of a carriage. They left me with my reticule and my d-dress, but they took my cloak and bonnet and parasol. The occupants of the carriage were very kind. There were actually two carriages. They were a troupe of traveling actors and offered to take me with them. But they were going in the wrong direction. They did give me a cloak and bonnet, though, from the trunk that contained their stage costumes."

The eyes of all three rose at the same moment to gaze at the plumes of her bonnet.

"It *is* a monstrosity, is it not?" she said and smiled.

"But the cloak has kept me warm and wearing this bonnet has been marginally less shocking than going bareheaded. May we go inside?"

Mr. Watkins cleared his throat, and the other man exchanged glances with the woman.

"Oh," Stephanie said. She had omitted something, of course. "Mr. Munro very kindly took me up in his carriage when he saw me trudging along the side of the road. And he has very generously brought me the whole way." She looked them all very directly in the eye. She would omit none of it. Let them make of it what they would. "That was three days ago. Without his help it would have taken me a few weeks to walk here, I am sure, and I might well have perished on the way. I have enough money in my reticule to buy only one small loaf of bread, you see."

"Mr. Munro?" Mr. Watkins said, looking sharply at that gentleman and frowning. "*Munro?*"

"Yes," Mr. Munro said. It was all he said.

"He insisted on bringing me all the way here," Stephanie said, "even though I have brought him out of his way. I owe him a deep debt of gratitude. *May* we go inside?"

"Horace—" The woman spoke for the first time, laying her hand on the arm of the man who had not yet spoken.

Horace cleared his throat. "How do we know you are who you say you are?" he asked. "If you will forgive me for saying so, Miss . . ."

"Gray," she said. "Stephanie Gray. I suppose I do look like a-an actress. Is this proof enough?" She opened her reticule and took out the letter Mr. Watkins had sent her. She handed it to him.

Mr. Watkins took it and opened it and appeared to be reading it, just as if he had not seen its contents before.

"But how do we know," the woman said, "that you

did not find this somewhere? How do we know that you and this . . . this *gentleman* were not the ones to attack Miss Gray and rob her?"

Mr. Watkins cleared his throat. "I believe I can vouch for . . . er . . . Mr. Munro, Mrs. Cavendish," he said.

"And I can vouch for Miss Gray, ma'am," Mr. Munro said, stepping forward and offering Stephanie his arm. She smiled at him gratefully, even though his voice had sounded very much as if there were ice dripping from it. "Shall we step inside, Miss Gray? It occurs to me that you do not have to stand here waiting for permission to do so."

"Thank you, sir." She took his arm.

The other three came up the steps behind them. But she had little time to think about them or the awkwardness of her arrival. Soon they were stepping through the doorway into a marble, pillared hall that quite robbed her of breath. She had expected the whole house to be smaller than just the hall was proving to be.

"Oh," she said and glanced up at Mr. Munro. His face looked strangely like the marble by which he was surrounded. The hall must have taken his breath too, she thought.

But there was another man standing in the hall, obviously a gentleman rather than a servant. He was younger than the other three, of medium height, almost bald, bespectacled. Stephanie smiled at him.

"Peter," Mrs. Cavendish said, "this is her. Miss Gray."

"Yes," Peter said, his voice and whole manner stiff and disapproving. "I heard everything, Aunt Bertha. You came with this . . . gentleman, Miss Gray? Alone with a stranger?"

"For three days," Bertha Cavendish added.

Stephanie could feel the certainty growing in her. Horace was her grandmother's nephew. Bertha Cavendish was probably his wife. Peter was their nephew—her intended bridegroom. Her spirits, already hovering on the lower end of cheerful, took a steep dive. It was unjust to judge on such brief acquaintance that it was almost no acquaintance at all, but in her estimation Mr. Peter Whoever was a man without even a glimmering of humor. He frowned now.

"I do not believe—" he began.

"Sir." Mr. Munro cut into whatever it was Peter did not believe, his voice quite decisive enough to command everyone's attention. And there was no doubt about it now—there was pure ice there. He had turned to Mr. Watkins. "Perhaps Mrs. Cavendish would be good enough to present herself and these other two gentlemen to Miss Gray. And perhaps she would then escort Miss Gray to the drawing room or a salon for tea. Miss Gray has been traveling for many days. I have been her companion for three of those days. I believe it would be appropriate if I had a private word with you."

Mr. Watkins bowed.

"Well—" Mrs. Cavendish began, her bosom swelling. But Mr. Munro wheeled on her and raised to his eye a quizzing glass that Stephanie had never noticed on his person until now. She remembered the early impression she had had of an arrogant and toplofty gentleman. It was all back, that impression, and clearly Mrs. Cavendish was cowed by it.

"Well," she said with considerably more civility, "if *you* are satisfied, Mr. Watkins, I daresay we must be too. But how foolish of you, my dear Miss Gray, to leave your employer's home without the proper escort. And how rash of you to accept a ride with a gentleman when you did not know him and had no maid with you."

"It seemed preferable, ma'am," Stephanie said, allowing herself to be led toward a magnificently curved staircase, "to dying of exposure and starvation."

Mr. Munro had disappeared with Mr. Watkins. She

had not had a chance to speak with him first and to invite him to come to the drawing room afterward or wherever it was that they were to take tea. She must have a chance to thank him properly before he left. And she must offer him dinner and lodging for the night. It would be quite proper to do so when there were obviously other gentlemen staying at the house in addition to Mrs. Cavendish.

It was all very bewildering. But she had arrived at last. The worst was over.

And it was hers. This was all *hers*—if she was married, within the next four months, of course. That might be tricky. She was not going to marry Peter Whoever-He-Was. She had made up her mind on that already. He had been about to say that he was not willing to take on a woman who had just spent three days in company with another man and had doubtless been behaving in quite unseemly fashion with that man.

How dare he.

The very idea!

She would rather go back to being a governess than marry such a man.

Though she hoped—oh, how she hoped—it would not come to that.

5

HE WAS FEELING ALMOST AMUSED. HE REALIZED THAT it was a feeling that would not last—that it was only shock that enabled him to see the humor of a situation that was not in any way humorous for him. But feeling amusement was preferable to feeling stark horror, he supposed.

He followed Mr. Watkins, the solicitor, into a private room leading off the hall—it appeared to be a combination office and library—and waited for the man to close the door behind them.

He had rushed with wide open eyes into a trap of his own making. That had been obvious to him soon after he had helped her down from the carriage. At first he had felt blinding anger against Miss Stephanie Gray. If only she had thought of telling before now the story of the stolen bonnet and cloak and the one about the actors. It seemed to him that she had told him almost every detail of her life history except that one. And it was the one detail that made all the difference.

But perhaps not. Perhaps he would have taken it as one more brazen and clever invention. And he could hardly blame her for not telling him. She was not a prattler. She had talked to him, yes. She had done most of the talking during their days of travel. But everything she had told him had been spoken in answer to his questions. He had not thought to ask her what had happened during that one night she had spent out of doors.

He should have thought of asking. It *did* make all the difference. Without the cloak and bonnet, he realized now when it was too late, she looked to be exactly what she had said she was—a governess living on the edge of poverty. *Why* had he not set more store by her gloves, which actually had holes worn in them, and on her plain gray dress and shabby reticule?

He had built his whole fanciful image of her around such flimsy evidence as a fuchsia cloak and a pink bonnet with its multicolored plumes.

Oh, yes, he had set the trap for her with careful deliberation, and then he had proceeded to walk smiling into it himself. Yes, it really was funny. Hilarious.

Mr. Watkins cleared his throat. "Mr., er, Munro?" he said. "Are you not the head of that family, er, sir? I have seen you in town once or twice, I believe. Are you not the Duke of Bridgwater?"

"I am," His Grace said, turning before the fireplace and setting his hands behind his back.

Mr. Watkins made him a hasty and rather ridiculous bow. "This is an honor, Your Grace," he said. "And an honor for Miss Gray, too. I cannot imagine why—"

"I will, of course," Bridgwater said, bringing one arm forward in order to toy with the handle of his quizzing glass, though he did not lift it to his eye, "be marrying the lady."

He knew even as he spoke, even before he saw the surprise on the solicitor's face, that it was a quite unnecessary gesture. His rank would have protected him. She would have suffered embarrassment and even a measure of disgrace, unless the four people who had greeted her all agreed to say nothing about her manner of arrival at Sindon Park. He would wager that the morally outraged Peter would agree to no such thing—unless he was bound and determined to marry her at all costs. But nobody would censure the Duke of Bridgwater for walking away from the woman. Nobody would expect him to do anything as drastic as offering for her.

But he had known as soon as the truth dawned on him that he had no choice. There was the annoying matter of his honor.

"You wish to *marry* Miss Gray?" Mr. Watkins said, his eyes starting from his head.

"But of course," His Grace said haughtily, taking his glass more firmly in his hand and lifting it, though not all the way to his eye. "Do you believe I would so thoroughly have compromised her, sir, unless I intended to make her my wife?"

He was thinking about the law of averages. His best friend and those other two friends of his had all been forced into unwanted marriages—though that was not quite true of Carew, who had married for love only to discover that his bride had married for another reason altogether. All three of those marriages had turned out well. Indeed he might almost use that dreadful cliché of them and say that the three couples were in the process of living happily ever after. He knew—he had just spent a few weeks in their company. Three out of three success stories. Now there were going to be four such marriages. It was too much to hope that there would be four out of four successes. The law of averages was against him.

"I believe," he said, "that according to her grandfather's will Miss Gray must be married within the next four months if she is not to forfeit her inheritance?"

"That is correct, Your Grace," the solicitor said. "But Sir Peter Griffin—"

His Grace set his glass to his eye, and Mr. Watkins fell silent.

"I think not," the duke said quietly. "I feel a certain

aversion to the idea of allowing another man to marry my chosen bride. Miss Gray is my chosen bride."

Sir Peter Griffin could go hang, he thought. He was probably dangling after her fortune and this impressive property, but he would never let her forget the impropriety of her arrival at Sindon, dressed like a prize ladybird and with a male companion in tow. The man had looked severely displeased at his very first sight of her and had done nothing to hide his irritation.

Though why he should press his point when there was such an easy solution to his dilemma, the Duke of Bridgwater did not quite know. Miss Gray could marry the baronet, he could be on his way to town and his family and the Season, and they would all live happily ever after. No, she would not live happily. He could predict that with some certainty. And he would not have done the right thing.

He wished suddenly that he had not been brought up always to do the right thing, or that he had rebelled against his boyhood education as he had rebelled during his childhood. Good Lord, he had just spent six years being very careful indeed that nothing of the like would ever happen to him.

But he had walked into just such a situation like a lamb to the slaughter.

Mr. Watkins cleared his throat again, perhaps disconcerted by the silence that had stretched a little too long for comfort.

"We will discuss the marriage contract," the duke said. "I wish it to stipulate quite clearly that Miss Gray retain ownership of this property and of whatever fortune she has been left besides. I gather, sir, that her choice of husband must be approved by you and by a relative. That would be Mr. Horace . . . Cavendish, I presume? He is the lady's husband?"

"Yes, Your Grace," the solicitor said.

"We will have him down here, then," Bridgwater said briskly, "and have his approval. Then we will proceed to business. I am expected in London and have no wish to delay. I take it I have your approval, sir?" He raised his eyebrows and favored the poor solicitor with a look that had been part of his early education and had stayed with him ever since, a look that brooked no denial and no insubordination. He did not even use his quizzing glass.

"Oh, y-yes, i-indeed," the solicitor said, visibly flustered. "It is a g-great honor, Y-your Grace. For Miss Gray, I mean. And indeed f-for—"

"Mr. Watkins," His Grace said, "Mr. Cavendish?"

The solicitor scurried to the door in order to summon a servant.

Lord, the duke thought. Amusement was fading fast. Indeed, it had faded to nothing long ago, he realized. Lord, he was about to marry a governess. A governess-turned-heiress. A stranger. Someone for whom he felt nothing. Nothing at all except a certain lust. And that now seemed embarrassingly inappropriate. Good Lord, she was undoubtedly a virgin—a twenty-six-year-old virgin. A virtuous woman whom he had been planning to take back to London with him as his mistress.

Good Lord! He dropped the handle of his quizzing glass lest he inadvertently snap it in two.

HER CLOAK AND her bonnet had been whisked away— she fervently hoped that she need never see them again, though she felt woefully her lack of belongings. She had been taken by Mrs. Cavendish, who had requested rather stiffly that she be called Cousin Bertha, upstairs to her room. Actually, it was a whole suite of rooms, quite overwhelming to someone who had made her home in a small attic room for the past six years. She had been given time only to wash her hands and pat her hair into better shape after the removal of her bonnet. Then she had been taken down to the drawing room for tea.

Mrs. Cavendish, Cousin Bertha, presented her properly to Mr. Cavendish, who explained that he was her grandmother's nephew, son of Grandmama's sister, and that she must call him Cousin Horace. And she was presented to Sir Peter Griffin, who bowed stiffly and frowned darkly and explained that he had the honor of being Cousin Bertha's nephew and that he also had the honor of being at her service in the ticklish matter of her grandfather's will.

It was, Stephanie supposed, his way of offering her marriage. She tried not to be awed by his title. He was the only titled gentleman she had ever met. But apart from the title itself, there was nothing impressive, nothing awe-inspiring about the man. She could overlook his lack of good looks. Though she would prefer a handsome husband if she had the choice, she had to admit, she had been taught from childhood on that a person must not be judged on looks alone. But she could not and would not overlook bad temper. And if Sir Peter Griffin was frowning at her the very first time they met, then one could hardly expect him to smile his way through the rest of the lifetime they might spend together.

Her experience of life might be limited, Stephanie thought, but even she knew that marriage was no easy business, that even the happiest of brides and grooms eventually had to work at achieving contentment and compatibility. Her parents had succeeded, though she could remember arguments and tight-lipped disagreements; Mr. and Mrs. Burnaby had not.

Her companions at tea were at least polite, she found. They appeared to have accepted her story and to have overcome their suspicions that she was an impostor.

Cousin Horace was called away after a while, and she was left to converse with the other two. Cousin Bertha made an effort. Sir Peter concentrated on being silently morose. Perhaps he thought to impress her with a show of masculine power. She was not impressed.

She thought about Mr. Munro. She hoped he would not leave before she had had a chance to see him again. It would have been far better if he had done what she had suggested and allowed her to come by stage from the nearest town. Her arrival had been horribly embarrassing, and she was sure that he must have felt the embarrassment too. But all seemed to have ended well.

The thought of not seeing him ever again saddened her in a strange way. He had been kind. He had been a gentleman, even if he had felt temptation when it had presented itself and had shown signs of being willing to give in to temptation. But after he had understood the misunderstanding, he had been the perfect gentleman. She hated to think of such a man going out of her life forever. She had met with so little kindness in the last several years. Perhaps things would change, of course. She was an heiress now—except that she had to marry within four months, and she had already made up her mind not to accept the suitor who was there and ready to oblige her.

The opening of the door heralded the return of Cousin Horace with Mr. Watkins. Stephanie looked eagerly beyond them for Mr. Munro, but he was not there. She hid a stabbing of disappointment. Had they not even invited him to tea? Or had he refused? There were still a few hours of daylight left. He could be well on his way to London before darkness fell.

Mr. Watkins cleared his throat. "Miss Gray," he said, bowing to her with at least a decent show of respect, "would you care to join the, ah, the gentleman below stairs? He would like a word with you. He is in the library. The servant in the hall will show you the way."

She jumped to her feet, a smile on her lips, and realized too late that her reaction had perhaps seemed too eager a one, considering the suspicions the other four occupants of the room must have about her and Mr. Munro. But she did not much care.

"Horace—" Cousin Bertha said, also getting to her feet.

But Cousin Horace held up a staying hand. "No, Bertha," he said. "It is quite all right."

Stephanie left the room without a word and ran lightly down the stairs. She felt a fluttering in her stomach again at the realization that this was all hers—or would be hers if . . . But she did not spare much thought for that little problem. Her eyes sought out the servant, who was standing across the hall before a large doorway. He opened the door as she approached him and smiled at him. She stepped inside the library.

He was standing with his back to the fireplace, his hands clasped behind him. He was not smiling, but then he had not smiled a great deal during their journey. He looked more—oh, what was the word? He looked more *imposing* than he had during their days together, though she remembered the impression she had had of him at first as a haughty, rather bored gentleman. She remembered his gloved hand tapping rather impatiently on the window of his carriage before he had decided to take her up.

If she were seeing him for the first time now, she thought, she would be a little afraid of him. But she was not seeing him for the first time. She hurried across the room toward him, both her hands outstretched. He took them in his.

"Mr. Munro," she said, "I am so glad you did not slip away before I had a chance to speak with you. You cannot know how grateful I am to you. Words are not always adequate vehicles for the expression of feeling. You cannot know, perhaps, what it is like to be a woman stranded without money or friends far from either her place of origin or her destination. Frankly, it is terrifying. I might have died—or worse. I will repay you. I swear it. I will find a way. But I will not offer you money. It would be vulgar, would it not?" She smiled brightly at him.

"It would be vulgar," he agreed. "Miss Gray, you are in need of a husband—very soon. Sir Peter Griffin is, I believe, the man to whom you referred during our travels?"

"Yes." She would say nothing to make him feel the burden of her problem.

"He would make you a miserable husband," he said. "He would make you feel like some inferior insect. I do not doubt he would beat you."

She had not thought of that. But it might well be true. "He has not stopped frowning since he set eyes on my gorgeous plumes," she said, laughing. "Poor man, he was quite disconcerted by them, was he not? I will be kind to him. I will refuse his offer."

"Good," he said. "Then I have no rival. You will marry me, Miss Gray, if you will be so good."

At first she felt only incredulity. Then she understood. She laughed again. "Oh dear," she said, "have they been threatening you? Have they backed you into a corner? Have they persuaded you to do the honorable thing, sir? What nonsense. I shall say no. No, thank you very much. There. Now they must be satisfied. You have offered, and I have refused. I daresay they will find someone else for me within four months. I do believe I must be far wealthier than even I thought if this house and park are anything to judge by. I will attract fortune hunters if no one else."

She smiled reassuringly at him. How unpardonable of her cousin and her grandfather's solicitor to make him feel that he had compromised her and must offer her marriage. When he had been so very kind. When he had come out of his way in order to make sure that she arrived safely. When he had saved her life.

"Miss Gray." He had tightened his hold on her hands. "I think it unlikely that in four months you will find a husband to love—that one and only mate created for you in whom one is tempted to believe from time to time. You said yourself that you were prepared to accept an arranged marriage, that almost any marriage was preferable to you than the alternative. You have known me for only three days. It has been a very brief acquaintance, though the fact that we have spent every moment of each day together has perhaps made it seem longer. Do you have any violent objection to me as a husband? Can you not bring yourself to accept me?"

She could feel herself flushing. She was suddenly almost overwhelmed by temptation. In three days she had not once thought of him in terms of matrimony, except perhaps to envy the Mrs. Munro who clearly did not exist. But now that she *did* think of it, she could see that it was a very attractive idea indeed. Almost irresistibly so.

She frowned. "I told you so, did I not?" she said. "I warned you. I knew how it would seem if you brought me all the way here. But you were too gallant to allow me to travel the last short distance by stage, and I was too weak to insist. But you need not offer for me, you know, despite what Mr. Watkins and Cousin Horace may have said to you. Perhaps I have my chance to repay your kindness now, long before I expected to have any opportunity. I release you from any obligation you may feel, sir. You are free to leave and return to your life in London. There. It seems a small thing to do to repay such a debt, but it is really not so small, is it? Marriage is for a very long time—a lifetime. I once overheard one of Mr. Burnaby's guests refer to marriage as a life sentence. He was right." She tried to withdraw her hands from his, but he held on to them.

"Has it occurred to you, Miss Gray," he asked, "that I did it all deliberately? That I have developed an attachment to you during the past few days, that I knew you must find a husband soon, that I maneuvered matters so that you would choose me?"

"But why?" She searched his eyes and found no answer there. "Do you mean that you fell in love with me?"

"I spoke of an attachment," he said. "I have grown fond of you. *Will* you marry me?"

It was impossible. How could he have developed an attachment to her? She was a nothing, a nobody. Until a week ago she had been treated rather like dirt beneath the feet of her employers. It was six years since she had felt fully a person. How could he like her enough to wish to marry her? *He* was not obliged to marry within four months, after all. Then she had a thought.

"Are you impoverished?" she asked and then flushed painfully once more at the impulsive, dreadfully rude question. But she had the right to ask it of him under the circumstances, did she not? "Is it my fortune, sir?"

"I have made a tentative marriage agreement with your solicitor," he said. "I have insisted that none of your property or fortune will come to me in the event of our marriage. They are yours to enjoy while you live and to will to whom you choose. I have a quite adequate fortune of my own, thank you very much."

"You really wish to marry me, then?" she said. "It is not because of the pressure they have put upon you?"

"There has been no pressure at all, Miss Gray," he said. "*Will* you marry me?"

It was too wonderful to be true, she thought, feeling dazed. She had known him for only three days. Indeed, she did not know him at all. He had told her nothing about himself. But she had learned to like him, to trust him. And he was so—beautiful. She despised the thought, but she was honest enough with herself to know that it made a difference. She would have a handsome husband after all. And really, if she needed an argument to finally clinch the answer, she knew she was going to give anyway—there was no time in which to be cautious. Four months really was not a great deal of time at all.

"Yes, then," she said. "If you are quite sure, sir. Because I owe you so much. Everything, in fact."

He raised her hands one at a time to his lips. She felt his warm breath on her hands and realized something that self-discipline had kept from her conscious mind for three days. In addition to being handsome, he was *attractive*. He was going to be her husband. She was going to have an intimate relationship with him. She felt slightly breathless.

"It is time I introduced myself properly to you, then," he said. "I have told you only half. Alistair Munro, Duke of Bridgwater, at your service, Miss Gray."

Her stomach felt as if it whooshed up into her throat, whipped itself upside down, righted itself once more, and slid back down into its appointed position. The whole exercise left her breathless, wobbly-legged, and fuzzy-headed. She clung to his hands, which suddenly felt very much warmer than her own.

"No," she said.

"Yes." He half smiled. "I am afraid so. You will be nothing as mundane as Mrs. Munro, you see. You will be the Duchess of Bridgwater."

"No." She succeeded in freeing her hands. She turned her back on him. "Oh, no. That is quite impossible. I could not possibly be. I would have no idea— What would I even call you?" She turned to look at him in deep dismay. "What *do* I call you? My lord?"

He clasped his hands at his back. It was there plain to see now that she was looking for it. It was quite unmistakable. He was every inch the aristocrat.

"Other people address me—and will address you—as 'Your Grace,'" he said. "You may call me Alistair, Miss Gray."

"No," she said. "Oh, no, sir . . . Your Grace. This is bizarre."

"I am to be rejected, then," he asked, "merely because I had the misfortune to be born heir to a dukedom? Have pity on me."

"I grew up in a vicarage," she said. "For six years I have been a governess in the home of people who have only a small claim to gentility. I believed a short while ago that Sir Peter Griffin was the only titled person I have ever met, and I despised myself for almost feeling awe. But you are a *duke*. It is impossible, sir. You and I have lived in different universes."

"You are afraid," he said, "that you will be unable to fit into my world, Miss Gray? And yet you own all this?" He lifted one arm to sweep in a wide arc that seemed to include the room and everything beyond it. "Your grandfather has already moved you into a new world. My mother will help you move comfortably in mine—and my sisters. They will be delighted."

It was the first personal detail she had learned about him. He had a mother and sisters.

"I must return to London without further delay," he said. "But I will have Mrs. Cavendish bring you to town within the week. She and my mother will take you shopping. We will have the announcement of our betrothal and imminent marriage announced in the morning papers. My mother will take you about to all the correct social functions. And soon—well within the four-month limit—we will marry at St. George's, Hanover Square. Have you heard of it? It is where almost all the fashionable marriages of the Season are solemnized. And then you will be my duchess."

"No," she said. She was terrified—and terrifyingly excited.

"You said no to me on another occasion," he said, "and I believed you and left you. Must I believe you now too? Will you not marry me? Would you prefer Sir Peter?"

She bit her lip.

"Say yes," he said. "Please?" He smiled fully, an expression she had seen only once before. Usually he only half smiled, using his eyes more than the rest of his face.

"Yes, then," she said. "You have been so kind from the start. You are the only one who has shown me respect and believed in who I am since I was forced to wear those embarrassing clothes."

"Splendid." His smile disappeared, and his manner became brisk and businesslike. "We will go to the drawing room, Miss Gray, and make our announcement and swift arrangements for your coming to London. I must be on my way then. You will find, though, I believe, that you will be treated here with considerably more respect than was accorded you on your arrival. If you are not, you must insist on it. And if you are still not, I will want to know the reason why of your relatives and your solicitor when they bring you to town next week."

She felt suddenly like a child who had no control whatsoever over her destiny. He swept into command as to the manner born. It seemed for the next half hour as if she said nothing except "Yes, sir," and "No, sir"—she could not seem to bring herself to call him "Your Grace." And it seemed to her as if everyone else said no more than the same words, either, though they all addressed him correctly.

And then, long before she had worked the bewilderment from her brain, he had her back down in the hall, and he had both her hands in his again, and he was bowing over them and lifting them to his lips and reminding her that he would do himself the honor of calling upon her in London in one week's time.

"Yes, sir," she said.

His lips quirked briefly so that for a moment she was reminded of the man with whom she had traveled for the past three days. Her feeling of unease lifted. But then he straightened up and left the house without another word or backward glance.

Stephanie took a deep breath and held it for a long time. She felt as if she had been caught up in a whirlwind one week ago and was still spinning helplessly about, waiting to be dropped to earth again. She wondered if it would be a soft landing or if she would be dashed quite to pieces.

Somewhere along the way she seemed to have lost herself. It was a bewildering thought.

6

THE MARCHIONESS OF HAYDEN AND THE COUNTESS of Greenwald were sitting with their mother, the Duchess of Bridgwater, in the drawing room of her town house. The Duke of Bridgwater was present too, though he was on his feet, pacing more than he was sitting down. They were waiting for the arrival of Mrs. Bertha Cavendish and Miss Stephanie Gray to take tea.

"Do sit down, Alistair," his mother said, looking up from her embroidery at him. "You remind me of a bear in a cage."

"I beg your pardon, Mama," he said stiffly, seating himself in the nearest chair.

"I still cannot believe what you have done, Alistair," the marchioness said, frowning. "A parson's daughter. A governess. And you a duke. You know very well that a duke rarely looks below an earl's daughter for a bride."

"But she *is* an heiress, Lizzie," the countess said gently. "A very wealthy one, apparently. And she is a gentleman's daughter. You speak as if she were entirely beyond the pale. I am sure she is quite lovely and quite refined. Else Alistair would not have offered for her."

"Thank you, Jane," the duke said dryly, getting to his feet again and taking up a brief stand before the fireplace.

"But we know very well, Jane," the marchioness said,

"that he offered because he felt he had compromised her. How can a duke compromise a governess? I would like to know. Hayden says—"

"I offered," the duke said firmly, fingering the handle of his quizzing glass and looking rather haughtily at the elder of his two sisters, "because I wished to, Elizabeth. And I do not recall granting you—or Hayden—permission to question my wishes. Miss Gray is no longer a governess. She is, as Jane has pointed out, a considerable heiress, owner of Sindon Park. And she is soon to be the Duchess of Bridgwater. You will doubtless keep those facts in mind when she calls."

"The only significant fact," the duchess said, setting her embroidery on a small table beside her, "is that Alistair is betrothed to Miss Gray and that her cousin has brought her to town and is accompanying her here this afternoon to make our acquaintance. We will remember, all three of us, that within a month Miss Gray will assume my title as Alistair's wife, that she will be the leading lady of this family, superseding even me. I will be merely the *dowager* duchess. We will treat her accordingly, both this afternoon and for the rest of our lives. I trust that is understood?"

"Yes, Mama," the countess said, smiling. "I am sure I am going to love her. I have been despairing of you, Alistair."

"Of course, Mama," the marchioness said more briskly. "You can always count on me to behave with good breeding and to do what is correct. Hayden always says—"

"Ah," the duchess said as the drawing room door opened, "here is Louise at last."

Lady George Munro, the Duke of Bridgwater's sister-in-law, hurried into the room, bent over her mother-in-law to kiss her cheek, and smiled a greeting at everyone else.

"I thought I might be late," she said. "Caroline is cutting teeth and was fretting at being left with Nurse. But I would not have missed coming here for worlds. Alistair, you are looking positively green. George says he cannot understand what possessed you. You are always so very high in the instep—his words, not mine, I assure you." She laughed lightly. "We thought perhaps you were waiting for an available princess, having judged every other lady beneath your notice."

The Duke of Bridgwater's hand closed about the handle of his quizzing glass, and he raised it to his eye, pursing his lips as he did so.

"Ah," he said, "then you have been proved wrong, Louise, have you not? You and George both."

But she only laughed merrily. "Oh, do put the glass down," she said. "You cannot cow me with it, Alistair. Henry can imitate you to perfection, you know. He can have us in stitches with laughter."

The duke lowered his glass and raised his eyebrows. His eleven-year-old nephew was growing into too impudent a wag for his own good. And George and Louise were encouraging him in such insubordination? So much for favorite nephews and the gratitude they owed a doting uncle.

The ladies settled into a dull and cozy chat about children. Among the three younger ladies, there were enough children to provide topics of conversation to last a week or longer. But they were not content with just their own.

"Cora is in town with Lord Francis and the children," the countess said. "Did you know, Mama? I was delighted beyond anything when she called yesterday. Do you remember the Season when she stayed here with us and you brought her out? The year Charles and I became betrothed? The year she married Lord Francis? And what a famous heroine she was?" She laughed at her memories even before the others began discussing them.

"Dear Lady Francis," Lady George said fondly. "She saved Henry's life. How could I ever forget her? How are her children, Jane? Four, are there not?"

But Bridgwater was no longer listening. He had crossed the room to the window and stood looking down on the square below, waiting for the appearance of another carriage.

In his mind's eye he could see her rather tall, slender figure. He could see her auburn hair thick and wavy like a cloud about her head and shoulders, as it had been that first night, which he had expected to spend with her. He knew that her eyes were hazel with golden flecks. He remembered that she had a dimple in one cheek—the left?—and very white teeth. He remembered that her smile lit up her face. He knew that she was pretty.

But he could not for the life of him put the pieces together in his mind in order to form a clear image of her. He even wondered foolishly if he would recognize her when he saw her this afternoon.

It had been ten days.

Ten days since he had fallen into his great madness. It seemed unreal, looking back. It was hard to believe that it had actually happened—all of it. That strange journey south with a bright bird of plumage, whom he had mistaken for a ladybird with a vivid imagination. His insistence on seeing the adventure through to its end so that he might enjoy her discomfiture when all her lies were finally exposed for what they were. His sudden realization, after they had arrived, that everything she had told him was true, and the accompanying realization that he had hopelessly compromised a lady. His offer. His insistence that she accept it.

Yes, he had insisted. She had tried more than once to refuse. She had quite categorically released him from any sense of obligation he might feel. She would not have been ruined if she had. The other occupants of the house would have kept their mouths shut—even Sir Peter Griffin. Yes, he especially. He would have kept his mouth shut in the hope of marrying her himself.

And yet the insistence. And her final acceptance.

He had not even corrected her on the assumption that had seemed to be at the heart of her acceptance. She had assumed that he had behaved throughout their acquaintance with the utmost gallantry. She had called him kind. She had thought his decision to take her all the way to Sindon had proceeded from his concern for her safety. She had said he had been the only person to treat her with respect for who she really was since she had acquired those atrocious garments. Lord, if only she knew!

He had not disabused her. It had seemed unmannerly to do so. It would have hurt her. Besides—dared he admit it?—she would have thought the worse of him if she had known.

He felt a little guilty for not admitting he was not quite the hero she thought him.

Yes, it was hard to believe that it was all true. Except that the memories of shocked disbelief among his family were very fresh indeed and very real. His mother, who now appeared to have accepted the inevitable, had been worst of all. He could not possibly so disgrace his name. She would not believe it of him. But she had believed eventually and had decided to stand by him.

And now the female members of his family were gathered behind him, waiting to meet his betrothed. The announcement was ready to go into tomorrow's papers, and St. George's had already been booked for the wedding in one month's time.

He watched almost dispassionately as a plain carriage entered the square and drew to a halt before the doors of his mother's house. He watched the steps being put down and two ladies being helped to the pavement—one middle-aged, one young. Neither looked up. Both ascended the steps of the house and disappeared inside.

He had intended calling on them yesterday or this morning. Yet, when he had made inquiries late yesterday afternoon, they had still not arrived at the Pulteney. This morning Mrs. Cavendish had sent a card to his mother, and his mother had sent word to him. He was to come here this afternoon, she had written. Mrs. Cavendish and Miss Gray were coming to tea. And so he had waited for the afternoon. He wished now that he had made arrangements to call for them and to escort them here.

He had been very firmly head of his family for longer than ten years. No one, least of all he, had been in doubt about that. But today he felt like a boy again, unsure of himself, subject to his mother's will. He drew a deep breath and let it out on a silent sigh. The door had opened behind him, and his mother's butler was making the expected announcement. He turned. All the ladies were rising to their feet.

He stood at the window like a spectator. She and her cousin both curtsied. His mother hurried toward them, greeted the older lady courteously, and then held her hands out to the younger, who took them.

"Miss Gray," his mother was saying graciously, "what a pleasure it is to meet you. The past week has seemed interminable. I do hope you had a comfortable journey up from the country and that your hotel is to your taste? You must tell us all about it. Allow me to present you to my daughters and my daughter-in-law."

They buzzed. They talked. They laughed. Mrs. Cavendish buzzed and talked and laughed back.

And then his mother turned to him, a smile on her face. "Alistair?" she said.

He came forward at last. "Ma'am?" he said to Mrs. Cavendish, bowing over her hand. "Miss Gray?" He took her hand in his and raised it to his lips. It was cold, even a little clammy.

Her dress was pale blue rather than gray. Her hair, dressed in a simple knot behind, was slightly flattened from the bonnet she had left downstairs. Her face was pale, her eyes slightly shadowed. There was not a glimmering of a sign of her dimple or her white teeth.

"Your Grace," she said in a voice that was little more than a whisper.

She looked every inch a governess.

He felt the nervous urge to laugh. Where were the fuchsia cloak and the plumed bonnet? Without them she seemed to be robbed of identity.

"Alistair," his mother was saying, "you will show Miss Gray to a chair? Mrs. Cavendish, do take the seat beside Lady George. Here is the tea tray."

He seated her on a love seat. He should have taken the place beside her. The occasion called for it. He should have engaged her in a tête-à-tête conversation, as far as politeness would allow. It would be expected of him. Instead, he walked to the fireplace a short distance away and stood with his back to it, his hands behind him.

She was a stranger. She was a clergyman's daughter, a governess. He did not think of her as his social inferior— just as his social opposite. He was a duke. There was a whole way of life his duchess would be expected to fit into with grace and ease. This woman just would not be able to do it. She already looked like the proverbial fish out of water.

By insisting that she marry him, he had ensured her unhappiness—and his own. He pursed his lips and set himself to being sociable, the perfect host. The role was second nature to him.

COUSIN BERTHA AND Cousin Horace had fawned upon her for longer than a week. Unkind as the word was, Stephanie could think of no more suitable one.

She was to marry a *duke,* the Duke of Bridgwater. They did not seem to tire of exclaiming over the fact and reminding her of her good fortune. How provident it was that they and Mr. Watkins and Sir Peter Griffin had all been at Sindon to witness her arrival with His Grace. Had there been no one but servants at home at the time, he would doubtless have withdrawn quietly and dear Cousin Stephanie might never have netted him. But he had seen how disconcerted they were, of course—how could they help but be outraged even if he *was* a duke and everyone knew that members of the aristocracy were a law unto themselves? For very decency's sake he had been forced to offer for dear Cousin Stephanie. She had done very nicely indeed for herself.

They had a week to get Cousin Stephanie ready to go to town and show herself worthy of being a duke's bride. Everything about her needed transforming. Gracious heavens, what must His Grace have thought of her in that dreadful cloak and bonnet? And in the even more dreadful gray dress? She needed new clothes, she needed to dress her hair differently, she needed to learn how to curtsy and how to converse in polite society. She needed to learn to *impress* people. How were they ever to be ready in time?

The village seamstress was brought to Sindon Park and kept a virtual prisoner in an attic room until she had produced a number of new clothes, which would have to do until Cousin Bertha had a chance to take Cousin Stephanie to a more fashionable modiste in London. A former ladies' maid, who had a reputation as an artistic dresser of hair, was engaged and set to work to show what she could do with Cousin Stephanie's unfortunately red and unfortunately unruly hair.

All the dresses except one—the one Stephanie had insisted upon for day wear—were so bedecked with ribbons and frills and flounces at Cousin Bertha's insistence that Stephanie swore privately she would never wear any of them. They made her look as if she were masquerading as a sixteen-year-old—a sixteen-year-old without any taste whatsoever. And the curls and ringlets with which her new maid loaded and decorated her head made her look so grotesque that she always brushed them out as soon as she was able and knotted her hair in its usual comfortable style.

"You have no *idea* how to go on, my love," Cousin Bertha said in despair the day before they left for town. "You will appear a veritable *bumpkin* to His Grace. I would not doubt he will quietly dissolve the betrothal. You look like a *governess*."

Perhaps he really would dissolve the betrothal, Stephanie thought. Surely he would. He must have had second thoughts—and third and fourth thoughts—by now. He must have realized what a dreadful mistake he had made. As had she.

She could no longer remember what he looked like. She had only disturbing and vague memories of a tall, handsome, rather arrogant figure. The memories terrified her as did the knowledge that he was a duke. Was a duke not next to a prince in rank? Above earls and marquesses and barons? How could she enter that world? Just a couple of weeks ago she had been a governess.

Several times—usually during the nights, when she awoke from disturbing dreams—she was on the verge of writing to him, telling him that she had changed her mind, telling him that she would release him from his promise, so hastily and rashly given. He would be as relieved as she, she told herself.

But always before she could write the letter—though once she actually started it—she remembered how little time she had. Less than four months during which to find a husband. Or else she must go back to being a governess. Sometimes the prospect of that familiar and drab life was less daunting than the one that actually faced her.

And now suddenly—it all seemed to have happened to her without her exercising any control at all over events—here she was. In London. At the Duchess of Bridgwater's house. Feeling numb and terrified all at the same time.

They were almost late. When she had gazed at her image in the glass at the Pulteney Hotel, and Cousin Bertha and her new maid had stood behind her, exclaiming on what a pretty picture she made, she had been almost paralyzed with horror. She looked grotesque! Despite the protests of her maid and the cries of dismay from Cousin Bertha, she had almost torn off the pink dress in her haste, and she had dragged a brush through her hair until tears stood in her eyes. And so at least she felt comfortable—oh, no, she did not!—in her plain blue dress and with her hair dressed as she had always worn it at the Burnabys'.

The Duchess of Bridgwater, his mother, was an elegant, gracious lady. She looked like a duchess. The ladies with her—his sisters?—all had illustrious-sounding titles. She felt overwhelmed, totally out of her depth. Suddenly, she was almost grateful for the six years of frequent humiliations she had been made to suffer. Those years had taught her always to be calm and dignified, never to crumble in a nasty situation.

She could not even remember the names of the ladies after the duchess had finished presenting her. Yet they were to be her sisters-in-law. The idea was so ludicrous that she almost laughed in her nervousness.

And then *he* was there before her—she had not even noticed him until that moment—taking her hand in his, bowing over it, kissing it. And she remembered in a rush that, yes, of course, this was how he looked. He was tall and elegant. His face was handsome and proud. He was not smiling. His pale gray eyes seemed cold. He had been *kind* to her, she thought desperately. For three days she had talked to him and felt at ease with him. But the thought was crowded out by the knowledge that he was a duke. This grand house belonged to his mother. These ladies—she seemed to remember that one of them was a marchioness, and all of them had titles—were his sisters.

She was his betrothed. No, it was impossible. As she allowed him to lead her toward a love seat, as she seated herself, she felt that the room was without sufficient air. She wanted nothing more than to jump to her feet and race from the room, down the stairs, and out the front door. She wanted to run and run and run. But where? Back to the Pulteney? There was nowhere else to run. London was bewilderingly strange and new to her. At the Pulteney she would have to wait for Cousin Bertha's return. Reality would have to be faced eventually.

Better to face it now.

Cousin Bertha had launched into loud speech. She was telling her audience about the expenses of their journey, about the high cost of rooms at the Pulteney and the exorbitant cost of meals there. She was telling them that she had brought her own bedsheets with her because one could never trust inns and hotels to have changed the linen after the last guests—not to mention the possibility of damp.

"One can never be too sure," she said, dropping her voice confidentially, as if whole armies of hotel servants might be standing with their ears pressed to the drawing room door to hear themselves maligned. "And I thought His Grace would thank me for protecting dear Stephanie from chills and fevers. He would not want to have a bride with the sneezes and a red nose on her wedding night, would he?" She simpered.

Someone had placed a cup and saucer in Stephanie's hand. She did not know quite how they had got there. The cup was filled with tea. She touched the handle with the fingers of one hand, but she knew that she would not be able to lift the cup successfully to her lips. The duke was commending Cousin Bertha on her careful nature and reminding her that the Czar of Russia had stayed at the Pulteney a few years ago.

"Miss Gray." One of the younger ladies—not the marchioness—was smiling at her. She had spoken up determinedly before Cousin Bertha could open her mouth again. "I understand from Alistair that you inherited Sindon Park only very recently and saw it for the first time less than two weeks ago. That must have been exciting. Are you pleased with the property?"

"Yes, thank you," Stephanie said. There was an expectant pause, during which everyone's eyes were on her, including *his*. There must be more to say. She could not think of a single thing.

"Of course she is pleased with it," Cousin Bertha said. "Are you not, my love? She is rather shy, you know. But how could she not be pleased? The furnishings and draperies alone are enough to pay a king's ransom."

"I understand that the park is somewhat celebrated," the duchess said. "Do you admire it, Miss Gray? How would you describe it?"

The park. For one moment she could not bring a single image of it to mind, though she had spent hours every day for a week strolling about it, drinking in the wonder and the beauty and the peace of it all.

"It is very pretty," she said. And then she remembered what she had missed. "Your Grace."

"The rhododendrons were planted there at great expense," Cousin Bertha said. "And the roses must have cost a minor fortune, I declare. There are two large rose arbors, Your Grace. Not one, but two. But then money is not lacking for such extravagant shows at Sindon. Mr. Cavendish always says that the visitors who come by the dozens every year to view the park should be charged for the privilege. But I always declare that those who are wealthy should be willing to share a little of their wealth free of charge. Would you not agree?" She smiled about at the ladies and at the duke.

The Duke of Bridgwater gravely agreed and mentioned the lime avenue at Sindon as a feature of the park he had particularly admired.

"Miss Gray," one of the younger ladies said—also not the marchioness, "do have a cake. Let me set your cup and saucer on this little table beside you so that your hands will be free." She smiled warmly.

"Thank you," Stephanie said, relinquishing the cup and saucer with some relief. And then the plate of cakes was offered. "No, thank you."

She had used to visit in the parish with her mother—and alone after her mother's passing. She had even visited frequently at the big house, where Squire Reaves had six daughters as well as a son, some of them older than she, some of them younger. She had never had problems conversing with people of any age or social level. Visiting had always been one of her greatest pleasures. Even during her years as a governess she had occasionally taken the children visiting or received visitors in the nursery. She had always accomplished both with the greatest of ease.

She sat now in the Duchess of Bridgwater's drawing room as if she had never learned any of the social niceties at her mother's knee. She could seem to volunteer nothing to the conversation. When questions were asked her in an attempt to draw her into the conversation, she could seem to make only monosyllabic answers. Her mind was blank and paralyzed with dismay—something that had never happened to her before.

She was horrifyingly aware of the ghastly impression they were making, she and Cousin Bertha. Cousin Bertha was embarrassingly loud and vulgar, but Stephanie could not censure her—at least she was making an attempt to converse. Stephanie, on the other hand, was saying almost nothing. She was painfully aware of her appearance in contrast with that of the other ladies, and of her muteness.

They were all being exceedingly polite. But what must they really think of her? And of the Duke of Bridgwater's betrothal to her?

She half raised her eyes to look at him, but found at the last moment that she did not have the courage to meet his eyes. Suddenly, she wished fervently that she was back at the Burnabys'.

He had actually kissed her once. His lips had touched hers.

And she was to marry him within a month. They were to live together in the intimacies of marriage.

And then Cousin Bertha was on her feet and signaling Stephanie with significantly raised eyebrows that it was time to take their leave. Stephanie half stumbled to her feet.

The Duke of Bridgwater spoke at the same moment. "Miss Gray," he said, "perhaps you would do me the honor of driving in the park with me later this afternoon?"

"She would be delighted, Your Grace," Cousin Bertha said. "Would you not, my love? It is Hyde Park you speak of? It is only fitting that the future Duchess of Bridgwater be seen in London's most fashionable spot as soon as possible. You must wear your pink muslin, my love. You will have more frills than any other lady there, I do declare. But then the dress cost a fortune."

"Not today, Alistair," the duchess said, stepping forward with a smile and linking her arm through Stephanie's. "One can see that Miss Gray is still fatigued from her journey. And tomorrow will be a busy one for her. You will be moving here tomorrow, Miss Gray. It will be the best arrangement. It will give us an opportunity to get to know each other at our leisure before your wedding. I am sure Mrs. Cavendish will be delighted to be able to return to her husband far sooner than expected. You will, of course, return for the wedding one month from now, ma'am?"

Stephanie felt too numb to feel fully the dismay she knew she would feel soon. She could not do this. She just could not. Cousin Bertha exclaimed and protested and finally—because she really had no choice in the matter—muttered something about Her Grace being too kind.

"I will walk you downstairs, Miss Gray," the duchess said, retaining her hold on Stephanie's arm. "Alistair will escort you, Mrs. Cavendish."

Stephanie wished desperately to redeem herself before leaving. She had never felt more like an utter dolt in her life. But the duchess spoke again before she could think of anything to say.

"I was the daughter of an earl," she said quietly. "But I had lived all my life in the country—a very secure but very sheltered existence. I can remember the bewilderment with which I faced my first Season in town and the courtship of Alistair's father. I thought I would never be able to measure up to the demands of being a duchess. But it is amazing what can be accomplished with a little courage and a little determination."

"I suspect that more than a little is needed, Your

Grace," Stephanie said, beginning at last to find her tongue.

The duchess patted her hand. "You are quite right," she said. "Sometimes with the passage of time we belittle the efforts we once had to make. With a great deal of courage and determination, then."

"Yes, Your Grace," Stephanie said. When she tried to smile, she found her facial muscles obeying her will for the first time in what seemed to be hours.

The Duke of Bridgwater took her hand in his again as she was leaving and raised it to his lips once more. "Good afternoon, Miss Gray," he said.

"Good afternoon, Your Grace."

She wondered if it would be possible to write that letter to him after all this evening. Or was it too late? She had the feeling that she was being swept along by events quite beyond her control.

7

LORD FRANCIS KNELLER WAS INDEED IN TOWN. THE Duke of Bridgewater met him at White's the following morning. He was looking healthy and sunbrowned, just like a country squire, the duke noticed, though he had not lost his taste for brightly colored and exquisitely tailored coats. This morning's was lime green.

Lord Francis appeared quite happy to set aside his paper in order to converse with his longtime friend. "Bridge," he said, getting to his feet and shaking the duke heartily by the hand, "how are you, old chap? Er, do I congratulate you or commiserate with you?" He grinned a little uncertainly.

Bridgwater raised his eyebrows and fingered the handle of his quizzing glass. "I would hope for congratulations," he said. "Thank you."

They both sat down. "I can remember your saying," Lord Francis said, "that you were going to become a recluse. That you would never again so much as make eye contact with a single young lady for fear that somehow you would be trapped into a match not of your own choosing. It was just before I married Cora—and you were blaming yourself. But apparently it, ah, happened to you anyway."

His Grace paused to take snuff and ignored the last

comment. "And how is Lady Francis?" he asked. "And the children? Well, I hope, after the stay in Yorkshire and the long journey home?"

"Blooming," Lord Francis said with a grin. "We were fortunate that the last one was a girl. Cora was beginning to wonder aloud if it was my ambition to produce a cricket team. And I must admit that one feels remarkably clever to have begotten a daughter. I will have to be very careful not to spoil her quite atrociously."

It was a marriage that had turned out remarkably well, considering its very inauspicious beginning, the duke thought somewhat gloomily. Lord Francis Kneller, son and brother to a duke, had been forced to offer for the daughter of a Bristol merchant after twice publicly compromising her—both times quite inadvertently. And Bridgwater *had* blamed himself. Cora Downes had been his mother's protégée at the time, and it was the duke himself who had presented Kneller to her and asked him to dance with her and bring her into fashion.

During the six years since then, His Grace had met them on a number of occasions, most recently in Yorkshire at the Earl of Thornhill's. There was no doubt that there was a fondness between the two of them and a contentment—and probably even that elusive something called love.

"We had been home at Sidley for only two weeks," Lord Francis said with a sigh, "when Cora began her annual rumblings. It was not right for her to force me to rusticate just because she is most contented in the country and the country is the best environment for the children. I must come to town for a month—and she must come too because she cannot bear to be a whole month without my company, and the children must come too because she could not possibly live through a whole month without them. I have learned from experience, Bridge, that one does not argue with Cora when her mind is bent on selflessness and sacrifice. It is pointless for me to argue that I am most happy when pottering about my own estate and partaking of my wife's companionship and romping with my sons—Annabelle is too young to be romped with yet." He sighed again and then chuckled.

"A month," the duke said. "You must come to my wedding then, Kneller. At St. George's, of course."

Lord Francis sobered. "Of course," he said. "Thank you. Cora will be pleased. Your betrothed is in London, Bridge? Miss Gray, is it? Yes, of course Miss Gray. I read the announcement in the paper just before you arrived."

"She arrived two days ago," the duke said. "She put up at the Pulteney, but she is moving to my mother's house this morning." His mother had been going to fetch her. And no, it would be best if he did not accompany her, she had told him when he had suggested it.

"We will see her this afternoon, then?" Lord Francis asked. "In the park? I will be sure to be there with Cora. We are both eager to meet her—dying of curiosity is how Cora puts it. You will escort her to the Burchell ball this evening?"

"No," His Grace said. "Neither, in fact. She is, ah, still tired after her journey. And this morning's move will fatigue her further." It was not a convincing excuse to give, he realized even as he gave it. What sort of a delicate blossom would still be tired after a journey made two days ago—from Hampshire? And how fatiguing would it be to drive in his mother's carriage from the Pulteney to his mother's house? Servants would look after her luggage, after all.

Lord Francis looked uncomfortable. It would be general knowledge throughout the polite world of London by now, of course, that he was marrying in haste a woman he had met and compromised only two weeks ago, a woman who was a considerable heiress, but one who had been a governess for the past six years and a mere country clergyman's daughter before that. Curiosity about her and about their relationship must be rife. He wondered if it was also general knowledge that they had spent three days and two nights together on the road. He did not doubt that it was.

"As soon as she is receiving," Lord Francis said, "Cora will call on her at your mother's house. She will probably go with the Countess of Greenwald, her particular friend. Have you been to Tattersall's this week, Bridge? I wandered about there for an hour or two and was almost tempted to bid on a pair of cattle I have no need of whatsoever. That is what the tedium of town life does to a man."

The conversation moved into comfortable channels, until they were joined by a group of other gentlemen, all intent on congratulating the Duke of Bridgwater on his betrothal.

He walked home alone a couple of hours later. He would change and call on his mother—and on Stephanie Gray, of course. He drew a steadying breath. His female relatives had been swift in their judgments the afternoon before as soon as he and his mother had returned to the drawing room.

"Alistair," his sister Elizabeth had said, blunt and severe as always, "she is quite impossible. That dreadfully unstylish dress. And her hair! I have known governesses who are more elegant. And she has no conversation whatsoever."

"Oh, Lizzie," Jane had said reproachfully, "she was *shy*. And she really is rather pretty. I am sure she will acquit herself better next time."

"It must have been somewhat daunting," Louise had said, "paying her first call on Mother and finding all of us here too. But that dreadfully vulgar creature who came here with her! I was waiting for her to ask the cost of the tea service."

"You are talking," the duke had said, standing very still just inside the door, feeling fury clutch with cold claws at his insides, "about my betrothed. And about her relative. I will have nothing said against her. I will have her spoken to and about only with the respect due my future duchess. Is that clearly understood?"

Their faces had told him that it was. But his mother had come into the room behind him. She had proceeded unhurriedly to her chair and sat down. She had invited him to do likewise.

"It is not well-bred to criticize people behind their backs," she had said, "especially when they are people who are to have close ties with this family. On the other hand, Alistair, there are certain truths that cannot be swept under the carpet, so to speak. Miss Gray is not at the moment anywhere near fit to be your duchess. And Mrs. Cavendish is in no way fit to be her chaperon during the coming month. Do sit down, dear."

He had leapt to his feet at her words, ready to vent his spleen once more. She had waited for him to overcome his fit of fury and seat himself once more before resuming.

"Miss Gray is Alistair's betrothed," she had said. "However rashly done it was, the fact is that he offered for her and was accepted. The announcement has already been delivered to the papers and will appear in tomorrow morning's editions. We cannot alter the facts, even if we wished to do so. Miss Gray is to be Alistair's wife, my daughter-in-law, and everyone else's sister-in-law."

"But Mama—" Elizabeth had said.

His mother had held up a staying hand. "The only thing we can do to alter the situation and make it more to everyone's liking," she had said, "is to make sure that by the time of the wedding in one month's time Miss Gray is fit to be Alistair's bride. She will move here tomorrow, and I shall take her under my wing. The task is not hopeless. She does have some beauty, as Jane pointed out. And I would also agree that she is shy, that perhaps it was a mistake to invite her to tea with all of us when she had never met even me and had not seen Alistair for a week and a half. I will see what can be accomplished during the coming month. I am confident that a great deal can."

"I will not have her changed, Mama," the duke had said stiffly. "I like her well enough as she is."

"Alistair!" Elizabeth had said in disbelief.

"For her own good there must be some changes," his mother had replied. "Even if you are too stubborn and too loyal to admit in public that she will just not do as she is, Alistair, you must surely see that she will be miserably unhappy if someone does not take her in hand. I will do that. You may trust me not to be harsh or contemptuous with her. She is to be my daughter-in-law, my son's wife, the mother of some of my grandchildren. I hope to have a relationship of affection and respect with her for many years to come. Go home, dear, and go about your daily activities as usual. I shall summon you when she is ready for you."

"I shall come with you to the Pulteney to fetch her here tomorrow, Mama," he had said.

"No, dear," she had told him quite firmly. "She will be bewildered. She is in a strange city and will be leaving a cousin who is still strange to her in order to take up residence with another stranger. She will not need the discomfort of your taciturn presence."

"I was *not* taciturn," he had protested, realizing even as he spoke that it should have been beneath his dignity to argue with his mother. "It seems to me that only I made an effort to converse with Mrs. Cavendish."

"And you virtually ignored your betrothed," his mother had replied.

Because he had felt horribly as if he had been on public display. How must she have felt, then?

"I will take her driving in the park tomorrow, then," he had said. "She will need to be introduced to the *ton*. That will be a fairly informal setting for her first appearance. Less intimidating than a soirée or a ball would be."

His mother had clucked her tongue. "Alistair," she had said, "how would the *ton* treat her if she appeared in the park dressed as she was this afternoon? Or in what I would guess to be the monstrosity of pink frills Mrs. Cavendish made mention of? We must be fair to her, dear. When she appears for the first time, she must look presentable. I look forward to seeing her lovely hair dressed properly—what a glorious color it is. Did you not admire it, Louise? No, Miss Gray will not appear in the park or anywhere else for at least a week. I would suggest that you stay away from her for that time too, Alistair, until she feels more the thing and can greet you with more confidence."

"No," he had said. "Absolutely not, Mama. She is my *betrothed*. I will call on her here tomorrow afternoon. You will wish to chaperon her, of course. But I would be obliged if you will contrive to leave us alone for a short while."

He had refused to allow her to shift him from that decision. And so now, walking home from White's, he planned his visit and wondered how awkward it would be to sit in his mother's drawing room and try to make conversation with Miss Gray while his mother listened. Would she leave them alone?

He had been quite as dismayed as the ladies during yesterday afternoon's visit. She had appeared quite unlovely and quite without character, sitting mute and ex-

pressionless in her unstylish blue dress, her hair scraped
back into an unbecoming bun. She had not eaten a bite
or even sipped her tea. She had spoken only when questioned directly, and then had answered in monosyllables. She had not once looked into his eyes. She had
given him no chance to converse with her, even if he
had wanted to.

He had felt panic. *This* was the woman with whom
he had committed himself to spend the rest of his life?

But neither the dismay nor the panic had lasted. He
had been saved partly by the unfavorable reactions of
his relatives. How dared they stand in judgment on her
when he was the one who had trapped her into this and
when she had so clearly been desperately uncomfortable? And he had been saved partly by memory.

He thought of her now as she had been during those
three days—garish and vulgar in appearance, but refined in speech and manner. Oh, yes, he could see that
clearly now that he knew the truth. The vulgarity had
never extended beyond those unspeakable outer garments. He thought of her smiles, which he had interpreted as coquettish at the time, but which he now
realized had been merely smiles. He thought of the stories she had told him, talking with warmth and anima-
tion about a very ordinary childhood and girlhood,
talking with intelligence about books and about children and teaching.

How could he ever have made the mistake he had
made? It seemed unbelievable now that he had based his
whole opinion of her on a fuchsia cloak and on a brightly
plumed pink bonnet. Was he to base his new opinion
of her on an unstylish blue dress and a mute social
manner—and on the vulgarity of her companion?

He owed her better than that.

And he remembered too—of course—the ravishing
woman he had glimpsed that first night, leaning back on

her arms on the bed, her face lifted in ecstasy, her wavy auburn hair swaying from side to side against her back.

Oh, no, she was not unlovely. Not by any means. It was still easy to feel a stirring of the intense desire he had felt for her on that evening.

But who was the real Stephanie Gray? He did not know. But he must get to know. If his marriage was to stand any chance whatsoever of being a workable one, he must find out who she was, and he must learn to respect and even like what he found. His mother must not be allowed to change her too drastically.

He quickened his step. He was becoming distinctly nervous about this afternoon's visit, just as he had been about yesterday's.

SHE WAS WEARING her blue dress again. The duchess had suggested that she wear something different today, but even Her Grace had agreed after inspecting her meager wardrobe that after all the blue was the only possibility.

"The gray is just too plain and even shabby," Her Grace said. "And the other dresses are . . . well, monstrous, if you will forgive plain speaking, dear. Do I detect the hand of Mrs. Cavendish in the selecting of them?"

"Yes, Your Grace," Stephanie said. "She assured me that they were all the crack, though I loathed them even before they were made." She felt disloyal saying so, but she was appalled to think that the duchess might think they represented her taste.

"I have a few maids who will go into transports of delight over the prospect of owning them," Her Grace said. "And would you be more comfortable calling me Mother? Perhaps you would more easily forget that I am a person who inspires awe in you."

Stephanie was not sure a name would make any difference. It was the regal grace and the unconscious arrogance and the self-assurance of her future mother-in-law that awed her. "Yes, thank you," she said, "Mother."

"I will call you Stephanie," the duchess announced. It was not a question. "It is a pretty name."

And so only the blue dress would do until tomorrow, when she was to spend all day—the duchess had stressed the fact that it would be *all day*—at a fashionable modiste's, being outfitted from the skin out for every possible occasion that might present itself for the next six months or so.

"We will not look beyond that," Her Grace said in a quite matter-of-fact voice. "If all is as it should be, you will need larger, looser clothes for the following six months."

It took Stephanie a few moments to grasp her meaning. She blushed scarlet when she did so.

Her Grace was to hire a maid for Stephanie—the maid from home was paid handsomely and sent back there. In the meanwhile, the duchess's own maid was brought to Stephanie's dressing room to dress her hair. The curls and ringlets that resulted were not as grotesque as the ones produced yesterday had been. They actually made her look elegant and even handsome. The duchess viewed the final effect with her head to one side and a thoughtful look on her face.

"No," Stephanie said at last. She had vowed last night at the Pulteney, during a long and sleepless night, that she was not going to be awed into incoherence again. But that was more easily said than done, of course. She was trembling now. "It is very fine, Marie. Is it not, Your Gr . . . Mother? But it is not *me*. I . . . No, I cannot."

"Perhaps for a ball," the duchess said. "Certainly it shows off your finest feature to advantage. But if you would be happier with something a little simpler for the afternoon, then Marie will oblige you. But not yesterday's or this morning's severe knot, Stephanie. Let us compromise on something between the two extremes, shall we?"

They did so, and both seemed pleased with the result. Stephanie's hair was brushed smoothly but softly back from her face and curled simply behind.

"Yes," Stephanie said. "Yes, I like it. Thank you so very much, Marie. How clever you are with your hands. I am afraid I have given you a great deal of work, forcing you to change the very skilled style you gave me first." She smiled at the maid in the looking glass.

"It will do quite nicely," Her Grace agreed and nodded dismissal to the maid. She waited for Marie to leave the room and close the door behind her before speaking quite kindly. "There is no need to thank servants, Stephanie. A cool compliment now and then is quite sufficient. Certainly one does not need to be apologetic about the amount of work one is causing. Servants are hired and paid to work."

Stephanie, still seated on the dressing table stool, stared at her future mother-in-law's image. She flushed. How gauche she must seem. And yet she did not know that she could ever become oblivious to servants as many employers, even the Burnabys, seemed to be. Servants were people.

"I am sorry, Mother," she said.

Her Grace smiled. "You are to be a duchess, Stephanie," she said. "You will be expected to look and act the part. Much of it is nonsense, of course, but that is life. You must learn to tread the fine line between pride and conceit. You must expect to be looked up to by everyone except royalty. You will accomplish that by always being gracious but never being overfamiliar. It will be easier for you in future if you can cultivate the correct manner from the start. It will be a week before we can have enough clothes made for you to enable you to mingle comfortably with your peers. We will use that week to prepare you in other ways too. It will not be as daunting as you perhaps fear. Once you have accepted in your mind and your body and your emotions that you are no one's inferior—you are to be Alistair's *bride,* his *duchess*—you will no longer fear having to meet the *ton.* Most of the *ton* will be your social inferiors."

"You knew that I was afraid yesterday?" Stephanie asked.

The duchess raised her eyebrows. "I *hope* you were afraid," she said. "I would hate to think that you can do no better than you did then."

Stephanie grimaced.

"Even now," Her Grace said, "you are by no means a nobody. Your father was a gentleman and your mother a lady. And you are a wealthy woman—an independently wealthy woman, which is a rare distinction. There are not many women who are the sole owners of properties like Sindon Park. Alistair is coming to tea, dear. He will be here soon. He was brought up from birth to know that one day he would be a duke and head of his family. He has been both for almost eleven years since the death of my husband. He has all the pride of manner and all the stiff dignity that have been bred into him. He is very like his father. In order to please him, you must become his equal. You will not do that by cowering before him and being afraid even to look him in the eye. It will not be a good marriage, Stephanie, if it is an unequal one. I shall leave you alone for half an hour this afternoon. You must converse with him."

Her Grace had not mentioned until now that he was coming to tea. Stephanie had thought she would not see him again until she was deemed presentable. He must have been very displeased with her yesterday. His manner had been aloof, even though he had been perfectly polite, especially toward Cousin Bertha, whom the other ladies had all but cut.

Was it true, what the duchess had said? If she made herself into the person the duchess wanted her to be, would she please him? Would she find it easier to lead the life she must lead as his duchess? Would her marriage have a better chance of success?

But did she want to change herself? She had always been conscious of her imperfections—how could she not be as the daughter of a clergyman?—and she had always striven to become a better person. But on the whole she had been satisfied with the person she was. Was she now to make herself into an imitation of her future mother-in-law? Was she to think and feel and move and behave toward others as if she were superior to everyone but the royal family? Her father had always taught her to think of herself as the equal of everyone, but to behave as if she were the lowliest of servants even to the poorest of the poor. Her father had exaggerated the matter, of course, but even so—arrogance and the assumption of superiority seemed alien to her nature.

Did she want to change that much?

Did she want to please him? But she *must* please him. His kindness and his courtliness had led him to this—to having to marry a woman who was in no way suited to be his wife.

She would give anything, she thought—almost anything on earth—to release herself from this terrible mess. She felt as if she were living through a nightmare.

And yet the idea was laughable. She had been a governess and was now a wealthy, propertied woman. She had been a clergyman's daughter and was now to be a duchess. She had been a lonely spinster of six-and-twenty and was now to marry a handsome, influential man. And it was all a nightmare?

"Come, Stephanie," the duchess was saying, "we will

go down to the drawing room and await Alistair's arrival. Lift your chin, dear? Ah, yes. Already you look more the part. Remember always to keep it raised. You are *someone*. You are going to be the Duchess of Bridgwater in just one month's time."

And she was going to see the Duke of Bridgwater in just a few minutes' time, Stephanie thought. She wondered if he would seem as much a stranger to her as he had seemed yesterday. She shivered and remembered to keep her chin up as she followed her future mother-in-law down the stairs.

8

SHE WAS WEARING THE SAME DRESS AS SHE HAD WORN the day before. Her face was still pale, and she still had dark smudges beneath her eyes, as if she had not slept well for several nights. Probably she had not, he thought. Neither had he. She was still unsmiling. Only her hair was different. Not a great deal, it was true. It was still combed straight back from her face and over her head and knotted at the back. Except that it was not scraped back quite so severely. It seemed softer and shinier. And the knot was composed of a few small, discreet curls.

She still looked like a governess.

But today she looked almost pretty again.

"Miss Gray." He bowed over her hand—it was as cold as it had been yesterday—and raised his eyes to hers. Today she looked back at him. Today he remembered those unusual golden flecks in her eyes.

"Your Grace," she said almost in a whisper.

They were no further forward than they had been yesterday at this time.

"Do show Stephanie to a seat, Alistair," his mother said. "And be seated yourself. You may stand and look impressively ducal when you are delivering a speech in the House of Lords, but here you are my son—and my guest."

Ah. So his mother was calling her Stephanie already, was she? It was more than he was doing. He wondered if his mother truly believed that the task she had set herself was a possible one.

They talked at some length about the weather, which was cloudy and chilly and no different from what it had been for the past week or more. They talked about the Pulteney Hotel, since it had been mentioned, and he and his mother told Miss Gray about the visit to which he had alluded yesterday. The Czar of Russia and his sister had stayed at the hotel while in London with other European dignitaries, celebrating Europe's first victory over Napoleon Bonaparte—before Waterloo. And he spoke of Waterloo until his mother fixed him with a sharp glance, and he remembered that a battle did not make suitable drawing room conversation for the hearing of ladies.

Stephanie Gray spoke today in more than monosyllables, though not significantly more. For half an hour his mother and he carried the weight of the conversation, until his mother got to her feet and he jumped to his. Half an hour and he was being treated as a guest. It was time to take his leave. But that was not his mother's intention.

"I have some business to take care of abovestairs," she said, smiling graciously. "Perhaps you will keep Stephanie company, Alistair, until I return. We would not wish her to feel lonely on her first day here, would we? I will be no longer than half an hour."

Ah, so she had remembered. He was glad of it, though he did not know what they would talk about. But good Lord, they had spent almost three days together not so long ago and there had been very few silences, and none of those had been uncomfortable.

He hurried across the room in order to hold the door open for his mother. She smiled reassuringly as she passed him. He closed the door and stood facing it for a moment, considering his next move. But when he turned, it was to find Stephanie Gray's eyes full upon him.

"It is just not going to work, is it?" she said. "I believe it would be better if I went back to Sindon and we forgot all about this disaster of a betrothal. It *is* a disaster, is it not?"

He walked slowly back across the room, resisted the temptation to stand before the fireplace, where he would feel in control, and took a seat close to hers. "It is because you are shy?" he asked. "This has been an ordeal for you?"

Her lips twitched, but she did not quite smile. "I have never been shy," she said. "No one has ever said it of me before. I just do not know this world, Your Grace. It is quite alien to me. Trying to live in it would be an embarrassment to me and worse than that for you. You have been kind to me. I still consider myself deeply in your debt and always will. I still feel responsible for this situation. But it just will not do. I will tell Her Grace so myself. I will explain to her that none of the blame must fall upon you. You have acted throughout as a true gentleman."

There was color in her cheeks again and light in her eyes. She looked more like his fuchsia ladybird again, though he must not encourage himself to think of her in those terms. Guilt gnawed at him for a moment. She was *not* responsible. The blame was his.

"You are awed by titles and fashionable dress and manners," he said. "It is understandable, but they are all superficial, you know. People are people when all is said and done."

"I think," she said, half smiling again, "you really believe that. You are wrong. You would not like having me as your duchess, Your Grace. And I would not like being a duchess. It would be foolish, then, to press on with this betrothal merely because at the time it seemed to you the honorable thing to do to offer for me. And because I was weak enough to consent."

Her eyelashes, he noticed when she lowered her eyes to look at her hands, were darker than her hair. They were thick and long.

"The betrothal has been announced," he said. "The notice was in this morning's papers."

"Yes, I know." She looked up at him again. "And so another notice must be sent correcting the first."

"There would be scandal," he said.

"I care nothing for scandal," she said. "And *you* will not be touched deeply by it. Your rank will protect you. I shall return to Sindon and be far enough away. I shall see if Mr. Watkins can find another husband for me within the next three months or so—one whose rank will not intimidate me."

"No one," he said softly, "will marry a woman who has just scandalized society with a broken betrothal."

She bit her lip. It was quite apparent to him that she had not known that. "Then I shall go back to my old life," she said. "I shall take another governess's post."

"Do you think," he asked, "that your former employers will give you a character when you walked out of their house early one morning without even giving notice?"

Her face was pale again. The shadows beneath her eyes were noticeable. Her eyes were fixed on his.

Why was he so diligently dissuading her from doing what she so clearly wanted to do? he wondered. He had felt the impossibility of it just as powerfully as she— especially since yesterday afternoon. Was it because he dreaded the scandal the breaking of the betrothal would bring on him? Or was it because, as he had just explained to her, she was in an impossible situation? He could *not* let her go.

She got to her feet suddenly and hurried across the room to stand facing one of the windows, where he had stood the day before watching for her arrival. He stayed where he was and watched her. She looked even more slender than she had during those three days. He wondered if she had been unable to eat as well as to sleep during the past week and a half. He remembered the trembling eagerness—though she had tried hard to hide it—with which she had eaten her soup on that first day.

He wondered briefly how innocence would feel beneath him on a bed on his wedding night. He had only ever known experienced women. And he remembered his assumption that she was very experienced indeed. If all had been as he had thought it was, she would have been his mistress now for almost two weeks. He would have been almost as familiar with that tall, lithe body as he was with his own. Well, in one month's time he would begin the lifelong acquirement of familiarity.

It was not by any means an unpleasant thought. If only that were all that was involved in his marriage!

"You will adjust to your new life," he said. "You have a lady's birth and education, after all. And my mother will be a good teacher. You can learn everything you need to know from her. She has not been . . . harsh with you today, I trust?"

"No," she said quickly, without turning. "No, of course she has not. She has been very kind. This must not be easy for her. She must be hating every moment. She must have had high hopes for her elder son."

He got to his feet and walked toward her. "She will be proud of you," he said, "and she will grow to love you. Over the coming week she will help you be fitted for clothes suited to your new station and she will help you learn some of the basic facts of a duchess's life. After that we will introduce you to Society between us. I look forward to it. You will take well. You are very lovely."

She lowered her head for a moment, but she did not immediately respond in words.

"Very well, then," she said at last. "I will learn how to dress and how to behave so that I will not shame you as I did yesterday, Your Grace. I will learn how to be a duchess."

He grimaced. "You did not shame me," he said. "I and my mother and sisters understood that you were somewhat overwhelmed by the occasion. It was thoughtless of me to have allowed it. I should have waited on you first at the Pulteney. I should have presented you first to my mother alone."

"You were not to know how it would be," she said, hunching her shoulders briefly. "Any lady from your world would have known what to expect and how to behave. She would not have been overwhelmed by the occasion."

He set his hands lightly against her upper arms. "You did not shame me," he said again. "And you will quickly learn to feel more comfortable in your new world. We will all help you—my mother and I, Jane, Louise . . ." He hesitated, but did not add Elizabeth's name.

She laughed and hunched her shoulders again. "Jane, Louise," she said. "I do not even know who they are. I do not even remember their titles or their other names. I am not even sure I would recognize them if I saw them again. I—"

"Give yourself time," he said.

She stood very still, her head down before nodding and turning to face him. "A week," she said. "We will have to hope that I am an apt pupil. We will have to hope that at the end of the week, when I leave this house to appear in Society, I will have learned enough not to disgrace you."

His hands had returned to her upper arms after she

had turned. They were almost thin. "Promise me something," he said, looking into her eyes.

"What?" she said. "Have I not promised enough?"

"Promise me that you will sleep at night and eat at mealtimes," he said. "You have not been doing much of either, have you?"

She smiled fleetingly. "I wonder," she said, "how much Cinderella ate and slept in the weeks prior to her wedding."

"Try," he said. "Promise me that you will try."

"Very well," she said. "I promise."

He remembered touching his lips to hers briefly that first night at the inn, when he had expected that his kiss would be the mere prelude to the full feast, when he had thought that she had openly invited him to the feast. He remembered that he had been sexually aroused even before the kiss. She had looked so achingly lovely and so mouth-wateringly desirable arched back on the bed with her face lifted and her eyes closed.

"May I kiss you?" he asked.

Her eyes widened, and she flushed.

"We are betrothed," he said. "May I kiss you?"

He thought for a moment that she would not answer at all. Then she nodded almost imperceptibly.

Her lips were closed and immobile. Warm. She smelled of soap, he thought as he lifted his own away from them. He had not realized until that moment how much he associated sexual passion with strong perfumes. He liked the soap smell. He preferred it.

Her eyes were on him. Wary.

He set his arms loosely about her before kissing her again, one about her waist, the other about her shoulders. She lost her balance and came swaying against him, her hands spread against his chest. There were no voluptuous curves, he thought, and yet she felt utterly feminine. She had long, slim legs. He kept his kiss light and undemanding, though he parted his lips to taste her and ran his tongue once slowly across the seam of her lips.

"You have never kissed before," he said as he lifted his head and released his hold of her. He wished immediately that he had not said it—he had done so only because the delightful novelty of it had somewhat dazed him. It was one more humiliation for her. He could see it as soon as her eyes dropped from his.

"The only chances I have had to kiss," she said, "have been with gentlemen who wanted a great deal more than just kisses."

He wondered if she too was remembering that first night.

"You will not be subjected to such indignities or to such humiliation ever again," he said softly. "My honor on it."

"This too," she said equally quietly, looking down at her hands, "I will learn in time with you as my teacher. I will try to be a diligent pupil, Your Grace. I am ignorant in so many ways, am I not?" Her voice sounded a little bitter.

"Ah, but it is ignorance," he said, "or rather innocence that a man hopes to find in his bride, Miss Gray. Do not apologize for yours. Yes, I will teach you. And you will teach me. We will each learn how to please the other. Now, I believe I will take my leave even before my mother returns. I believe you would appreciate some time to yourself, some time to sleep perhaps before dinner?"

"Yes," she said. "Thank you."

"Come," he said, "I will escort you to the stairs. I will leave word for my mother that you are resting."

He drew her arm through his and set his hand over hers. A few moments later he watched her climb the stairs to her room before he descended to the hall and left the house after giving his message to a footman.

He had no more idea than when he had arrived if this thing was going to be possible or not. All he did know was that it was impossible to go back or to try to change the situation. Like it or not, he was going to be a married man by this time next month. He was going to be married to Miss Stephanie Gray. She was an intelligent woman, he thought, with a natural refinement of manner, even if she had little confidence in her ability to be a duchess. His mother would see to it that she was brought up to snuff within the next week. And together he and his mother would polish the product and prune away its raw edges in the three weeks that would remain before the wedding.

Yes, she would take, he thought. He really did feel more confident than he had felt yesterday—considerably more confident. And there was something else too that helped him sit back in his carriage and relax against the velvet seats.

He was going to enjoy the intimate side of the marriage. As the flamboyant actress he had taken her for, he had wanted her. But as Miss Stephanie Gray, his betrothed, she was just as desirable. Perhaps more so. He really had found her innocence—her total lack of understanding of what a kiss could be—almost erotic.

Yes, today he felt considerably more cheerful.

SHE FELT LESS cheerful than she had felt before his visit—if that was possible. Until then, she realized afterward, she had never been quite convinced that her betrothal was irrevocable. Bad as things had seemed, she had been able to tell herself that she could put an end to it, find herself another husband within the appointed time, or even go back to her old way of life as a last resort.

Now she knew that there was no going back. Only forward. But how could she go forward? It was impossible. Only by changing herself completely could she fit herself for her new life. And how could she change herself completely when she was already six-and-twenty? And when certain principles and attitudes and ideas were ingrained in her? And when she basically liked herself the way she was?

But change she must. And if she must change, then she would give herself a good reason for changing—a really good one. She would change for *him*. She would never forget how he had saved her from certain misery and terror and from possible death just two weeks before. And she would never forget how courteous he had been—except for that one small lapse when she had inadvertently tempted him. Of how he had treated her like a *person* even when others were looking askance at her because of her appearance. She would never forget how he had insisted on taking her all the way to Sindon Park, even though he had obviously realized that he was going to feel honor bound to offer her marriage. And she would never forget how he had urged her to accept and how he had continued to urge her today, just so that she would not suffer disgrace.

She owed him everything, even her life.

And yet, she was quite sure that he must be as reluctant about this marriage as she could possibly be. He was a young and a handsome man. He was a wealthy man and a duke. He had everything with which to attract any woman he cared to choose as a wife. Yet he had been forced—by his own gallantry—to take her. She wondered if he had ever had dreams of love. She did not know a great deal about men, but she imagined that they must have such dreams just as much as women did.

She would change for him then—in order to make him a worthy duchess. And in order to . . . please him. That was the term he had used. They would teach each other, he had said. They would each learn to please the other. She knew nothing about pleasing a man. But she drew comfort from the fact that he had told her men hoped for ignorance and innocence in their brides. He would have both in full measure with her. She knew nothing.

She had been shocked to the core of her being by his kiss. His lips had been parted—she had felt the warmth and moisture of his mouth against her lips. She had tasted him. And he had touched her with his *tongue*. Perhaps what had shocked her most, though, was her reaction. She had felt the kiss not only with her lips. She had felt it with her body, with a rush of strange sensation to her breasts and to the most secret parts of her body. Her legs had almost collapsed under her.

Oh yes, he would have his innocent, right enough.

She would change for him—for his sake.

And so the following day—and again four days after that—she stood uncomplaining for hours on end while the duchess's own modiste measured her and pinned fabrics to her and showed her endless patterns and bolts of fabric and lengths of trimmings. She listened meekly to Her Grace's advice and to the modiste's and only occasionally insisted on disagreeing. She felt incredulity at the number of different clothes for all occasions that were deemed the bare essentials for her during the next six months—of course she was expected to be *increasing* by that time. But she said nothing.

At home—at the duchess's home—she sat for more hours on end unmoving while Patty, her bright and talkative and skilled new maid, dressed and redressed her hair in a dizzying number and variety of styles. And she listened to Her Grace's judgment on each and resisted the urge each time to grab her brush and pull furiously at the elegant creations.

At home too she trailed about the house after the duchess, listening to that lady's conversations with her housekeeper, her cook, and her butler. She memorized both Her Grace's manner of speaking and her way of taking command of her own household. She genuinely admired the quiet firmness with which Her Grace treated all her servants, but she wondered if there would be any harm in a little more warmth. She quelled the thought. If this was how a duchess ran her household, then she would learn the way. She would not disgrace him when the time came by trying to make friends of his servants.

In the duchess's private sitting room, where they often sat for long stretches of time stitching away at their embroidery—Stephanie preferred that to the endless piles of mending and darning with which she had been expected to occupy her evenings at the Burnabys'— she listened and learned about the *ton,* about Society manners and morals. She learned all the small details that would help her avoid embarrassment and awkwardness—like the fact that at a ball she must dance with the same gentleman, even her betrothed, no more than twice in one evening, or that the sort of curtsy with which she might greet a lady or gentleman of no title must differ from the one with which she would show respect to a dowager countess or duchess. And her curtsies now, when she was merely Miss Stephanie Gray, must be more deferential to all than they would be when she became the Duchess of Bridgwater.

She learned that after her marriage she must expect to see little of her husband. It would be considered bad *ton* if they lived in each other's pocket. Men had their own pursuits and did not appreciate clinging, possessive wives. If her husband chose to keep a mistress after his marriage—Her Grace spoke about it quite as matter-offactly as she had spoken about everything else—then she must pretend not to know. It was ill-bred to be jealous. And if she chose to take a lover, it must be done with the utmost discretion and only *after* she had presented the duke with a son.

"It is my hope, of course," Her Grace added, "that Alistair will be faithful to you. But he is a grown man and head of this family. He will make his own decisions. I say these things only so that you will understand the rules, Stephanie. It is of the utmost importance that you know the rules and abide by them."

She learned the rules, carefully and meticulously committing them all to memory so that she would not make any gauche blunders when she appeared in Society herself. She would not make mistakes. She would not shame him.

He did not call upon her again during that week. Neither did anyone else. Apart from the two lengthy visits to Bond Street and Her Grace's modiste, she spent the week inside the duchess's home, seeing no one except Her Grace and the servants.

But the day finally came when a staggeringly large number of parcels was delivered to the house and the modiste arrived at the same time. Stephanie's new wardrobe was ready. She had to try on every one of the clothes while the duchess and the dressmaker looked critically at them and a few minor adjustments were made.

Stephanie, it seemed, was ready to meet the *ton*. There was to be a ball the following evening at the home of the Marquess of Hayden. It was a ball being given in honor of the Duke of Bridgwater's betrothal to Miss Stephanie Gray.

The Marchioness of Hayden, Stephanie remembered belatedly, was the duke's sister.

"I could have wished for some smaller, quieter enter-

tainment for your first appearance, Stephanie," Her
Grace said. "But it is as well to start this way, perhaps.
And you are quite ready, my dear. I have seen during the
past week that you learn fast and that you have made
every effort to learn. I am very pleased with you. Alistair
will be equally delighted. He will come tomorrow to escort us to Hayden's for dinner and the ball to follow it."

Stephanie drew a slow breath. She would not disgrace
him, she thought. He would look at her and be pleased.
He would watch her through the evening and be satisfied.

Oh, she hoped she would not disgrace him. She owed
him so very much. She must repay him at least in this
very small way.

The thought of seeing him again set her stomach to
fluttering. It was neither a wholly pleasant nor a wholly
unpleasant feeling.

9

$\mathcal{H}$IS MOTHER HAD WORKED MIRACLES IN THE COURSE of a week. That was the Duke of Bridgwater's first reaction when he saw Stephanie on the evening of the Marchioness of Hayden's ball.

He was standing in the hall of his mother's house. He had been told that the ladies were almost ready to leave and had waited for them to come downstairs. His mother came first, looking her usual almost regal self in purple satin with matching plumed turban. He took her hands in his and kissed her on both cheeks.

"As usual, Mama," he said in all sincerity, "you look far too young and far too beautiful to be my mother."

"But," she said, "only a son of mine would have learned so to flatter me, Alistair."

She had come down ahead of Stephanie Gray, he knew, so that all his attention could rest on his betrothed as she descended the staircase. He looked up now to watch her come. And yes, he thought, definitely a miracle had been wrought.

She wore pale green. The underdress was cut low at the bosom and was high-waisted, with one deep flounce at the hem. The overdress was of fine lace. She wore pearls at her throat and about one gloved wrist. Her hair was dressed smoothly at the front and sides, though curled tendrils at her temples and neck softened any suggestion of severity. He could see elaborate curls at the back, even though he had as yet only a mainly frontal view of her.

He could recognize his mother's superb taste in both the deceptive simplicity of the gown and the style of her hair. She looked impeccable and elegant. She would far outshine any of those ladies at the ball—and there would be many of them—who would think to draw attention and admiration by the fussiness of their appearance.

But it was not just the hair and the clothes that made him think of miracles. There was something about *her* that had transformed her from a governess to a duke's fiancée. He had never thought of her as having poor posture, yet there was something now about the set of her shoulders and the straightness of her back that suggested almost a regality—like his mother. And she held her chin high in an expression of pride that stopped well short of conceit.

Her posture and her gown combined emphasized all that was best in her appearance—her tall slimness, her swanlike neck, her long slim legs, clearly outlined as she walked.

"Miss Gray." He waited for her to reach the hall before taking a few steps toward her and stretching out his right hand. When she placed her own in it and curtsied, he bowed over it and raised it to his lips. "I almost did not recognize you." He turned to look at his mother. "You have performed a miracle, Mama."

"Stephanie has been the easiest pupil any teacher could wish for," his mother said. "It is no miracle, Alistair. Hard work has done it."

He looked back to his betrothed. "You are nervous about tonight?" he asked her. She had been half smiling as she descended the stairs. The smile had vanished now.

"A little, I suppose," she admitted.

He squeezed her hand, which he had not yet released.

"You need not be," he said. "You look magnificent, as I am sure your glass and my mother have both informed you. If you remember everything that I am sure she has told you during the past week, you will do very well this evening. If you feel a little uncertain at any time, remember who you are. Remember that you are my betrothed and that soon you will be the Duchess of Bridgwater."

"Yes, Your Grace," she said. "I will remember."

But he knew that she was still nervous. Her eyes had lost some of the sparkle they had had a minute before. Her face looked paler. He felt an unexpected rush of sympathy for her and of protectiveness too. This must all be very difficult for her. He did not doubt that the closest she had ever come to a grand ball was a country assembly when she had still been living at the parsonage. He hoped his mother had thought to brush up on her dancing skills. But he was sure she would not have forgotten something quite so elemental.

His mother led the way out to the carriage while he followed with Miss Gray, her arm resting along the top of his own. He looked reassuringly at her. "Do not fear," he said. "No one seeing you tonight would ever guess that until three weeks ago you were a governess. My sisters will be amazed and delighted by the transformation in you."

She looked up at him briefly before he handed her into the carriage, but she said nothing.

He would have to be careful, he thought. He knew that the temptation would be to hover over her all evening, to try to protect her from the ordeal he knew she would be facing. He must not do it. Nothing would be more certain to make her appear like a gauche rustic who had neither the manners nor the conversation required by the role she was about to assume in Society. He must not ask Elizabeth to seat him next to her at dinner. He must dance with her only twice, and he must not take up his place at her side between sets more than once or twice.

He must trust his mother to see to it that she got through the evening unscathed.

He listened to his mother talk as the carriage made its way through the streets of Mayfair and to Stephanie Gray replying more briefly. She addressed his mother as "Mother," he was interested to note. He did not himself participate in the conversation. He was feeling nervous about the coming evening, he realized—and just a trifle depressed. Why was it that good manners always ensured that one kept one's distance from the very people with whom one would most like to spend most of one's time?

He was surprised to find that in some ways he was beginning to look forward to being married. They seemed to be able to relax a little more when they were alone together than they could when in company with others. He wanted to hear her talk again as she had talked to him in his carriage. He wanted to get to know her. And—the thought seemed strangest of all—he wanted her to get to know him. He had always been a very private person. Nobody, he felt, really knew him. And he had liked it that way—until now.

The carriage slowed outside the doors of his brother-in-law's mansion on Berkeley Square.

THE EVENING WAS going well. She had not yet set even one foot wrong, so to speak. She had done nothing to embarrass herself and nothing to shame either the Duke of Bridgwater or his mother. She had sat next to the Marquess of Hayden at the head of the table at dinner; her future brother-in-law, older than his wife by at least ten or fifteen years, was a man with an enormous sense of his own consequence. She had stood in the receiving line between the marchioness and the duke, since the ball was in honor of her betrothal, and had smiled and curtsied and tried to memorize the names of a seemingly endless stream of guests. She had danced the opening quadrille with the duke and every set thereafter with a different gentleman. She had remembered the steps of every dance and had executed them without mishap. Between sets she had stood with the duchess and a number of other ladies and gentlemen. She had never once been alone.

It was going well. Or so Her Grace assured her. The duchess was pleased with her. She was taking well, it seemed. She looked quite strikingly beautiful—Her Grace's words—and she looked poised and confident without in any way appearing conceited. It did not matter, the duchess assured her, that she had little conversation. The important thing was that she smiled at those who spoke to her and encouraged them with polite questions and responses. Shyness, provided it did not border in any way on muteness or sullenness, was no disadvantage at all in a lady. Quite the contrary. Everyone would know, after all, that she was being elevated on the social scale by her betrothal to Bridgwater. Her shyness would be considered becoming modesty.

All was going well. Except that she was not enjoying herself. She tried, whenever the demands of conversation were not occupying her mind, to understand why this was so. Did she feel uncomfortable? No more than was to be expected. In fact, she was finding that she need behave not very differently from the way she had behaved throughout her years as a governess. Quiet dignity, self-containment, the ability to listen while saying little—these had been a way of life to her for six years. Did she fear that she had failed, then, that she had somehow let the Duke of Bridgwater down? No, she did not feel it. And if she did, she could not disbelieve what his mother told her. Her Grace would have been fast enough to point out any glaring shortcoming.

Everyone had been polite to her. Many had been kind and even friendly. She had not been a wallflower as she had feared she might. She had not lacked for company between sets. No one had treated her with contempt or even noticeable condescension.

The ballroom, with its many mirrors and chandeliers, with its numerous floral decorations, was beautiful. It was filled with elegant, beautiful people. It was the perfect scene she had always dreamed of—the sort of setting she had always imagined for Cinderella's ball. And in many ways she was the personification of the fairy-tale heroine.

Why, then, was she not quite enjoying herself? Was it because after the first set the Duke of Bridgwater had not danced with her again or come near her between sets or even shown any sign that he was aware of her presence in the ballroom? He danced every set. He mingled easily with the company, conversing with people whose identities she had forgotten. He looked thoroughly at home in this, his own environment. And he looked exquisitely elegant and handsome in black evening clothes with gleaming white linen.

Was she hurt by his apparent lack of interest in her? No, she told herself. She had learned from the duchess during the past week—and she had partly known it before that—that it was not considered good manners among the *ton* for a man and his wife or betrothed to cling together as if they could not bear to be out of each other's company in order to enjoy that of others. His behavior was no personal affront to her, but merely evidence of his perfect manners.

She just wished perhaps that occasionally his eyes would alight on her, that he would perhaps smile at her. He had not smiled at her all evening.

She was not allowed to waltz. It seemed that no lady was allowed to perform the dance in London until she had been approved by one of a select group of ladies. It seemed absurd that the rule applied to Stephanie, since she was six-and-twenty years of age, but the Duchess of Bridgwater had told her during the week that it would be unwise to do anything that might raise polite eyebrows—at least until after her marriage.

And so she did not waltz. It was the only set before supper that she missed. But she was not left alone to watch everyone else dance. A lady to whom she had been introduced earlier as the wife of a particular friend of His Grace's—she could not for the life of her remember the lady's name—took her arm and smiled brightly and warmly at her.

"I can remember being wild with fury during my first few balls not to be allowed to waltz," she said, "even though I had already passed my majority. I still think it foolish beyond belief that a few social dragons can have so much power, but I have learned by now to laugh in private—or with only Francis for an audience—at such stupidities. Francis is dancing with Jane because he forgot this was a waltz and should therefore have been mine—I shall make him suffer for that later. Come, Miss Gray. You and I will stroll outside and pretend that we would not waltz even if our respective menfolk were on their knees begging us." She laughed heartily.

Francis, Stephanie thought frantically, allowing herself to be led away. He was Lord Francis Something. Lady Francis Something looked at her as they left the ballroom and crossed the terrace to descend the steps into the garden. She laughed again.

"Oh, that remembered look," she said. "That *who the devil are you, but I do not dare to ask* look. I am Lady Francis Kneller, Miss Gray, but I would far prefer to have you call me Cora. Titles used to terrify me, and so it is rather ironic that I married one. You did need rescuing, did you not? Just for a short while? I could see it. And of course the Duke of Bridgwater would never do anything as improper as spend the evening at your elbow. He used to awe me into incoherence—I lived at the duchess's home, you know, for part of one Season while she attempted to find me a husband. Not Francis—I am a merchant's daughter and could not think of looking so high. But Francis had the misfortune to decide to amuse himself by bringing me into fashion, and dreadful things happened to force him into offering for me. Can you imagine a worse fate?"

Stephanie felt rather as if she had been caught up in a whirlwind. Lady Francis Kneller was taller than she and far more amply endowed. She was not pretty—her features were too bold—but the word "handsome" leapt immediately to mind.

"No, I cannot," Stephanie said.

Lady Francis looked sharply at her. "Oh dear," she said, "I have opened my mouth and stuffed my slipper—my lamentably *large* slipper—into it, have I not? How Francis will shake his head ruefully and refrain from scolding me when I tell him what I just said to you. It is exactly what happened with you and His Grace too, is it not? We were quite incredulous when we heard. His Grace has always been very adept at avoiding matrimonial snares and fortune hunters. And so he was snared accidentally by a wealthy heiress who happened to be a governess before she inherited. You cannot imagine how *pleased* I am, Miss Gray—may I call you Stephanie? You are just what he needs. Someone to throw him slightly off balance, so to speak. He has always been just too perfectly *balanced* for his own good. That is why I have always stood in awe of him, though not so much lately. Francis has derived so much amusement over the past six years from the great dithers I go into when I meet a title—especially in light of the fact that he is himself a duke's son—that I have learned to laugh at myself too. It is either that or bash his head in, Stephanie, and how could I do that to my beloved Francis?" She laughed gaily.

The strange thing was that Stephanie found herself laughing too, with genuine amusement. How refreshing it was to find that there was someone human at the ball—she did not stop to ponder the strange thought. And she remembered now that Lord Francis Kneller was the gentleman with the coat of a delicate spring green satin and with the laughing eyes. He had been notice-able in a ballroom full of gentlemen who were wearing either black or dark sober colors. It was no wonder his eyes laughed if he lived with Cora, she thought.

Lady Francis squeezed her arm. "All will be well, you know," she said. "I promise you, though it is very stupid to do so when I cannot know the future. But when two people are forced into marriage, each feels guilty and apologetic to the other, and both make an extra special effort to make the marriage work. If you think a governess-turned-heiress and a duke an unpromising combination, as I am sure at present you do, then imag-ine what my situation was, Stephanie. A merchant's daughter and a duke's son and brother. But Francis and I are now the dearest of friends and hold each other in the deepest affection. You must not allow them to in-timidate you, you see. The Duchess of Bridgwater is a wonderful lady—she was remarkably kind to me all be-cause I had apparently saved her grandson's life—but she can be intimidating. I found her so, and I can readily believe that she is ten times more so to someone who is about to marry Bridgwater. She means well. But you must not allow it to happen. You must remember that there is nothing wrong—and nothing inferior—about being a governess or a merchant's daughter. I have no patience with snobbery."

Stephanie smiled. "You are very kind, Cora," she said. "I am much obliged to you for suggesting that we come outside for some air. I feel considerably better."

"There," Lady Francis said, squeezing her arm, "you will feel the better for getting all that off your chest. A person always does. I have been only too glad to lend a sympathetic ear. I will call on you, Stephanie, and you must call on me. I shall like it of all things. I sometimes feel a little lonely in town—lonely for adult company, that is. I have four children, you know, all below the age of six, and I dote on their company. But when in town I insist that Francis go about all those dull gentlemanly pursuits that gentlemen set such store by, even though he always tries to be noble and insist that he would be far happier with me and the children. One has to understand men, Stephanie. They do not understand themselves half the time, I do declare."

Stephanie was chuckling again. She found that for the first time all evening—perhaps all week—she was relaxing and even feeling a measure of enjoyment. But the music of the waltz wafting from the ballroom into the garden had ceased. That particular set was at an end, it seemed.

"Ah," Lady Francis said, cocking her head to one side and listening, "it is time to go inside again. Time for me to scold and sulk over the fact that Francis danced our waltz with Jane. No matter that she is one of my closest friends. He is not to be forgiven."

When they had entered the ballroom and Lord Francis joined them immediately, bowing and smiling at Stephanie and extending his arm for his wife's, the latter tapped the arm with her fan and scowled.

"I am in a towering rage," she said. "Am I not, Stephanie?" But she immediately gave the lie to her words by grinning broadly at her husband and linking her arm through his. "Stephanie is terrified of the Duke of Bridgwater, Francis. I have been consoling her."

"Oh dear," Lord Francis said and grinned back at his wife before looking a little uncertainly at Stephanie.

It was not clear to Stephanie whether his concern was over her mythical terror or his wife's consolation. But she caught the duchess's eye at that moment, smiled at Lady Francis, and made her way across the room. Now that she was inside again, though, she felt even more discontented than she had before. It was something Lady Francis had said, she thought. She frowned to bring back the relevant words. Lady Francis had said a great deal altogether.

You must not allow them to intimidate you.

There, that was it.

They were intimidating her. Both of them. Oh, they were both kind, just as Lady Francis had said. But intimidating too.

Suddenly, Stephanie could not bear the thought of standing next to the duchess for more endless minutes, smiling and listening to the conversation of those who came to make her better acquaintance. She could not bear the thought of dancing again just yet, nor could she bear to watch the duke, her fiancé, quite oblivious to her presence, converse with everyone, it seemed, except her and dance with yet another lady. It seemed to her that the evening was interminable, that it would never end.

"Excuse me," she murmured to Her Grace, "I shall be just a few minutes."

But she knew even as she hurried away to the ballroom doors and through them that she had no intention of returning until she felt she could avoid doing so no longer. It was the occasion that was overwhelming her, she thought as she tried to find a place in which to be by herself for a while. But all the small rooms on either side of the ballroom and the landing itself were occupied. She hurried down the stairs, trying to look as if she had a destination in mind. Perhaps, she thought belatedly, she could have gone back out into the garden. There had not been many people out there when she had strolled with Lady Francis. But she could not go back to the ballroom now and out onto the balcony without the risk of being seen. Perhaps she could find her way out from downstairs.

She did not find the garden door. But she did find something even better—a conservatory that was both dimly lit and deserted. She found a large plant almost as big as a palm tree and sank down onto a chair conveniently placed behind it, hiding her from the door.

All week she had been oppressed by a sense of obligation to the Duke of Bridgwater. She had felt deeply in his debt. She had thought to try to repay that debt at least in some small way by making herself into the sort of woman who could be his duchess. She had worked hard. Except in one or two very minor matters concerning her clothes, she had argued over nothing. She had accepted whatever the duchess had told her. She had absorbed everything and had adapted her own behavior and attitudes to what was now expected of her.

She had dressed earlier this evening in a flutter of nerves. Not so much nerves over the ball—though there had been that too, of course—as nerves over what he would think of her. She had imagined how he would look at her, what he would say. Surely, he would be pleased. She had tried so hard.

Had he been pleased?

Yes, he had. She had seen approval in his eyes when she was coming down the stairs. When he had taken those few steps toward her as she reached the bottom and stretched out his hand for hers, all had seemed worthwhile. She had been like a child waiting for a parent's coveted praise.

Miss Gray. I almost did not recognize you.

Praise would follow. He would applaud her taste in dress and hairstyle—both were slightly plainer than Her Grace had wanted, though her own wishes had been respected.

You have performed a miracle, Mama.

Yes, Stephanie thought now, staring ahead of her, oblivious to the beauty of the exotic plants about her. Yes, she had forgotten. But that was what had prevented her from enjoying the evening—just that—long before they had even arrived at the Marquess of Hayden's mansion. She felt hurt all over again, as she had felt hurt then.

It was his mother who was to be applauded. Just as if she, Stephanie, was an object. Just as if everything had been done *to* her and nothing *by* her.

You look magnificent . . . If you remember everything that I am sure she has told you during the past week, you will do very well this evening.

Now she could not stop remembering.

If you feel a little uncertain at any time, remember who you are. Remember that you are my betrothed and that soon you will be the Duchess of Bridgwater.

Was that her identity, then? Her sole identity? She was his betrothed, his future duchess. But yes, of course. That was what the past week had been all about, had it not? Erasing everything else about her that was not that one thing. All her lowly and embarrassing past was to be blotted out as if it had never been.

And she had concurred in the transformation.

Did she regret it, then?

She sat for a long time without knowing the answer. She lost track of time. Although the music from the ballroom was clearly audible in the conservatory, she failed to notice when the one set ended. It was a voice that finally startled her back to the present.

"Miss Gray?" the voice said.

He was alarmingly close. Of course he would have to be. From the doorway he would not have seen her. He had come right inside, looking.

"Miss Gray?" the Duke of Bridgwater said again. "You have been gone from the ballroom for a long time—since well before the start of the last set. I grew concerned. So did my mother. This is not quite the thing, you know."

She drew a deep breath and looked down at the fan she had been clutching unconsciously in her lap. She had the choice between ripping up at him, or apologizing, she thought. It would be unfair to do the former—what he said was quite right. It was one of those rules that had been instilled into her all week. But she would not apologize. *You must not allow them to intimidate you.*

"No, Your Grace," she said, looking up into his eyes. "It is not, is it?"

10

IT FELT STRANGELY EXHILARATING TO BE AT A LARGE squeeze of a ball with his betrothed—to be at his betrothal ball. Though as a younger man he had dreamed of love and happily ever afters, and as a more mature man—just a few weeks ago—he had considered the necessity of making a dynastic marriage in order to secure his line, he really had not quite expected that he would marry. Marriage was for other men, not for him.

And yet here he was at Hayden's and Elizabeth's, betrothed. He was to be married in three weeks' time. And rather than feeling depressed or even panicked because he had been forced into a betrothal with a stranger—a woman almost from outside his own world—he was feeling exhilarated.

He no longer felt nervous. She was beautiful. He had known that before, of course, but now she was a beautiful ornament of the *ton*. She fit her surroundings perfectly at the same time as she outshone them. He had received a dozen compliments or more on her beauty before the evening was half over. More important, she had somehow acquired the poise and dignity to appear quite at her ease in the ballroom. She smiled at everyone, conversed with everyone, though he noticed that she did so more by listening and looking interested than by talking. And she danced with grace and confidence.

He felt enormously relieved. He had so feared that she would look as out of place and behave as awkwardly as she had in his mother's drawing room a week ago. His heart would have bled for her. He would have felt forced to take her away and marry her quietly and keep her in the country for the rest of their days so that she would not have to face the humiliation of such ordeals again. It would not have been a situation conducive to happiness or contentment for either of them.

He felt so very guilty about the way his own stupidity had trapped her and given her no choice at all of husband. And about allowing her to go on believing it had been all her fault. She had had little enough choice as it was, time being so short for her. But he had taken away even that little. And he had brought her into a world she had never experienced before.

He was relieved to know that, after all, her birth and education had made it easier for her to adapt than he had feared. He was proud of her. Apart from his mother and perhaps his sisters and sister-in-law, only he knew how much effort it had taken for her to appear thus tonight.

Like a gauche and eager schoolboy he wanted to stay by her side all evening. He wanted to dance with her all evening. At the very least he wanted to watch her, to feast his eyes on her. But he could do none of those things, of course. He could not humiliate her by making it appear that she could not cope alone in a social situation.

But he watched her covertly. At every moment of the evening he knew where she was, with whom she talked and danced. It was a new feeling for him. Even when he was younger and had had flirts, he had never been so aware of them as he was of Stephanie. He was pleased when she stepped out of doors with Lady Francis Kneller during the waltz. He had been about to cross the room to her and take her walking himself. But he had engaged her for a set after supper. It would be too much to walk with her now as well.

He saw her leave alone after saying a few quick words to his mother. He watched for her return as he danced a country set and apparently gave his attention to his partner. His anxiety grew as the set progressed. Where was she that she was gone so long? Had she met someone outside the ballroom who had kept her talking?

His mother was worried too.

"I have just looked in the ladies' withdrawing room," she told him when he joined her at the end of the set. "She is not there, Alistair. And nowhere else that I can see."

He looked into all the rooms on the ballroom floor. He wandered out onto the balcony and down into the garden. She was nowhere to be found. Soon her absence would be noted, if it had not already been. He reentered the house through the garden door on the lower level and made his way to the hall, where a few footmen stood on duty.

"Miss Gray stepped this way?" he asked nonchalantly, his eyebrows raised, his hands clasped behind him. "The lady in green?"

"She is in the conservatory, I believe, Your Grace," one of the footmen said, bowing deeply and hurrying ahead of the duke to open the door for him.

It was not in total darkness, but it seemed quite deserted. He almost turned back to resume his search elsewhere. But it was clear to him by now that she was either hiding or had left the house altogether. And if she was hiding, she would hardly sit in full view of the conservatory door. He strolled inside.

She was sitting very quietly behind a potted palm, staring ahead of her. Apparently, she was quite unaware of his presence. She must have been here for longer than half an hour—quite alone and unchaperoned. Yet this was her betrothal ball.

"Miss Gray?" he said.

Her head jerked up, confirming his first impression, though she did not turn to look at him. He felt suddenly angry.

"Miss Gray?" he said again. "You have been gone from the ballroom for a long time—since well before the start of the last set. I grew concerned. So did my mother. This is not quite the thing, you know."

For a while he thought she was not going to answer him. She still had not looked at him. Rather, she directed her gaze at the fan she held in her lap. But finally she spoke.

"No, Your Grace," she said coolly, and finally she turned her head. "It is not, is it?" She spoke quietly. Why, then, did her words sound like a declaration of war?

He would not rip up at her, he decided, and then was surprised that he had even had to curb the urge. He never ripped up at anyone. He did not need to. He had learned as far back as boyhood the art of imposing his will by a mere look or quiet word. He must certainly not be angry with Stephanie. Doubtless she had been awed by the occasion. He moved to stand in front of her.

"You have been overwhelmed by it all?" he asked her gently.

She lifted her shoulders, but did not answer him. She was gazing at her fan again.

"You have done remarkably well," he said. "Your manner has been as poised as if you had been accustomed to this way of life for years. You are lovelier than any other lady present. I have had numerous compliments on your beauty."

She raised her eyes again. "Have you?" she said. There

was an unidentifiable edge to her voice. He waited for her to continue, but she did not do so.

"Talk to me," he said. "How can I help you if I do not know what ails you?"

Again he thought she would not speak. He remembered the way she had talked and talked in his carriage, her face animated and framed by the foolish bonnet. Somehow it was hard to realize that this was the same woman.

"'You have performed a miracle, Mama,'" she said so quietly that he thought he must have misheard.

"What?" he said, frowning.

"'You have performed a miracle, Mama,'" she repeated a little more loudly. "It is what you said earlier, Your Grace. Almost your first words, in fact."

Oh, good Lord. She was right, was she not? That was what he had said. He had been so delighted at his first sight of Stephanie, so . . . dazzled, that he had spoken without thinking. Words of congratulation to his mother. None to Stephanie herself. Surely, he had congratulated her too? But he could not remember saying anything. It was his mother who had pointed out that the transformation was the result of hard work rather than of a miracle.

He went down on his haunches before her and rested his wrists over his knees. "You are quite right," he said. "I gave you no credit at all, did I? Will you forgive me? I know—I knew at the time—that it was you who made the miracle happen, that my mother merely guided and advised. You have worked incredibly hard during the past week. And I spoke as if it was all my mother's doing. Forgive me, Stephanie." It was, he realized, the first time he had used her given name. He had not asked her permission—another error uncharacteristic of him.

"Of course," she said. "Are you pleased then, Your

Grace? Will I do? I have not embarrassed or shamed you tonight?"

"You know you have not," he said. "And you must know that I am pleased—even if I was doltish enough to phrase my pleasure quite wrongly at the start of the evening."

"Then the hard work has been worthwhile," she said. "I have done it for you, you see, because I am so very deeply in your debt. I believe I owe my life to you."

"No." He felt distinctly uneasy. He reached for her hands and held them tightly. He rested one of his knees on the floor. "You owe me nothing. I seem to have caused you more misery than anything else."

She smiled at him for the first time. He was startled anew by her dimple, by the sunshine of her smile. "There are thousands of women who would give all they possess for such misery, Your Grace," she said. "Have I been gone very long? I meant to sit here only until the set had ended. But I believe I lost track of time. You cannot know, perhaps, how bewildering this is for me. All my life I have been accustomed to quietness and even to solitude. I enjoy both and must have them occasionally."

He squeezed her hands. "I will remember that," he said. "But you will, of course, learn when solitude is appropriate and when it is not. It is not appropriate in the middle of a ball, especially when you are the guest of honor."

"Yes." She visibly drew breath. "I still have much to learn, Your Grace. I will try to achieve perfection. Will my absence have been remarked upon? Will I have brought disgrace on you?"

"By no means," he said, bringing one of her hands to his lips. "We will return to the ballroom from the garden and balcony, and it will be assumed that we have taken some time to stroll together. It is quite unexceptionable to do so since we are betrothed. And it will be understood why we have done so during this particular set. It is another waltz."

She listened to the music, which was quite audible. "Yes," she said. "So it is." It seemed to him that she sighed.

"Do you know the steps?" he asked.

"Yes," she said. "I was required to teach them to the eldest daughter at the Burnabys'. I always thought it would be wonderful to waltz with a real gentleman at a real ball."

"Am I real enough?" he asked her, getting to his feet and retaining his hold on her right hand. "Is this ball real enough?"

Her smile was rueful. "I am not allowed to waltz here," she said. "Her Grace said that perhaps it would not be quite improper since I am well past the age of majority, but she also said that I must be very careful not to give anyone even the slightest reason to frown."

"She is quite right, of course," he said. "You must never risk censure unnecessarily. But I meant here. Our own private ballroom. Shall we?"

Her smile grew slowly and caused strange fluttering sensations in the regions of his heart and stomach. He could not understand now why he had once thought it was the smile of a coquette. There was too much of pure joy in the expression for it to proceed from anything else but innocence. He was beginning to find innocence far more alluring than experience had ever been.

He took her hand in his and set his arm about her slender waist.

WALTZING WITH A pupil while playing the role of the male partner, and waltzing with a gentleman were two entirely different experiences, Stephanie realized immediately. His shoulder was well above the level of her own and felt solidly muscled beneath her hand. His hand was large and warm. She could feel his body heat, smell his cologne. He held her very correctly so that she touched him only at the hand and shoulder. But she knew instantly why so many people had been dubious about the morality of the waltz not so many years ago.

It was an intensely intimate dance.

He waltzed expertly. After the first few moments she found that she no longer had to concentrate on counting steps and following his lead. All she had to do was move her feet and float and enjoy the moment.

She did not believe she had ever enjoyed any other moment as she was enjoying this one. She closed her eyes and trusted that he would prevent them from colliding with plants and chairs.

"Come," he said after several minutes, "confession time, Stephanie. You have not been a teacher of general instruction for the past six years. You have been a teacher exclusively of the waltz. You dance it superbly."

She was so very susceptible to praise from him, she thought as she opened her eyes to smile up at him. Just as she had been easily hurt by his unintentional slight at the start of the evening. But perhaps the reason was that her life for so many years had been starved of praise or even approval.

"I am merely good at following the lead of a superb partner," she said.

He laughed, and she realized how rarely he did so and how very attractive he was when he did. Not that he was unattractive even when he was at his most poker-faced, of course.

"Touché." He stopped waltzing even though the music continued from somewhere above their heads. "When we are seen entering the ballroom from the garden, you know," he said, "it will be assumed that I have stolen at least one kiss from you. I would be thought a remarkable slowtop if I had not tried."

She had dreamed all week about his kiss, about what he had done with his lips and tongue. She had relived, with some guilty shame, the effects his kiss had had on her body. She had wanted to be kissed again. She had wondered what the intimacies of the marriage bed would feel like.

"May I?" he asked.

She nodded.

She had grown up in the country. She knew what happened between male and female, though she was not quite sure how exactly it was done between man and woman. For years she had longed to find out and had expected never to do so. In three weeks' time she would know finally—with this man. Unsuspected muscles deep inside her contracted and left her shaken and breathless.

He kissed her as he had kissed her the week before, briefly and lightly on the lips before lifting his head and looking into her eyes. Instinct told her that she wanted to feel him with her breasts, that tonight she did not want her hands to be trapped against his chest. She slid them upward and clasped them behind his neck. She let her body sway against his as his arms came about her waist. She could feel him from her shoulders to her knees. All warm, solid masculinity. She closed her eyes.

Yes, the kiss continued as before—his slightly parted lips, his tongue touching the seam of her own lips, the sizzling sensations in other parts of her body. But she wanted more. She parted her own lips tentatively and felt his tongue come through them to stroke the soft, sensitive flesh behind. She opened her mouth.

After that her mind ceased making a running commentary of what happened. It was only afterward when she thought about it—she spent all night thinking of nothing else—that she remembered sucking inward on his tongue until he moaned. And his mouth against her throat and her breasts, which his thumbs had bared by drawing her dress down beneath them. And his hands spread firmly over her buttocks, holding her against masculine hardness. It was only afterward that she thought to feel shock—and shame.

He was breathing hard, his face turned in against her hair, when his hands covered her breasts with her gown again. He held her by the shoulders for a few moments and then put her away from him and turned his back on her.

"The music has stopped," he said, his voice sounding quite normal, if a trifle breathless. "Thank God. Miss Gray, did your mother never warn you against situations like this? Or my mother?"

A pail of cold water flung in her face could not have more effectively brought her back to the present.

"Yes," she said. "And experience has taught me how to handle situations like this. A governess is often prey to lascivious attempts at seduction, Your Grace. I thought this was different. I thought I need not fight. You are my betrothed." If truth were known, she had not even considered fighting.

"We are not married," he said. "It would be folly indeed to anticipate the marriage bed, Miss Gray. What if I should die before the day? What if I should leave you with child? Even failing that, what if I should leave you a fallen woman?"

Hurt and anger—and shame—warred in her. And confusion about which was uppermost held her silent.

He turned to look at her. "I am sorry," he said. "Deeply sorry. The fault was all mine. I asked a kiss of my betrothed and then proceeded to use you as I would a—" He stopped to inhale deeply. "Forgive me. Please forgive me. It will not happen again."

"No." She brushed past him on the way to the door.

"It will not, Your Grace. It seems I have more to learn than I have realized. It seems I have more in common with a whore—that *is* the word you stopped yourself from saying, is it not?—than a true lady. But I will learn. By the time I am your duchess, I will behave like a duchess. I will remember that kisses are meant to be brief and decorous."

"Stephanie—" he said, coming after her.

"We must return, Your Grace," she said, "before the next set begins. If we leave it longer, the *ton* will no longer think that you have been stealing a kiss. They will think you have been tumbling me, and my reputation will never recover. You and your mother will be disgraced."

"Stephanie," he said again, drawing her arm through his even though she tried to resist, and leading her out through the garden door she had been unable to find earlier. "What I said was unpardonable. I was horrified by my own lack of control and blamed you. I seem to have done nothing but insult you this evening. It was unpardonable. I will not even ask your pardon. I will bear the burden of my own guilt. But please do not blame yourself. Not in any way. When you look back later, as you surely will, you must take none of the blame on yourself."

He was leading her quickly up the steps onto the balcony and across it to the French doors into the ballroom. Almost without thinking she smiled. She was on view again.

The point was, she thought, that she would not have considered their embrace in terms of guilt or shame if he had not made her see that both were needed. It had felt right. They were betrothed, soon to be married. Attraction—physical attraction—between them had seemed desirable. Without ever thinking of it in verbal terms, she knew that she had embraced him with a feeling close to love. She had believed, naive as she was, that he had felt the same. There had been no question—surely there had not—of anything happening that might have left her ruined or with child. That was for the marriage bed. They had been standing in the conservatory.

But it seemed that there was guilt and there was shame. Such things as physical attraction and passion were quite inappropriate between a duke and his duchess—they were acceptable only between a duke and his mistress. And of course the word "love" was probably not even in the ducal vocabulary.

Well, then, she thought almost viciously as His Grace led her toward his mother and they all smiled as if nothing untoward had happened all evening—well, then, she would learn.

If it was the last thing she ever did in life, she would learn.

SHE SEEMED LESS shy today, he thought. Less shy with other people, that was. He was driving her in his curricle in Hyde Park during the fashionable hour, and she seemed in no way intimidated by the crush of people that the sunshine had brought out—not that the *ton* needed sunshine in order to gather for the daily ride or stroll and for the polite gossiping and ogling. Only a downpour of rain would keep them away.

She was looking extremely lovely in a pale blue muslin dress of simple, elegant design and a cornflower-trimmed straw bonnet. Her blue parasol was the only article that was in any way fussy. She twirled it above her head as they drove along. She smiled.

In the park she spoke to everyone who stopped to pay their respects. Unlike last evening she did not merely listen and encourage more talk with her smiles. Today she participated fully in the conversations. He knew that she was succeeding in charming the gentlemen and perhaps making the ladies faintly envious. She was far more lovely than anyone else there, after all. He did not even pause to wonder if it was partiality that led him to such a decisive conclusion.

He had been foolish to worry that she would just not be able to learn in time what she would need to know to be his duchess. There would be a great deal more, of course, than merely to look fashionable and to converse with ease and charm. But those things certainly helped. And if she could learn those so quickly and so thoroughly, then surely she could learn everything else too, given a little more time.

He was pleased with her. He was proud of her.

And he was uncomfortable with her and still ashamed of himself. He had scarcely slept during what had remained of the night after he took her and his mother home from the ball.

If the cessation of the music in the ballroom had not somehow penetrated his consciousness when it had, he thought, he might not have brought that embrace to an end until it had reached its logical conclusion. He had been drawing up the skirt of her gown, bunching it in handfuls about her hips when he had realized what was happening—and what had already happened.

If one thing had characterized his life for the past eleven years, and even longer, it was control. He had always felt fully in control of other people and events and—most important—of himself. Last evening had bewildered him. He had insulted her right at the start in a way that was inexcusable, especially since he had not even realized it until she had pointed it out. And later, he had insulted her in such an unpardonable manner that he had shuddered over it all night and all morning—he had blamed her for his own loss of control.

The trouble was that his dream—his long abandoned

dream—had leapt to life for a few mindless minutes while he held her and kissed her. For those few minutes she had been that dream of love. She had felt like the other half of his soul—the half he had always known was missing, the half he had always yearned to find.

It had been a ridiculous feeling. All that had happened was that he had lusted after her, his own betrothed. He had behaved unpardonably.

And so today he was uncomfortable with her. And today her bright charm seemed more like a shield than anything else. She talked to him incessantly on the way to and from the park—about the weather, about the flowers she had received from various gentlemen who had danced with her last evening, including his orchids, about the kindness Lady Francis Kneller had shown her last evening and the amusement she had provided, about a hundred and one topics that held back the silence between them.

Silence, when there had been silence between them in his carriage during that journey, had been a comfortable thing. No longer. Not that either of them put it to the test today.

"Miss Gray," he said when he had lifted her down from his curricle and led her inside and refused his mother's invitation to come upstairs for tea, "I told you last evening that I would not ask your pardon for what was unpardonable. I have changed my mind. *Will* you forgive me?"

"Of course, Your Grace," she said, smiling warmly. "I believe you were right to put at least part of the blame on me, though you were gallant enough to retract what you had said. I am gradually learning the rules, you see. I hope to have them all by heart by the time of our nuptials."

She offered him her gloved hand, and he took it and raised it to his lips.

"Until this evening, then," he said, "and the theater."

"I am looking forward to it," she said.

He knew what was wrong as soon as he stepped out of the house and climbed back to the high seat of his curricle. Although she had smiled and although her voice had been warm, there had been no gold flecks in her eyes. Strange, ridiculous notion. How could eyes change?

But hers had. There had been a certain blankness in their smiling depths.

11

SHE HAD BECOME TWO DIFFERENT PEOPLE—SHE WAS uncomfortably aware of that realization during the three weeks leading up to her wedding—two quite distinct people.

When she was alone—but how rarely she was alone during those weeks—and during her dreams at night she was Stephanie Gray, vicar's daughter. She was the girl and young woman who had kept house for her father. She was the general favorite of the villagers and even of the squire's family. She visited everyone and was a friend of everyone, young and old, rich and poor alike. She took gifts of baking and needlework to the sick and elderly. She refused a marriage offer from Tom Reaves, the squire's only son, though they had been playmates all through their childhood and friends in more recent years. She refused because she knew he had offered out of pity, for her father had died and left her poor and she was compelled to seek employment elsewhere. Friendship seemed not a strong enough basis for marriage.

When she was alone and when she dreamed, her life at the vicarage became idealized. It was always summer there. The sun always shone. The flowers in the garden always bloomed. The villagers always smiled. Tom always seemed a little dearer than just a friend. And his sisters seemed more like her sisters too.

When she was alone, she liked who she was. She was the woman her parents had raised her to be. She was the woman she wanted to be. She was herself.

But when she was not alone—most of the time during those weeks—she was the betrothed of the Duke of Bridgwater. She dressed the part, always expensively elegant. And she lived the part, every word, every action, every reaction consciously chosen. There was no spontaneity at all in this Stephanie. She seldom made a mistake. After the gentle scolding meted out by the duchess following that first ball— "Everyone feels the occasional need for solitude, Stephanie. But a duchess recognizes that she is a public person. She learns to live without solitude." —after that there were no more scoldings and only the occasional reminder. Like the time she apologized and smiled too warmly at a milliner's assistant who had patiently taken out more than a dozen bonnets from their hat boxes only to find that she had not after all made a single sale— "A duchess *never* apologizes for giving a servant work, Stephanie."

With her betrothed she behaved as a future wife should behave. Never again would he have cause to compare her to a whore—though he had stopped himself from using that word at the Marquess of Hayden's ball, she knew it was the word he had almost said. She conversed with him when they were alone together on any genteel topic that leapt to mind. When they were not alone, she gave her attention to other people. No one would ever accuse her of clinging to the coattails of her husband.

He did not kiss her again during those weeks, except for her hand. Had he asked for another kiss, she would have offered her lips while keeping her hands and her body—and her emotions—to herself. When they were married, she would offer her body. But only as a genteel wife would. She would offer herself for his pleasure—

never her own—though she knew that he would probably get most of that elsewhere. Most important, she would offer herself as a bearer for his legitimate offspring. She would give him his heir. Her Grace had already told her that this would be her primary duty.

She would give him a son, God willing, she thought. A life in exchange for a life. She would give him a son and heir, and perhaps then she would feel it possible to take back her own life. Perhaps she would feel that she had repaid the huge debt she owed him.

Perhaps . . . Oh, perhaps one day she could be herself again. Or was self always lost in marriage? Even when one did not owe one's life to one's husband, one became his property after marriage. All that one possessed became his.

No, that was not true in her case. He had insisted in the marriage settlement he had made with Mr. Watkins and Cousin Horace that Sindon Park and all her inheritance was to remain hers. He had been kind to her even in that—unbelievably kind.

She was constantly aware of his kindness. Had she merely owed him her life, she might have come to hate him during those weeks. She might have rebelled, despite herself. But in saving her, he had been kind to her. And *after* saving her, he had continued kind. And had given up his own freedom in order to take her safely home.

When she was not alone, she was the person she had been trained to be by her future mother-in-law. She was the person she had chosen to become, because of an obligation that lay heavily on her. But she felt like a stranger to herself.

Only occasionally and all too briefly did she break free.

They were at the Royal Academy art gallery one afternoon in company with Lord and Lady George Munro and the Earl and Countess of Greenwald, her future in-laws. Her arm was drawn through the duke's. They were all sedately viewing the crowded tiers of paintings and commenting on their various merits and demerits. Stephanie judged with her emotions. If a painting lifted her spirits, she liked it. She did not try to analyze her feelings.

But His Grace smiled when she explained this to him. "Then you miss a whole area in which you might exercise your mind," he said. "You do it with books, but not with paintings, Miss Gray? You surprise me." And he went on to analyze a Gainsborough landscape she had admired in such a manner that she was enthralled and felt that she had simply not seen the painting at all before.

"Oh," she said, "and I thought it was merely pretty. How foolish I feel."

"I must confess," he said, "that I react to music much as you do to painting. I suppose sometimes we need to allow our intellects to rest in order that we may merely enjoy."

She smiled at him.

And then beyond him, she spotted two couples standing before a canvas, absorbed in viewing it. Her eyes fixed on them and widened. It could not be—but it was. She forgot everything but them. She withdrew her arm from the duke's, took a few hurried steps across the gallery, and stopped.

"Miriam?" she said uncertainly. "Tom?"

She had not seen them for six years. For a moment she thought she must have been mistaken. But when all four people turned their heads to look inquiringly at her, she saw that she had not. Tom Reaves stood before her—and Miriam, his sister, the one closest to Stephanie in age—looking hardly any different at all than when she had last seen them.

"Stephie?" Miriam questioned, her eyes growing as wide as saucers. "*Stephanie?*"

And then they were in each other's arms, hugging and laughing and exclaiming.

"Steph?" Tom was saying, loudly enough to be heard above them. "Good Lord!"

He caught her up in a bear hug, swinging her off her feet and around in a complete circle. She was laughing helplessly.

"What on earth are you doing here?"

"You look as fine as fivepence—as *seven*pence."

"I cannot believe it!"

All three of them spoke, or rather yelled, at once. All three laughed.

"I cannot believe it," Stephanie said again. "To meet my dearest friends again, and in London of all places. How very wonderful!"

"Steph, you look . . . like a duchess," Tom said, his eyes sweeping over her from head to toe.

"What on earth are you doing here?" Miriam asked again. "You are supposed to be in the north of England, teaching. What a *fortunate* coincidence to run into you here, Stephie."

"We are here for a month of sightseeing," Tom said. "With our spouses, Steph. This is my wife, Sarah." He smiled at the young lady standing beside him. "And Miriam's husband, Perry Shields. Stephanie Gray, my love. She grew up close to us at the vicarage. The best female cricketer it has ever been my misfortune to know. She had a formidable bowling arm."

They all laughed merrily. And then the two couples looked inquiringly beyond Stephanie's shoulder. She was brought back to reality with a sickening jolt. Oh dear, she thought. She had abandoned him in the middle of the gallery and had proceeded to shriek and laugh like a hoyden—or a country bumpkin—with people who were strangers to him. She had hugged Miriam with unbecoming enthusiasm. She had allowed Tom to sweep her right off her feet and swing her around.

The Duke of Bridgwater was looking at her with raised eyebrows when she turned.

"Oh." She felt herself flushing. And then the part of her that no longer did anything impulsively or spontaneously felt the awkwardness of a dilemma. If one should meet an acquaintance while in company with someone else, the duchess had taught her just a few days before, one ought to avoid introducing the two people unless permission has been granted beforehand by the socially superior of the two. Thus one avoids putting that person into the regrettable situation of having to acknowledge an unwanted acquaintance.

But she had no choice in the matter now. He had followed her across the gallery room, as his sister and brother had not. That meant, surely, that he wished to be presented. Or did it merely mean that he had come in the hope of preventing her from making a further spectacle of herself?

"Your Grace," she said, "may I present Mr. and Mrs. Shields and Mr. and Mrs. Reaves? Miriam and Tom are dear friends from my girlhood."

He bowed his head in acknowledgment of the introductions.

"May I present His Grace, the Duke of Bridgwater?" she said, looking at her friends. Their faces registered an almost embarrassing degree of surprise.

"I am pleased to make your acquaintance," the duke said. "You are in town for long?"

"For ten more days, Your Grace," Tom said. "We have come to see the sights. The ladies have come also to shop."

"Oh, and the gentlemen too," Miriam said, "though they hate to admit it."

"Perhaps," the duke said, "you can be persuaded to extend your stay by a few days. Miss Gray and I are to be married in two weeks' time. Yet it seems that the guest list consists almost entirely of my relatives and friends."

Miriam's eyes had widened still further if that was possible.

"Oh, Stephie," she said, "is this true? I am so happy for you. *May* we, Perry?" She looked eagerly at her husband.

"Will you like it, my love?" Tom was asking his wife at the same moment. "Shall we stay?"

It was all arranged within the next couple of minutes, before His Grace took Stephanie's arm in a firm clasp and led her back to their companions, who were discreetly viewing another portrait, their backs to the other group. Miriam and her husband and Tom and his wife were to attend the wedding. The duke had asked for their direction—they were staying at a hotel not frequented by the elite of the beau monde—and had promised that an official invitation would be sent there the same day.

Foolishly, although they went to Gunter's for ices after leaving the gallery and then walked home so that there was all the time in the world for conversation and even for some private words since the six of them did not all walk abreast in the street, Stephanie talked determinedly on a number of topics, but did not once mention the meeting with her friends.

She felt a little like crying. It was almost as if her dreams of her youth had conjured up Miriam and Tom. She felt a huge nostalgia for those days, for her parents, for the vicarage, for the simplicity and happiness of her first twenty years.

But she felt embarrassed too. She had forced the duke into an acquaintance that was not of his choosing. By describing Miriam and Tom as her dearest friends, she had perhaps made him feel obliged to issue the invitation to their wedding. Surely, he could not want them there. Although of gentle birth, they did not move in *ton* circles.

And she felt unhappy at the implied snobbery of her embarrassment. Was she ashamed of her friends? No, of course she was not. They were most dear to her because they had filled her childhood with friendship and happiness. She was merely concerned that they would be treated with condescension and even perhaps downright contempt at her wedding. And yet even that thought suggested uncomfortably that she *was* perhaps ashamed of them. Would she have preferred it if they had refused, if they had used their planned departure for home as an excuse not to attend?

She realized afresh how wide apart her two worlds were, the one to which she was about to belong, and the one to which her heart cleaved.

It was the Duke of Bridgwater himself who mentioned them as he was taking his leave of her in the hall of his mother's house.

"I shall send the invitation to your friends as soon as I return home," he said. "They seem pleasant people."

"Yes," she said. "Thank you, Your Grace."

He held her hand silently for a few moments longer, gazing into her eyes as he did so. Then he raised her hand to his lips and took his leave of her.

Her uninhibited exuberance had probably disgusted him, she thought as she climbed the stairs wearily. She should have excused herself quietly, talked with Miriam and Tom quietly, and then returned to her group quietly. Quietly and decorously, in a manner to embarrass no one. That was what Her Grace would have expected of her. But she had spied her friends and had forgotten everything she had learned in the past two weeks.

She would not forget again, she vowed.

But she did forget again only a little more than one week later.

THE DUKE OF Bridgwater had been delighted to hear that his closest friend, the Marquess of Carew, was on his way from Yorkshire with his wife and children. The wedding invitation had been sent, of course, but the duke had not really expected that they would come. They rarely came to town, claiming that life was too short to be spent going where one *ought* to go when one loved no place on earth better than one's own home.

But they were coming to his wedding. So were the Earl of Thornhill and his family.

"We have all been telling one another to the point of tedium that we really ought to join you and Francis and Cora in London for a few weeks of the Season," the marquess had written. "And then your announcement and your invitations arrived. There is to be no keeping us away now, of course. Expect us to arrive in plenty of time to look over your bride and give our approval. Samantha declares that it is high time. I leave you to interpret that comment for yourself. She has persuaded me to allow her to travel, by the way, despite the almost-imminence of the event that must have been obvious to you when you were here."

They arrived, the four of them plus their families, true to their word, one week before the wedding. The Earl of Thornhill had opened his town house. He and his countess invited the Duke of Bridgwater and his betrothed to dine with them two days later in company with the Carews and Lord and Lady Francis Kneller. It felt like a reenactment of a few weeks before except that circumstances had changed. And Stephanie had not been in Yorkshire.

It was an awkward evening, though Bridgwater was not sure that anyone but him felt the awkwardness. Stephanie looked beautiful in a gold evening gown with a simplicity of design he was beginning to recognize as characteristic of her. She was poised and charming and apparently quite at her ease in the company. His friends treated her warmly. Conversation throughout dinner was lively.

"A beauty, Bridge," the Earl of Thornhill said when the ladies had retired to the drawing room and the gentlemen had settled for a short while with their port. "And she certainly knows what to wear to show off that hair."

"And a charming lady," the marquess added. "I hoped she would not be intimidated by us all as I remember Cora was when she first met us."

Lord Francis grinned. "I still see that twinge of panic in Cora's eyes when there is a new title to meet," he said. "She is fond of Miss Gray, Bridge. She has kept Cora company a few mornings in the park with the children after I have been banished to enjoy myself at White's. The children even refer to her as Aunt Stephie, for which familiarity I was advised not to scold them. It seems that Aunt Stephie requested it."

The rest of the evening progressed just as smoothly as they conversed and played cards and took tea in the drawing room.

But the Duke of Bridgwater found the evening uncomfortable. Actually, he found every day and every evening uncomfortable. He had hurt her and insulted her on the evening of his sister's ball, and he knew that she had not forgotten, even though he had apologized—with deep sincerity—and she had given her forgiveness. There had been a barrier between them since that evening that had proved insurmountable.

It was not that she was sullen or even silent. Quite the

contrary. She never lacked for conversation. He could not fault her on any detail of her behavior either with him or with society in general.

But there was not the slightest hint of anything personal in their relationship. The warmth and the smiles he remembered from those days on the road—how long ago they seemed now—were gone. The shy uncertainty of those first days in London and the hints of feeling, even of passion, had disappeared.

He had tried to make their conversation more personal when they were alone. He had tried to get her to talk about her girlhood again. He had failed utterly. She always turned the conversation. He had hoped when they met her friends at the Royal Academy—how totally enchanted he had been by the bright vivacity of her manner there—that perhaps he had found the answer. He had hoped she would talk about them, suggest that they call on them at their hotel. But there had been nothing.

She had shut him out of her world. He was being punished, he thought, for daring to criticize her behavior at his sister's ball. How he longed for a repetition of that behavior. And now that it was too late to go back and do things differently, he wondered why he had been so alarmed and so ashamed. She was, as she had pointed out, his betrothed. It was to be hoped that as man and wife they would find each other desirable, since for the rest of their lives they would find that sort of pleasure only with each other or not at all. They had found each other desirable three weeks before their wedding—and he had accused her of wantonness and himself of an unpardonable lack of control.

But it was too late to go back. And there was no chance to repeat the embrace and do it all differently. She gave him no chance. She behaved so correctly that sometimes it seemed to him that she was inside an invisible casing of ice.

Having seen his friends again, he felt the hopelessness of his own case. They had overcome the odds against contentment and even happiness, all three couples. It seemed impossible, just too good to be true, that the same might happen to him. And yet seeing his friends had made him realize how desperately he wanted to capture that dream he had had as a young man.

How he longed to love her. To have her love him. To become her closest friend. To make her his. To live with her in companionship and intimacy and contentment for the rest of his days.

He remembered the disorienting impression he had had during that notorious embrace that she was the missing half of his soul. He had been wrong, of course. They were two strangers about to spend the rest of their lives together. They were of two worlds that would only rarely touch and perhaps never would.

But perhaps he could make things a little easier for her, he thought. She appeared to like his friends, and they seemed to return the feeling. She already had a personal friendship with Lady Francis. She must like the children if she had asked them to call her aunt. And she was from the country. She must miss it after three weeks spent in London, moving from one fashionable drawing room or ballroom to another.

"Will you all join Miss Gray and me for a picnic in Richmond Park tomorrow afternoon?" he asked before they took their leave. "The children too, of course. I shall have my cook provide sufficient food."

"Cricket," Lord Francis said. "I shall provide the bats and balls and wickets. Splendid idea, Bridge."

"Trees to climb," Lady Francis said in a voice of mock gloom, "especially for the youngest, who will be able to climb up but not down again."

"We will allow you to rescue them all, Cora," Lord Thornhill said dryly.

They all knew that Lady Francis was terrified of heights, though neither that nor her fear of water had ever daunted her from rushing to the rescue of anyone she perceived as being in distress.

"The outdoors again almost before we have arrived in town," Lady Carew said. "Bliss. What a wonderful idea, Alistair. Thank you."

"We will be there," the Countess of Thornhill said. "I hope you realize, Miss Gray, that you are going to be surrounded by no fewer than nine children. And none of them, except Samantha's Rosamond, can be described as shy."

"Not by any stretch of the imagination," the marquess said with a laugh.

"I shall look forward to meeting them all tomorrow," Stephanie said. "I am fond of children."

"I can vouch for that," Lady Francis said. "A picnic. How we will look forward to it. Will we not, Francis? Though it will deprive you of one of your precious days in town."

Lord Francis grinned and winked at the Duke of Bridgwater as soon as his wife turned her head away.

It was settled then, the duke thought. A picnic might be just the thing—with his friends and their children— in the rural surroundings of Richmond Park. Perhaps he could get past that barrier with her again. Perhaps he could get their relationship onto a more workable footing.

There was so little time left. Only five days.

His stomach lurched at the thought. In five days' time they would be man and wife. They would be irrevocably bound together. But then they already were. A betrothal was quite as binding as a marriage.

12

RICHMOND PARK. IT WAS CLOSE TO LONDON, AND YET it was pure countryside. There were even deer grazing among the giant oak trees. And there were long stretches of grass. Stephanie loved it. It helped too that after the gloomy weather of much of the past month the sun shone from a cloudless sky.

She felt relaxed and happy almost from the start of the afternoon. The Marquess and Marchioness of Carew and their children traveled with them in the Duke of Bridgwater's carriage. Despite their somewhat daunting titles, Stephanie had found both of them to be sweet and kindly the previous evening. And the marchioness immediately set her at her ease during the afternoon.

"Oh," she said after Stephanie had greeted them, "do I have to be 'my lady' all afternoon? It sounds so pompous for a picnic. And does Hartley have to be 'my lord'? I am Samantha, Miss Gray. And you are Stephanie?" She smiled. "You will hear Jenny call me Sam, but Hartley prefers what he calls the more feminine form of my name."

It was agreed, as it was later with the Earl and Countess of Thornhill—Gabriel and Jennifer—and with Lord Francis Kneller, that they be on a first-name basis. Stephanie felt warmed, as if she had been accepted and welcomed by the people who were perhaps her future husband's closest friends. She also felt a little awkward. His Grace had at one time told her that she might call him by his given name, but she had never done so. He had called her a few times by hers, but not during the past two weeks. Were they to be formal today only to each other?

The marquess and marchioness's little girl, three-year-old Rosamond, a blond and pretty replica of her mother, was extremely shy. But Stephanie sat forward in her seat and had soon won the child's confidence sufficiently to draw her onto her own lap. They played at counting fingers while five-year-old James told the duke how his riding skills had improved during the weeks since His Grace had left Highmoor. His father rested his left hand on the boy's head and gently ruffled his hair. He smiled sweetly.

"He has wanted to ride during every waking hour since you told him he had a splendid seat, Bridge," he said. "We have a famous equestrian in the making."

The other carriages were close behind the duke's with the result that they all arrived together at the park, and all spilled out together to great noise and confusion and much laughter.

"Michael," the countess said to her eleven-year-old son, "remember that you are the oldest. I am trusting you to behave responsibly and not lead the younger ones into trouble."

"Yes, Mama," he shouted over one shoulder as he raced for the closest tree.

"Francis," his wife called. She was holding baby Annabelle, who was squirming to be put down. "Andrew is off."

"Ho!" Lord Francis shouted, and he sprinted after his two-year-old, who had already covered an admirable distance for one with such short legs.

"Andrew has never yet heard of curves or corners,"

Lady Francis explained to Stephanie, "or of walks either. He runs—and always in a straight line."

"Yes." Stephanie laughed. "I had noticed once or twice before."

"Papa," five-year-old Jonathan demanded of the earl, "I want to play cricket. You said Uncle Frank was bringing the things."

"My dear lad," his father said, "might we at least wait five minutes? Might we be permitted to catch our breath?"

"Yes, cricket!" five-year-old Paul Kneller cried with enthusiasm. "I want to bat first. I get to go first because the bats are mine."

"And the manners are decidedly not," his mother said sharply. "Oh, thank you, Stephanie. She is *such* an armful." She flashed Stephanie a smile as Annabelle was lifted from her arms. "You may pull Aunt Stephie's hair for a change, sweetheart."

"You can bat first, Paul," Jonathan conceded magnanimously. "But I get to be on Uncle Frank's team."

"It looks as if your afternoon has been mapped out for you, Frank," the earl said as Lord Francis returned to the main group, tossing his shrieking son up in the air and catching him as he came down.

"While we ladies are relegated to watching the toddlers," the marchioness said with a mock sigh. "The world never changes."

But the duke had other ideas, and soon enough order had been restored to the scene of cheerful chaos. Those who wished to play cricket were to gather about Lord Francis and be organized into two teams of near enough equal strength and skill. He himself had no intention of being drawn into the game, and he believed he spoke for the earl and the marquess too.

"They are all yours, Frank," he said. "Hart, you had better take Rosamond since she will doubtless not come to either me or Gabe. Annabelle can go with Gabe. Andrew, my lad, you may ride on Uncle Alistair's shoulders if you promise not to pull my ears. When you grow tired, you may run to your heart's content or until you have exhausted me. Ladies, I will spread the blankets on the grass before I leave, and you may relax and enjoy the game or a quiet conversation."

"Well!" the countess said. "A man after my own heart. Gabriel—"

"I was about to suggest the exact same thing," the earl said, winking at the duke as he took Annabelle from Stephanie's arms and immediately had his hat knocked to a decidedly rakish angle. "But Bridge spoke faster."

"I do believe," the marchioness said, "Alistair is tactfully taking note of my condition. I shall be eternally grateful."

The gentlemen set off on their walk with the younger children as soon as the blankets had been spread for the ladies. But Lord Francis had a problem on his hands. Every prospective cricketer wanted him on their team, but as he pointed out, he could not divide himself in two.

"And even if I could," he said, "someone would have to take the left-hand side and therefore the useless side."

"But—"

"But—"

The chorus came from all sides.

Stephanie got to her feet and coughed for their attention. "If it is an adult who is wanted on both sides," she said, "I could offer my services."

Everyone—including Lord Francis to his discredit—turned to stare at her as if she had two heads.

"I was the champion bowler of my county for years," she said rashly. "Of the girls anyway," she added more quietly. "I shattered more wickets than anyone could possibly count."

"I can count to a hundred, Aunt Stephie," four-year-old Robert Kneller announced.

"More than that," she said. "Well, here I am. Take me or leave me."

"Stephanie," the countess said with a grimace, "you really must not feel obliged—"

"I am going to sleep with the sun on my face," Lady Francis announced, stretching out her full length on the blanket and determinedly closing her eyes.

But Stephanie was in the game—on sufferance, she realized when she saw the glum faces of her team members. Lord Francis, of course, was on the other team.

Gloom turned to exuberance when her turn at bat came and she got a good hit off the first ball Lord Francis bowled at her. She suspected that he had thrown it deliberately slowly, as he had done for Robert and Jennifer's Mary. She laughed and whooped as she hitched her skirts and ran between the wickets. Her team cheered wildly. The other team looked accusingly at their hero. Samantha and Jennifer applauded.

"Oh, very well done, Stephanie," Jennifer called.

After that success Stephanie threw herself even more wholeheartedly into the game. She cheered and coaxed and coached her own team; she jeered and taunted the other team—the oldest member of it, anyway. She pulled off her bonnet and tossed it to the blanket. She tucked her dress a couple of inches up beneath the ribbon under her bosom so that she would not trip over the hem as she ran. She lost hairpins. She gained color.

She had not enjoyed herself so much for ten years or more.

And then came her moment of greatest triumph. Her team was leading by only two runs, and Lord Francis, the final batter for the other side, came in to bat.

"Move your fielders back, Aunt Stephie," he called,

taking the bat in both hands and flexing his wrists. "Here comes a certain hit."

Cheers from his side.

"Stay where you are, fielders," Stephanie commanded, "so that you may have a better view of the wickets shattering."

Cheers—considerably more halfhearted—from her side.

But it happened just as she had predicted. Luck was with her, of course, as she would have been the last to admit. The ball took an awkward bounce on the grass before the bat and hopped over it, while Lord Francis sawed at the air. It sent the wickets toppling with a satisfying thud.

"Yes!" Stephanie pumped both fists in the air and then fell backward as her team threw themselves at her, all shrieking enough to break eardrums. She laughed and hugged them and wrestled with them. Lord Francis, she noticed as guilt suddenly struck her, was also prone on the grass with his team on top of him. Considerable laughter came from their direction.

A few minutes passed before the children dispersed, intent on sharing their triumph with mothers. Stephanie, still laughing, struggled to her feet and brushed ineffectually at the grass clinging to her muslin skirt. Her hair must be similarly full of it, she thought, lifting her hands to the ruin of curls that Patty had created just a few hours before.

And then she saw that the children were talking excitedly at the blankets not only to mothers, but to *fathers* too. And Annabelle was crawling on the grass, trying to pull the head off a daisy.

Reality came crashing back as she found him at last with her eyes—leaning against the trunk of a tree a short distance from the blankets, his arms folded across his chest, his eyes focused on her. In his dark green superfine coat and buff pantaloons and black Hessians, he looked about as immaculate as a man could possibly look. He was not smiling. *Of course he was not smiling.*

An hour or so ago he had left the ladies to sit on the blankets. Being decorative. Being dignified. Behaving as ladies should behave. And the other three ladies had done just that.

"Bravo, Stephanie," the earl called to her.

"Francis may never forgive you, Stephanie." Lady Francis was laughing gleefully.

"Oh, Stephanie, your poor dress," the marchioness called.

"We thought only Cora ever acted above and beyond the call of duty," the countess said, and everyone laughed, including Lady Francis herself.

Stephanie scarcely heard them. She swallowed. He was coming toward her. He stooped to pick up something from the blanket as he passed it—her reticule. He looked at her unsmilingly.

"Your friend Mr. Reaves did not exaggerate about your bowling arm," he said. "That was quite a show."

"It was a game," she said. "For the children's sake." In a sense it was true. It had started out that way. But quickly enough she had become one of the children.

Her dress was still tucked up awkwardly and covered with grass. She could see tendrils of her hair that had no business being visible. She felt hot and flushed. Goodness only knew how long he had been standing there, watching her. His words suggested that he had seen her bowl out Lord Francis at the least. That meant he had also watched the exuberant aftermath of the win. He had seen her roll and wrestle in the grass, laughing helplessly.

She could not feel more at a disadvantage if she tried for a thousand years, she thought.

"Your reticule," he said, handing it to her. "Come. We will take a short walk."

So that she could be scolded privately, she thought, taking his arm and not even looking back when he called to the others that they were going to take a short stroll before tea. To be informed that her behavior had just fallen far short of what was expected from any lady. That it was totally unacceptable in a lady who was to be a duchess within one week.

She wondered if he would turn her off. No, she thought immediately, he would not do that. It was too late. There would be too much dreadful scandal, for him as well as for her. Besides, he was far too kind to turn her off.

She was beginning to hate kindness.

And she was beginning to hate herself for hating it.

HE WAS FEELING rather as if he had been slapped across the face—the same sort of shock and humiliation—and pain.

He had scarcely been able to believe his eyes when he had returned from the walk with the other men and with the younger children, who would have given the ladies no rest if he had not devised a plan for taking them out of the way for an hour.

One of the ladies was playing cricket with Kneller and the children.

It was Stephanie, of course. The words that damnably good-looking old friend of hers had spoken at the Royal Academy had returned immediately to mind. It was Stephanie with her elegant muslin dress pulled up to show far too much ankle for propriety, with no bonnet and auburn hair in an untidy halo about her head. It was Stephanie, flushed and exuberant and laughing and totally absorbed in the game.

He had never seen a woman look so startlingly beautiful.

And she was his. All that beauty and vitality and uninhibited joy in life was his. He had felt a rush of pure lust for her. Though he had realized as soon as the word formed in his mind that he was doing himself an injustice—and her too. It was more a feeling of delighted possessiveness. No, even that was not quite accurate.

He was in love with her, he had thought at last—delighted with her and proud of her. Proud that his closest friends were looking at her too and seeing what a very *right* choice of bride he had made.

He had imagined her playing thus with his children—with *their* children. And this time the feeling really was pure lust.

He had arrived toward the end of the game and had got himself positioned a little apart from the others just in time to see the lucky result of the rather wild overarm pitch she made to Kneller. Kneller had been showing off too, of course, hitting out when he should have been protecting his wickets. Bridgwater had propped one shoulder against a tree and watched the children of Stephanie's team bowl her right off her feet onto her back and pile on top of her. He watched her laugh and hug them and roll good-naturedly on the ground with them, making for them a perfect afternoon. He had even noticed her glance at Kneller and his losing team to make sure they were not dejected.

How wonderful she was, he had thought. He could not imagine any other lady of his acquaintance risking her appearance and her dignity for the sake of children who were not even her own. And for the sake of her own enjoyment too, he suspected. It saddened him somehow to think that exuberance, spontaneity, even laughter were stamped ruthlessly out of the lives of children of gentle birth as soon as they began to grow up.

Gentlemen and especially ladies were expected to behave with quiet dignity at all times.

He had, he realized, quite without any merit to himself, found just the right bride. Perhaps she would help him relax the habit of years. Perhaps she would help him enjoy life again. Perhaps she would teach him to laugh in public.

And then the children had scattered, abandoning their heroine in order to take the glory to themselves by boasting to their parents. She had got to her feet, had begun to brush herself off—and then had seen him.

She had changed in a flash. At one moment she was vibrant with laughter. At the next she was frozen-faced and tight-lipped. She looked incredibly untidy.

That was when he felt as if he had been slapped.

He had taken all the joy out of her day.

How she must hate him.

He could think only that she was also going to be embarrassed in another moment to be seen as she was. She needed to tidy up. She needed some privacy in which to do it. He acted from instinct, walking toward her, picking up her reticule as he passed the blankets—perhaps she carried a comb inside it.

He wanted to tell her how splendid she had been, what a good sport. He wanted to tell her how proud he was that she had made the children so happy. He wanted to tell her how beautiful she looked to his partial eyes. He wanted to tell her that he loved her. But he was hurt. He felt bruised. She did not like him. He merely commented on her bowling skills and took her arm and led her away toward some of the ancient oaks.

He felt stiff and uncomfortable. Rejected. Hated.

"You will wish to tidy yourself before tea," he said.

"Yes." They were already out of sight behind the trees. She slipped her arm from his and pulled at the waist of her dress. He could see then why so much of her ankles had been showing. She had tucked up some of the fabric behind the ribbon under her bosom. She looked up at him briefly as he stood a foot away watching, his hands clasped at his back. It seemed to him to be a look of pure hatred.

"No *lady* would ever dream of doing such a thing, would she?" she said.

"Turn," he said. "Your back is covered with grass."

She turned obediently, and he brushed firmly with one hand, trying to make the action as impersonal as possible, but feeling her warm curves with every stroke.

"Your hair needs attention," he said when she turned again. "Do you have a comb in your reticule?"

"Yes," she said, more tight-lipped than ever. Perhaps she was embarrassed even with him, he thought. She probably was, in fact. Perhaps that was all this was—embarrassment, not hatred. He watched her take the pins from her hair and set them between her lips before combing quickly through her hair—thick and wavy. He remembered it from that first night at the inn and swallowed convulsively. She kept her eyes lowered.

"You have made the children very happy this afternoon," he said.

"The *children,* yes," she said around the pins in her mouth. She was knotting her hair at the base of her neck with sure, practiced hands, and he was reminded that she was a woman unaccustomed to the attentions of a maid. She slid the pins deftly into place.

He could not quite read her expression. He did not know quite what point she had been making with the three words. But they did not encourage him to continue.

Ah, God, and they were to be man and wife within a week.

She looked up at him with expressionless eyes. "Will I do now, Your Grace?" she asked him.

He could hear the hatred quite clear in her voice this time. Despite the pretty lemon muslin dress, she looked like a governess again—a hard-eyed governess who would stand for no nonsense.

"Yes," he said. "You will do."

And he felt suddenly and unaccountably angry. Though perhaps not quite so unaccountably either. What had he done to incur her hatred? He could think of a few things, perhaps, but they were in the past, and he had apologized for them and had tried to make amends. They were not the only couple the world had known who had been forced into a marriage not quite of their own choosing. She might give them a chance. She might try to like him at least. She might surprise herself and find that it was not altogether impossible. He was no monster, after all.

Without pausing to ponder the wisdom of what he was about to do, he took a few steps toward her, backing her up against the trunk of a tree. He set his palms against the trunk on either side of her head, brought his body hard against hers, and found her mouth with his own. It was not a gentle kiss. Unashamedly, he used his expertise to demand with his lips that she part her own, that she open her mouth. When she did so, he thrust his tongue inside to its full length and stroked back over the roof of her mouth with its tip.

And he lifted his head.

"Perhaps," he said, and he was amazed and a little alarmed to hear the cold haughtiness in his voice, "you would do well, Miss Gray, to reconcile your mind to the fact that you will be my wife in less than one week's time. The Duchess of Bridgwater. I will expect your attitude to change."

He did not know where the words came from. He certainly had not planned them. He listened to their echo as if they had come from someone else. He was, he realized, quite out of his depth. He had always been in perfect control of his own life. It was the fear of losing that control that had driven him into virtual hiding for the past six years. But it had happened anyway.

His dream had happened too, but it was a nightmarish parody of the dream with which he was to spend the rest of his waking life.

Her lips looked just kissed—itself an irony. "It will, Your Grace," she said, her head still back against the tree, her arms and hands pressed against it at her sides. "I will not forget again."

Her eyes brightened with tears, and he turned away, deeply ashamed. He seemed to have behaved at his worst with Miss Stephanie Gray right from the first moment.

"Come," he said. "We must return to the others. I am supposed to be the host, yet I have abandoned my guests before serving them tea. You and I must learn to rub along together somehow. Shall we resolve at least to try?"

"Yes, Your Grace," she said, taking the arm he offered.

He would give anything in the world, he thought foolishly, to hear her call him Alistair.

13

She had rarely worn white. White, she thought, was a young girl's color. Yet as a young girl she had worn more practical colors as the busy daughter of the vicar. Between the ages of twenty and six-and-twenty she had worn only gray and brown and black. In the past month she had worn colors that both she and the duchess agreed looked good with her hair.

Today she wore white—white satin, made heavy and stately with its pearl decorations. But no frills, no flounces, no bows. White flowers and green leaves were twined into her hair. She wore white gloves and slippers. She carried a posy of gold rosebuds.

The duchess looked her over carefully from head to toe and nodded. "You will do very nicely, indeed," she said. "You are a bride fit for a prince, Stephanie."

"Mother—" She was cold all the way through to the heart. Cold with terror—with the certain knowledge that she was doing the wrong thing. But that it was quite, quite unavoidable. Foolishly and suddenly, she wanted her own mother and her father too. She wanted to be hugged, cried over. She was so cold. She was surrounded by coldness and had been for a month. With kindness and ice, an unlikely but all too real combination.

But it was only her nerves that made her imagine such

things. That was obvious even as panic threatened to engulf her. Her Grace's lips twitched, her eyes grew unexpectedly bright, and she stepped hastily forward—the only time Stephanie had ever seen her do anything that might be called impulsive.

"Oh, my dear," she said, hugging Stephanie and laying a cool cheek against hers. "Make him happy. He is so very dear to me, my son. And be happy yourself."

And then she was standing apart again, looking cool and regal once more. "There," she said, "I risked squashing your flowers. Forgive me. Your cousin will be waiting downstairs, and I must be on my way to the church. In less than two hours' time you will have my title, Stephanie. Carry it as proudly as I have. But I am sure you will. You have worked hard during the past month. You have surpassed all my most optimistic hopes."

And with a half smile she was gone.

Cousin Horace exclaimed over the transformation in her appearance and reminded her of her extreme good fortune in having netted a duke for a husband. His Grace had shown her the sort of condescension for which she must be grateful for the rest of her life. And she must not forget too that from this morning on— once the wedding ceremony was over and the register signed—she would be secure in her inheritance. She would be an independently wealthy woman.

She should, she was told, consider herself the happiest and most fortunate woman in the world.

She felt cold to the heart.

And colder still when they reached St. George's on Hanover Square and walked through the path left clear by the curious gathered outside to watch a Society wedding. And even when they were inside and the organ began to play and she became aware of the pews filled with all the cream of the beau monde. Somewhere in the crowd—she did not even try to find them with her eyes—were her own two friends, doubtless feeling awed and perhaps even intimidated by the company in which they found themselves. The only two friends of her own present. Yet since she had met them two weeks ago, she had not even tried to see them again.

And then she saw him. He was waiting for her at the altar rail. He was watching her walk down the aisle on Cousin Horace's arm. Straight and tall and proud, he looked as cold as she felt. He was dressed all in white and silver. She had never seen a man dressed all in white before. He looked magnificent. And cold.

But his eyes, his silver eyes, when she was close enough to see them burned into hers with cold fire.

She stood beside him, quietly dignified as she had always been as a governess, proud of bearing as she had been taught to be by the duchess. She spoke the words she was told to say. She listened to him say what he was told to say. She felt his hand hold hers—warm and steady in contrast with his icy appearance. She watched as he slid the bright and unfamiliar gold wedding ring onto her finger; he had to coax it over her knuckle. She lifted her face for his kiss—warm, closed lips pressed firmly against her own while an almost soundless murmur passed through the congregation behind them.

She was his wife.

She was the Duchess of Bridgwater.

Her inheritance was safe.

She felt as cold as the marble floor of the church.

She realized why she had so dreaded her marriage for the past week and even longer than that. It was not just that she was losing her freedom to a man who did not want her, but was marrying her out of a sense of obligation. It was not just that she felt she was losing her identity in that of his duchess. It was not just that she felt bound and confined to the point of suffocation by the rules that she must not on any account break. It was not just that she was being rushed at dizzying speed from a dull but familiar world into a frighteningly new one. It was not just any of those things.

It was that she loved him—and was unloved in return.

If she could have remained indifferent to him, she thought, merely grateful to him and under an obligation to him, she could have borne all the rest. What freedom had she known for the last six years, after all? And what happiness and self-respect?

But she had not remained indifferent.

And then the rest of the service was over and the register signed, and she was walking slowly back up the aisle again, her arm resting along the top of her husband's. There were smiling faces wherever she looked. Cora, sitting almost at the front, was red-faced and openly sobbing and taking a large white handkerchief from Francis's hand. Jennifer, beside her, was smiling and teary-eyed. Gabriel was winking. Miriam, almost at the back, was wet-faced and brightly smiling.

And then they were outside and being greeted by the rowdy cheers and the bawdy comments of the small crowd gathered there. Her husband led her through it to his waiting carriage, handed her inside, and climbed in beside her. The carriage lurched into well-sprung motion as the first guests began to leave the church. The wedding breakfast was to be at the duke's town house— Stephanie had never yet been there, though her trunks and her maid had been taken there even before she had left for the church. The duke and his duchess must be there ahead of their guests in order to receive them as was proper.

As was proper.

"My dear," her husband said, taking her hand and setting it on his sleeve again—her bright new wedding ring shone up at them—"you look more beautiful today than I thought it possible for any woman to look. I wish you to know how proud I am of you."

Yes, she had learned her lessons well—with one or two rather nasty lapses. They would grow fewer and fewer as time went on, until they disappeared altogether.

"I have tried," she said. "I will continue to try so that you may continue to be proud of me, Your Grace."

His free hand covered hers. "Stephanie," he said quietly, "my name is Alistair."

"Yes." She closed her eyes for a moment, beguiled by the intimacy of the carriage interior and by the softness of his voice, imagining that she heard tenderness in it. "Alistair."

"There is nothing improper about a man and his wife sharing the intimacy of their given names," he said.

"No." She opened her eyes again. "If it is not improper, it may be allowed, then." She hoped he had not heard the bitterness she tried to keep out of her voice.

Everything by the rules.

Very well, then. Everything by the rules.

HE HAD INTENDED to remain in London with his bride until the end of the Season. It was the proper thing to do, after all. As the Duchess of Bridgwater she would need to be presented at court to the queen. His mother would act as her sponsor. And she would need to establish her new position as his duchess and his hostess. They would need to entertain—dinners and soirées and one grand ball. Besides, she had a position of her own to establish. She was now undisputed and independent owner of Sindon Park and the fortune left her by her grandfather.

The proper thing to do was stay. It was what he had planned. But London appeared to be suffocating her. It was suffocating him. Suddenly, he wanted to be away from it, away from the social obligations. He wanted to take her into the country. He wanted to be alone with her, perhaps rashly. She hated him. She had not once smiled at him, though it was their wedding day, and she had smiled at everyone else. Even when she had come to stand beside him at the church rail she had not smiled.

Had he? He could not be sure he had. He had felt choked with a deep emotion he had been forced to keep under control. Half of the beau monde was looking at him—or at her. Probably at her. Everyone looked at a bride. Who was interested in a mere bridegroom? But he could not be sure anyway that he had smiled.

When he rose from his place at the wedding breakfast to speak to his guests, he announced that he would be taking his duchess to Wightwick Hall in Gloucestershire on the morrow. He did not look at either his wife or his mother to observe their reactions. He thanked his guests for attending both the wedding and the breakfast and for making the day a special one.

"I will send instructions without delay to your maid to leave your trunks as they are," he said quietly to Stephanie after he had sat down again. "She will unpack only what you will need tonight and tomorrow."

Tonight she would become fully his wife, he thought, watching the slight flush of color that stained her cheeks.

"Yes, Your Gr . . ." she said. "Yes. Thank you."

He wondered if he had been very foolish. The summer alone at Wightwick would be a long one if they began it this early. They could invite guests to join them there, of course, or they could take themselves off to Brighton for a few weeks. But for a while at least they would be virtually alone together. Was there any chance at all of making a viable marriage out of what they had begun? He doubted it. Their relationship seemed to have deteriorated steadily through the month of their betrothal. For the past four days—ever since the day of that wretched picnic—there had been nothing at all between them except cold formality.

It was his fault, he knew. There had been his dream, his longing for a marriage that would bring love and warmth and companionship and happiness into his life. But there had never really been the possibility of anything but the dream. All his education had been designed to make him into a dignified, controlled figure of authority. There had been love—certainly a fondness between him and his parents, between him and his brother and sisters. But love had always been a cool thing in his life, and for most of his life it had taken second place to dignity and duty.

He was capable of feeling love. He had always known that, and he knew it now with painful force. But he had never been taught a way of showing love—or of inspiring it.

He had inspired gratitude and respect and obedience in Stephanie, under largely false pretenses. But there was nothing more. She hated him, though he guessed that she must feel guilty at her feelings and would spend the rest of her life fighting them. He did not doubt that he had married a dutiful duchess.

He did not want duty. He wanted love.

Perhaps, he thought, at Wightwick . . .

But there was no further time for dreaming. There were guests to entertain for the rest of the afternoon and on even into the early evening. He scarcely saw his wife and had no chance to exchange even a single word with her. He glimpsed her talking with his relatives, his friends, her friends. She had acquired a great deal of the regal manner that had always characterized his mother, but to it she added her own brand of beauty and charm. He spoke with as many people as time permitted.

It was, of course, the correct thing for his wife and him to remain apart as they entertained guests. It was the way things would have continued if he had not made the impulsive decision to leave for Wightwick in the morning. A rider had already been sent, he gathered, to gallop hell-for-leather to his country seat to warn the staff there of his imminent arrival. There would be panic there for a few days, he did not doubt.

The thought brought a smile to his face.

But finally he was alone with her. They dined alone together; both had changed from their wedding clothes into evening dress. They conversed as smoothly as any well-bred couple might. They continued the conversation in the drawing room both before and after she had played for him on the pianoforte and he had played for her. They drank tea together.

And then he escorted her upstairs to the door of her dressing room, bowed over her hand, and told her he would do himself the honor of visiting her half an hour later.

He went into his own dressing room and flung himself into the closest chair. He propped his arms on the rests and steepled his fingers beneath his chin. He closed his eyes.

And remembered her as she had been that night at the inn. Warm and beautiful and inviting and willing—or so it had appeared. He wondered what would have happened if she had been what she had seemed. She would have been his mistress for a month now. They would be comfortable together, contented together. Would he have tired of her yet? Would he have ever tired of her?

Foolish, pointless thoughts, of course. She had not been as she had seemed. And he could no longer think of her in terms of sexual gratification alone. She was his wife, his life's partner.

He drew a deep breath and let it out slowly. It was time to summon his valet. He must not keep her waiting beyond the appointed time. She was probably nervous.

SHE WAS NOT afraid. It would be foolish for a woman of six-and-twenty to fear a physical process that would probably become almost as familiar as breathing to her over the coming months and years. She reminded herself that she was fortunate it was to happen at all. For years she had not expected that it ever would. But she had always wanted it to happen. She had always wanted children of her own—quite passionately.

He was a man she found physically attractive. He was a man she loved. She was not afraid.

She just wished that he could have stayed simply as Mr. Munro. She had liked him. He had been so very kind. He would have been of her own world. She would not have had to change. She would not have had to consider her every word and action to be sure that everything that was proper was said and done. She would not have come almost to hate him because she lived constantly in fear of shaming and disappointing him.

She did almost hate him. She also loved him.

Tonight she would be the duchess he expected—calm, gracious, unimpassioned. She would not find it too difficult. She was not afraid, after all.

She looked up with cool welcome when he tapped on her door and came inside. She stood still and relaxed as his eyes moved down over her loosened hair and her white silk and lace nightgown to her bare feet.

"Come in, Alistair," she said. "Let me pour you a glass of wine." She had thought to have some sent up. She poured a glass for herself too and handed him his. She wanted him to see that her hand was steady, that she was no shrinking bride unworthy of her position.

"So that we may toast our health?" he said. "And our happiness, Stephanie? To our health, then, and our happiness." He raised his glass.

She touched hers to it, and they drank. He held her eyes with his own as he did so. She wished he would smile at her. She longed to smile at him. But she would not risk appearing coquettish.

"Perhaps," he said, "we will be happy. Will we?"

To hide her longing from him, she took his empty glass and set it down with her half-full one on the tray.

"I shall try," she said, "to make you happy, Alistair. Always. Tell me how."

He half smiled at her then. One side of his mouth lifted. It was an expression she had not seen on him before.

"Ah, yes," he said. "You will too, will you not, Stephanie? We will make the best we can of it, then. And I will try to see to it that you never regret the events of this morning—and tonight. It will be my recipe for happiness. We will both try."

"Yes." She wanted suddenly to reach out with one hand to cup his cheek. But it was not the sort of thing one did with the Duke of Bridgwater. Even if he was her husband.

"Come, then." He reached out a hand for hers, his eyes probing hers at the same time. "Come to bed, Stephanie."

"Yes," she said. She moved too fast toward it and deliberately slowed her pace. She was perhaps a little nervous, after all. Since it was his mother who had instructed her, she had not liked to ask questions. Perhaps she would not have anyway. Should she raise her nightgown herself or wait for him to do it? Should she touch him with her hands or rest them on the bed? Should she say anything afterward or keep quiet? It was embarrassing at her age to know so little.

She decided on total passivity. At least she could do no real wrong that way. Perhaps he would tell her what he wanted. She learned fast; she had proved that to him in the past month. Soon enough she would learn what was expected of her in their marriage bed. At least she knew what he did *not* want. She had not forgotten the lesson learned in Elizabeth's conservatory.

He blew out the candles after she had lain down. She was glad of that. She was a little embarrassed as well as nervous. Her body had been so very much her own private property all her life. Even the presence of a maid during the last month had embarrassed her. But a maid was at least her own gender.

He lay down beside her, leaned over her, and kissed her. In the way he had kissed her twice before—she did not even want to remember that last kiss against the oak in Richmond Park. She should have been prepared for the same results. Her breasts tightened almost instantly, and she felt a rush of raw aching pain to her womb. She had disgusted him at Elizabeth's ball by giving in to her passion. She reminded herself of the fact, deliberately verbalizing it more than once in her mind. Not again. It would not happen again. She pressed her palms against the mattress and fought her body's needs.

Should she part her lips? His tongue pressed through, and the decision was taken out of her hands. Should she open her mouth? *Tell me what to do,* she pleaded silently. She opened her mouth.

She had never had a nightgown that buttoned down the front. Both her mother-in-law and her modiste had guided her to ones that did for her wedding clothes. In her naivete she had not realized why until her husband began to undo the buttons while he kissed her. The front opening was a long one.

His hand came inside against her bare flesh. He brushed his palm and his fingers over her very lightly. He touched her breasts. They already felt swollen and sore. She bit her bottom lip hard when his thumb touched and pressed lightly upon her hardened nipple.

The ache that had been in her womb and between her thighs had become an insistent throbbing.

And then his hand was there too, and his fingers were probing—very gently. She could not have borne the pain of a firm touch. She shut her eyes very tightly and pressed her fingertips hard into the mattress. She wanted to squirm and cry out. She wanted to throw her arms about him and beg him to stop or to— But she did not know what. She held her breath. And through it all she felt embarrassment and humiliation. She could both feel and hear wetness.

"Let your breath out," he said quietly against her ear. "Relax. You will soon grow accustomed to it."

She felt so ashamed. That she had had to be told! Her breath shuddered out of her quite audibly. But he had moved over her and was lowering himself onto her body. It was almost a relief to feel his knees between her own. She did not resist as he pushed her legs wide. Her nightgown, she realized, was already up about her waist. She need not have worried about that either. There had been no awkward moment.

Despite herself, she drew in her breath and held it again. His hands were beneath her. She could feel him position himself.

And then he came into her. She had prepared herself for pain. But pain did not come immediately. She had not expected the incredible stretching sensation, the sense of being invaded, of having her body taken over by someone else. Then came the pain, the momentary panic. And the hard deep occupation of her secret depths.

She let out her breath slowly. This was it, then. What she had yearned for for so long. The completion of her femininity. The uniting with man. The hope of being fruitful. The pain had gone and the panic and the strange, unexpected outrage at being violated. Wonder replaced them all. Wonder that such a thing could be. Wonder that she held him so much deeper inside than she had expected. Wonder that there was no sense of embarrassment or humiliation. She relaxed completely.

It felt wonderful.

She knew what was to come. Or had thought she knew. She lay still, allowing it to happen, holding herself open to his pleasure, taking to herself as much secret pleasure as she dared without losing herself in passion as she had in Elizabeth's conservatory. She wanted to tighten inside muscles as she had during that embrace. She wanted to tighten about him and feel her pleasure. She lay relaxed and still as he pumped firmly and repeatedly into her. She could feel the heat of him—all over her, inside her. She could hear his labored breathing against her hair. She could smell his cologne and his heat and his sweat.

She wanted to lift her legs and press her inner thighs hard against his lean hips. She wanted to tilt herself so that she could bring him deeper. She wanted to wrap her arms about the firm muscles of his chest and waist. She lay still, spread-eagled beneath him, giving herself in marriage.

When his pace quickened and deepened and then he sighed and relaxed and she felt the heat of his seed inside her, she swallowed and fought tears. She lay very still. She had been told that she might find it unpleasant. She had been told that she might in time find it pleasant. She had not been told that it would be the most wonderful feeling in this world. And she had not been told that she would want to cry when it was over because she would want it to go on and on until . . . Oh, she did not know until when.

She felt cold when he moved away to lie beside her. She felt his hand lower her nightgown and raise the bedcovers. She felt his hand take her own; his was very warm and damp. He was still breathing rather heavily.

"Did I hurt you very badly, my dear?" he asked her.

"No." Her voice sounded high-pitched. She brought it back to normal. "Hardly at all, Alistair. I hope I pleased you." She was pleased with the calm, matter-of-fact tone she had achieved.

He did not answer for a few moments. "You pleased me," he said at last. "I thank you. You will find it less painful tomorrow and perhaps a little less . . . over-whelming."

"I was not overwhelmed," she said quickly, turning her head toward him. But she could not see him clearly in the darkness. "I tried. I . . . I liked it." Perhaps she ought not to have said that. Perhaps it was the wrong thing to say. "I hope I can bear you an heir within the year, Alistair."

He sat up on the edge of the bed, his back to her. His back seemed hunched. She guessed that his elbows were resting on his knees. She could see his fingers pushing through his hair. And then he was on his feet and bending over her. She felt the backs of his fingers light beneath her jaw.

"I will leave you to your sleep," he said. "You have had a busy day, and tomorrow we will be traveling all day. Thank you for today, Stephanie—for marrying me, for entertaining our guests, for . . . this. I shall try to be a good husband. Good night."

"Alistair—" she said as he moved away. But when he stopped and turned back to her, she could not think what to say. *Please come back to bed? Please let me admit to you how wonderful it was for me? Please let me love you?* "I will try too. All my life I will try."

"Good night, my dear," he said.

"Good night, Alistair." *Good night, my love.*

She could feel the soreness and the discomfort that the

consummation of their marriage had left behind. She felt cold with his body heat removed. She could smell him on her pillow and on herself.

At first the sound of a noisy sob startled her. Then she turned her face into the pillow and indulged in a good self-pitying weep.

There was no one to see her loss of dignity and control, after all. She was tired to death of dignity and control.

She wondered how an act of such unbelievable intimacy could leave her just a few minutes later feeling lonelier than she had ever felt in her life.

14

THEY WERE TRAVELING IN THE SAME CARRIAGE AS they had during that other journey. He tried to feel the sameness. He tried to feel relaxed, amused, totally in control of the situation as he had felt then.

Of course, she had sat on the seat opposite him during those three days. He had been able to watch her the whole time—the accomplished actress, fully aware of the lure of her beauty and charm. Spinning him a tale that was so unbelievable and yet so full of predictable clichés that he had enjoyed vastly the exercise of anticipating what she was about to say—and being right almost every time.

He had fallen in love with her as far back as then, he thought now in some surprise. Though there was nothing profound about falling in love, of course. Loving was a different matter altogether. He wondered which applied to him now. Was he merely in love with her? Or did he love her?

He half turned his head to look at her. She was dressed all in light spring green, even down to her slippers and gloves, which were lying on the seat opposite. She looked quiet and composed. She had been a bride just yesterday, he thought. She had lost her virginity last night. There was no sign in her bearing that such momentous events in her life had happened so recently. She smiled calmly back at him. She met his eyes, but did not blush.

He had hoped for blushes this morning, for lowered eyes, for some sign that she remembered their intimacy of the night before. But she had arrived at breakfast only moments after him. And she had sat and conversed easily with him and had eaten a breakfast of respectable size. There had not been even a tremor in her hands.

Of course she had behaved much the same way in bed. There had been none of the passion he had hoped he might rekindle, though her body had responded at least sufficiently to minimize the pain of his entry. There had been only the slight nervousness, which had caused her to tense just before she had been mounted for the first time—and the dignified, unresisting acquiescence in the performance of the marriage act.

He, of course, had been fiercely aroused by her tall, shapely slimness. By the almost athletic firmness of her body—a strange word to think of in connection with a woman.

"Tell me about your friends," he said. "The Reaveses, that is." Perhaps somehow he could recapture the charm of that other journey. He almost wished, absurdly, that she were wearing the flamboyant plumed bonnet again—and sitting opposite him.

"There are seven of them," she said. "Six girls and Tom. I am closest in age to Miriam and so was most friendly with her. And with Tom."

She had sat with Thomas Reaves and his wife for almost fifteen minutes yesterday, talking animatedly with them before moving away to mingle with their other guests.

"I was encouraged to be friendly with them," she said. "Mrs. Reaves said it was because only I could keep peace among the girls. Mama said it was because I was better born than they and Mrs. Reaves had social ambitions. But I think not. They were far wealthier than we were. None of that mattered to us when we were children, anyway. We played and played. We used to climb trees and swim in the stream and dive in the lake—all forbidden activities. I was . . . Mama once called me a hoyden. I am afraid she was right."

"Anyone who plays cricket as well as you must have been a hoyden," he said. Absurdly, he wished he had known her then. In the month of their acquaintance he had had only a few tantalizing glimpses of the daring, exuberant girl she must have been.

"When I grew older," she said, spreading her hands in her lap and looking down at them—her wedding ring looked startlingly new and bright—"Papa suggested that I redirect my energies. And so I worked with Mama for as long as she lived and then alone in performing parish duties. But I did not mind. I loved the life."

She had talked about all this during that other journey, but he had listened in a different way then. He had thought then that she was spinning an amusing yarn.

"And the friendships faded?" he asked.

"Not really," she said. "They matured. The hardest thing to accustom myself to when I took employment with the Burnabys was the loss of those friendships. I was not allowed to receive personal letters at the Burnabys more than two or three times a year. I missed them, my friends. I missed Miriam."

"And Tom?" he said. "Was there never a romantic attachment between the two of you?" Surely, there must have been. They must be close in age. They were both handsome people. He wished then he had not asked the question.

"Not really," she said. "We had been friends all our lives. It would have been difficult to see each other differently. Of course it was hard saying good-bye and knowing that we would probably never meet again. And

he felt bad about my having to become a governess—
they all felt bad."

"But he did not try to stop you?" he asked.

She smiled at her hands. "He offered me marriage,"
she said. "I refused."

"Why?" he asked.

"Because he offered out of kindness," she said. "He
did not love me. And I did not love him. It would not
have been the marriage I had always dreamed of."

He felt uncomfortable suddenly. She might have been
describing their own marriage. Except that she had been
unable to say no to him.

"What was the marriage you had always dreamed
of?" he asked almost unwillingly.

She looked up at him suddenly with cheeks that were
at last slightly flushed. It was as if she had just realized
the turn their conversation had taken.

"Oh." She laughed. "It was the dream all girls and
very young women dream, I suppose. It seems foolish
now and would appear even more foolish to a gentleman—to a duke in particular. I dreamed of romantic
love. I believed in that quite ridiculous notion that
somewhere for all of us there is that one perfect match,
that . . . Oh, it does not matter. But I am glad I did not
marry Tom. I would have always felt that I had"—she
winced and caught at her bottom lip, but she had no
choice but to complete what she had started to say—
"that I had coerced him into it. I would always have felt
th-that I owed him an obligation I could never fully
repay. I . . ." She foundered to a halt after all.

It was how she felt about him, of course. She believed
she had coerced him into marriage. She believed she had
an obligation to him she could never repay. Her marriage was a burden to her. She could never be happy
with him.

What would she say if she knew that he had mistaken

her for an actress and a whore? That he had taken her all the way to Sindon not out of kindness and concern, but . . .

"Tell me more," he said, "about those games you played, about the exploits and the mischief." He was hungry to know her. Although she had told him a great deal more than he had ever told her, he still felt that she was a stranger—a stranger who was his wife and his duchess, a stranger with whom he had been intimate last night and would be intimate tonight and tomorrow night and so on through their lives.

"They were not dignified," she said, smiling quickly at him so that for a moment he had a dazzling glimpse of her dimple and gold-flecked eyes. "Some of them were downright dishonorable, like the time we all crept out at night—Tom, Miriam, Agnes, and I—because Tom had heard and believed the strange story that fish swam on the surface of the stream at night and might be caught in the hands. I believe I was eight years old. We did not see a single fish, let alone catch any, of course."

He smiled. She told him several more of her adventures that he had not heard before. It was clear that Tom Reaves had been the leader, with Stephanie a close second. He thought of his own childhood. He had been much like Tom, only perhaps considerably worse, until his father, despairing of ever grooming him to take on the ducal title and responsibilities eventually sent him off to school at the age of ten. It seemed to him that he had spent a large portion of his childhood bent over his father's desk trying not to hear the whistle of his father's cane, which was always the harbinger of stinging pain.

Let George be the damned duke, he could remember yelling once, dancing from foot to foot in a vain attempt to alleviate the stinging of his rear end. *All I want to be is a damned soldier or a damned sailor.* All he had got for his act of shocking defiance, of course, had been a thunderous order to bend over again. And school very soon after that. He had wondered how many people, knowing him now, would guess that he had been such a child.

Would his own eldest son be such a rebel? And would he handle the problem in the same way his father had handled it? His father had been stiffly dignified and humorless, though not lacking entirely in love. Was he like his father? His mother and his sisters said that he was.

He reached out suddenly and took Stephanie's left hand in his own. It was something he had been wanting to do for an hour or more. She had beautiful hands, with long slim fingers. He set a thumb and forefinger against her ring and twisted it on her finger.

"I believe you will like Wightwick Hall," he said. "The park is so large that you need hardly be aware of the farms unless you ride out to them."

"I am sure I shall like it," she said. She made no effort to reclaim her hand. "I suppose it is much larger than Sindon Park. I shall do my best to fulfill my duties there, Alistair."

"It is a safe, spacious place for children to grow up in," he said. "Six generations of my family have grown up there. Our children will be the seventh."

"Yes," she said. "I know that the Dukes of Bridgwater have not been without a male heir in all that time. There is a portrait gallery, is there not? Your mother told me that there are portraits of all your ancestors. I look forward to seeing them. And I shall try to see to it that the tradition is not broken. I hope to bear you an heir within the year."

It was coolly said, without a blush. He wished she would blush, thinking of how the begetting of an heir was to happen. She had shown passion once in Elizabeth's conservatory. There had been times since when he had wished he had carried that embrace to its conclusion, dangerous as it would have been in an unlocked room during a ball and grossly improper as it would have been when they had been merely betrothed. Their relationship might have taken a wholly different course if he had not remembered propriety and then reminded her of it in a particularly insulting manner.

He wondered what last night had meant to her. He wondered how she had felt, not just in her body, but in her emotions. He wondered what thoughts had gone through her mind as he had first fondled and then mounted and then worked in her. He wished he could ask her. Why could he not? But there was no point in asking himself the question when he knew that the answer was simply because. Because there was no closeness between them and he did not know how to bridge the gap.

"My mother will have told you," he said, "that that is your main duty as my duchess—at least until it has been accomplished." He half smiled at her, but she had looked away. He still thought George would make a quite creditable Duke of Bridgwater, and George already had healthy sons. He wanted children with Stephanie because he wanted a family. His dream was beginning to revive, though it would doubtless have to be a dream based on reality. She did not love him.

"Yes," she said. "I will begin my other duties as soon as we arrive, Alistair. You must not fear that I will be inadequate to the task. I shall be a diligent mistress of your home. I will visit all your tenants and laborers. And once you have presented me to your neighbors, I will entertain and call upon them as is proper. I believe you will not be displeased with me."

He brought her hand to his lips and held it there for a few moments. "I am not displeased," he said. "I am confident you will acquit yourself admirably."

"Your mother mentioned a summer fête," she said.

"With games and exhibits both in the village and in the park. And an evening feast and dancing. She described my responsibilities there. I shall look forward to fulfilling them."

He made sure he was at home each year for the fête. He never particularly enjoyed it since it was an entertainment designed entirely for the local people, and he was no longer able to mingle with them as he had done as a boy. He had been a duke for longer than ten years. He was too far separated from his people socially, even though he was fond of them and he believed that they in their way were fond of him.

It had been different when he was a boy, of course. Even though school had quelled much of his rebellious high spirits and he had learned to be his father's son even when at home for the holidays, there had still been moments of escape. It had been at one of the fêtes, late in the evening, when his seventeen-year-old self had lost his virginity. He had gone into the hay barn—he was still not sure who had done the leading and who the following—with a merry widow eight years his senior and had emerged three or four hours later with his virginity several times gone, if that were possible. He had been swaggering, thinking himself one devil of a virile fellow, though the memory now of his four vigorous performances during those hours brought a rueful smile to his face.

"The fête is to be enjoyed, Stephanie," he said.

"Oh." She turned her head and smiled dazzlingly at him. "I shall see to it that everyone does enjoy it, Alistair. I shall begin planning it as soon as we arrive, though I know there are numerous traditions regarding it that I must follow. You must not worry about it. I shall plan it all myself. You will find that you have a competent duchess."

He had heard very little. The smile had dazzled him.

He acted without thought. He leaned across her and set his mouth to hers. She was his bride of two days and one night, he thought, and they had traveled side by side for almost a whole day like polite strangers. He had plied her with questions, and she had spoken cheerfully about duty. About bearing his son, as if doing so meant no more to her than a duty that was expected of her.

He lifted his head and looked into her eyes. She was perfectly composed, her hands clasped lightly in her lap. She smiled placidly at him. She was being his dutiful duchess. She was fulfilling an obligation she believed would never quite be fulfilled.

"How do you feel about me?" he asked her.

Her eyes widened. "Alistair," she said, "you are my husband."

As if that was an answer.

"What do you wish me to say?" she asked when he continued to search her eyes with his own. "I have learned during the past month what will be expected of me as your duchess. But I realize that something has been missed. No one has tried to tell me how to please you personally, except for a few general principles." She blushed more rosily this time. She would have been told to be obedient and submissive, he thought—particularly in bed. "I want to please you, Alistair. Tell me how. I owe you everything."

"Perhaps," he said, "I have only one request, Stephanie. That you stop thinking that. It is untrue, you know. You owe me nothing." Words that were being spoken one month too late.

"I had enough money left to buy a small loaf of bread," she said. "During that one night I spent alone outdoors I very narrowly escaped having everything stolen—even my virtue. I was not so innocent that I did not realize they would have taken that too before leaving with my meager belongings. I would have faced other such nights. Looking as I did when you first saw me, I would not have escaped again. I saw the way everyone looked at me—everyone but you. You were the only one who treated me with respect as well as kindness. And you took me all the way home rather than abandon me to the risk of danger again. Even though you knew that in doing so you would sacrifice your own freedom. I owe you my life and, just as important, my virtue. And you must ask how I feel about you?"

"No," he said, sitting back again so that he would not have to look into her face. He drew a deep breath. "This will not do."

"I have tried and am trying," she said, her voice unhappy now. "I did not please you, did I? But I knew nothing, Alistair. Tonight perhaps I will do better. Please tell me how I may better please you. Pleasing you is the dearest wish of my heart."

"Stephanie," he said, "I felt no more respect for you than anyone else. I saw the abominable bonnet and the tasteless cloak and I saw nothing else. And heard nothing else. I thought you were at best an actress and at worst a whore. Probably both. I will not say I intended from the start to have you. I did not. I kept you with me because the parcel of lies I thought you were telling me amused me no end, and I wanted to see your embarrassment when I finally backed you into a corner and exposed you for what you were. That first night I thought you a clever tease and out of my own boredom decided to play your game. But before we reached Hampshire and Sindon Park, I fully intended to have you for my mistress—after I had taken you there and watched to see how you would handle the situation. I trapped myself. *Now* tell me how much you owe me. Now tell me that pleasing me is your dearest wish."

It was something he had thought never to tell her. He had convinced himself at first—perhaps with some compassion—that doing so would only humiliate her. But he had seen since that his silence had actually caused something worse. She had been trapped, suffocated, made intensely miserable by the debt she had thought she owed him. He had released her at last. Too late? How was she going to react? But he could not feel sorry that he had spoken the truth.

He turned his head to look at her when she did not immediately speak. Her body was quite rigid. Her hands, still clasped together in her lap, were white-knuckled. Her face had lost all vestige of color. Her eyes were closed.

"It would be absurdly inadequate," he said, "to beg your pardon. But I am the one, you see, Stephanie, who has atonement to make. You did not have a great deal of freedom anyway, but I took away even the little you had."

"You believed nothing I said?" She was whispering.

"No," he said. "A bright bird of paradise standing on a dusty and deserted road told me that she was on her way to Hampshire to take up her inheritance, and I was amused."

"I was not shown to the wrong room that night, was I?" she said. "It was the right room. I was to share it with you."

"Yes," he said.

"I was to share the bed with you too," she said. "You were going to do to me what you did last night."

"Yes," he said.

He heard her draw a sharp breath and hold it. It shuddered out of her after a while.

"Why did you not?" she asked. "Two nights in a row it happened, then. I had narrow escapes twice. Why did you let me escape?"

"For the reason I mentioned a short while ago," he said. "I thought you had outmaneuvered me, and I chose to humor you."

"It was not simply because I had said no?" she asked. Her voice was so soft that he could scarcely hear her.

He thought for a moment. "Yes," he said, "for that reason too. I would never force myself on a woman who had said no."

"Does your wife qualify as a woman?" she asked.

Oh, good Lord! He thought about it. "Yes," he said at last, as softly as she. "Are you going to say no tonight? And tomorrow night?"

She said nothing for so long that he thought perhaps she intended never to speak to him again. But she spoke at last.

"I suppose," she said, "I must be thankful for that bonnet and that cloak. If I had been my usual gray self— gray like my name—you would not have afforded me even a second glance. You would not have stopped to take me up. I would have starved and perhaps died. I would probably have been ravished. Your error saved me." Bitterness was heavy in her voice. "But despite that, I need no longer feel beholden to you. I believe, when I have recovered from my shock, I may find that fact enormously freeing. Why did you tell me? You might have kept it secret for the rest of our lives. I would never have suspected. I would have been your willing slave for a lifetime."

His own voice too was bitter when he spoke, though he knew he had no cause for bitterness. "Perhaps I do not want a slave," he said. "Perhaps I want a wife."

"Oh, you have that," she said. "I married you yesterday, if you will recall. We shared a marriage bed last night. I tried so very hard to please you, because I thought you were like a god. I might have better spent the time pleasing myself."

"By sending me away?" he said. "By saying no?"

"No," she said and laughed harshly. "Oh, no, not that."

They must be nearing the inn where they were to spend the night. He looked out through the window for familiar landmarks. He had traveled this road hundreds of times. Neither of them had spoken for several minutes. He wondered why he was feeling strangely calm. And he realized with a grim smile that it was because he now for the first time had a real relationship with her. A disastrous relationship, perhaps—no, probably. But real, nonetheless. It was better than what he had had with her before.

He would rather live without her than have her as a slave. It was a surprising and quite bleak realization.

"We will be at the inn soon," he said. "I have had a suite of rooms reserved. You will have your own bedchamber. You will be under no compulsion to receive me there. You will not be relegating me to a distant attic if you say no."

She said nothing. She was sitting straighter than before. She was less relaxed.

"May I come to your bed tonight?" he asked.

"No," she said after a slight hesitation. "Not tonight, Alistair. Maybe not tomorrow night either. I do not know. I need some time."

He nodded. "I will ask again tomorrow," he said.

His carriage was making the turn into the large stable yard of the Bull and Horn, and ostlers and grooms were converging on his familiar carriage.

15

IT WAS A RELIEF TO ARRIVE AT WIGHTWICK HALL, PRINcipal residence of the Duke of Bridgwater in Gloucesterhire. If they had arrived just this time yesterday, Stephanie thought, it might have been no relief at all. If she had been amazed at the sight and size of Sindon Park a little over a month ago, she would have been awed to incoherence by Wightwick with its massive stone gateposts and wrought iron gates, its twin gatehouses, which seemed almost small mansions in their own right, by the seemingly endless curved driveway flanked by oak trees, by the three-arched stone bridge over a river or stream, and by the long, sloping lawns and groves and flower arbors leading past the large stone stable block up to the stately Palladian house.

She would have been awed by the sight of grooms in livery lined up on the terrace—far more than would be needed to tend the four horses and the carriage, and by the almost regal figures, dressed all in black, of the butler and housekeeper, standing at the foot of the marble steps leading to the main entrance doors. She would have been overwhelmed by the high domed grand hall and by the sight of two motionless lines of house servants awaiting her inspection.

She was not awed—only relieved. Relieved to be away from the oppressive silence of her husband's presence.

Not away exactly, of course. He walked slightly behind her right shoulder, presenting her to his head groom, who had handed her down from the carriage, and then to the butler and housekeeper. He followed her along the lines of servants and spoke quietly to a few of them as she had a word and a smile for each one.

He and his wife had scarcely spoken all day. After she had assured him that yes, she had slept very well, thank you—she had not—and that yes, the sky did look overcast but no, it did not look quite as if it would rain, there had been no further conversation at breakfast. Through the day in the carriage he had tried a few times to draw her into conversation, but her monosyllabic answers had discouraged him each time.

It was not that she was being deliberately sullen. It was just that she was totally bewildered. All the worlds she had ever known, and now this new one into which she had tried so hard to fit—all of them had crumbled. She no longer knew who she was or where she belonged.

"You will wish to see your apartment, Your Grace," the housekeeper murmured when the inspection had been completed, "and freshen up. I will have tea served in the drawing room in half an hour's time."

Stephanie smiled at her.

"Her Grace has had a tiring journey, Mrs. Griffiths," her husband said. "She will take tea in her private sitting room. Parker will bring something more appropriate to me in the library."

Stephanie expected that he would remain downstairs. But he stayed just behind her as Mrs. Griffiths led her up four flights of marble stairs and along a wide carpeted corridor toward what must be the ducal suite at the front of the house. He followed her while the housekeeper showed her the large, luxuriously appointed sitting room, which was, it seemed, exclusively hers, and the spacious dressing room in which Patty and two other maids were already busy opening trunks, and the bedchamber, the largest, most luxurious room of all.

"I shall leave you to your maid's care, then, Your Grace," Mrs. Griffiths said, inclining her head with gracious respect. "I shall have tea sent up."

"Thank you." Stephanie smiled and watched the housekeeper leave the room. Her husband remained behind.

She turned to look at him, her chin raised, her hands clasped loosely before her. He looked so very handsome, as he always did. She was very aware of the large canopied bed behind him. What would happen now that they were—home? She was, after all, his wife. She had vowed to be obedient to him. She would not break her vows. Would he break his?

"Welcome home, my dear," he said softly.

The words took her by surprise and almost took away her control. She had not realized until that moment how close to the edge of control she had been living for the past twenty-four hours.

"Thank you." She drew a slow breath and smiled at him. "It is magnificent, Alistair. More so even than I expected."

"It is my pride and joy," he said.

The old cliché touched her in some strange way. But she did not want to be touched in any way. Not yet. She needed to think. But so far even her mind had deserted her. She had been unable to think for a night and a day. She lowered her gaze and said nothing.

"Stephanie," he said, "will you answer one question before I leave you to rest alone?"

"Yes." She looked up at him again.

"If I had told you," he said, "on that day in Sindon Park, would you have married me?"

No, of course not. But she held back the words. Would

she? The arguments in favor of their marriage would have been just the same. Her options would have been just as limited. How could she know what her answer would have been? The point was, he had not told her. He had allowed her to believe in his kindness and gallantry—in his self-sacrifice.

"I do not know," she said. But she had to be honest with him. Only through honesty now could she hope to regain herself. "Yes. I believe I probably would have. I had tasted something better than what I had known for six years, you see, but to keep it I had to marry soon. It is difficult deliberately to give up something desirable once one has tasted it. I wanted wealth. I wanted Sindon Park."

He nodded.

"I would probably have married you anyway," she said, "but perhaps I would not have sold my soul if you had told me everything at the start."

"What do you mean by that?" he asked.

She lifted her chin. "I wanted to be worthy of my savior," she said. "I have spent the past month changing myself into someone worthy to be your duchess. There was nothing equal in our union, Alistair. All the giving, all the stooping, all the condescension were on your part. I was totally inferior—in every conceivable way. It did not need to be that way. I could and should have been your equal in everything except rank. You took that away from me."

"I did not want to humiliate you by telling the truth," he said.

She smiled. "Or yourself?"

He hesitated. "Or myself," he admitted.

They stood looking at each other. She wondered if she still loved him. Or if she ever had. How could one love a god? One could only serve a god. But he was not a god at all. She did not know what or who he was. He was a stranger to her. She touched her wedding ring with the thumb of her left hand. And her mind touched on the brief and secret pleasure she had known in her marriage bed. He had been inside her body.

But he was a stranger.

"Where do we go from here?" he asked. "Is this the end, Stephanie? Is there no chance for our marriage?"

She had not faced such a stark question yet. It frightened her to hear it thus put into words. Surely, it was not this they were facing? Two days ago had been their wedding day.

"I do not know," she said. "Alistair, I do not know you. I know only a few things *about* you, and not even many of those. I do not know you at all. You have told me nothing. You are a stranger to me."

"And do you wish to know me?" he asked. "Or is it too late?"

She wanted to know him, she realized suddenly. Now that he was no longer a god, he was knowable. Despite his impressive title and his wealth and his enormous dignity, he was a man. A man just as she was a woman. She wanted to know him. She wanted to know whom she would reject—or accept. But was it too late to make such a decision after their marriage? He was standing still and quiet, waiting for her reply.

"I want to know you," she said.

She could see him draw breath. "Then you will know me," he said. "For the next days and weeks, Stephanie, I will do the talking. It will not come easily to me. I have been accustomed to self-containment, you see. It was part of my upbringing. It has been the dominating fact of my adulthood. But for you I will talk. I will try to teach you who I am."

"Is this marriage so important to you, then?" she asked.

"Yes."

He answered without hesitation, but he did not explain in what way it was important, though she waited. It would be humiliating for him to have a broken marriage almost before it had begun. It would be dreary for him to be locked for life into a non-marriage. It would be disastrous for him to be in a marriage that offered no possibility of an heir—unless he intended to break his promise. Or perhaps the marriage was important to him in some other way, some more personal way. She did not know. She did not know *him*.

She would not wait for him to ask the one remaining question, she decided. "Alistair," she said, "you may come to me tonight if you wish." No matter what happened, no matter what her final decision, she realized, she would give him his son if she was physically capable of doing so.

"Thank you," he said. "You are tired, my dear. I shall leave you to rest. I shall come to your dressing room to escort you down to dinner."

"Yes," she said.

He took a couple of steps toward her, took her right hand in both of his, and raised it to his lips.

Then he was gone.

She understood one thing during the couple of minutes she stood where she was before going to her dressing room. It was the first really clear thought that had formed since his staggering revelation of the day before. She was glad he had told her. A great deal had been destroyed. She was not sure if anything could be rebuilt. She was not sure of anything—except one realization. She was glad he was no god. She was glad he was merely a man.

She brushed the fingers of her left hand absently over the back of her right hand, where his lips had just been.

CONVERSATION CAME EASILY to him. It was a necessary accomplishment for any lady or gentleman of *ton*. It was an art, perhaps, but one he had practiced for so long that he no longer had to give it conscious thought. He knew almost by instinct to whom he should speak about books or ideas or politics or economics or fashion or gossip. By the same instinct he knew with whom he must lead the conversation and with whom he could merely follow.

He had never feared silences. Sometimes silence could be comfortable and companionable. And when it was not, he always knew how to fill it.

The silence throughout this day had suffocated him. It had been something loud and accusing, something painful and impenetrable.

Conversation at the dinner table, though there was scarcely a moment of silence, was equally uncomfortable. One topic had never been part of his conversations, he realized now that he had committed himself to it for the coming days and even weeks. He was quite unaccustomed to talking about himself. It was as if, in becoming reconciled to the very public nature his life must take as the Duke of Bridgwater, he had shut away the private part of himself, hidden it away so that no one would take that too away from him.

"George was my dearest friend and my worst enemy," he told her, beginning abruptly without stopping to consider exactly where he should start. He could hardly begin with his birth, after all, though in more ways than one that had been the most significant event in his life. "I loved him and I hated him."

"It is something I have always found perplexing," she said, "but it is something that seems quite natural. I longed and longed to have sisters and brothers. Yet it seems that those who do, spend their childhoods fighting with them."

"I resented him quite bitterly," he said. "He was born barely eleven months after me. I never forgave him for waiting so long. If only he had been born eleven months before me. I am not sure I still do not resent him."

Her place had been set at the foot of the long table in the dining room. They would have had to raise their voices to converse. He had had her moved beside him.

Her knife and fork remained poised over her plate for a moment. "Is it not usually the other way around?" she asked. "Is it not the younger son who is supposed to resent the elder? Eleven months cut your brother out of the title and the fortune and Wightwick Hall."

"Even as a child," he said, "I felt the bars about my cage and knew that for George there were no bars, no cage. Ungrateful wretch that I was, I raged against my bars. Yet strange as it may seem, I do not believe that my brother ever raged against me or the fate that made him the younger."

He knew that he had started in the right place. If he had told her all the facts of a happy, carefree childhood—and the facts were there in abundance—he would not have told the essential truth. He would not be enabling her ever to know him.

She leaned a little toward him, her food forgotten for the moment. "I cannot picture it," she said. "You and your title and position seem to be one and indivisible."

"They are now," he said. "I am talking about my childhood—my rebellious childhood. I knew very early that life would offer me no choices, you see. Now who would complain about that when he could be secure in this for a future?" He indicated with one hand the room about them. "Only a foolish child, of course. A man learns to accept his fate, especially when it is a fate that brings along with it such luxury and such security and such power."

"But who can blame a child," she said, "for wanting to be free? For wanting to dream."

Ah, she understood. No one else ever had. No one.

Not that he had talked about such things for eleven years. No, longer than that. Not since boyhood. He had never really entrusted himself to anyone. He felt suddenly vulnerable, almost frightened. He concentrated on his food for a while.

"Very few people are free," he said. "Almost no one is, in fact. It is something one learns as one matures. Something one comes to accept. Yet many people's cages are poverty or ill health or—other miserable factors. My father was right to call me an ungrateful cur and to squash my rebellion as ruthlessly as he did. He must have been bewildered by me. We must hope that our eldest son will not be so perverse."

"If he is," she said, "we must hope that his father will give him the benefit of his understanding."

He smiled at her. They spoke as if there were a future. Was there? The future was in his hands, he suspected. He had to help her to get to know him. He had to hope that she would like him, that she would wish to spend the rest of her life with him. She must already know that he would never force her either to live with him in the intimacy of marriage or to remain with him in the facade of an empty marriage. She was independently wealthy, with a sizable home of her own.

And he had begun by pouring out the foolish, ungrateful self-pity of his childhood self.

For the rest of dinner, and for a while in the drawing room afterward, he told her happier stories of his childhood, choosing the amusing ones involving mainly him and George. Elizabeth and Jane had been born some years after them and had never really been playmates. He was rewarded with smiles and even with laughter.

"Tomorrow," he said finally when he could see that she was tired, "I will show you the house, Stephanie, including the state apartments and the portrait gallery. If the weather is fine, I will show you the park too. We will take tomorrow for ourselves. The day after you can begin being the Duchess of Bridgwater here if you wish."

"Yes," she said, "I do wish, Alistair. But tomorrow we will spend together. It is important that we do so."

He was leading her up the stairs. He paused outside her dressing room door. "I may come to you tonight, then?" he asked.

She nodded, and he opened her door and closed it behind her when she had stepped inside.

He had not told her what a dreamer he had been. There had been the two totally different sides to his nature—the mischievous, energetic, rebellious boy on the one hand, and the lone, moody dreamer on the other. Both had infuriated his father. Both had been quelled, totally repressed.

He was not sure he could share the second aspect of his nature with Stephanie. He was not sure there were the words. He was not sure he could so bare his soul even for her. And yet, he thought bleakly as he prepared for her, something told him that his only chance with her was in total honesty. Was he capable of it?

SHE WAS STANDING at the window, looking out, though her head turned back over her shoulder when he came inside the room. It was not a studied pose, he realized—he knew far more about her innocence than he had known on his first acquaintance with her. But if it had been, it could not have been more provocatively done. Her auburn hair, caught by the candlelight, lay in heavy waves down her back. The turn of her body, clad in a fine silk and lace nightgown, emphasized its lithe slimness.

She turned completely as he crossed the room toward her, and her hands reached out for his. She had said he might come, and she was not going to stint her welcome, he saw. She lifted her face to his.

He tried to keep his hunger in check, but she opened her mouth as his lips lightly explored hers, and he slid his tongue into moist heat and gathered her closer. She came, arching her body to his, bringing her hands up to rest on his shoulders. He wondered if it was merely duty, but he could feel the heat of her body through his night-shirt and her nightgown.

He kissed her throat, her ears, her temples, her eyelids. Her mouth again.

He had hurt her, he thought. He had admitted to her that at first he had believed the evidence of his own eyes above the story she had told him. He had told her in effect that she had been a toy to him, a creature of fun. One he had used for his own amusement and had planned to use for his sexual pleasure. He had denied her personhood.

And now she had the power to hurt him, to bring shattering down about him the house he had built for himself over the years so carefully that he had not even fully realized it himself. The house inside which he had hidden so that no one would find him and reveal to him the emptiness of his existence.

Stephanie had found him, whether she realized it or not.

"Come and lie down," he said.

But he stopped her when she was beside the bed and about to lie down on it. He lifted his hands to the top button of her nightgown.

"May I?" he asked her, looking into her eyes.

For a moment she glanced aside to the single candle that burned beside the bed. There was a whole branch of candles on the mantelpiece. She nodded almost imperceptibly, and he undid the buttons one by one until he could lift the gown away from her shoulders. She did not even try to hold on to modesty by bending her arms at the elbow. She held them loosely at her sides so that the single garment slithered all the way to the floor.

She was all slim, taut beauty. She watched him, her face calm, her chin high, as his eyes roamed over her. He pulled his nightshirt off over his head and tossed it aside.

"Lie down," he said.

He hesitated for only a moment. But he did not extinguish the candles. And before joining her on the bed, he stripped back the bedclothes to the foot of the bed. Perhaps he was sealing his own doom, he thought, but if she was going to allow the continuation of their marriage, then perhaps it was as well that she understood the full physical, carnal nature of what they would do together in her bed. He rather suspected that on their wedding night she had hidden behind darkness and closed eyes and beneath bedcovers and inside the instructions on duty that his mother of all people must have given her.

There could be no more hiding for either of them. Every day now, he realized, and every night, he would risk losing her. But he could only come out into the open with her and take the risk.

He slid an arm about her shoulders, but did not draw her close. He raised himself on his elbow and leaned over her to kiss her. With his free hand he explored her and fondled her. After a while he lifted his head away and watched what he did. She watched his face.

He could see and feel and hear her body's response. Her nipples hardened. She grew almost hot to the touch. She was breathing quickly and rather raggedly. But she lay still and relaxed and continued to watch him.

He slid a hand beneath her leg and lifted it. She followed his unspoken direction and raised both legs, setting her feet flat on the bed. When he slid his hand between her knees, she let her legs drop open. He fondled her with his hand, parting, stroking, teasing with light fingers while he leaned forward to kiss her breasts and her flat abdomen. He would not move his head lower. Not yet. She was not ready for that kind of extreme intimacy. Perhaps she never would be.

She was slick with wetness. Ready for him. He slid a finger in and out and listened to the erotic sucking sound. When he looked into her face, he found that she was still looking at him. But her eyes were heavy-lidded, and her lips were parted. He knew that she was listening too and that tonight she was not embarrassed by the sound.

She would not hide from any of it, he decided. She would not use his body as a blanket. When he moved over her, he knelt between her thighs and lifted her legs up over his and positioned himself. Her eyes dropped from his eventually when he paused and waited for her. She watched. He pushed himself slowly inside until he was fully embedded. And drew out again almost his full length and pushed inward once more. She was watching.

"Touch me," he said to her as he leaned over her and set his hands on either side of her head, holding himself above her with straight arms. "Put your arms about me." Her arms were lying flat on the mattress beside her as they had on their wedding night.

She set her hands on either side of his waist. He watched her swallow and move them to his hips and around to touch his buttocks briefly. She rested them against his waist again and closed her eyes at last as he resumed his movements in her. She was soft and hot and wet. He closed his own eyes and held himself above her while he worked. He could smell her. Pure woman.

He waited for her body to move beyond arousal into the beginnings of fulfillment. He stroked her firmly for a long time, holding back his own pleasure. But he knew finally that it was not going to happen. There was no tension in her, only relaxed acquiescence, even though her legs were still twined about his and she was rocking to his rhythm. He could have moved her on to the next stage by sliding his hand between them and caressing a part of her she was probably unaware of. But he sensed that she did not want to abandon control. Control at the moment must be more important to her than almost anything else.

But she was not even trying to hide her quiet enjoyment of what was happening. She liked what he did to her, as she had two nights ago. It was enough. For now it must be enough.

He lowered his weight onto her and thrust deeply and quickly and repeatedly until release came and his seed spilled into her. He heard himself sigh against her hair.

He set his hand over hers after he had uncoupled them and moved to her side. She drew her legs together and lay quietly on her back.

"Thank you," he said.

She turned her head to look at him. "It is very pleasant, Alistair," she said. "I always expected it would be, but it is even more pleasant than I imagined. I want you to know that it was for myself that I said yes tonight. Not just because of duty and not because of . . . of you. It was for me. I decided to be selfish. So I must thank you too, you see."

He leaned over her and kissed her mouth. He was surprised to find that he was feeling almost amused, almost lighthearted. Did she realize that she was turning the tables on him? That she was making him her slave? That she was punishing him most effectively? Should he tell her?

"You may be selfish any time you wish, my dear," he said, "if the results for me are so very pleasurable."

She smiled at him tentatively as he smiled back. It was enough. Hope was born in him as he kissed her again and then reluctantly removed himself from her bed to return to his own room.

16

$\mathcal{L}$IFE BECAME SO BUSY FOR STEPHANIE OVER THE FOL-lowing month that she had blessedly little time for thought. She was mistress of Wightwick Hall, a daunting task even for a bride who had been brought up to expect such a life. The only experience she had of running a home had been gained at the vicarage after her mother's death. It was pitifully inadequate as preparation for what faced her now. The month-long training given her by her mother-in-law helped a great deal. But she found that she had to learn to do the job in her own way. She had been taught to remember who she was and refuse to be intimidated by a regal housekeeper and a despotic cook. Yet she forced herself to remember too that her servants were people, that they had lives and dignity and pride of their own. She had to learn to command through a combination of firmness and kindness.

Sometimes she envied her husband, who needed to use neither. His word was everyone's command. He never raised his voice, never spoke harshly to anyone. Often he did not even have to speak at all. A lifted forefinger at the table would bring a footman smartly hurrying with the coffeepot. Raised eyebrows would send the instant message that a door should be opened or that one course of a meal might be removed and the next brought on.

But she could not be like him. She had to learn to live her new life her own way. She no longer needed to feel guilty about deviating from some of the instructions she had been given.

There were neighbors to meet, visits to make, entertainments to plan. There were tenants to be called upon and laborers too. There were the sick and elderly and very young to identify so that she might learn to give them extra attention. There were the rector and his sister to be seen and parish concerns to be discussed.

There were letters to write. After the restrictions imposed upon her by the Burnabys, writing and receiving letters were among her greatest pleasures. But there were so many. The dowager duchess wrote to her as did Cousin Bertha, her sisters-in-law, Jennifer, Samantha, Cora, Miriam, and Tom's wife.

There was her own estate with which to concern herself. She summoned her steward to Wightwick and spent hours with him over four separate days, asking questions, looking at ledgers, listening to advice, making decisions. She was very tempted to ask her husband to oversee the estate for her since she knew that he was more than competent with his own. And she knew that he waited to be asked, even though he said nothing but merely entertained their guest with his usual correct, rather austere courtesy. But she did not give in to the temptation. It was her property, and perhaps she would wish to live there one day—perhaps soon.

And there was the summer fête to organize. There were to be stalls and competitions and maypole dancing in the village, and cricket and races in the park. There were to be refreshments all day in the park and a grand ox roast there in the evening to be followed by an outdoor dance. All the celebrations in the park for years past had been organized by the dowager duchess. Now the task fell upon Stephanie's shoulders. The fête was the biggest event of the year in the neighborhood. She knew she would be judged harshly if it was poorly organized.

She might have busied herself with her tasks as Duchess of Bridgwater from the time of her early rising until bedtime, she sometimes thought, and still not feel that everything was done. But there was another major area of her life too, and it took at least half her time. She had a new marriage to work on.

Strangely, it was not difficult. It might almost have been idyllic if she had wanted it to be, she thought. Her husband made time to spend with her, though her mother-in-law had warned her that she must not expect to see a great deal of him once the marriage had been solemnized.

He was the one who showed her the house the day after their arrival, though Mrs. Griffiths seemed somewhat taken aback. He took her through the state apartments, rooms that awed her with their size and magnificence. He took her to the portrait gallery on an upper floor and spent longer than an hour there with her, pointing out his ancestors to her, telling her their stories. He paused longest before a portrait of his mother and father, painted soon after their wedding. His mother was beautiful then as she still was now.

"Oh," Stephanie said, going one step closer, "you are very like your father. You might almost *be* him." The former duke stared back at her from the canvas, proud, aloof, almost arrogant—and very handsome.

"Yes," her husband said quietly. "Perhaps that was part of the trouble. Because I looked so like him, I was expected to be like him in all ways."

She turned to look at him. "You did not love him?" she asked incautiously.

"Oh, yes," he said, "I loved him. And he loved me. Perhaps that was part of the trouble too."

He did not elaborate, but he was not silent with her. He talked to her almost constantly, telling her about his life, about his heritage.

He loved his home, she thought. Perhaps more deeply than he realized, though he had once described it as his pride and joy. If he had wanted none of it as a child, he certainly loved it now.

"You love Wightwick," she said to him, smiling at him. "If you had been the younger son, it would have been George's now."

"Yes." He looked about him. "Yes, and so it would."

He walked about the park with her, showing her its most obvious attractions, taking her on walks that had been carefully laid out to give both a picturesque route and unexpected and glorious prospects of greater distances. He took her on a shady walk through a grove of trees until they reached a small, secluded lake she had not suspected was there.

"Hartley—Lord Carew—redesigned the park for me several years ago," he said, "before his marriage. He has great talent as a landscape gardener. Indeed, when he and Samantha first met, she mistook him for the gardener of his own estate."

"Oh," she said, "I hope he disabused her as soon as he realized what had happened."

"No." He smiled ruefully. "We men do not always do what we ought, Stephanie."

He took her riding. She had ridden as a girl, though not a great deal since her father had kept only one horse and that exclusively for the cart. She had not ridden as a woman. But he chose a gentle mare for her and rode patiently at her side while she cautiously walked the horse and eased it into a canter until the world seemed to be flying past at a dangerous pace to either side of her. Once she caught him laughing at her—it was when she had taken her horse to a canter for all of thirty seconds across a perfectly level meadow and then hauled back on the reins before blowing out her breath from puffed cheeks.

He looked like a mischievous boy when he laughed. She wondered how he had looked when he was nine or ten—when he had got up to some of those wild escapades he had told her about. She could not imagine his doing anything wild.

He always attended her in the drawing room when she was entertaining, even if it was just some of the ladies to tea. He made pleasant, courtly conversation with them. He always accompanied her on visits, even to his tenants. She suspected that he drank more tea during the first month of their marriage than he had drunk in the whole year previous to it.

He came to her bed every night. She was sometimes alarmed by the thought that she might be becoming addicted to what happened between them there. She found herself anticipating it with eagerness all day long, and willing it not to end while it was happening, and then fighting bleakness after he had returned to his own room at the thought that there was the rest of the night and all the next day to live through before it would happen again. The marriage act was the most enjoyable activity the world had to offer. She was convinced of it.

She was disturbed by her enjoyment, felt guilty about it. Sometimes she wondered if she stayed just for that. How would she live without it now that she had experienced it?

How would she live without *him*?

On the surface the marriage was not an unhappy one. Their neighbors and acquaintances had a way of looking at them—with a sort of amused indulgence—that suggested they were seen as a newly married couple living through a honeymoon. And in many ways they were. Stephanie found that even her need for quietness and privacy was waning. A couple of times during the evenings after dinner she had retired to her own sitting room with a book, feeling the need to be away from his eyes and his voice. Feeling the need to be herself. And yet the second time it happened, remembering how the first time she had been unable to concentrate on her reading or do any constructive thinking either, she took her book and went back downstairs. She found him in the library, also reading.

"May I join you?" she asked.

He had got to his feet as she entered; he always stood when she came into a room. He was always the perfect gentleman.

"Of course, my dear," he said, indicating the comfortable-looking leather chair on the opposite side of the fireplace from his. He waited for her to seat herself before resuming his own place.

At first she was self-conscious and read and reread the same paragraph without comprehending a single word. But after a while she looked up with a slight start, wondering for how long she had been absorbed in her book. He was reclined in his chair, looking very comfortable, clearly absorbed in his own reading. They sat, silently reading, for a few hours before he put his book down and suggested that she ring for the tea tray.

It had been a strangely seductive evening. They had not spoken, and yet his very presence had relaxed her and enabled her to enjoy one of her favorite pastimes.

"It is getting late," he said and half smiled.

She glanced at the clock on the mantel. They would drink their tea, and it would be time for bed. Within the next hour . . . She felt the now familiar aching sensation in her womb and between her thighs.

"I am sorry," she said, getting to her feet. "I have been neglecting my duty." But his words had not been scolding, and her answer had not been apologetic.

Sometimes she wondered why they were not completely happy. She would look back on her life with the Burnabys and shudder inwardly. She would picture life alone and free and independent at Sindon Park—she knew he would not try to stop her from going there if she decided to do so—and felt a bleak chill.

By her own request their marriage had continued to be a real marriage. She was proving both to her husband and to herself that she was capable of being his duchess. They communicated. She knew that she pleased him in bed. He pleased her there too. It was too soon to know whether she had conceived during this first month of their marriage—she had had her monthly period only just before her wedding and did not know yet if the next one would happen. But he had come to her each night except the second. She loved perhaps best of all, although it came at the end of what she never wanted to end, the heat of his seed passing deep inside from him into her.

Yet there was in both of them at the end of their first month together a sense of waiting—a sense of a decision yet to be made. It was strange, perhaps. They were married. The decision had been made. She was his property, to do with as he wished. She had vowed obedience and would not break her vow. But she knew that there was a decision to be made and that he would allow her to make it and would live by whatever she decided.

She was perhaps unique among women.

She was married, yet she was free.

She did not have that freedom by right. He had given it to her.

It was a thought that made her angry at first. Why could women not be free as men were free? Why did they have no right to freedom?

But it was also a thought that began to dominate her thinking, that began to haunt her night and day. He had her in his possession. All the forces of law and religion—as well as his superior masculine strength—were behind him to back up his claims. No one—*no one*—would ever blame him for holding on to her for the rest of their lives and forcing her into submission to his will. Yet he had given her her freedom. He had exposed himself to the possibility of censure and ridicule—he would receive both in plenty if he allowed her to leave him—and given her freedom.

He had treated her during that journey to Hampshire with contempt veiled in courtesy. He had been no different from anyone else she had seen while dressed in those clothes. He had judged by appearances and had dismissed everything she had said, everything she *was,* with an amused cynicism. He had been quite prepared to amuse himself with her during their nights on the road and to set her up in some love nest for his future pleasure.

Her shock at being so dismissed as a person deserving a hearing, deserving some respect, was still deep.

But he *had* helped her. And he *had* been courteous. And he had *not* tried to force himself upon her once she had uttered that one word—*no*. And finally, when he had fallen into his own trap, he had taken the consequences with his characteristic courtesy and sense of honor.

And now he was *still* giving her the choice of saying no. No to whatever he wished to do to her or with her. No to being his wife in anything but name. No to living with him.

And even when they were still at Sindon Park, he had insisted that the marriage contract state that her inheritance remain independently hers.

Sometimes it seemed foolish and childish—and even downright insane—to refuse to forgive him.

Sometimes when his body was joined with hers in her

bed, she would hold him with tenderness and try to persuade herself that it was merely with pleasure and that it was a pleasure she took for herself without regard to the pleasure he might be taking too.

But it was tenderness.

She was not sure that she could allow herself to feel tenderness for him. She was not sure she could respect herself if she did. But it was something she had to work out for herself.

It was a lonely feeling. Freedom is a lonely thing, she thought with some surprise.

THE SUMMER FÊTE had never been his favorite day of the year even though he had always made it a point to be at Wightwick for the occasion. He had always felt it important to watch his people celebrating, to stroll among them, talking with them, encouraging the participants in the various contests, congratulating the winners, commiserating with the losers, eating with them. Even dancing with them. His mother, of course, had done all the organizing and had busied herself throughout the day, going from the village to the park, making sure that she was always available to judge the contests in baking and needlework and to hand out the prizes in all the races and other competitions. It was something she had done with grace and apparent ease and with perfect, unruffled dignity.

This year was to be different. He knew it almost before he had swallowed the first mouthful of an early breakfast. Fortunately, he had seen from the window of his bedchamber, the day promised to be sunny and warm, a luxury this year. Stephanie came hurrying into the breakfast room, smiled quickly at him, smiled more dazzlingly at the footman beside the sideboard, and asked him if he would please bring her two eggs and two rounds of toast. Oh, and some coffee, please, James.

She always smiled at their servants. She always said please and thank you. She always sounded genuinely grateful for their service. She often asked the servant—by name—about a particular detail of his or her health or of his mother's health or that particular item he had been looking to purchase. She knew each of their servants personally, he was sure. His mother would be alarmed. He was charmed.

"Alistair," she said, turning her smile on him, "you are to be captain of one of the cricket teams this afternoon. You did know? I did remember to tell you?"

"No, actually, my dear," he said. "Are you sure you would not prefer to do it yourself?"

"No." Her smile was almost a grin. "I have to be busy about other things. I have to make friends of a few women by awarding them prizes for their embroidery and netting and cake-making and so on, and make a few dozen enemies at the same time."

He had never joined in the cricket match, which was the highlight of the day for many of the men. His mother had not considered that it would be dignified for him to do so.

"Very well, then," he said. "But if you *do* decide to play, it must be on my side. A husband's orders."

It was the only command he had given since their wedding, even in joke.

"And you must give the prizes in the village this morning," she said. "Will you, Alistair? It is not fair that I judge the contests and award the prizes. And I am sure the winners will be far prouder of themselves if their prizes are presented by the Duke of Bridgwater himself."

Good Lord! "Very well, my dear," he said. "If you wish it."

"Oh, Alistair." She leaned across the table toward him, her face eager and animated. "There is to be dancing about the maypole. Why is dancing about a maypole so much more magical than dancing anywhere else? I used to love it of all things when I was a girl. I remember Mama being doubtful and thinking perhaps it was not quite proper for the vicar's daughter to join in, but Papa said I might. I would have *died* if it had not been allowed."

He had to resist the impulse to lean back slightly. He was dazzled. She was as excited as a girl. She was *enjoying* this. His mother had never enjoyed it. She had treated it as one more duty that must be perfectly executed.

"Alistair," Stephanie said, "give me your opinion. Will it be undignified for the Duchess of Bridgwater to dance about the maypole?"

His mother would have an apoplexy. So should he.

"Not unless it is undignified for the Duke of Bridgwater too," he said. "I intend to dance about it with you, Stephanie. I hope it does not coincide with the cricket match?"

"Oh, no." She laughed. "There have to be men to dance. It is to be afterward. Before the ox roast. And then the dance. I can scarce wait. I have never danced out of doors during the evening before."

"There is a breeze to ruffle your coiffure," he said, "and stones to cut against your slippers, and night chills to raise goose bumps on your arms."

She laughed. "And stars for candles," she said.

"Yes." There was a curious ache about his heart. "And stars for candles, my dear. We will dance beneath the stars. We will *waltz* beneath the stars. Shall we?"

"Yes." Her hand came half across the table to him, but she had drawn it back before he could cover it with his own.

"I must fly," she said, getting to her feet before he could rise to draw her chair back for her. "I promised to be in the village early."

"Before eight o'clock?" he said.

She laughed. "Is it that early?" she said. "But I still have to change my clothes and have my hair dressed. No respectable lady can accomplish those tasks within half an hour, you know. Will you ride with me, Alistair? Perhaps I will need advice on some of the judging."

"I am the world's foremost authority on embroidery," he said.

She laughed.

"But I will come, of course," he said.

He would go anywhere in the world she cared to ask him to go—if she would but go there with him.

17

THERE WAS A STRANGE, HAPPY, CAREFREE FEEL TO THE day, even though there was so much to do every minute of it and there should have been so much anxiety that something would go wrong. There was an excitement about the day, a sense of a turning point. Everything since her marriage and her coming to Wightwick had been leading up to this day, Stephanie realized. It was as if there had been a tacit agreement between her and her husband to postpone their personal problems until after the summer fête. To postpone any decision.

Tomorrow loomed like a great empty void in her life. She could not look beyond today. And while she lived today, she did not want to look beyond. It was such a very happy day.

She moved several times during the course of the day between the village and the park and house, sometimes with her husband, sometimes alone. She wanted to be everywhere at once. She wanted to miss nothing. She judged the ladies' and the children's contests, then smiled and applauded while her husband presented the prizes. She switched roles with him during the races and complained to him that judging races was very much easier than judging who had baked the best currant cakes.

She even joined in one of the races, when there was an odd number of children wishing to participate in the three-legged race. She partnered a thin, timid little girl, and they narrowly won the race when the leaders-by-a-mile fell in a tangled heap just before the finish line and could not untangle themselves in time. Stephanie hugged her partner, laughing helplessly, and waved cheerfully to the rather large crowd that had suddenly gathered. She threw a half-laughing, half-defiant glance at her husband, and realized that just a month before she would have been horrified by her own behavior and would have been vowing never to behave thus again.

She coaxed her husband into buying her six lengths of gaudy ribbon from a peddler's stall in the village and then tied them into the newly washed, newly combed hair of the six young daughters of one of the poorer tenants. She drew him toward the tent of a gypsy, whom she suspected was no gypsy at all, insisting that they have their fortunes told. But at the last moment, after he had acquiesced, she changed her mind.

"No," she said, "not the future. This is today, and it is such an enjoyable day. Let us not find out about the future, even in fun."

"No," he agreed. "Let us enjoy today, my dear."

He too knew that tomorrow all might change.

She watched the cricket game and cheered unashamedly and partially for her husband's team. He was a talented player, as she soon discovered with interest. His steward, who came to stand beside her for a few minutes, informed her that His Grace had been on the first eleven while at Oxford University. That was one thing about himself he had not told her.

"You should have played at Richmond that day," she said accusingly when the game was over.

But he merely smiled and drew her arm through his. "When our children reach a suitable age," he said, "we will scrape together enough children from the neighborhood to make up two teams and we can captain one each."

"Mine will humiliate yours," she said.

"Yes, probably," he agreed pleasantly. "It *is* humiliating to know that one has completely annihilated another team and made them feel quite inept."

She looked sidelong at him to find that he was doing the same to her. She did not miss the assumption they had both made about the future. She wondered, as she had done several times during the past week, if she was with child. There was a definite chance, though she was always so irregular that it was impossible to know for sure. It would be foolish to hope yet—or to dread.

Usually after the cricket match, most people relaxed or strolled in the park until it was time for the feast to begin. Only the young people headed back to the village for the maypole dancing. But this year word had somehow spread that the Duke of Bridgwater and his new bride were not only planning to attend the event, but were themselves intending to dance.

No one had ever seen a Duke of Bridgwater or his duchess or any of his family dancing about the maypole. No one could quite imagine it. Everyone needed visual evidence to believe that it could possibly happen. And so late in the afternoon the main street of the village was crowded with people, and the village green was surrounded by a milling, curious, laughing throng.

Stephanie took off her bonnet and her gloves and set them aside with her parasol. There was a smattering of applause, and one brave anonymous soul whistled. Her husband took off his hat and his coat, as he had done for the cricket match, and rolled up his shirt sleeves to the elbows. He eyed the maypole and its many-colored ribbons with some misgiving, Stephanie saw.

But he knew the steps, as he proved as soon as they and the other dancers had all taken a ribbon in hand

and the violins began to play. The crowd ringing the green clapped and stamped in time to the music. Only once did the ribbons become snarled and the music pause for a few moments. The crowd jeered good-naturedly. Stephanie smiled as her husband laughed, apologized abjectly, untangled the ribbons, and laughed again.

If she closed her eyes, she thought, as she performed the intricate patterns of the dance, concentrating on both her steps and the movements of her hand with its green ribbon, she could almost imagine herself back in her girlhood, in that golden time before all the harsher realities of life had intruded. She could picture her mother smiling, her father clapping to the rhythm and nodding encouragement to her. She could picture Tom whooping with enthusiasm and catching the nearest pretty girl about the waist when the dancing was finished and twirling her about.

But this was not her girlhood. She turned her head to watch her husband, who was grinning and lifting his arm higher as one of his tenant's young daughters stepped with her ribbon beneath his and around him. Stephanie was doing the same thing with the man closest to her. She smiled at the man, and he smiled back—a smile of warmth and admiration and respect.

This was not wrong, she thought. It was not undignified. She was glad she had decided to do things her way, though she would always be grateful for the training her mother-in-law had given her. She was glad she was free. She was glad she had found out in time that she need be no slave to an obligation that could never be repaid.

He might have held her in thrall for the rest of her life. She would never have known. There would have been no danger of his secret ever being disclosed. No one but Alistair had known.

What a great and wonderful wedding gift he had given

her, she thought so unexpectedly that she almost lost her step and almost dipped her ribbon when she was supposed to raise it.

The dancers were treated to enthusiastic applause when the dancing was over.

"My mother," the Duke of Bridgwater said when they were walking back to the house to prepare for the evening festivities—they had not brought the carriage this time—"will suffer an apoplexy if, or when, she hears about this, Stephanie. She will believe she failed utterly with you and that I have fallen into bad company."

Oh, my dear, make him happy. He is so very dear to me, my son.

Stephanie could almost hear her mother-in-law say those words, as she had done on her wedding day. One rare glimpse behind the armor of dignity and propriety and grace the dowager duchess had worn perhaps all her life. Stephanie was not so sure her husband was right. But right or not, he sounded quite uncontrite.

"Alistair," she said, "there is nothing as exhilarating as dancing out of doors, is there? And look, the sky is still quite clear of clouds. We really will be able to dance beneath the stars tonight, will we not?"

She was even, she thought, beginning to be able to contemplate the prospect of tomorrow coming. But she would not let her thoughts dwell on it yet.

IT WAS A day in which great happiness had warred with desperate depression.

He could not remember a day he had enjoyed so greatly. A day in which he had felt so free or so uninhibited by his rank and consequence. Or so in love.

She had changed in the month since their marriage. It was only today, looking back on the month and considering the month preceding it that he realized how different she was. All the stiffness and timidity and seriousness and submissiveness had disappeared. In their place was a warm, charming, fun-loving woman who seemed to know by some inner instinct how to deal with people.

She said and did all the things that should have lost her the respect of both her peers and her servants—according to his mother's rules. And yet the opposite seemed true. He suspected that even after just one month she was adored by everyone who knew her. And yet he had seen beyond any doubt that it was she who commanded his home, not either Mrs. Griffiths or Parker.

And he, of course, was no exception. He adored her too.

He understood the change in her. He understood that during this month he had had the privilege of becoming acquainted with the real Stephanie Munro. He understood that during the month before their marriage she had been awed into trying to change herself so that she would be a worthy duchess for him. She had thought at the time that she owed him everything.

What he had seen during the month, culminating in today's fête, was a woman who had become free and independent, a woman who had asserted her own character and personality and who liked herself. A woman he had allowed to be free because he could never have lived out his life with one who was his merely by rights of possession.

It was a realization that terrified him. And he knew something would change tomorrow or very soon. Everything until now had been focused on the fête. After tonight there would be nothing to focus upon except the fragile, uncertain state of their marriage.

He opened the outdoor ball with his wife, dancing a vigorous country dance with her. He danced with three of his neighbors' wives before leading her out again—

for a waltz beneath the stars. He could not say afterward that he had enjoyed it. It was too agonizingly sweet. They scarcely spoke. They did not once look into each other's eyes. Tension and awareness rippled between them.

When it was over, he could no longer bear to smile and converse and continue to lead out the wives of his neighbors and tenants. He slipped away. It was not the thing to do, but he was beyond caring too deeply. It was late in the evening. The ball would play itself out, and people would begin to wander homeward. It was unlikely that he would even be missed.

He walked through the trees to the lake, always a favorite haunt of his when he wished to be alone. He never felt the healing power of nature as strongly as when he was at the lake. The moon was shining across it in a silver band tonight. There was hardly a ripple on the water.

He leaned his back against a tree, propped one foot against it, and folded his arms across his chest. He drew a deep breath, let it out slowly, and closed his eyes.

IT WAS DIFFICULT to see everyone in the darkness, despite the moon and stars and the colored lamps strung in the trees. At first she thought he must be somewhere beyond the range of the light available. But after she had danced two sets without once seeing him, she realized that he had left the dancing area. She asked the butler at the refreshment table, but it was only by chance that the village blacksmith, who was trying to cool himself with a glass of punch, overheard and mentioned seeing His Grace walk into the trees. He pointed to the spot.

He must have gone to the lake, she thought. But why? The evening was not over. He had appeared to be enjoying himself. But she knew why. She had felt the tension between them like a physical thing as they had waltzed. She had been unable to look at him or speak to him— even though they had lived in the intimacy of marriage for a whole month. It had been the most wonderful dance of her life and the most dreadful.

He would want to be alone. Otherwise, he would not have gone off by himself without a word to anyone. She would be the last person he would want disturbing him. She must wait for him to return. Tomorrow they must talk. The time had come. But not tonight.

"Oh, will you please excuse me?" she asked, smiling warmly at their closest neighbor who had asked her to partner him in a quadrille. "There is something I must do."

After that she could not just stand there or even mingle with those who did not dance. Mr. Macy would believe she had merely offered an excuse. She turned and crossed the lawn to the trees. After a moment's hesitation she stepped along the dark path, having to feel her way from tree to tree. Very little light penetrated from the sky above. She hoped she was going the right way. She had been to the lake only once before and that had been in daylight with her husband as a guide.

And then she saw light—moonlight on the lake. She stopped for a moment when she reached the bank, her breath catching in her throat. Surely nothing on earth could be more beautiful.

"It *is* breathtaking, is it not?" he said quietly from somewhere to her right.

He was leaning back against a tree, she saw. He made no move to come toward her.

"You wished to be alone," she said. A foolish thing to say. If she knew it, why had she not stayed away and respected his privacy? His head was back against the tree. She thought his eyes were closed, though she could not see him clearly.

"I have been dreaming an old dream," he said.

"What?" she asked.

"I was a dreamer as a child," he said. "I dreamed all sorts of impossible things. Ridiculous things, all involving adventure and personal freedom. Because I knew that the pattern of my life had been marked out for me from birth, I suppose. Part of the general rebellion that characterized my childhood. I grew to recognize and to accept reality and even to rather like it. But there was one dream that clung during my late boyhood and early manhood. It took longer to die than the others."

He stopped talking, but she did not prompt him. She stood looking at him.

"I dreamed of living here," he said. "You were right that first day, you see. I do love it. It is a part of my very being. But I dreamed of living here not just as the Duke of Bridgwater with responsibilities to the land and the people on it. I dreamed of living here as a man. With a woman. And children."

She felt an ache in her chest and throat. She had never seen him so vulnerable. He had told her a great deal about himself during the past month. But she had sensed that he still kept the deepest part of himself locked away.

"I was still young enough," he said, "to believe that somewhere out there was the woman who had been meant for me before either of us was even conceived. It was a lovely dream. But naive and sad too. It finally had to be abandoned."

"Why?" she asked him. She had taken a few tentative steps toward him. "Do you no longer believe in love?"

He opened his eyes and smiled at her. But he said nothing.

"I think," she said—and she had moved close enough to touch him though she did not do so—"that you are the most loving man I have ever known." Her words took even her by surprise. But as she listened to the echo of them, she knew that they were true. And she knew that the answer to all her questions had been staring her in the face ever since the day after her wedding, ever since that dreadful revelation in the carriage.

He chuckled without humor.

"My father's favorite biblical text was the one about laying down one's life for one's friends," she said. "You know? 'Greater love hath no man than this'? You gave up everything for me the day after our wedding, Alistair."

"I merely confessed to something I should have told you a month before," he said. "And in so doing I made you miserable and myself miserable."

"No." She shook her head and spread her hands against his chest. She saw him flinch. "You gave me the gift of knowledge and freedom, Alistair. You have given the same gift continually every day since then. You have allowed me to get to know you and your home and your people. You have let me into your life. But you have put no restraints on me. You know, do you not, that tomorrow I may ask for the use of the carriage to take me and my belongings to Sindon Park, and that I may stay there indefinitely."

"Don't go," he said. His head was back against the tree again. His eyes were closed again.

"But you will not stop me if I decide to go, will you?" she asked.

She heard him swallow. He did not answer for a long time. She waited.

"No," he said at last.

"Why not?" She dipped her head and set her forehead against his chest between her hands.

"I will not hold you against your will," he said.

"Why not?" Her eyes were closed very tightly.

"Because I would rather live without a dream than with a spoiled one," he said. And more softly, "Because I love you."

She was crying then. Just when she wanted to say something, she was crying instead. She felt his hand light against the back of her head, his fingers stroking through her hair. She felt him lean his head downward to kiss the top of her head.

"Don't cry," he said. "It is all right. Everything will be all right."

"Alistair . . ." She looked up at him, all teary-eyed and wobbly-voiced. "It does not need to be a spoiled dream. I will live in it with you. You will never understand, perhaps, how wonderful it is to know that one may say no. How wonderful it is for a woman. For now I know beyond any doubt that I may say no to you, then I know too that I am free to say yes with all my heart."

Both his arms had come tightly about her. He was rubbing his cheek against the top of her head.

"Because I love you," she said.

She leaned against him in the long silence that followed and breathed in the familiar smell of him. This, she thought, utterly relaxed, utterly safe and secure, was happiness. This moment. She looked for no happily ever afters. She knew there would be none, that despite the beauty and essential reality of dreams, the real world could often be a harsh place in which to do one's living. But this now, this moment, was happiness, and this moment would take them forward into a future they would create for themselves for as long as they both lived—with love.

"Alistair," she said after a while, "I am very happy."

He chuckled unexpectedly and tightened his arms about her. "Stephanie," he said, "will you come somewhere with me?"

"Where?" She looked up at him. Even in the near darkness she could see the spark of mischief in his smile—the one she had seen very rarely in the two months of their acquaintance.

He took her hand firmly in his, but then abandoned it in order to set an arm about her waist. "You will find out," he said.

She set her head against his shoulder and her own arm about his waist, and allowed him to lead the way.

HE WAS LYING naked on his back on the hay in the barn, at the farthest side of it from the door, where there would be plenty of warning in the unlikely event that they were interrupted. Stephanie was astride him, her thighs hugging his sides. She was kneeling upright, her head thrown back, her hair hanging loose down her back. The faint light from the small window above them gleamed in a bar across half her face and one naked shoulder and breast.

She was riding to the rhythm of his deep thrusts, and he could feel her open enjoyment despite her initial shock at the posture he had chosen for their loving so that it would be his back scratched by the hay, not hers.

She was looking down at him then, and her face fell into shadow. "Alistair," she whispered. "Alistair."

"My love," he said.

He knew then why she had spoken his name and broken rhythm. Her body was tensing. With inner muscles she was clenching about him so that his thrusts met greater resistance.

"Don't fight it," he told her.

But she remained taut in every muscle as she threw back her head again and clasped his knees behind her. He held his rhythm, pushing into the tightness, coaxing her to move into the new world they could explore together for the remainder of a lifetime.

And then she cried out. The tautness remained for a few moments while he held still in her, and then she shuddered. He reached up to take her shoulders in his hands, and he drew her down so that she was crouched over him, her head on his shoulder. He held her while the tension shuddered into gradual and total relaxation, and gave himself up to the release he had been holding back for her sake.

A long time of panting silence passed. "It is ungenteel," she murmured at last.

He laughed softly. "Very definitely," he said. "Quite unduchesslike. Far worse than bowling in a cricket match or running a three-legged race or dancing about a maypole. And naked in a hay barn, Stephanie. Tut!"

"Ah, but it was so wonderful," she said.

"Very definitely," he agreed. He turned carefully with her so that she lay beside him, his coat half beneath her. He had not disengaged from her. "Shall I tell you why I brought you here?"

"Because it is very wicked?" she said. She sounded sleepy.

"Very," he said. *I lost my virginity here on a summer fête night many years ago.* He had been about to say the words aloud. He wanted her inside his soul, inside his secrets for the rest of his life. But perhaps, he thought just in time, there were some secrets best kept after all. "It is time I did something wicked. It was not enough to abandon our guests merely to take you to your bed, you see. Tonight you have earned a roll in the hay." He chuckled.

"Alistair!" She was wide awake now and bristling with indignation. "Are you suggesting . . . ?"

"Mhm," he said, his mouth against her hair. "Running three-legged races, cheering partially for one side in cricket, dancing about the maypole, looking lovelier than any duchess, or any *woman* for that matter, has any business looking—yes, you have deserved every roll you have been given or will be given tonight. I promise several more to come. Our guests may dance until they wish to go home. It is doubtful they will even miss us, and if they do, they are welcome to allow their imaginations to run riot. You have liberated me, you see, Stephanie, and now you must take the consequences."

She sighed and touched her tongue to his. "Oh," she said.

"Mm," he agreed.

She giggled suddenly, a sound he had not heard from her before. "Several more to come?" she said. "*Tonight?*" She pressed her hips closer to his. He knew she could feel him hardening inside her. "Is it possible, Alistair? I thought it could be done only once . . ."

"Let me prove how wrong you can be," he said. "My love." He drew one of her legs snugly over his hip and kissed her once more. "I am going to take you back to town soon. There is something I must buy you, and only a London designer could do it justice."

"What?" she asked. She gasped. "Oh, it *is* possible. Oh, that feels *so* good."

"A new bonnet," he said. "Pink. With three plumes. Pink, purple, and . . . what color was the other one?"

"Fuchsia," she said.

"Mm," he said. "Oh, yes, love, very good indeed. It can be done more than once in a night, you see."

"And a fuchsia cloak?" she asked.

"Mm," he said. "My bright bird of paradise. How fortunate that your gray cloak was stolen. I might not have noticed you."

"Wretch!" she said. "Was not my beauty more dazzling than a bright cloak and a plumed bonnet?" Her sigh was half moan. "Ah, I love you. Oh, yes, Alistair. Oh, yes. Oh, please."

It was his dream, he thought. And had he not been making love to her nightly for a whole month—without interruption? Ah, yes, it was his dream, right enough.

"Hush," he whispered against her ear. "Let me answer you this way. Mm, so beautiful, my love."

*Get ready to fall in love
with a brand-new series from Mary Balogh. . . .*

WELCOME TO THE SURVIVORS' CLUB.

*The members are five gentlemen and one lady,
all of whom carry wounds
from the Napoleonic Wars—some visible
and some not. These tight-knit friends have helped
one another survive through thick and thin.
Now, they all need the perfect companions
to teach them how to love again.
Learn how it all begins in:*

The Proposal

Featuring the beloved Lady Gwendoline Muir from
One Night for Love and *A Summer to Remember*.

Available from Delacorte in hardcover

Turn the page for a sneak peek inside.

1

GWENDOLINE GRAYSON, LADY MUIR, HUNCHED HER shoulders and drew her cloak more snugly about her. It was a brisk, blustery March day, made chillier by the fact that she was standing down at the fishing harbor below the village where she was staying. It was low tide, and a number of fishing boats lay half keeled over on the wet sand, waiting for the water to return and float them upright again.

She should go back to the house. She had been out for longer than an hour, and part of her longed for the warmth of a fire and the comfort of a steaming cup of tea. Unfortunately, though, Vera Parkinson's home was not hers, only the house where she was staying for a month. And she and Vera had just quarreled—or at least, Vera had quarreled with *her* and upset her. She was not ready to go back yet. She would rather endure the elements.

She could not walk to her left. A jutting headland barred her way. To the right, though, a pebbled beach beneath high cliffs stretched into the distance. It would be several hours yet before the tide came up high enough to cover it.

Gwen usually avoided walking down by the water, even though she lived close to the sea herself at the dower house of Newbury Abbey in Dorsetshire. She found beaches too vast, cliffs too threatening, the sea too elemental. She preferred a smaller, more ordered world, over which she could exert some semblance of control—a carefully cultivated flower garden, for example.

But today she needed to be away from Vera for a while longer, and from the village and country lanes where she might run into Vera's neighbors and feel obliged to engage in cheerful conversation. She needed to be alone, and the pebbled beach was deserted for as far into the distance as she could see before it curved inland. She stepped down onto it.

She realized after a very short distance, however, why no one else was walking here. For though most of the pebbles were ancient and had been worn smooth and rounded by thousands of tides, a significant number of them were of more recent date, and they were larger, rougher, more jagged. Walking across them was not easy and would not have been even if she had had two sound legs. As it was, her right leg had never healed properly from a break eight years ago, when she had been thrown from her horse. She walked with a habitual limp even on level ground.

She did not turn back, though. She trudged stubbornly onward, careful where she set her feet. She was not in any great hurry to get anywhere, after all.

This had really been the most horrid day of a horrid fortnight. She had come for a month-long visit, entirely from impulse, when Vera had written to inform her of the sad passing a couple of months earlier of her husband, who had been ailing for several years. Vera had added the complaint that no one in either Mr. Parkinson's family or her own was paying any attention whatsoever to her suffering despite the fact that she was almost prostrate with grief and exhaustion after nursing him for so long. She was missing him dreadfully. Would Gwen care to come?

They had been friends of a sort for a brief few months during the whirlwind of their come-out Season in London, and had exchanged infrequent letters after Vera's marriage to Mr. Parkinson, a younger brother of Sir Roger Parkinson, and Gwen's to Viscount Muir. Vera had written a long letter of sympathy after Vernon's death, and had invited Gwen to come and stay with her and Mr. Parkinson for as long as she wished since Vera was neglected by almost everyone, including Mr. Parkinson himself, and would welcome her company. Gwen had declined the invitation then, but she had responded to Vera's plea on this occasion despite a few misgivings. She knew what grief and exhaustion and loneliness after the death of a spouse felt like.

It was a decision she had regretted almost from the first day. Vera, as her letters had suggested, was a moaner and a whiner, and while Gwen tried to make allowances for the fact that she had tended a sick husband for a few years and had just lost him, she soon came to the conclusion that the years since their come-out had soured Vera and made her permanently disagreeable. Most of her neighbors avoided her whenever possible. Her only friends were a group of ladies who much resembled her in character. Sitting and listening to their conversation felt very like being sucked into a black hole and deprived of enough air to breathe, Gwen had been finding. They knew how to see only what was wrong in their lives and in the world and never what was right.

And that was precisely what *she* was doing now when thinking of them, Gwen realized with a mental shake of the head. Negativity could be frighteningly contagious.

Even before this morning she had been wishing that she had not committed herself to such a long visit. Two weeks would have been quite sufficient—she would actually be going home by now. But she had agreed to a month, and a month it would have to be. This morning, however, her stoicism had been put to the test.

She had received a letter from her mother, who lived at the dower house with her, and in it her mother had recounted a few amusing anecdotes involving Sylvie and Leo, Neville and Lily's elder children—Neville, Earl of Kilbourne, was Gwen's brother, and lived at Newbury Abbey itself. Gwen read that part of the letter aloud to Vera at the breakfast table in the hope of coaxing a smile or a chuckle from her. Instead, she had found herself at the receiving end of a petulant tirade, the basic thrust of which was that it was very easy for Gwen to laugh at and make light of her suffering when Gwen's husband had died years ago and left her very comfortably well off, and when she had had a brother and mother both willing and eager to receive her back into the family fold, and when her sensibilities did not run very deep anyway. It was easy to be callous and cruel when she had married for money and status instead of love. Everyone had *known* that truth about her during the spring of their come-out, just as everyone had known that Vera had married beneath her because she and Mr. Parkinson had loved each other to distraction and nothing else had mattered.

Gwen had stared mutely back at her friend when she finally fell silent apart from some wrenching sobs into her handkerchief. She dared not open her mouth. She might have given the tirade right back and thereby have reduced herself to the level of Vera's own spitefulness. She would not be drawn into an unseemly scrap. But she almost vibrated with anger. And she was deeply hurt.

"I am going out for a walk, Vera," she had said at last, getting to her feet and pushing back her chair with the backs of her knees. "When I return, you may inform me whether you wish me to remain here for another two weeks, as planned, or whether you would prefer that I return to Newbury without further delay."

She would have to go by post or the public stagecoach. It would take the best part of a week for Neville's carriage to come for her if she wrote to inform him that she needed it earlier than planned.

Vera had wept harder and begged her not to be cruel, but Gwen had come out anyway.

She would be perfectly happy, she thought now, if she *never* returned to Vera's house. What a dreadful mistake it had been to come, and for a whole month, on the strength of a very brief and long-ago acquaintance.

Eventually she rounded the headland she had seen from the harbor and discovered that the beach, wider here, stretched onward, seemingly to infinity, and that in the near distance the stones gave way to sand, which would be far easier to walk along. However, she must not go *too* far. Although the tide was still out, she could see that it was definitely on the way in, and in some very flat places it could rush in far faster than one anticipated. She had lived close to the sea long enough to know that. Besides, she could not stay away from Vera's forever, though she wished she could. She must return soon.

Close by there was a gap in the cliffs, and it looked possible to get up onto the headland high above, if one was willing to climb a steep slope of pebbles and then a slightly more gradual slope of scrubby grass. If she could just get up there, she would be able to walk back to the village along the top instead of having to pick her way back across these very tricky stones.

Her weak leg was aching a bit, she realized. She had been foolish to come so far.

She stood still for a moment and looked out to the still-distant line of the incoming tide. And she was hit suddenly and quite unexpectedly, not by a wave of water, but by a tidal wave of loneliness, one that washed over her and deprived her of both breath and the will to resist.

Loneliness?

She never thought of herself as lonely. She had lived through a tumultuous marriage but, once the rawness of her grief over Vernon's death had receded, she had settled to a life of peace and contentment with her family. She had never felt any urge to remarry, though she was not a cynic about marriage. Her brother was happily married. So was Lauren, her cousin by marriage who felt really more like a sister, since they had grown up together at Newbury Abbey. Gwen, however, was perfectly contented to remain a widow and to define herself as a daughter, a sister, a sister-in-law, a cousin, an aunt. She had numerous other relatives too, and friends. She was comfortable at the dower house, which was just a short walk from the abbey, where she was always welcome. She paid frequent visits to Lauren and Kit in Hampshire, and occasional ones to other relatives. She usually spent a month or two of the spring in London to enjoy part of the Season.

She had always considered that she lived a blessed life.

So where had this sudden loneliness come from? And such a tidal wave of it that her knees felt weak and it seemed as though she had been robbed of breath. Why could she feel the rawness of tears in her throat?

Loneliness?

She was not lonely, only depressed at being stuck here with Vera. And hurt at what Vera had said about her and her lack of sensibilities. She was feeling sorry for herself, that was all. She *never* felt sorry for herself. Well, almost never. And when she did, then she quickly did something about it. Life was too short to be moped away. There was always much over which to rejoice.

But *loneliness*. How long had it been lying in wait for her, just waiting to pounce? Was her life really as empty as it seemed at this moment of almost frightening insight? As empty as this vast, bleak beach?

Ah, she *hated* beaches.

Gwen gave her head another mental shake and looked, first back the way she had come, and then up the beach to the steep path between the cliffs. Which should she take? She hesitated for a few moments and then decided upon the climb. It did not look quite steep enough to be dangerous, and once up it, she would surely be able to find an easy route back to the village.

The stones on the slope were no easier underfoot than those on the beach had been; in fact, they were more treacherous, for they shifted and slid beneath her feet as she climbed higher. By the time she was halfway up, she wished she had stayed on the beach, but it would be as difficult now to go back down as it was to continue upward. And she could see the grassy part of the slope not too far distant. She climbed doggedly onward.

And then disaster struck.

Her right foot pressed downward upon a sturdy looking stone, but it was loosely packed against those below it and her foot slid sharply downward until she landed rather painfully on her knee, while her hands spread to steady herself against the slope. For the fraction of a moment she felt only relief that she had saved herself from tumbling to the beach below. And then she felt the sharp, stabbing pain in her ankle.

Gingerly she raised herself to her left foot and tried to set the right foot down beside it. But she was engulfed in pain as soon as she tried to put some weight upon it— and even when she did not, for that matter. She exhaled a loud "Ohh!" of distress and turned carefully about so that she could sit on the stones, facing downward toward the beach. The slope looked far steeper from up here. Oh, she had been very foolish to try the climb.

She raised her knees, planted her left foot as firmly as she could, and grasped her right ankle in both hands. She tried rotating the foot slowly, her forehead coming to rest on her raised knee as she did so. It was a momentary sprain, she told herself, and would be fine in a moment. There was no need to panic.

But even without setting the foot down again, she knew she was deceiving herself. It was a bad sprain. Perhaps worse. She could not possibly walk.

And so panic came despite her effort to remain calm. However was she going to get back to the village? And no one knew where she was. The beach below her and the headland above were both deserted.

She drew a few steadying breaths. There was no point whatsoever in going to pieces. She would manage. Of course she would. She had no choice, did she?

It was at that moment that a voice spoke—a male voice from close by. It was not even raised.

"In my considered opinion," the voice said, "that ankle is either badly sprained or actually broken. Either way, it would be very unwise to try putting any weight on it."

Gwen's head jerked up, and she looked about to locate the source of the voice. To her right, a man rose into sight partway up the steep cliff face beside the slope. He climbed down onto the pebbles and strode across them toward her as if there were no danger whatsoever of slipping.

He was a great giant of a man with broad shoulders and chest and powerful thighs. His five-caped greatcoat gave the impression of even greater bulk. He looked quite menacingly large, in fact. He wore no hat. His brown hair was cropped close to his head. His features were strong and harsh, his eyes dark and fierce, his mouth a straight, severe line, his jaw hard set. And his expression did nothing to soften his looks. He was frowning—or scowling, perhaps.

His gloveless hands were huge.

Terror engulfed Gwen and made her almost forget her pain for a moment.

He must be the Duke of Stanbrook. She must have strayed onto his land, even though Vera had warned her to give both him and his estate a wide berth. According to Vera, he was a cruel monster, who had pushed his wife to her death over a high cliff on his estate a number of years ago and then claimed that she had jumped. What kind of woman would *jump* to her death in such a horrifying way, Vera had asked rhetorically. Especially when she was a *duchess* and had everything in the world she could possibly need.

The kind of woman, Gwen had thought at the time, though she had not said so aloud, *who had just lost her only child to a bullet in Portugal,* for that was precisely what had happened a short while before the duchess's demise. But Vera, along with the neighborhood ladies with whom she consorted, chose to believe the more titillating murder theory despite the fact that none of them, when pressed, could offer up any evidence whatsoever to corroborate it.

But though Gwen had been skeptical about the story when she heard it, she was not so sure now. He *looked* like a man who could be both ruthless and cruel. Even murderous.

And she had trespassed on his land. His very *deserted* land.

She was also helpless to run away.